An Angel's Unintentional Entanglement

by

Tena Stetler

Demon's Witch Series, Book 4

An Angel's Unintentional Entanglement

COPYRIGHT © 2018 by Tena Stetler

Cover Art by *Kristian Norris*

The Wild Rose Press, Inc.
PO Box 708
Adams Basin, NY 14410-0708
Visit us at www.thewildrosepress.com

Publishing History
First Black Rose Edition, 2018
Print ISBN 978-1-5092-2142-4
Digital ISBN 978-1-5092-2143-1

Demon's Witch Series, Book 4
Published in the United States of America

Sunrise brought an orange glow
spreading over the top of Independence Pass, bathing the valley in warm golden sunlight. He stood on the ridge with wings spread, brushing the breeze and absorbing the sun's warmth. *Feels better than yesterday. Finally, I'm gaining some strength back.* It was time to move on to Maroon Bells and the lake to enjoy summer in the Rocky Mountains. Carefully, he tucked his wings in and picked his way down the trail. Dislodged rocks and sticks bounced down the path ahead of him as he stopped to admire the view and noticed something in the brush.

A woman lay naked, battered, and beaten several yards off the trail. Her long, straight black hair fanned around her head, tangled with twigs and bits of grass. He moved silently toward her, stopped, and picked up a Bureau of Indian Affairs ID a few feet from where she lay. He stuffed it in his pocket while watching the surrounding area for signs of her attackers.

Kneeling at her side, he saw scratches and bruises on her high-sculpted cheekbones and her full lips had a tinge of blue around them. He placed his hand lightly on her chest, felt a weak heartbeat, and sensed a brave soul unwilling to give up. *God, this is the last thing I need.*

Praise for Tena Stetler

Dedications

To my family and friends
for their continued unwavering support.
~*~
To my husband
for his dedication and support.
~*~
To my editor extraordinaire, Lill.
You Rock!
~*~
To The Wild Rose Press
a fantastic publishing house.
~*~
To my fellow authors at the Wild Rose,
always ready to lend a hand.
What a great team!
~*~
To Darla,
in the wilds of Wyoming
whose information has been
invaluable to the research of this book.
~*~
To my wonderful readers,
I can never THANK YOU enough!

Chapter One
Intervention

Screams of terror accompanied by mournful howls pierced the crisp night air as Caden Silverwind settled into his chair in front of a crackling campfire. Shadows from the flames danced across the dark tree trunks, curling and twisting in mesmerizing shapes. He had heard it all before, but tonight the usual ceremonial chants ended with menacing growls and a sudden eerie silence, rather than the quiet winding down of previous nights.

Maybe he should investigate the unearthly sounds that echoed against the canyon walls, but he just couldn't. The last battle with dark demons had nearly destroyed his body and shattered his soul. He'd known it was coming for nearly a year. The darkness seeped into his consciousness a little more with each battle.

He talked with his legion commander who ultimately decided the feeling would pass. It didn't. At least he hadn't endangered the mission when he'd failed to act. Once shimmering marble-gray wings, now hung charcoal black. At first, his muscles were weak. He was barely able to bring them forth from his back to brush the air. Even the slightest movement causing severe pain and fatigue.

Against the advice of his superiors, he'd chosen an indefinite sabbatical in the Colorado Rockies. The rugged strength and majestic beauty allowed him the serenity to pick up the pieces, face his fears, and contemplate the future. If there was one. *Perhaps I should've remained among the warrior angels and used the facilities above to heal physically and repair what is left of my damaged soul.* He shook his head slowly taking in the bounty of nature around him. With daily exercise, his wings were getting stronger and his stamina increasing, still he had a way to go. N*o, I made the right decision.* Leaning back in his chair, he relaxed and watched the dancing flames consume the logs until glowing embers were all that remained in the fire ring.

He stood and stretched his arms above his head, letting out a jaw-popping yawn as he walked over to a five-gallon bucket of water. He tossed the water on the embers, trod up the steps to his home and fell into bed. Tossing and turning, dreams kept him awake for most of the night.

Sunrise brought an orange glow spreading over the top of Independence Pass, bathing the valley in warm golden sunlight. He stood on the ridge with wings spread, brushing the breeze and absorbing the sun's warmth. *Feels better than yesterday. Finally, I'm gaining some strength back.* It was time to move on to Maroon Bells and the lake to enjoy summer in the Rocky Mountains. Carefully, he tucked his wings in and picked his way down the trail. Dislodged rocks and sticks bounced down the path ahead of him as he stopped to admire the view and noticed something in the brush.

A woman lay naked, battered, and beaten several yards off the trail. Her long, straight black hair fanned around her head, tangled with twigs and bits of grass.

He moved silently toward her, stopped, and picked up a Bureau of Indian Affairs ID a few feet from where she lay. He stuffed it in his pocket while watching the surrounding area for signs of her attackers.

Kneeling at her side, he saw scratches and bruises on her high-sculpted cheekbones and her full lips had a tinge of blue around them. He placed his hand lightly on her chest, felt a weak heartbeat, and sensed a brave soul unwilling to give up. *God, this is the last thing I need.*

Summoning medical help was futile. The altitude at 12,092 feet, combined with rocky terrain, made it difficult for most rescue vehicles. They'd be too late to save her. He slid his hands under her body. At his touch, a scene unfolded in his mind of snarling wolves, the valiant fight she waged against a male until she was too weak to defend herself any longer, then blackness. Anger surged through him as he carried her along the rocky path to the fifth wheel trailer he called home.

Settling her gently on the bed, he retrieved a sponge, a washcloth, and small tub of warm water from the bathroom. He began gently cleansing the deep gashes inflicted by canine teeth along with several long deep rows of claw marks. Turning her over carefully, he swore, wincing as he wrung out the sponge exchanging it for a soft washcloth. It appeared she'd been dragged a long distance over rough terrain leaving small rocks and gravel embedded in her back. She'd lost a large amount of blood and her backside was a raw bleeding mess. Without his intervention, she wouldn't survive.

Still healing himself, he wasn't sure if he had the strength to heal her on his own, or what it would cost him, but there was no other choice. He finished cleaning her wounds and shrugged out of his shirt and jeans, slid his warm muscular body next to her frigid one, then wrapped his arms around her, lifting her gently. Finally, he wrapped his wings around both of them. His dark hair fell across his forehead, and a subtle silver light enveloped them as the sun rose high in the sky.

When he awoke, the full moon was drifting across the star-strewn western sky. As he lay staring out the bedroom window, he considered the situation. Above the jagged mountain peaks streaks of pink and orange mingled in the dusky-blue sky. Dawn had arrived. Somehow, they'd both survived the night. Her breathing was regular, her body warm and relaxed against him. She was still unconscious.

Slowly, he opened his wings and carefully slid away from her. A bright patchwork quilt lay folded at the bottom of the bed. He drew the quilt over her, stood, stretching his arms above his head, then leaned over and placed his palms flat on the floor, willing his stiff muscles to relax.

After several minutes, he straightened, rolling his shoulders, and tucking his wings gingerly into his back while pulling on a pair of jeans. Wearily, he dropped into a chair beside the bed to wait. He picked up her Bureau of Indian Affairs ID from the nightstand, turning it over repeatedly, considering the possibilities. Leaning back in the chair, his body relaxed, but his stomach rumbled loudly. He pushed up out of the chair.

Warm sunlight streamed through the kitchen window as he stirred a pot of oatmeal on the three-burner stove. A low moan came from the bedroom and he breathed a sigh of relief. She was coming around, finally. He flipped off the burner, poured the oatmeal into two bowls, grabbed a couple of spoons, and silently ascended the three stairs. He shouldered the curtain aside that separated the bedroom from the bath and living areas. Huge chocolate- brown eyes wide with terror watched him enter and move slowly to the side of the bed. Using his powers of persuasion, he created an aura of calm around her.

"Don't be afraid. You're safe here," he murmured. "You've slept a long time. Hungry? I've a warm bowl of oatmeal ready. It'll put you right, I guarantee." Smiling he eased himself down on the foot of the bed and put one bowl on the floor beside him. The other bowl and spoon he extended toward her.

Warily, she watched him, carefully licking her swollen, cracked lips. Slowly, she reached for the small bowl. He slid up the bed, placing it in her hand, his hand supporting hers.

"Can you sit up a bit?" He wanted to slide his hands under her, but the fear in her eyes, made him reconsider.

She nodded, pushing herself up with a groan, keeping her eyes on his as she reached for the spoon.

He picked up the bowl from the floor and scooped a spoonful into his mouth, savoring the warm oatmeal sprinkled with brown sugar and cinnamon. He swallowed the bite and glanced sideways at his patient. She hadn't touched her food yet. "Eat. I'll get you a glass of water and be right back. Oh, by the way, I'm Caden, and you are?" He gave her a friendly smile, held up one finger, then disappeared around the corner.

When he returned with a bottle of water, she

blinked at him as if to clear bleary vision while she studied him. After several minutes, in a hoarse scratchy voice, she blurted. "I'm Mystic…Mystic Rayne." Her bronze cheeks pinked when she glanced down at her naked body. Grimacing, she yanked up the quilt to cover herself. The bowl of oatmeal careened off the bed, he caught it before the dish hit the floor and offered it to her. A quiet moan slipped from her lips as she eased back on the bed, then reached for the bowl.

Wincing, he watched the pained expression cross her face. He moved to the closet, took out a well-worn flannel shirt and gently tossed it to her. Returning to the bed, he picked up his oatmeal bowl. "Be right back, then we can talk. Okay?"

Not waiting for an answer, he popped another spoonful of lukewarm oatmeal in his mouth and left the room. Frowning, he cradled the bowl in his hand and padded down the stairs into the kitchen. He shoved the bowl in the microwave for a minute then took it out and grabbed another bottle of water from the fridge and returned to the bedroom. He twisted the cap from one bottle and set it on the nightstand next to her.

Sitting on the edge of the bed, his eyes met hers for a brief moment. He took a swig of his water and shifted his gaze out the window, hoping the lack of direct eye contact would make her feel more comfortable.

He listened to the metal spoon scrape the ceramic bowl as she ate. When the sounds stopped, he ventured a look in her direction. She watched him intently while taking a sip from the water bottle.

In a gentle voice, he asked, "Feel like a little conversation?" Shifting his body farther onto the bed, he spooned up another bite, this one hotter than hell. He sucked in a breath.

She shook her head slowly and leaned against the pillows.

"Don't want to talk? I understand, but there are a few questions that need answered to assure our safety in the short term." He gave her his best devastatingly charming smile as he tucked the blanket around her legs, noting the shirt he'd offered her still lay on the bed. "Who did this to you? Will someone come looking for you possibly to make sure you're dead or finish the job?"

"I don't know," she murmured. A single tear rolled down her cheek. Sighing deeply, she turned her face away from him and stared out the window. After a few minutes, she closed her eyes.

"Okay." He patted her leg, took her empty bowl, and stood. "Get some rest. I'll be back in a little while."

He returned to the kitchen, washed the bowls and spoons, and set them in the drainer to dry. He gulped down the remainder of his bottle of water, tossed it in the trash. Pausing at the door, he flipped the lock from the inside, stepped outside and closed the door quietly.

What now? His breath fogged in the early morning air. Spring was slow in coming to the lands above timberline, but small greens shoots were quickly covering the barren ground. He let his mind wander away from the problem lying in his bed and took a deep cleansing breath in the crisp mountain air.

Independence Pass intrigued him. Part of the Continental Divide where the watersheds divided flowing downward in opposite directions to the Pacific and Atlantic Oceans, the pass offered the solitude he craved during off-season, but the winters were too harsh even for him.

Well not personally, but it took more than divine intervention to keep the trailer's lines from freezing. The haul truck was a bit cantankerous about starting at thirty to forty degrees below zero. Not to mention the large amounts of snow the pass got all winter long. He'd spent the winter at a lower elevation and recently returned.

He walked around the trailer, touching the sleek insulated panels fondly. At one time, he considered renting a comfortable cabin somewhere in the Rockies, but he was too restless to stay in one place. Instead, he chose a thirty-eight foot, three-axel, deep burgundy fifth-wheel trailer, with matching haul truck. It was the right choice.

He enjoyed the panoramic rear window offering spectacular views from one of two frosty gray upholstered recliners that sat on either side of the window. An oak coffee table with pole lamp attached to the floor held his drink of choice. He was comfortable here, and no one bothered him, yet. Another month the area would be crawling with tourists and he'd move on.

The trailer was equipped with a generator and solar panel charging system. He didn't depend on typical campgrounds for services. He was free to pick a campsite anywhere his rig fit that allowed overnight or long-term camping.

He divided his time between primitive camping areas or campgrounds around Maroon Bells, and occasionally wandered as far as Cripple Creek. All this to avoid contact with humans or other creatures and the problems they created. Yet, here he was smack dab in the middle of one hell of a mess. Lifting his eyes toward the heavens, he shook his head slowly. "Just couldn't leave me alone in peace."

Tapping his hand once more on the trailer, he turned on the balls of his feet and silently sprinted down the trail surveying the surrounding area. The physical activity helped clear his mind and relax his body. After running a couple miles, trees dotted the landscape and he slowed his pace. Suddenly icy fingers shot up his spine. Soundlessly, he spun on his heel checking the immediate area then ducked behind a huge tree. Agitated male voices rose in the wind as he crouched listening.

"Yeah, boss we got a problem. We found where she apparently bled out, but there is no body." One of the voices said. Then a couple minutes of silence hung in the air. "I know she didn't disappear into thin air, but there are no signs of her either."

"Got it." The man cursed loudly and ended the call.

"You hung up on the boss?" the other voice inquired incredulously.

"Yeah."

"What did he say?"

"He said don't fucking come back until we find her, if we value our skins." The first voice was clearly angry.

"We look some more," the second voice stated. "We gotta be missing something."

"No. We just don't go back. This is Ethan's mess let him clean it up. He shouldn't have attacked her in the first place. Especially in front of the tribe."

"Where do we go? He'll hunt us down and dispose of us."

"Not if the law finds him first."

"What are you saying, we turn him in?"

"Not yet. He's in Wyoming, busy with casino business. He can't leave right now. Find out how many of the tribe members were present last night and remember what happened. Most were shit-faced."

"That's just stupid. Got a death wish? I sure don't."

"Shut up. Let me think."

He crept down the trail toward the voices, careful to stay out of their line of sight. All he could think about was getting a good look at these men, so he could sketch their faces for Mystic. Rounding a bend in the path, a small clearing spread out in front of him. He froze like a deer in the headlights for a beat, backpeddled, then stepped to the side of the path. Crouching low, he hid behind a clump of evergreen shrubs and a huge tree.

Approximately forty feet in front of him stood two individuals. They were darker skinned, one with short black hair, tall and muscular build. The other man had long stringy dark hair, short and stocky. Both dressed in jeans and T-shirts with faded writing on the front and jean jackets, they stared menacingly at each other.

The stringy haired man said, "Don't tell me what to do. I'm going to clear out of here and disappear for a while."

"You're not going anywhere. We gotta stick together, if we're going up against Ethan. Which is the only way we won't end up like her. Unless of course…" The black-haired man shoved a finger into the other guy's chest causing him to stumble backward. "…you know where the body is."

Lunging forward, he grabbed the front of the other man's shirt. "Ya know damned well I don't."

Wrenching the guy's fingers from his shirt, the taller man shoved the other man to the ground and stepped over him. "Let's get back to the car and get out of here."

The second man got up and dusted himself off, glancing around nervously, then followed.

Gravel crunched under foot as they headed directly toward him. He held his breath and watched as they drew closer. Sweat beaded up on his brow. They made a sharp right not more than four feet in front of him, followed the path up to the road and away from him. He wiped the sweat from his forehead with the sleeve of his jacket and leaned back against a tree.

It seemed like an eternity before he heard the roar of an engine and squeal of tires on pavement. He bounced on the balls of his feet, his wings still too weak to carry him very far and took off at a run toward his home. At last, the trailer came into view, he slowed to a walk, his muscles aching as he trudged up the path. He stopped just outside the door to compose himself and listen for any movement. Silence.

The key turned in the lock with a click. He walked through the door quietly, and over to the stairs. Glancing to the right, through the open curtain to the bedroom, he saw her still asleep. Relieved, he tiptoed to the couch, reached underneath it, and pulled out his sketchpad. He sat down, toed off his shoes and swung his legs onto the couch, bending his knees to prop the pad against his thighs.

Though the subjects of his sketches weren't of a pleasant nature, the action itself felt good. It had been a long time since he'd spent any time with his sketchpad and pencils. In fact, the last sketch he'd done was for

Alaia, his legion commander's wife. She'd asked him to do a portrait of Nathanael. The year before, Nathanael requested that he do a portrait of Alaia in her gown on their wedding day. The pictures would hang side by side in the privacy of the couple's bedroom.

Nathanael had taken a mortal woman as his wife before it was forbidden, and prior to his appointment as Legion Commander. Even then, it had caused a rift between the warrior angels and their superiors. The superiors wanted the warriors available at a moment's notice, not distracted by a wife and possible family on earth. In their eyes, it was too dangerous to have a warrior's attention divided, whether they were in battle or merely on patrol. Ultimately, the Angel Tribunal decided to forbid all warrior angels from fraternizing with mortal women.

He shook his head. It was a tumultuous time for the elite legion. Many warrior angels left the ranks, unable to abide by the decision. Mortal women were popular with the warriors, whether to take their mind off their duties or for a more permanent relationship.

Now Nathanael and Alaia had a beautiful, yet precocious, little girl, that kept them both very busy. He smiled at the way Nathanael's daughter had him wrapped around her tiny finger. When at home, he was very different from the battle tough warrior he knew. The superiors were still miffed. *They are a bunch of control freaks.* He brushed aside the twitchy feeling of irritation.

Because of their long friendship, he had spent quite a bit of time at Nathanael's home and in fact had confided in him when he felt he wasn't fit for duty any longer. Nathanael counseled him that this was probably just a phase and would pass. But it didn't.

The sketches finished, he sighed and pushed himself up, leaned against the corner of the couch. He'd forgotten just how much he enjoyed drawing. Flipping through the many pages of his pad, he stared at all the sketches he'd created before the evil he battled had taken its toll.

He closed his eyes and then opened them again and sat up, feet on the floor. *Enough of this.* There were more immediate things demanding his attention, like the woman lying in his bed at this very moment. *Who wanted her dead?*

A soft moan came from the bedroom, followed by rustling of bedding. In the blink of an eye, he was at her side. Her warm, chocolate brown eyes opened and stared at him.

A slight smile played around the corners of her bruised, split lips. She winced. "Not quite ready to smile, I guess." Shyly, Mystic put her hand to her mouth.

"Maybe not, but it was sure nice to see you try. How are you feeling? Your color seems better, your cheeks are almost pink." He drew a stick of lip balm out of his pocket and handed it to her.

Blood rushed up her neck and spread across her still pale face as she took the lip balm. "Better, I think." She removed the cap and twisted the bottom of the tube gingerly smoothing it across her lips.

"Good. During my walk, I discovered a couple of men searching the area where I found you. It sounded like they were involved with what happened to you. Feel up to looking at a couple of sketches to see if you recognize them?"

Her eyes rounded, and she drew her bottom lip though her teeth. "I don't know," she said wincing again, her voice trembling.

He considered her response for a moment. "Well, I'm afraid, you really don't have a choice. Someone wants you dead and enlisted the help of the two men I saw to make sure the deed is done."

Any color that had returned to Mystic's face drained away. Her eyes filled with tears that threatened to spill down her cheeks. She blinked rapidly but was past the breaking point. The battle was lost as tears trickled down. She wiped them away with the back of her hand. "Sorry."

"Nothing to be sorry about. Most people don't come back from the brink of death without some kind of emotional release." He touched her arm gently.

She looked up at him and relaxed a little, some of the fear left her eyes, replaced by caution. "Thanks."

"You bet ya. Now about those sketches."

She leaned forward. "I'll take a look."

"Great." He bounded down the steps to the living room, picked up the sketchpad, returned to the bedroom, and handed her the pictures.

Her gaze slowly left his face and shifted to the pad. One look and Mystic's eyes flew open. She flipped to the next picture on the pad and sucked in a breath, starting to tremble again. "Yes." She laid the pad on the bed next to her. Her voice shook as the words tumbled out. "These are members of my tribe. Kinda lowlifes, hang with a rough crowd. Last I heard they were working security for River Winds, the tribe's casino in central Wyoming."

"Yep, that fits with what I heard. You know a man

named Ethan?"

She drew her mouth into a thin line. "Yes," she said in a flat tone. "He's the one responsible."

"You knew your attacker." His eyebrow winged up. "Mind if I ask what happened?"

She leaned back against the headboard and closed her eyes. "I guess I owe you that much."

Chapter Two
Secret of the River Winds Casino

Caden remained quiet and waited for Mystic to answer his questions.

After a few minutes, she opened her eyes and pulled herself to a sitting position. "I work with the Bureau of Indian Affairs and the Wind River Agency. I grew up on the Wind River Reservation in Wyoming and now try to help my people navigate the government's bureaucracy."

"You work for the government."

"Not exactly. I'm an independent contractor in an advisory capacity. Well, until recently."

His brows lifted in question. "What happened to change that?"

"My father died. He was the tribe's Shaman and Tribal Leader. I came home to take care of his affairs, as he would have wanted, and wound up accepting his place on the Tribal Council. His position as Shaman is still technically open until I either accept or decline the position. Theoretically, I guess I'm still with the Agency." She rested her head against the bed headboard and sighed.

"But don't you have to be a healer or something to replace a Shaman? Most tribal councils are still a good old boys network. Aren't they?"

"Some, but things are changing. They must, to

keep up with the modern world, or lose the young people. They're the tribe's future. My father trained me to follow in his footsteps since I could walk. He said I had the touch and the talent. Unfortunately, I rebelled, left the reservation, and went off to college. I didn't want to live in his world. I wanted to prove I was as good and smart as anybody else." She picked at the loose strings on the comforter with her fingers.

He scooped up the sketchpad, flipped the pages closed and tucked the pad between the bed and nightstand. "He didn't try to stop you?"

"No, he was a wise man. He knew I had to try my wings before I'd be satisfied with my destiny." Mystic shifted her body and looked at the long fingers on his broad hand as he leaned on the bed.

"Yet, you wound up right back where you started."

"Yes, as it was meant to be. I studied hard, graduated in the top of my class, and was accepted to Harvard Law School. It was a tough road there. The students assumed I was accepted because I was Native American and not on my merits. I proved them all wrong." She sat up a little straighter and smiled, her eyes meeting his. "I graduated top in my class and had numerous offers from prestigious law firms."

Caden let out a low whistle. "Some people would kill for those opportunities. But…obviously you didn't take any of the offers."

She nodded her head slowly, then winced. "I did, for a few weeks. It was all wrong. Rather than being ecstatic as I thought I would be, it was miserable. I hated playing the political games, missed the personal contact, and I missed my father. I gave my notice and returned home.

My father understood, in fact, he expected me and welcomed me back. He suggested that I use my knowledge to assist the community. Here I am." Mystic spread her arms then grimaced, slowly letting her arms fall back on the bed.

"From where I sit, it appears the community didn't appreciate your help." He frowned.

"No, that wasn't the problem, exactly." She hesitated for a beat. *Why on earth am I telling this stranger my life story? He did rescue me…and he's real easy on the eyes.* Her gaze met his, and her heart fluttered as she listened to the smooth cadence of his voice.

"What are you doing in Colorado when your tribe is in southwestern Wyoming?" He shifted on the bed to face her fully.

"My father along with several tribal members purchased land in this area years ago. They use it for special occasions and to just get away from…things."

"Oh. Was it a celebration that brought you here?"

"Of sorts, at least it started out that way." She looked down at the large bruises on her arms and closed her eyes, slumping down on the bed. "It ended badly. I'm tired now."

"I know you are," he said in a gentle voice. "But I must repeat, there are people out there who want you dead. You must tell me what happened. I can't help you any other way."

"I know." She sighed blinking back tears. "The short version, I spurned the advances of the man who wanted to take my father's position on the council. Refused to marry him. Ethan didn't love me, all he wanted was power." She sniffed, rubbed the back of her hand across her eyes as the heat rose in her face.

"I questioned his management of the tribe's casino and informed him that I, not him, would be taking my father's place on the council," she said reliving the indignity she'd suffered at his hands. "I reminded him the tribe owned the River Winds, and our council would be requesting accountability from him." Her body trembled as she tried to rein in the anger. "He lost his temper during..." Her eyes rounded as she sucked in a breath. *Oh God, I almost confided the tribe's darkest secret.* She let the air out slowly. "He lost his temper and attacked me."

Caden nodded his head, narrowing his eyes. "You're not telling me everything. Like how is it the injuries you sustained are bite and claw marks, besides the injuries obviously caused by being dragged on the gravel path and left for dead?"

She stared at her hands, refusing to meet his eyes. *Should I trust this stranger with my tribe's secrets? The secrets I've learned from childhood never to divulge. Will he think I'm crazy? Does it really matter? Caden is right. Ethan tried to kill me and probably will try to finish the job. If he finds out I'm still alive.*

"Well...are you going to help me or not?" Caden asked. "I know there's more to it than you're telling me."

"Ethan lost his temper when he shifted and couldn't control himself. I'd already changed in an effort to escape," she blurted out and then brought her eyes to his, gauging his reaction.

His facial expression neutral, he stated, "Your people are shapeshifters."

"Yes. The ones that possess the gene." She sighed

with relief. "You're not freaked out or think I'm crazy?"

"Nope. You'd be surprised at the things I've seen. Nothing shocks me anymore. It may surprise you to learn that my heritage is a lot like yours. Only I had an Irish mother, and my father was Lakota. This caused more than a few awkward moments for our family and tribe. My mother's people disowned her. The tribe took her in, because of my grandfather and father's standing in the tribe. She was accepted. Grandfather was a Shaman training my father to follow in his footsteps."

Mystic's hand flew to her mouth as a small gasp of surprise escaped. "You understand exactly where I'm coming from." Her eyebrows drew together, and her head tilted slightly to one side. "I try to give people the benefit of the doubt. Sometimes…it's hard. Are your parents still alive?"

"I understand more than you know," he said getting to his feet. "Now get some rest. We probably should move to another location soon. I was preparing to transfer to the Maroon Bell's area for the summer before you arrived, anyway."

"I don't want to be a burden. I'll be better in a couple of days and be on my way." Using her arms to scoot up higher on the bed, she tried to swing her legs to the edge. She sucked in a breath, pain zinged up her back, making her eyes water.

"A couple of days…we are leaving now. You're not a burden. I'm enjoying the company. Besides I'd like to help you bring these people to justice. Especially Ethan, what's his last name?"

"Nix. I'll give it some thought." She yawned wide, let her body slid down in the bed. "I think I'll just take a little nap. Then I can help…" Her voice faded away as her head laid back.

"Good idea." He tucked the bright hand-made comforter around her and pulled the rich maroon curtain between the bedroom and living room shut behind him.

****

He paced the living area, his gut told him to check out the River Winds Casino and Ethan, but leaving her alone was risky.

Caden looked up the phone number to the River Winds Casino, tapped in the numbers on his cell phone and stepped outside the trailer.

"River Winds Casino," a pleasant female voice greeted him.

"Oh, sorry must have dialed the wrong number." Caden said, his voice deep and smooth. He got a lock on the location from her voice and teleported into the casino before the conversation ended.

"That's quite all right," the female voice said and disconnected.

Luckily, the casino was full of people, intent on their endeavors at the card tables and Roulette wheel. No one seemed to notice his appearance, dressed in jeans and a T-shirt he blended in seamlessly. He strolled through the casino looking for an inconspicuous place from which to disappear and a more secluded place to use for teleportation later. He froze, then backed into an alcove. A man passed by him and stopped. Standing not five feet from Caden was the man he'd seen in Mystic's mind. This was Ethan Nix.

He stepped behind a slot machine, positioning himself to get a good look at the low life, without anyone noticing him. Mr. Nix stood about six-foot tall, broad shoulders, straight black hair that touched his shoulders, and beady dark eyes. His high cheekbones accentuated his deep-set eyes, making his face look hard.

He followed at a safe distance, drifting into Ethan's mind.

The melodic sounds of slot machines and friendly chatter surrounded Ethan as he strode across the casino floor. Nodding in acknowledgment to employees and regular customers, he smiled asking, "How's it going?"

"Fine Mr. Nix."

He didn't bother to acknowledge the response. His step quickened as he headed down the empty corridor leading to his office. Caden followed silently remaining in the low life's mind, though his revulsion made his stomach churn.

Last night had been a terrible mistake. Ethan kicked open the door to his office, strode through, and slammed it so hard the lock failed to catch, and it bounced open. Caden slipped to the side of the door blending invisibly into his surroundings. The scent of old leather and cigarette smoke permeated the air. Ethan wrinkled his nose and slid open a window. He looked around the room. There was no sign that Ethan smoked, but obviously some of the customers did.

Ethan flopped down in his worn leather chair and glanced across the desk. The message light on his business phone was flashing, and he quickly ran through the messages. Nothing from the enforcers he'd sent out to mop up his mess. *Damn*!

The man's arrogant attitude and dispassionate thoughts had Caden clenching and unclenching his fist.

I'd love to plow my fist into that man's face. He smirked, Nat, his legion commander would not approve. He continued to listen to the man's thoughts and observe using his angel talents blending in to remain invisible.

Pausing for a moment, Ethan glanced around then blew out a breath. The dumb asses should know better than to call his work phone anyway. He reached into his jacket pocket and pulled out his cell phone, no messages there either. Ethan had been so sure Mystic would be amicable to joining with him once he'd made his intentions known, that he had no backup plan.

The surprise was his. She had made it quite clear she didn't want to be anyone's mate, especially his. She intended to take her rightful place on the Tribal Council of Elders as well as tribe's shaman or whatever the hell she thought was her right. A position he'd assumed would be his after she agreed to be his wife. He'd lost his temper and control as he had shifted from man to wolf. She had it coming.

That was it. *I'll kill him.* He took a step forward, and a sharp voice permeated his thoughts. *Unacceptable, Caden. You may be on sabbatical, but rules still apply.* He blocked his legion commander's intrusion, stepped back, and continued monitoring Ethan's thoughts.

Running a scarred hand through his hair, Ethan rubbed the back of his neck, rolling his shoulders as he stood then began to pace around the office. His pants chafed against the bites and scratches she'd inflicted during their fight. The starched shirt grated against the gauze bandage he'd used to cover the claw marks across his chest and abdomen.

He pumped a fist in the air. *Good for Mystic. This man is a piece of work.*

No wonder, Ethan was one big ball of tension, and it was entirely her fault. He blew out another breath and shook his head slowly. Walking over to the little office bar, he opened the crystal paneled cabinet door, grabbed a glass, and poured three fingers of his good whiskey into the glass. After downing half, he winced as it burned his throat and strode back to his cherry wood desk.

Overseeing the casino was Ethan's responsibility, one he took seriously. The current members of the tribal council let him run things as he saw fit. After Mystic spurned him, she insinuated that the council, which she would be a member, needed to take a more active role. This meant he'd be accountable to them, have to sit down with a council member monthly to review the books, upcoming events, and approve expenditures.

Damned if he'd let a woman interfere with his business. Especially one who thought she was his equal. Well…he'd solved that problem, now he had to minimize the collateral damage.

Caden shook his head, his temper flipped back to simmer. *This man was a piece shit.* He relaxed against the wall still listening to the miscreant's mind.

When the people he'd hired brought her body back, he'd give it a proper burial and close the chapter on Mystic Rayne. *The witnesses, and there were plenty, won't dare cross me. Would they?* It wasn't his fault, he reasoned. *The damn bitch had it coming for her arrogant display.* Ethan slammed his fist onto the desk, splintering the wood and sending piles of papers skittering to the floor. His claws unsheathed and sliced

24

the palms of his hands. "Shit," he muttered aloud, grabbed a roll of paper towels out of the drawer, and wrapped his hands. All she had to do was agree to his proposal, but no. What should have been a celebration of their union, instead turned into a fight to the death; her death.

The clock on the wall chimed two o'clock. Ethan bent over, picked up the reports on the floor and arranged them in a neat pile on his desk. Taking his cell phone out of his pocket, he checked for messages, then tossed it on the desktop. "Shit." Where were Dane and Ian? They'd had plenty of time to find her by now and destroy the evidence. His cell phone buzzed and vibrated across the desk. "Finally." A single bead of sweat trickled down the side of his face. He swiped at it as he snatched up the phone, his heart racing, and touched the screen. "It's about time. Where the hell are you?"

"Boss, there's been…uh…a complication."

"What kind of complication?" He roared, gripping the phone so tightly his knuckles turned white.

"We can't find her body. There is a lot of blood soaked into the ground just a few feet from the trail. It appears she dragged herself quite a way before she bled out, about a mile from the ceremonial site. Then nothing. It's like she disappeared into thin air."

Caden sighed in relief. He didn't think they were still searching, but confirmation eased his mind.

"Find her," Ethan bellowed, the vein at his temple pulsing. "That's what I pay you for. Unless you want to meet a similar fate." He ended the call and slammed the phone onto the desktop. "This is what I get for hiring thugs from the tribe rather than professionals. How far

25

could she have gone?" He slumped into his worn brown leather chair to gather his thoughts and consider an alternative solution to the situation. *Could she still be alive? This could end my career, if I don't act quickly.*

Methodically, he went over the events of last night in his head, jotting down on a legal pad who had attended, how many where inebriated, who posed the biggest threat of exposure and whose loyalty he could count on if this got messy. He stared at the paper as if memorizing it, then tore the sheet off and paused, a sardonic smile curving his lips.

Still invisible to the mortal, he waltzed across the room to glance over Ethan's shoulder at the list. *That list will go a long way to seal Ethan's fate.*

Stuffing the sheet of paper in the shredder, Ethan glanced at his watch. *Shit, I have a meeting with the state auditors in fifteen minutes, and I still have a new floor manager to train. Sage, was that her name?* A female not of his choosing. He cursed vehemently as he crossed the office floor.

He moved out of Ethan's way, pausing to see where he went next.

The tribal council decided that the ratio of men to women working in the casino leaned too heavily in the favor of men. They hired this woman he hadn't even met, because she was highly qualified with an impeccable résumé. She replaced his second shift floor manager who had simply disappeared. Ethan shoved his arms in the navy pinstriped suit jacket, straightened his silver and gray striped tie, and glanced at his reflection in the mirror. *Not bad, considering.*

Disgusted, Caden faded through the wall, materializing in the hallway. He tucked into an alcove and waited for Ethan to emerge.

****

"Mr. Nix, may I see you for a minute," a male voice sounded directly behind Caden. He jumped, pressed against the wall hidden from view. Using his powers to remain invisible had taken a toll. He didn't have the strength to continue and still return home.

"I have only a minute before my meeting. What do you need, Bobby?" Ethan asked impatiently.

"Archer Clearwater from the Wind River Tribal Council just called and wants to set an appointment with you to go over the day to day operations and review the books. When would be a good time?"

"Never. Tell them I'm too busy right now training the new floor manager they hired."

Bobby looked at the floor and then flicked his attention back to Ethan. "If you don't call with a date and time, he'll probably show up in the casino with the entire council in tow and unannounced."

"Fine, push the date out as far as he'll accept. Let me know." Ethan strode away without looking back. *This is all her fault.*

Caden disengaged from Ethan's mind, waited until he disappeared, then walked up to a scantily clad waitress. "Miss, where would I find the manager of this establishment?"

"You just missed him. Mr. Nix is on his way to a meeting."

"That's too bad, I have a proposition for him."

"You can probably catch him tomorrow morning in his office. It's at the end of the corridor, just left of the little alcove." She pointed to a corridor leading off the main gambling area.

Perfect. Now I know exactly where Ethan should be in the morning, provided he doesn't deviate from his schedule. "Thank you. I'll catch him tomorrow." He gave the woman a smile and walked down the hall. Anxious to return, he'd already been gone longer that he intended, Caden found an empty conference room and moments later materialized outside his trailer.

Chapter Three
Secret's Out—Now What to do About It.

Mystic woke up disoriented, feeling a bit fuzzy. She rolled from her side to her back and attempted to stretch her arms above her head. The pain was excruciating, and she recoiled into a fetal position, arms curled to her chest. Even that hurt so she straightened her back a little. Fully awake now, she recalled the recent string of events and shivered.

In an effort of self-preservation, her mind clicked back to the tender care Caden lavished on her, the trembling decreased to a tolerable level. A rumbling came from her stomach. "Caden," she called out softly. There was no answer. *He's probably outside.* She tried to bring herself to a sitting position and cried out in pain as she gingerly slid her legs off the bed. Mystic put her bare feet down on the plush deep burgundy carpet with frosty gray swirls running through it. She wiggled her toes in the lush fibers. *Apparently, my feet are the only part of me that doesn't hurt.*

Standing, she pressed her hand to the wall to steady herself. Stopping in the bathroom, she took care of business, then opened the door and stared down the stairs. Surely, she could shuffle the twenty steps or so to the kitchen and scrounge something to appease her hunger, without bothering or the needing assistance. Halfway to her goal, she collapsed on the couch, exhausted. *So much for that idea.*

She stiffened as the door handle turned, then smiled weakly at Caden as he ducked his head stepping inside the door. "I tried to find something to eat, but couldn't make it."

"Let's get you back to bed. Then I'll fix you something to eat. Feeling better?" He leaned over and put a hand under her arm to help her up.

The accidental brush of his hand on the side of her breast sent a warm tingle through her body. At his gentle touch, heat rose to her cheeks, she pushed his hand away and glanced up at him. "Yes, until I got up and walked down here. I'm still weak, I guess. Could I just sit here, while you fix something to eat? I'm tired of lying in bed."

"Sure. Would you like soup or something more substantial?" He bent down and brought out a pan from the cupboard under the sink.

The corners of her mouth turned up slightly then she asked, "What's on the more substantial list?"

He chuckled, placed the pan on the stove, and opened the refrigerator. "Let see, roast and potatoes—maybe, spaghetti and garlic bread. There's even a couple of T-bone steaks in here," he said opening the freezer and peering inside. "Yep, I have baking potatoes," he added glancing at the cupboard above the refrigerator.

"Surprise me." Her stomach rumbled again at the thought of food.

"You got it." He pulled the steaks out of the freezer and went outside to start the grill.

Eyelids heavy, she slumped down for a quick nap. Her last thoughts before drifting off were of the handsome man caring for her. *What a change from the men she'd dated.* Her dreams were filled with passionate moments with Caden, a man she hardly knew, then terrifying memories of what had happened to her at the hands of a childhood friend.

When she awoke, the delicious aroma of steak, baked potatoes, and fresh baked rolls wafted through the trailer. "How long was I asleep?" Her eyes met Caden's across a folding table set in front of the couch. She felt her cheeks heat as the memory of her dreams of him surfaced.

He arranged two plates filled with mouthwatering food next to steaming cups of coffee, and he'd cut her steak into bite size pieces. *You're too good to be true. Men in my world could take lessons from you.* Her mind wandered to the near-death experience at the hands of a man that she'd trusted. *Why do I always learn the hard way?* The sound of Caden's voice yanked her out of her thoughts.

"About an hour, give or take," he said nonchalantly. "Enjoy your dinner."

His deep, rich voice flowed over her like warm honey, sending shivers of delight up her spine. To distract herself, she grabbed a roll and buttered it. Biting into the soft bread, she chewed slowly and closed her eyes, savoring the taste. "These are really good." She opened her eyes and dropped the roll on her plate. She scooped up a piece of baked potato with butter and put it in her mouth.

"Thanks. A friend's wife made the dough, formed rolls, and froze them for me. All I do is thaw out a couple and pop 'em in the oven." He cut the steak, forked a piece, and slipped it into his mouth.

His movements were so smooth, deliberate, and exuded such confidence. Yet, she sensed an underlying kindness and caring to his nature. In her experience, those traits would be at odds with each other. Obviously, she'd been attracted to the wrong kind of male. She looked down at the bruises on her arms. *Never again.*

After dinner, he cleared the table and helped her back into bed. "You rest for a bit, while I get the trailer ready to move. You'll need to sit in the truck with me. Are you able to sit up for a while, or do you want me to make a bed in the back seat of the truck for you to lie down?"

She chewed on her bottom lip. "I'd rather sit for a while, but I don't know how long I can lean on my back comfortably."

"Okay, I'll take care of it. You rest now."

She started to lay back then sat up abruptly. "Caden. You didn't happen to find a cell phone or backpack in the area you found me, did you?"

Silent for a few beats, he eased down on the side of the bed. "No, but then I wasn't looking for one. I didn't see a phone when I ran across those men in the clearing either, but I didn't have time to take a good look. I take it you're missing one."

She nodded her head and relaxed back against the bed. "Yes. I'd like to let the people I work with and close friends know I'm all right. They are probably worried sick, or worse were told I'm dead."

He shook his head and braced his hand behind him on the bed, leaning back. "Without a body, that would be difficult to prove. Let alone, explain why someone thought you were dead. What were you doing out there anyway, if your tribal business is on the Rez or in Riverton?"

Mystic took a deep breath and let it out slowly. "Ethan wanted to take me to the area my father and others purchased. I hadn't been there since I was a little girl. Besides, he said when we got there, he had something to discuss with me. It would be a reason to celebrate."

She remembered the excitement she felt, when he proposed the trip. It'd been a long time since she'd set foot on the property. Her eyes glistened with unshed tears as she recalled what happened once they arrived. Viciously she willed them away. She brought her gaze up to meet Caden's.

"It wasn't the whole tribe that attended this celebration?" he asked. The vein at his temple pulsed as his jaw tightened.

"No. Just Ethan and a group of the younger tribe members that had never seen the land. Ethan was kind of a role model to some that had lost their parents or those whose guardians had a substance abuse problem and couldn't care for them. This was especially important for those who carried the gene."

"Some role model." Caden snorted. "If you don't like the way things are going, kill 'em."

"Yeah, that's kinda how it turned out. But something still bothers me. I know Ethan is quite capable of controlling his wolf during and after the shift. It's a difficult thing to learn at first, which is why some of the younger ones need a mentor. I just don't understand what happened."

"He wanted you out of the way. That's what happened." Caden shifted on the bed, sat up straight, bending his arm up and down at the elbow.

"Yes, he was angry because I had no intention of becoming his mate or wife. Ethan was extremely upset that I choose to take my father's place as Shaman, as well as, on the council. But never in my wildest dreams did I think him capable of..." Her voice trailed off as she glanced down at her battered body.

Caden said, "Let's get you some decent clothes. We'll be relocating near Maroon Bells. Aspen isn't too far from the area, maybe we should go shopping." He glanced at her dressed only in his old flannel shirt and sweat pants that were too large and smiled. His gaze shifted from her, then he cleared his throat returning his attention to her. "You probably should stay in the truck, until I find you something decent to wear. Then you can go into the stores and pick other things. I doubt we'll run into Ethan or any of his associates there. We can go early morning right as the stores open and be gone by the time other people arrive."

"Probably a good idea." She twisted her hands in her lap, paused for a couple beats. "Without my backpack, which had my wallet and phone inside, I don't have any way to pay for new clothes."

"Don't worry about it. You can reimburse me later. Do you remember where you last had your backpack? Did you leave it in Ethan's vehicle?"

"No, I remember taking it out and putting it behind the logs that formed the circle sitting area."

"When I heard those two guys talking, they didn't mention a back pack at all." He paused for a moment rubbing his chin. "Can you tell me exactly where this place is?"

"I can show you, but...well...it can't be far from

where you found me. I must have dragged myself there."

"No. Your injuries are from being dragged by someone quite a way, then making your own way off the trail. And you aren't going anywhere near that area."

She winced. "Still I can't believe it's that far."

"Can you describe the area or draw a picture of something that was unique? Maybe I can locate it that way."

"Are you crazy? It's dark outside. You'll never be able to find it in the dark."

"Oh, you'd be surprised. Besides, this is the only chance we have. We're leaving tonight. Now, how about it." He handed her the sketchpad and a pencil he'd tucked away earlier between the nightstand and bed.

She took the pad and drew a clearing lined with trees with a ceremonial circle inside. "Is that good enough?"

"Believe so. I'm familiar with the area you are talking about. I'll go look around." He stood and stretched his arms out from his sides. "I'm going to turn the lights out and lock the deadbolt in the trailer. You should be safe in here until I get back. I'd like you to stay in bed and remain quiet. Do you know how to shoot a gun?"

She nodded.

"Good." He took a .357 out of the bedside drawer, checked that it was loaded, that the safety was on, and handed it to her. "If someone tries to come in the door, shoot and ask questions later."

"What about you?"

He grinned and turned around, lifting the back of his shirt slightly. Tucked in his belt, at the small of his back was a holstered gun just like the one he handed her. "I'll let you know before I come in the door."

Chapter Four
Return to the Scene of the Crime, the Ceremonial Circle

Caden stepped outside to disconnect the hoses supplying water to the fifth wheel. *Ready to hookup and go when I return.*

Thankful the meal had renewed his energy level, he put his hands on his lower back, bent backward then forward, side to side and rolled his shoulders. It had been too long since he'd exercised his wings, and his back ached. Assured there was no one around, he walked a few yards behind the trailer and into a dense wooded area and stripped off his shirt, thankful he'd decided to camp below the tree line.

He shrugged his shoulders forward to allow his wings room to unfold. The tips brushed the ground as he stretched them to their full expanse and moved them gently forward and back. *No pain, no gain.* With a couple of beats of his wings in the evening breeze, he was air-borne soaring above the treetops on the wind currents. The pain was tolerable, a good sign. He circled high above the trailer and dropped back to the ground, not ready to explain, if Mystic looked out the window. His back and chest muscles ached with the activity but were much better.

Eyes closed, he envisioned the picture Mystic had drawn. Usually he liked to have a connection to the area he was going, but there was no time. In the drawing, she'd indicated the ceremonial circle and a stand of aspens about fifteen feet away. The trees should provide him with sufficient cover, on the off chance someone was there.

He silently materialized in the stand of Aspens, as planned. The place was deserted, food wrappers, beer cans, and whiskey bottles scattered everywhere. Ethan's group had left the area in a hurry. What a disgrace. He considered picking up but had no way to discard the trash. Besides, it would indicate to anyone returning that someone had been there. He carefully picked his way to the ceremonial circle and looked behind the log Mystic thought she'd stashed her backpack.

There it was, damp and dirty, but otherwise appeared to be undisturbed. He picked it up and surmised by the weight it still had something inside. Not wanting to invade her privacy by rooting through the pack, he slung it over his shoulder and returned to the trailer.

"I'm back," he called to Mystic through the closed door. "I'm going to get the truck hooked up, then come inside and get you."

He turned the key in the ignition, and the truck rumbled to life. He backed the truck under the hitch, careful to minimize any jolts. Caden used his down parka to cushion the back of the passenger seat. With the additional blankets he kept for emergencies, he arranged the back seat into a makeshift bed.

Finished, he pulled open the trailer door and slipped inside. Mystic was still groggy from sleep, so he gathered her up in the comforter and tucked her into the passenger seat of the truck. He dropped the backpack on the floor at her feet. She opened her eyes, mumbled something, and drifted back to sleep. The painkillers he'd given her earlier worked quite nicely.

Relief washed over him as he descended Independent Pass and turned the truck toward White River National Forest, near Aspen, Colorado. He certainly wouldn't get any sleep staying in the vicinity of the attack knowing people were looking for her.

Silver Bells campground would be a quiet place to stay for a few days. There they could discuss the situation and agree on a strategy. After that, he figured they'd head for Wyoming. Still, finding an isolated campsite in the White River National Forest might be better. He'd fill the water tanks before setting up camp, the solar panels and generator would provide all the creature comforts for a few days.

He looked over at her. She hadn't stirred since he put her in the passenger's seat three and half hours ago. The ride would get rough from here until he found a suitable campsite. Reaching over, he gently touched her shoulder.

She bolted up right. "What's wrong?"

He eased off the accelerator, slowing the truck and checked the road ahead before glancing over in her direction. "Nothing. We are almost to our destination and the road may be a little bumpy." He brushed the strands of hair off her cheek with the back of his knuckles, lingering only a second feeling her soft skin against his hand, and returned his attention to the road. An unexpected zing of desire rushed through him. *Not what I need right now. The entanglement a woman could bring to my life is unacceptable.* He shifted in the seat. "Relax. I fixed a makeshift bed in the back seat.

Want to move back there?"

"No, I'm fine." She pushed the comforter off and pulled the parka up around her shoulders. "Any luck finding my backpack?"

He raised an eyebrow. "You doubted my abilities? I'm hurt." He took one hand off the steering wheel and held his hand to his heart, grinning. "Of course I found your backpack. Spending the night in the elements, left the pack damp and dirty, but it didn't look like anyone messed with it. I didn't open it. It's on the floor at your feet."

"Oh, that's wonderful." She smiled wide, reached down, and winced, feeling around. At the edge of the seat, her fingers touched at the straps, and she tugged it up in her lap. "Would you turn on the cab light so I can see if everything is here and if my phone is okay?"

"I'd rather not right now. I need my night vision with the help of the full moon to find us a nice campsite. Decided not to stay in a campground."

"Okay." She reached into her backpack felt around for her wallet, pulled it out and held it up triumphantly. "It's still here. I've got money. Well—at least checks and credit cards."

"All traceable. Can't use them. It's in your best interest to remain missing."

"Oh." Mystic dropped her backpack to the floor and looked around. Nothing but trees lined the both sides of the road. "Are we staying in the forest?"

"Yep, less people see us the better, until Ethan makes his next move. If his amateurs don't return, he'll more than likely hire professionals. I'd rather we make the next move, take him off guard."

She shifted toward him, eyes wide. "What do you

propose?"

"Sticking around here for a couple of days. Get you some decent clothes. Then surprise Ethan on his own turf. We'll walk right into the casino. If you agree with my plan, calling your friends might not be a good idea right now."

The truck bumped along the gravel road as she appeared to mull over his plan. "Wouldn't it be better to even the odds. I could have some of my trusted friends meet us at the casino."

He cut his gaze to her quickly and then back to the road. *She was beautiful and smart. If he was looking for a woman, which he wasn't, she was darn near perfect.* He shook his head to dislodge such thoughts. "Are you sure you can trust anyone, after what happened to you?"

Chewing on her bottom lip, she was quiet for a couple of minutes. "Yes, I have a couple of childhood friends in the tribe I would trust with my life. I know they are worried sick about me right now."

"Well, the decision is up to you. But the less people who know you are still alive, the better." He slowed the truck and turned up a narrow dirt road. After about five minutes, he turned on the high beams. In front of the truck was a long flat meadow with trees off to both sides. He pulled the truck past the area and then backed in several yards from the road. "We'll spend the rest of the night here and see how it looks in the morning."

"Okay," she said doubtfully.

The truck engine was still running when he opened his door and motioned her to stay where she was. After walking the area, he came over to her side and opened the door, reaching across her to shut off the engine.

"Can you walk, or do you want me to carry you into the trailer. The ground it pretty flat, so you shouldn't trip."

"I'm not an invalid. I can walk," she said.

In the pale moonlight, the corners of his mouth turned up in an almost smile.

"What…what's so funny."

"Nothing…nothing at all. Let's get inside, I'm dead tired, and my big ol' bed will feel really good."

She followed him around the front of the truck to the door of the trailer. He pulled down the steps, opened the door, and offered his hand to help her inside. She grumbled to herself but took his hand anyway. Once inside, he flipped on the lights in the kitchen and living space, then settled her on the couch. "I'll be right back."

With a *click,* he shut the trailer door, twigs and gravel crunched beneath his feet as he walked to the bed of the truck, disconnected the fifth wheel, and parked the truck beside the trailer. Trudging up the stairs, he opened the door and flipped a couple of switches on the inside wall. The trailer slowly leveled itself. When he pushed another button, a soft hum sounded as one by one the four slides moved out and locked in place.

Climbing up the steps to the bed and bath areas, he turned on the light in the bathroom. "Give me a couple of minutes, and you can use the bathroom. It'll take the water heater a few minutes to heat the water, then you can take a shower."

"Sounds good."

"There are clean flannel shirts in the closet and more sweat pants in the top dresser drawer. Tomorrow, we'll get you some clothes that fit." He fell back on the bed and stretched out, heaving a heavy sigh.

"Does the couch make into a bed?"

He sat up and began to unlace his shoes. "Sure, but it's only a queen size. Would you like to sleep on this one? I can take the couch."

"Oh no, I've inconvenienced you enough, and you're exhausted. Just show me where the bedding is, and I'll be fine."

He kicked off his shoes, stood, and walked toward her. "Tell you what. I'll make up the bed, while you take a shower. Then once you're settled, I'll take a shower and go to bed. Fair enough?" Eyes sparkling with mischief, he grinned. "Unless of course, you need help in the shower."

A wary expression clouded her face.

He immediately raised his arms up in a gesture of surrender. "Only teasing, didn't mean to offend or scare you. Only wanted to see that brilliant smile of yours again."

She rolled her eyes and gave him a wan smile. "Thanks for the offer, but I can manage."

Geez, my social interaction skills are rusty. "Okay… But seriously, I'd like to clean your back and replace the dressings before you go to bed. Don't want to risk infection. Let me help you get them off." He paused for a beat. "I promise I won't peek."

With a snort she said, "I think you've already seen everything there is to see." She unbuttoned her shirt and turned around to allow him to remove the dressings.

Stopping her, he took her chin in his hand, tilted her face up to his and smiled. "You have been through hell, yet you're still feisty. I like that." *A hell of a lot more that I should.* He bent his face down to hers,

43

wanting to brush his lips against hers, instead, he kissed her on the nose. His hand slipped around her neck, careful not to touch the raw areas, and pulled her close. She melted into him.

She turned to rest her cheek against his chest, he felt her heartbeat increase. She pulled him closer, wound her arms around his waist.

Neither pulled away, though he knew it wasn't a good idea, he laid his cheek on the top of her head.

He cleared his throat. "This isn't getting your dressings removed, and we have an early day tomorrow." He pulled away slowly as her arms dropped to her sides.

"You're right of course. I was just enjoying your warmth. Seems like I just can't get warm."

"The shower should warm you through. If it doesn't, I'll see what I can do after I redress your back."

"That's for sure," she said with a groan, shrugging out of his shirt.

He carefully removed the bandages and examined her back. "Healing nicely. Now hop in the shower and call me when you are ready for me to wash your back."

She glared at him but moved through the doorway into the bathroom and shut the door behind her.

****

The next morning Mystic awoke with a start, then remembered where she was and what happened. The bright sunlight streamed through the window where the shade didn't quite reach the side of the window. It was warm and felt good. Kinda like Caden's embrace last night. *What was it called, the nightingale effect— transference or something like that?*

He was a kind, caring genuine human being, something she'd not experienced in a long time. The only male interest she'd received since her father's death came at a price. Either they wanted her place on the tribal council or the position of Shaman. Neither of which she was willing to give up. The tribe's good ol' boy network was about to go down in flames, if she had anything to say about it.

Somehow, Caden had managed to maneuver into the kitchen without waking her. Bacon sizzled in the pan, and mouthwatering aromas filled the trailer.

She rolled to her side. The folding door between the hall and the kitchen was open so she could see him. "Hey, you're pretty good at the domestic stuff."

"Live alone long enough and you learn to pick up after yourself or live in a pig sty. Learn to cook or starve. Me, I like a nice living quarters and good food. So…" He spread his arms wide and turned in a three-hundred-and-sixty-degree circle.

"Can I help?" she asked, sitting up stiffly and slowly sliding her legs off the side of the bed. "I'm stiffer this morning than I was last night."

"It'll get better as you move around. You can help me by getting dressed and eating breakfast. Then we are off to Aspen."

"Get dressed?"

"I laid out a pair of blue sweats that the dryer shrunk to micro size. You'll probably need to roll up the pant legs. The dryer fried the elastic around the legs so they're loose. Same with the waistband, but the drawstring should hold them up well enough." He shrugged his shoulders and jerked his head in the direction of the dresser. "I also found a soft sweater that

45

will look better than my flannel shirts for going out in public."

"Thanks." She made her way up the steps, closed the hallway folding door and changed clothes. "Hey, these aren't bad. But it'll be nice to get some clothes that fit."

The sweats weren't too bad, once she'd rolled the pant legs up several times and drew the drawstring as far as it would go. His sweater almost swallowed her whole. She'd rolled up the sleeves, and the bottom of the sweater hit her mid-thigh. She wasn't a small person by any means, at a little over five feet ten inches tall, but slender. Lost in clothes meant for a man well over six feet and extremely muscular, Aspen would shun her for sure.

She opened the door and stood for his inspection.

He nodded his approval, then grinned as she made her way down the stairs and eased onto the couch. "Not bad. You look much better today. More color in your face. What's that, a full-on smile?" he teased. "Don't worry first stop is at a sportswear shop. I'll find some cute sweats and socks. What size shoe to do you wear?"

"Eight and half, sometimes nine. Depends on the make. I'd like some jeans and shirts. I'm tired of sweats."

"Whatever you want, but I don't think the tender skin on your backside, arms and legs will appreciate jeans or fancy shirts yet. But we can get some for later."

"Yeah, you are probably right." She reluctantly agreed, then sat down at the table and enjoyed scrambled eggs, hash browns, toast, and orange juice.

When they finished eating, he washed the dishes. Mystic sat on a stool and dried.

After cleaning the kitchen, he asked, "Ready to go?"

"Yep."

He bounded down the trailer steps, then turned to offer her a hand coming down the stairs. She pushed his hand aside and negotiated the steps slowly on her own with help of the handrail. Getting into the truck proved a bit more challenging, and she accepted his assistance.

"It won't hurt you to accept my help for a little while longer."

She looked up at him and grinned. "It might."

Chapter Five
Unexpected Visitors—an Unwelcome Surprise

Just as they approached the Aspen Gap store, a parking spot opened right in front. She shook her head in amazement "Imagine that, a space opened up right in front of where you want to go."

"Great luck," he said with a shrug, then strolled into the shop. A friendly clerk met him after he came through the door. He held his arm up at about her height, the clerk nodded and smiled, walking toward the back of the store with Caden close behind.

She glanced out the window at the well-dressed shoppers strolling on the sidewalk while she waited for Caden to come back into view.

After a few minutes, he returned with the sales woman standing in the window holding up jogging suits in a rainbow of colors. Which ones, he mouthed to her. She laughed and pointed to a light pink jacket with dark pink satin piping down the sides and maroon pants. A turquoise set with beaded bling around the V-neck and down the front was her other choice. He nodded and handed the two outfits along with a shoe box to the store clerk who smiled broadly at their antics.

The clerk smiled pointedly at her. He turned and grinned mischievously then paid for the items and started toward the door. A display stand with colorful socks caught his eye, and he picked several pair off the rack and handed them to the clerk, never glancing at her. The clerk put them in the bag and handed it to him. He waved goodbye to the clerk, yanked open the door to the shop, and strode through.

Opening her door, he thrust the bags into her lap, then walked to his side and climbed into the driver's seat. "They have nice things in there."

She opened the bag and pulled out a black satin jogging suit with varying lengths of silver sparkle down the front and a deep scoop neck. "Caden, I didn't see this one. It's beautiful, but way too expensive."

"Yeah, well it wasn't too expensive for me."

Her eyes met his and glittered with defiance. "Then you wear it."

"Won't fit. Besides, you'll look much better in it than I will. Now, I want to get gas, and you can take one of your new jogging suits and shoes into the ladies' restroom and change. I'll try to find one with an outside restroom entrance. Then we'll go get something to eat. I'm starved. Shopping makes me hungry. How about it?"

"Sounds good. I don't want to draw attention dressed like this." She grimaced as she looked down at the sweater that could be a dress if it wasn't so wide at the shoulders. "I'm glad you didn't insist I go into the shop and change."

He grinned but said nothing as he pulled up to the gas pump.

She hurried into the ladies' room with her pink outfit, turquoise running shoes, and a pair of socks When she emerged, Caden nodded. Everything fit perfectly.

"This is so soft against my skin," she said climbing

into the truck. "Why are you doing this? You just met me."

"Let's just say I'm paying it forward. Someone helped me in my hour of need, so it's my turn. Some day you can do the same." He glanced up and down the street. "I see a restaurant a couple blocks down." He started the truck, put it in gear, and drove the short distance, locating a parking space only a few yards from the door.

"You should buy lotto tickets the way your luck is running." She snickered.

He snorted. "Too risky."

After they'd eaten their fill at the local restaurant, she purchased casual wear at a couple of boutiques on Galena Street. She also found a pair of over the knee leather boots she just couldn't live without, along with another pair of athletic shoes and casual flats.

Completely shopped out, she flopped in the passenger seat of the truck, tucked the sales receipt in her backpack. "I'm going to owe you a fortune. My saving account will never forgive me. I'm done, let's go home."

Caden shot her a look, his brows raised. "Home?"

"Oh, you know what I mean. Back to the trailer, I could use a nap. My back burns and itches all at the same time." She wiggled in the seat trying to scratch her back on the seat.

"That's a good sign, it's healing. You've pushed it to the limit. I've lotion at the trailer that should make it feel more comfortable, but you don't want to put your new clothes on after I put it on, it might stain them."

"Okay, I'll just put on the pants I had on this morning with one of your flannel shirts. I'm growing quite fond of wearing your clothes." She chuckled turning in the seat to face him.

****

For the first time since he found her, her laughter sparkled in her eyes. *God, she was beautiful. That kind of thinking will get me in all kinds of trouble.* He dragged his gaze from her tall, slender body. He'd love to wrap his arms around... *Okay that's enough.*

Reaching for the ignition, he turned the key, and the engine rumbled to life. He backed out of the parking space and yanked the steering wheel to the left guiding the truck onto the street and toward the highway. *That's better, think of something else, that won't cause discomfort and get me in trouble.* He shifted in his seat discretely to alleviate the growing discomfort in his crotch.

Casually, he tried small talk. "Overall I think our shopping expedition was a success."

"It was. I hope I don't need any party clothes for a while."

"Oh, you will when we get to the casino, but we'll do more shopping later."

"If you'd just let me call my best friend, Chinoah, she could meet me somewhere with my own clothes."

"Do you really think you can trust her, after all that's happened?" He slanted a glance at her for a moment and looked back to the road.

She nodded her head emphatically. "Absolutely. She wasn't involved, I bet my life on it. She's got to be worried sick about me by now."

"I think it best if we walk into the casino without contacting anyone. We're looking for shock factor. After that, you can call your friend and have her bring

51

you some clothes. I don't want to take any chances."

"How long are we going to stay here?"

"Until you can walk a mile normally without being tired. The short amount of time we spent in Aspen, wore you completely out. You limp pretty bad when you get tired."

He concentrated on the road. Once he reached the highway, he peered over at her. She was staring intently at him.

"What."

"Your body language is interesting. All day you've been relaxed even animated until we got back into the truck and talked about my back. Then you stiffened up, seemed distant and uptight. What's wrong?"

"Nothing. The recent events have finally caught up with me. I'm really tired."

"Oookkay." She drew out the word as if not quite convinced.

He underestimated her powers of observation. She wasn't buying his story. When he examined her back tonight, he'd be careful to keep his emotions in check.

By early afternoon, they'd arrived at the trailer. She promptly jumped out of the truck, grimaced a bit when she landed and turned around in time to catch his hand. "Let's go for a walk and see how I do. During the ride here, I rested up. My stamina seems to be coming back in waves. I'd like to ride this one 'til it crashes."

"You sure? I'd like to check your back first."

"I'm sure, and my back can wait. Once you've messed with it again, it will hurt for a while and tire me out. It's fine right now."

"The walk will probably do us both good. First one to the dead stump at the end of the trail has to cook dinner." He took off at a run.

She couldn't keep up with him after only twenty feet or so but did make it to the stump and plopped down. "Well that didn't take long. But it felt good to run even for a short distance."

"Better rest up. You're cooking dinner after I check your back."

She gave him a withering stare. "I don't think I'm the only one that needs to rest."

"Hey, who made it to the stump way before the gimp did?"

She swatted at him, lost her balance, then fell into him. He caught her, pulling her tight against him. She glanced up shyly. Bending over, he brushed his lips over hers, gentle at first, then he deepened the kiss. The tip of his tongue slid between her lips, exploring, caressing. Arms wound around his neck, her body melted against his chest, and her hips pressed against his. Her fingers explored the curves of his back, she traced the raised areas down both sides of his back. She paused then ran her fingers over the area again. "Wow what happened to you to cause such scaring?"

He drew in a breath and pulled away, leaning his cheek on the top of her head. "Mystic we can't do this."

"Why not, we are both consenting adults." She blinked up at him.

"Because there are things…well, there are just things." He unwound her arms from around him and took a couple steps away.

Her forehead creased, and she licked her lips nervously. "Did I do something wrong?"

"No, that's not it at all." He let out a little sigh and reached for her hand.

"Are you going to tell me what happened to your back?"

"Battle wounds," he said quickly taking her hand and tugging her up the trail toward home. "Let's go in so I can take a look at your back." He opened the door and extended his hand to help her inside.

She brushed past his hand and climbed the stairs unassisted. "This conversation is not finished. Not by a long shot."

Silent, he followed, his mouth set in a grim line. "Take your shirt off and sit down. I'll get the lotion and gauze. See if we can make you more comfortable."

Her heart still pounded, and he scented her arousal. *Oh God, what have I done.*

"You can try, but I don't think lotion is going to help," she said testily.

His forehead creased as his brows knitted together. "Why? Do you have new symptoms?"

"No, oh never mind." She unbuttoned her blouse and held it in front, her arms over her chest, and her back bare.

After he cleaned the area and gently applied lotion, he straightened. "It's amazing your backside is almost healed. I don't think I even need to bandage it, as long as you only wear soft material against it, so it doesn't get irritated."

"Great. Now it's your turn. Take your shirt off," she demanded.

"Why? There's nothing wrong with my back."

"Then why did you become so agitated at me when I caressed it?" She reached for the front of his shirt.

He backed away. "I don't want to talk about it right now. And you need to get supper started." He shot a triumphant grin over his shoulder and walked out the door, flipping the lock on his way out. Spring was in the air, and buds on the trees were dropping their covers. Green sprouts were everywhere on the forest floor.

His nostrils flared as he breathed in the crisp night air, letting it out slowly. In the blink of an eye, he disappeared into the wooded area behind the trailer and arched his back allowing his wings the freedom necessary to stop the infernal aching. He stretched them out behind him, the tips brushed the ground as he spread them out wide allowing the wind to ruffle the edges.

With powerful strokes of his wings, he was airborne hovering several feet above the ground, holding steady, testing the weakened muscles. Pleased with their performance, he floated silently to the ground, and his mind returned to the problem at hand.

What the heck am I doing? Sharing a kiss fanned the flames of a relationship that can never be. Running a hand through his hair, he rubbed at the back of his neck. He settled into one of the lounge chairs he'd set up around the fire ring for later. The rumble of an engine and gravel crunching under tires caught his attention. *Shit, now what?*

A black SUV turned down the bumpy dirt road, turned off and slowly rolled to a stop in front of his trailer. The driver cut the engine, and three men dressed in light colored suits emerged.

Caden shoved up from the chair and advanced toward the SUV. "What the hell are you doing here?"

"Nice to see you too. How have you been? Your wings still giving you trouble? Not enough exercise?"

The tallest man with dark brown hair and hazel eyes asked biting back a grin.

"Nathanael, you picked at poor time to visit." Caden looked toward the door wondering how he would explain if Mystic saw them. Then he nodded toward the SUV. "Isn't that a little over kill?"

"Contrary to your opinion, I timed it perfectly and to quote an old friend. "What the hell are you doing? Visit casino's much?" Nathanael nodded toward the young man with light brown hair and lanky build standing silently to his right. "Let me introduce your temporary replacement. This is Sean. He's a good warrior just lacks your years of experience."

Sean nodded to Caden and turned his gray eyes back to Nathanael, waiting instructions.

"Killian, your former partner, you already know." Nathanael slanted his eyes in the direction of the man with reddish brown hair, bright blue eyes, and stocky build of a bar brawler standing to the left of him.

"Cut the crap, Nat. Why are you here?"

"You know why I'm here. The Angelic Tribunal is not pleased." Nathanael looked over at his men and jerked his chin indicating they should disappear for a while.

"I don't think…" Killian started to object.

Nathanael, his thin lips set in a firm line, narrowed his eyes at Killian, who nodded grudgingly and sauntered down the path toward Sean.

"The tribunal is never pleased." He snorted. "Except for the centuries when I killed the highest number of dark demons. It didn't matter that with each kill, I lost a part of myself, until there was nothing left but hatred and darkness."

"True, we didn't realize the toll it took on single warriors' souls. Your situation has brought about changes that will benefit everyone, eventually. But that's not why I'm here."

"Okay…so…" He stood hands on hips.

"The woman, she's mortal. You are headed down a forbidden path, and nothing good can come of it."

"Technically she's not a mortal, she's a magical being, a wolf shape-shifter." He leveled his gaze at the commander. "You would know first-hand about that track. Huh? The path saved you from my fate, didn't it? How are Alaia and that young daughter of yours?"

Nat shook his head slowly and started at the ground. "Caden, don't do this." He brought his gaze back up.

"Do what, search for happiness? For someone that heals the darkness in my heart and soul? Who makes me smile and laugh, brings meaning to life I thought was lost forever?" He dropped his arms to his sides, flexed his hands into balls, then stretched them out again.

"Well, if that's true, then why haven't you been honest with her?"

"Planned to tell her tonight after supper. I know the situation has gone on too long. Originally, I wanted to make sure her injuries healed both physically and emotionally before, I added to them. Then I discovered the man that almost killed her is still looking for her. I wanted to see that situation to a close. But our feelings for each other could add another aspect to this situation."

"That's putting it mildly. You know, she'll have to make a choice of her own free will." Nathanael glared directly into Caden's eyes. "Nothing can influence that choice. Once she knows everything, that choice may not be what you want. Are you prepared for that?"

"I am."

"Are you sure?" It's a big decision, and one that will be fraught with difficulties. The tribunal being your biggest hurdle. They're adamant about enforcement of the mortal and warrior rule."

"Well, I'm outside their control on indeterminate disability leave. No longer a warrior. The choice to return to warrior status or live on earth the rest of my days was left up to me and me alone."

Nathanael rubbed his chin and nodded in agreement. "To tell the truth, I hadn't thought about that, but you are exactly right. Even if you win, the tribunal will require full disclosure to the woman and a guarantee of her silence. She's a lawyer, and that could be a problem."

"Her name is Mystic, and I don't think it will. She's a lawyer, but also a healer and Shaman foremost. She became a lawyer to help right the wrongs done to her people."

"With a rebellious streak a mile wide. You two are kindred spirits." Nathanael nodded in understanding. "From where I'm standing, it looks like she was wronged by her own people."

"Remember, not everything is as it appears. There is some truth in what you said, but this is a complex and deadly situation."

"The fact remains, that I can't leave here without being able to report to the tribunal you told Mystic everything and secured her silence. That's if I can get the tribunal to agree with your status and agree to waive the rule. A big if."

"I need more time. We have a little situation of someone trying to kill her. I'd like to get a handle on that situation before I dump everything else on her."

"Yes, I see your point. I'll try to buy you a few weeks, but you should tell her what you are tonight. If that goes well, then Killian, Sean, and I will hang around for a bit in case you need divine intervention. If she rejects you…"

"She won't," Caden said adamantly. "Now, please leave. She's probably already seen you, so that is one more thing I'll have to explain."

Nat shifted his gaze from Caden to the trailer door and back. "Okay, we'll leave now, but we'll be back tomorrow evening to officially meet her. I may bring Alaia along to help your situation. If I stick my neck out for you with the tribunal, I want to make damn sure all your ducks are in a row." Nat turned to leave, then hesitated turning back around to face Caden. "I really hope things work out for you."

"Great. Now go," he said pacing beside the vehicle.

Killian and Sean came trudging up the path. Nathanael clasped Caden on the shoulder, before they all got into the SUV. "You know I only want the best for you." Then he slid into the driver's seat, started the engine, and the vehicle disappeared down the road in a cloud of dust.

Mystic opened the door and stared at the dust from the disappearing vehicle. "Was someone here?"

Caden waved his hand dismissively, putting his foot on the first stair to the trailer. "Yes, they just stopped to ask directions."

She narrowed her eyes and watched him for a

moment. "Seemed pretty chummy to me to only be asking for directions," she muttered under her breath.

"Did you say something?" Caden asked absently climbing the rest of the stairs, well aware of what she'd said but choosing to ignore it.

"Yes, supper is ready. I hope you like pork chops, potatoes, and gravy. I couldn't find any veggies. You need to restock your fridge, if we're going to be here for a while." Mystic backed up and opened the door wider.

"I'll see to it tomorrow. I love pork chops, especially when I don't prepare them. By the way, you did really well in your sprint down the path today. Tomorrow we'll take a longer walk and see how you do." He closed and locked the door behind him.

"I'd like that. Now dinner is getting cold, so get over here." She walked over to the kitchen table and placed the roll of paper towels in the center of the table.

"The pork chops are delicious," he said around a bit of meat then dipped his fork into the mashed potatoes and gravy. After swallowing, he slipped the potatoes into his mouth. "Mmmm. You are a great cook."

"You've been on your own too long." She laughed, taking a sip of tea and watching him over the rim.

After they cleared the dishes and cleaned up the kitchen. He caught her hand and tugged her toward the door. "I've piled wood in the campfire ring and arranged our camp chairs around it. Would you like to relax around a cozy fire tonight?"

"I am kinda tired, but…that sounds like fun."

"We won't stay out too long. I'm beat too." He held his parka out for her. She slid her arms in, and he zipped the coat up. His fingers left the zipper and caressed her jaw line then he brushed the tip of her nose with his forefinger.

After building a blazing fire, to make sure she was warm, he said, "We need to talk."

She turned her attention from the crackling fire to his eyes. "About what?"

Chapter Six
Are Angels Among Us?

"What did you want to talk to me about?" Mystic asked pushing the embers around in the fire pit with a stick, the heat from the flame racing up her arm.

Caden stood and paced around the campfire. He took off his jacket and shirt, arched his shoulders and brought forth wings. All the while gazing directly into her eyes and watching her face.

She sat there round-eyed taking it all in and chewing on her bottom lip. A nervous habit. *Holy shit.* Rubbing her eyes, she stared at him. *I've got to be dreaming. Men don't have wings.*

"Well, say something," he said standing still for the first time since the conversation began.

She opened her mouth to speak, but nothing came out except a squeak.

"That's better than nothing. Words would be nice. I didn't know how to tell you, so I decided to show you."

"What do you want me to say?" Her mind jumbled, and her breath caught. *This isn't really happening. It was dream. That's it, a dream.* Finally, she gulped in air, and everything went black.

Mystic's eyes fluttered open, and she regained consciousness with a start. She was in Caden's lap on the couch. *How'd I get here?* His fingertip lightly traced her lips. Forehead creased, she watched him, and then she giggled. "I just had the strangest dream. You were standing in front of me with long wings and… Did I really faint? Never happened to me before, must be a culmination of everything that has occurred over the past several days."

Caden grimaced shifting her over to sit on the couch beside him, wrapping his arm around her shoulders. "I'm afraid it wasn't a dream. You fainted, and I carried you into the trailer. Let me try again. Remember the vertical scars you asked about?"

She nodded. Somehow feeling like this was an out of body experience, but peering at his facial expression told her it wasn't. This was real.

"It's part of my anatomy as an angel. My wings expand from that area. The skin disruption is minimal, I'm surprised you noticed."

"I may be educated as a lawyer, but my father trained me as a healer. I notice anomalies of the human body, or in this case the not so human body." She offered him a weak smile. *An angel? This can't be happening to me. I've lost it. Angel's belong in the spirit world, not here.*

A little sigh of relief escaped his lips. "You're not shocked?"

"Well of course I'm shocked. It's not often I meet an angel, let alone kiss one." She touched her fingers to her lips as if remembering the kiss. "Especially a kiss like that." She ran the tip of her tongue around her lips. "Besides, being a shape-shifter, I learned all kinds of things are possible. Just never expected to meet a— um—real angel on earth. There is magic all around, you just must believe, my father used to say."

"God bless your father." Caden didn't take his eyes

off her lips.

What was he thinking. Her gaze wandered lower, and it became apparent what he was thinking. Her lips formed an O as heat rose in her cheeks.

He cursed under his breath, shifting in his seat to relieve the obvious.

Seeing the uncomfortable look on his face, she asked, "Is something wrong?" Her forehead creased, then she covered her mouth with her hand before he saw her knowing smile.

"No."

"Okay…is that all you wanted to talk about?" She tried to sound convincing. Her whole world just flipped on its side, and she had no idea how to right it. She knew this man, um angel, cared for her, so she had to steady her world and fast.

"Yes." He sighed and leaned back on the sofa.

"And the men that were here before supper?"

He hesitated for a beat. "There's more."

Her eyes widened. "Isn't there always? Okay, spill it."

"The men are also angels, warrior angels to be exact. Nathanael is my legion commander. He is married to a mortal woman, Alaia, and they have one extremely precocious little girl."

"Married to a mortal? How does that work?" She stretched her long legs out in front of her for a beat then curled them under her, while her gaze held his.

"With difficulty. That's why the Tribunal of Superiors forbade all warrior angels from fraternizing with mortal women."

"If it's forbidden—I'm mortal. How can you—we?" She blew out a breath in frustration.

"I am getting to that." He ran his fingers through his long tresses and sighed. "One question at a time. The other angel with Nat, was Killian. He is my best friend and was my partner when I was a warrior."

"What about the other one, another partner too?"

"No. That is Sean. Nat introduced him as my temporary replacement. Don't know a lot about him."

"Temporary?" She arched a brow staring at him quizzically.

He told her what happened and about the decision he'd made to return to earth. Then explained how it was his decision alone whether to return to active status with the warrior angels. His eyes searched hers as if waiting for a reaction.

She threw up her hands. "Where does that leave us? If there even is an us. What are we doing? Friends? More than friends? Protector and protected? What?" *Oh geez, what am I doing. I learned to quit babbling on and on when I felt uncomfortable or not in control in law school. Clear, concise, and to the point. Did all my education fly right out the window, when an angel flew in?* The corner of her mouth twitched, and she blew out a breath. She had to get a grip. Thinking with him so close was impossible.

"Not sure where our relationship is going, but I damn sure intend to find out," he said.

"But if you are forbidden to associate with me…" She looked up at him, wriggled out of his hold and put some space between them on the couch. *There, that's better.*

"Nope. I'm no longer a warrior, nor do I intend to return. I can't be sure that I won't succumb to the dark demon influence again. Physically I'm not one hundred percent either. That makes me a liability in battle, and I'm not sure when or if that will ever change."

"I've fallen for a defective angel. Wouldn't you know it." She threw her hands up in the air then tried to stifle a giggle.

His heart took a leap, and his pulse quickened. "Did you?"

She wiped her sweaty palms on her pants. "Yep. And you know what?" She couldn't believe she was finally going to admit her feelings for him. Or should she? Her heart was saying one thing her brain was in denial. Emotionally, she was a friggin' mess. But the one thing she knew, without a doubt is that she was falling in love with him. By his racing heart and pulse he had feelings for her. At least she…

"No, what?" he said slowly his voice wavered with uncertainty.

"I don't regret it one bit. The only thing I regret is the circumstances that brought us together and the dangerous position you're in because of me." Well, she'd come as close to sharing her feelings as she could right now. Opening herself up for more hurt was something she couldn't do…shouldn't do… Too late.

He blew out a breath. "It's not your fault. I'm not a warrior anymore, but I'd love to show Ethan the error in his ways." His jaw muscles pulsed as his lips closed in a thin line.

"You can't do that. Can you?" she asked with more hope than she'd intended.

"Only time will tell." He grinned and tugged her back on to his lap. "If the tribunal sanctions our relationship, there is one more thing you need to know."

"There's more requirements to dating an angel, even a defective one, than taking the bar exam. Now what?" She grinned, cupping his chin in her hand to prevent him from constantly looking away.

"You must take an oath to never divulge that you are involved with an angel. Can't have mortals looking for favors. You understand?"

"Of course. And where is this oath taken, if I agree."

He turned his eyes heavenward.

"Really?"

"No," he said laughing. "Got ya. My commander will be here tomorrow to interrogate you. To make sure I've told you everything, and you understand exactly what you are getting yourself into."

She blinked at him, then punched his shoulder. "You're kidding, right?"

He shook his head solemnly. "Not this time. Nat also threatened to bring his wife, Alaia, with him so she can make sure you understand completely. No room for any doubt and all that stuff." He ran his fingers over her hair. "I know this is a lot to digest."

"That's an understatement," she said rolling her eyes, licking her lips again, partially to taunt him.

He sent her a warning glance as if he knew her intentions, then continued. "If you decide to walk away, I will still help you with the Ethan situation. No strings attached." He shifted again but failed to thwart his male reaction.

She grinned at his discomfort. "Are you kidding, give up my own personal angel? No way."

"I still want you to sleep on it and give me your decision tomorrow. Things may look different after you've had a chance to think about it."

"Okay. But I doubt I'll change my mind."

"I need to go check on the fire outside. If we are through sitting around the campfire, I'll put it out." He stood with her still in his arms, gently settled her on the couch and padded over to the door.

"Caden, could we go outside and enjoy the stars for a little while longer?"

"Sure. I'll throw more logs in the pit and get a roaring fire going to keep you warm. Then we can sit outside as long as you wish. It's a beautiful night. Would you like a blanket?"

"Yes, that would be nice."

"Give me a minute." He ran up the stairs to the bedroom grabbed the comforter off the bed and tossed it to her, turned around then headed toward the outside door.

She grinned up at him, her eyes sparkling with mischief. "If that doesn't work, I guess I'll snuggle with you on your lounge chair."

"I'd like that idea much better than a blanket. Give me that." He lunged for the comforter.

****

The sky was awash with bright orange mingled with fiery red as the sun rose in all its glory over the mountaintops. Rainbows bounced over the walls of the trailer as the sun filtered through the crystals hung in each window. To give her space, Caden spent the night on the couch, and she'd spent the night alone in his bed.

He stood in the doorway of the trailer, his arm around her as they silently enjoyed the spectacular sunrise, steaming mugs of hot chocolate held in their hands.

She sat her mug down on the counter and put her arms around his neck, molding her body to his. Her lips brushed his lightly.

His gentle kiss lingered on her lips, he wanted to commit it to memory. Their hearts beat in unison. He sat his mug down without looking and moved his hands to the small of her back holding her tightly against him as the kiss became more demanding. Her flavor spun into him as his tongue parted her lips slipping between them to dance sinuously with hers. Slowly, he pulled back.

Her eyes gradually opened, her soft full lips curving into a shy smile. "I thought about all the things you said last night. We both know you didn't try to influence me. Now I'm positive my decision is the right one." Closing her eyes again she laid her cheek on his warm chest.

Caden laid his cheek on top of her head and whispered, "And now you're sure?"

"Yes," she murmured.

"Care to share?"

"Not right now, I just want to enjoy this moment."

A crack of a shotgun shattered the silence. They both dropped to the floor. On his way down, he grabbed the door handle, pulled it closed, and flipped the dead bolt in place with his thumb. Her elbow caught the handle of the mug. It crashed to the floor spilling hot chocolate all over them and the floor. Another report sounded and then quiet.

What seemed like an eternity, but was only a few minutes, passed without a sound. He shifted to a crouched position and indicated she should stay on the floor. He moved to the panoramic window in the rear of the trailer and peeked out just above the window ledge. *Nothing*.

Turning he crept across the trailer, climbed the stairs to the bedroom and pulled the shade up enough to peer out the bedroom window. He still saw nothing out of the ordinary.

Tires crunched on the gravel road. The vehicle stopped in front of the trailer, leaving the engine running. A door slammed, and footsteps came closer. Mystic's eyes went wide as she pushed to a crouching position.

He moved to the bedroom window on the same side as the door. A forest ranger stood at the door, his gun holstered. He raised his hand and knocked on the door. He stealthily descended the stairs and sidled up to the side of the door. He motioned for her to move to the kitchen.

Without opening the door, he said, "Good morning, sir. Is there something I can do for you this fine morning?"

"I'm ranger Wolfe. I'd like to talk with you for a few minutes." He shifted from one foot to the other.

"Of course, but first, if you don't mind, would you hold your badge up to the window just left of the door? Then put your hands on the door, please."

"Okay," the ranger said pensively. Taking a step back, he held up his badge and ID, then hesitantly touched his hand to the door.

Caden pulled the gun out of his boot and laid his hand on the door so he could verify if the ranger was truly who he said he was. Sensing no deception, Caden unlocked the door. Holding the gun behind the door, he opened it only an inch or two. "What can I do for you?"

The ranger tucked his badge and ID into his front pocket. "I assume you heard the gunshots."

"Sure did." He tucked the gun in his waistband and pulled his shirt over it.

"We took down a poacher we've been after for some time about a mile from here." The ranger glanced back at his truck to where his partner stood between the truck and his fifth wheel. "He appeared to be working alone, but we are searching the surrounding area and warning campers. Mind if we look around?" The ranger leaned to the side as if wanting to look inside the fifth wheel.

"Not at all. He pushed the door open wider and backed away.

Ranger Wolfe climbed the steps as his partner moved closer to the trailer. He stepped inside and looked from one end of the trailer to the other.

"Feel free to look around. We've nothing to hide."

"How long you been here?" He took a couple of steps toward the bedroom, pulled the curtain aside and glanced around.

"We pulled in a couple nights ago. Decided the forest would be quieter than a commercial campground." He laughed. "Until we heard the shots."

She left the kitchen to stand beside Caden. "We were getting ready to follow the trail—see where it leads."

Wolfe returned to the door. "It's a pretty area, lots of great trails. Keep your eyes open, if you go hiking. We'll notify you if we find anything of concern. Sorry to bother you."

"Not a problem. Thanks for letting us know what's going on."

"Sure thing. If you see anyone acting suspicious, don't approach. Call the ranger station." The ranger took a card out of his pocket and offered it to him.

He took the card and set it on the counter. "We'll stay alert."

The ranger tipped his hat back and met his eyes. "The campers a couple miles down the road reported seeing a black SUV yesterday afternoon. Did you see it?"

"Our friends drive a black SUV and they were here yesterday afternoon. They'll be back this evening for dinner."

"Good to know. Wanted to be sure the poacher and SUV weren't connected. Be careful, and enjoy the rest of your stay." The ranger descended the stairs.

"Thanks." He closed the door and locked it and returned the gun to his boot.

Mystic leaned against the counter staring at his boot.

He let out a sigh of relief. "I think after Nat stops by tonight, it's time to pay Ethan a visit."

She nodded in agreement, walked to the couch, and sat down. "A gun in your boot too?"

"Yep, it's a backup."

She licked her lips nervously and looked toward the door. "Maybe we should forego our hike and watch a movie."

"Sounds good to me." He pulled a drawer open next to the TV. "Take your pick."

Perusing the large selection he offered, she plucked out a comedy. "Let's start with this one. Then see how we feel about a hike. I get antsy if I sit for a long time."

"Who said you'd be sitting all the time." He sat

next to her and put his arm around her shoulders pulling her body close. His nostrils flared as he drew in her scent of lemons and a floral fragrance. He kissed her cheek then nibbled his way down her neck. His fingers caressed the side of her breast in slow feather like touches, then continued down her belly in slow circles, stopping under the waistband of her pants. His breathing increased, and his gaze held hers for a long moment before his fingers inched lower. His lips claimed hers, and she deepened the kiss.

He felt her heart beat a tattoo in her chest as her pulse quickened. A moment of indecision crossed her eyes. She shifted away and put her hand over his, shook her head. "I think that's about far enough. I have lots of questions, before taking the next step in our relationship. Are you ready to answer them or do we wait for your commander and his entourage?"

He blew out a breath and reluctantly slid his fingers away from her waistband, resting his hand on her thigh. "Ask whatever you want."

"What if things don't work out? Do you erase my mind or something?"

He laughed. "Don't worry about it. Things will work out." His breathing returned to normal as he shifted to relieve the tightness in his crotch. "No, I don't have the ability to wipe your mind."

"Okay, let's go with that. What happens now?" She turned to face him, staring intently.

"The same thing that happens when you are attracted to a human male. I'm not so different."

"I noticed." Red patches bloomed on her cheeks as her gaze slipped to his crotch. "But you said our relationship must be approved. What if it isn't?"

"It will. They have no authority over me as long as I'm not among the ranks of the warriors."

"And if you decide to return, what happens to me? To us?"

"I don't plan to return."

"Sounds like they eventually want you back."

"That's why I'm here in the first place. I tried to do what everyone wanted, rather than what was best for me. The demons had more influence over me than they should, my rage and desire for vengeance at any cost, was wrong. Yet, I went into battle because it was expected." He shoved his fingers through his hair, leaving little furrows and frowned.

"Sounds kinda like if someone wanted to jump off the roof, would you too?" She pursed her lips drawing the bottom lip through her teeth. "Your duty knows no bounds?" She tilted her head to one side.

"It does now. Everyone said the feeling would pass and I'd be fine. Well, it didn't, I wasn't, and it almost killed me. No more." He pushed up from the couch and paced the floor, hands clenched and shoved in his pockets.

"Okay, so let's say they approve our relationship. Then what? What kind of commitment am I looking at? Do you have a job here? Do you return there? Will you split your time between here and there?" She turned her attention to the sky outside the window.

The corners of his mouth twitched. He turned so she wouldn't see the smile he couldn't hide. "I believe you are over thinking this just a bit. Life of any kind has no guarantee's, this is no different. Except once committed to me, dating if you will, there will be no other men, unless you ask to be released. I will never hold you against your will."

Making an exaggerated motion with the back of her hand to wipe her brow she said, "Whew, that's a load off my mind. As if you could hold me against my will." She smirked.

"Oh, Myst, never underestimate an angel, even a fallen one," he said with a mischievous grin.

"You do have powers us mere mortals don't have."

"I don't think you are a mere mortal. You're a shapeshifter with all the power required and then some. Shapeshifters are magical beings. Maybe not so much in the modern world, but in ancient times they possessed powerful magic. Now, they are like everyone else, busy trying to get ahead, becoming doctors, lawyers, engineers, and rocket scientists. They've lost the ability to call their magic."

Mystic frowned. "What a ridiculous statement. Magic, huh. You're changing the subject. Your abilities?"

"At the moment, my abilities are limited due to injuries and lack of trust in my own mind. Although being with you has helped a great deal."

"What can you do that mortal men cannot?"

"Other than being built to satisfy and one hell of a lover?" He tried to hold a straight face but failed and burst out laughing.

She leaned over to swat at him. He moved out of her reach, and she nearly fell off the couch. "I'm serious," she said as a soft giggle escaped her lips. "And isn't your language a bit rough for an angel?"

"Hey, I gotta be me." He shrugged, shot her an outrageous grin, then burst into gales of laughter again.

She shook her head. "I see."

He waited a couple of minutes until his laughter subsided and tried to give her an answer that would satisfy her. "As our relationship grows you'll learn the abilities I possess. Part of the fun of exploring a relationship is learning new things about each other. Ours will be no different. Nat will tell you the same, so don't try to wheedle information out of him. There is one more thing."

"Maybe Alaia will tell me." She batted her long dark lashes at him and smiled. "One more thing?"

"Nope she won't. I don't want you falling in love with me because of my abilities."

"As if. You really think I'm that shallow?" If looks could kill, he'd be dead on the spot.

"I didn't say that. That's not what I meant." He paused raking his fingers through his hair again and stood. "Since we're not watching the movie any way, let's get out of here. Go for a walk. The ranger didn't come back, so we'll be careful. Nat and his group will be here soon. Then we'll address the Ethan problem too." Grabbing her hand, he tugged her out of the trailer, locked the door and did a quick survey of the area.

"One more thing?" Mystic insisted as they ambled down the trail.

He sighed, not sure it was the time to discuss it, but Nat would probably bring it up eventually tonight. "If we choose to consummate our relationship physically, we would be mated for eternity. In other words, by Angel Tribunal law, you would become my mate. Before you consent to a physical relationship, think long and hard about the consequences. Because in the heat of the moment, I may not remind you."

Her eyes rounded, and she swallowed hard. "Just once and we're wed?"

"Yes."

She took a deep breath and nervously joked. "What if you're no good in bed?"

"I've never had any complaints." A slow sensual smile spread across his lips, he cupped the back of her neck with his hand, kissed her long and deep. Trailing his other hand down her back until he cupped her ass, he pulled her against him and pressed his erection against her body. His heart raced, and his growing excitement was restricted by his tight jeans. He released her with a low groan. *I am going to need a long cold shower after this.*

She blinked at him and managed to regain her composure. "You've had physical relationships before. What about the law?"

His lips twitched as he continued following the trail. "Only applies to a loving physical relationship with the partner that knows who and what I am. I've never had that," he said over his shoulder, and then added. "You can't imagine that I've spent a couple hundred years without female companionship. I am male after all."

"Well, no…of course not," she stammered. "But the way you put it at first."

He stopped her on the trail, took hold of her shoulders, and turned her to face him, his gaze sharp and assessing. "Was for shock value. I wanted to make sure you understood the seriousness of this particular situation. Eternity is a long time."

"It is," she said thoughtfully as she reached for his hand. They walked down the trail lost in their own thoughts.

The sound of Nat's SUV turning onto the gravel road caught his attention. "Myst, we better get a move on. We got company." He changed direction tugging her with him.

"Where?" Mystic glanced around the deserted trail, her brow creased.

"Back at the trailer." His steps quickened. In his mind, he saw the vehicle stop and three men in blue pinstriped suits step out, accompanied by a short slender blonde woman with a small toddler in tow.

Nathanael knocked on the trailer door. Then turned to the others. "Apparently they aren't home. Can't be too far away, Caden's truck is still here." He walked over to the chairs arranged around the fire pit. "Let's just make ourselves comfortable until they return. Killian, would you get the play yard out of the car and set it up for Kaitlyn, we don't want her escaping." Nat's daughter tugged at her mother's hand trying to break loose.

Caden snickered to himself as the scene played out in his mind. "Kat has Nat wound around her little finger."

"What?" Mystic said looking perplexed.

Shit, I said that out loud. "Nat's at the trailer. He's brought his wife and daughter, Kat."

"How do you know?"

Shrugging, he said absently, "A talent," and tuned back into the scene playing out at the trailer.

Alaia glanced in her husband's direction. "Nat, we need to take Kat for a walk before expecting her to settle down in the play yard. She's just been on a long car ride." Just as the girl broke free, Alaia caught her squirming child around the waist.

He hesitated then shook his head. "Well, I'd like to wait 'til Caden gets back."

Kat threw her head back and wailed at the top of her lungs. Alaia glanced from the child to Nat. Ignoring the screaming for a moment, she said, "Besides, I'd like to talk to you…alone. The guys can wait for Caden." She leaned over and swung the child from side to side.

"My legs could use some stretching too." He smiled down at his wife. He took his sobbing daughter and set her down on the path.

Kat bolted up the trail as fast as her little legs would carry her, squealing at the top of her lungs. Alaia started after her.

Nathanael caught her arm and pulled her back. "Let her go, she'll be fine. No way she'll get lost making that much noise. Besides, like you said she needs to burn off some of that energy. What did you want to talk to me about?"

"You didn't finish explaining why you insisted I come along. I'm always excluded from your business. I like it that way. You said something about Caden causing a problem or had a problem. How's that different?"

"Because the problem is that Caden saved a woman's life, and now I believe he's falling in love with a mortal woman, well, not exactly mortal."

A twinge of guilt stabbed at his conscience, but not so much that he backed out of Nat's mind.

Her eyes flew open wide, her hand flew to her mouth. "What? That's forbidden. Even he knows that."

"He's never been involved with a woman like this. I know the signs very well." Nathanael winked at her and squeezed her hand. "He's not going to give her up."

"Why am I here?"

"Luckily, Caden has found a loop hole. The tribunal has no jurisdiction over him because he's not a warrior…at the present time. Since he was badly injured, both physically and emotionally, then released from duty indefinitely, they won't have any power over him in the foreseeable future."

"Thank goodness. I like him, but he has always been one of your toughest challenges," she said, brushing the strands of her hair away from her face.

"And my best warrior. I blame myself for not taking to heart the things he said to me before he nearly died. If I'd listened to him, really listened, I'd have known he wasn't fit for duty." Nat lowered his head, his lips pulled tight, shoulders slumped, and let out a heavy sigh. "I owed him that much. He is my oldest and dearest friend. He was asking for help, and I failed him."

"Don't be so hard on yourself. No one knew that angels were susceptible to that type of thing, until it happened to him." She gently caressed her husband's cheek with her hand. "This is why you are hell-bent on helping him now, even though you're close to breaking the rules yourself."

Caden shook his head, he knew he should withdraw from Nat's mind. This was an invasion of privacy, against the rules, but he had to know what he was up against and if Nat was going to support him. Besides knowing Nat felt guilty could work in his favor. He turned back into the scene promising himself to make his presence known.

Nat nodded his head. "Caden deserves to be happy.

He's spent all his life mortal and angel being a warrior. If this woman makes him happy, I'll do everything possible to make sure nothing stands in his way. That's where you come in."

The light dawned on her face, and she shook her head. "You want me to check her out, see if she is playing with him or has real feelings for him? You want me to interfere. I won't do it. They'll need to work things out for themselves."

Nathanael smiled. "Close but no. I want you to explain to her what you've been through. Tell her what she can expect. I want her to know just how difficult it can be. If she is up to the task, then like you said, it's up to them to work it out."

Caden glanced over at Mystic. *Would she bolt when she learned the truth?* He blew out a long breath. *Nat's here to force my hand.* He tuned into what Alaia was saying.

"I can do that. Only because I wish someone would've done that for me. I wouldn't have changed my mind, but I might have done a few things differently."

"What? I thought you liked our life." His brows furloughed, concern filled his voice.

"I do, but I would have liked to be your wife longer before having your child. Sometimes I would like more time to ourselves. Early on, I know it was hard on you getting used to a wife and then suddenly a child too and dividing yourself between us and your job."

"Wise woman." He gently trapped her against a tree with his body and kissed her hard, his hand wandering over her body as he checked his peripheral vision for Kat.

Caden eased out of his commander's mind, giving Nat privacy, though he could still hear their voices and see them through the bushes.

"If you want more time for us, I can make arrangements for someone to watch Kat. I'd like that, a lot. Not that I don't enjoy fatherhood, I do, but I'd like you all to myself sometimes."

"Stop it, what if someone sees us. We're not horny teenagers."

"Speak for yourself." He laughed seductively. "There's no one around. I checked, and Kat is up the trail a few yards destroying a pinecone. Relax and enjoy. I know I am."

Amused, Caden couldn't help himself, he slipped into Nat's mind. *Mystic and I are on the other side of the path and will be in range of sight within a minute or two. We'll slow down our pace a bit to give you more time.*

Smartass. Nathanael responded in kind.

As he and Mystic rounded the bend, Kat sat in the middle of the path a few yards in front of her parents, throwing rocks down the slope in front her.

"Don't ask, you don't want to know. Caden and his girl are headed up the path toward us, and I don't want to be caught fondling my wife."

"I believe you already have." She snickered.

"Kat stop throwing rocks, what if someone is coming up the path and you hit them. Wouldn't you feel bad?"

"Ony Cadn," Kat said quickly. "He no mind."

"He deserves it," Nat said under his breath.

"But his friend doesn't," Alaia said sternly to her husband.

"Agreed." He strode forward, reached for his daughter's arm, and pulled her to a standing position, brushing the dirt from her bottom. "Run on down the path and find Caden, Kat."

Kat looked up at her father and then tore off down the trail as fast has her chubby little legs would carry her. "Cadn, Cadn, I get you."

"Not if I get you first," Caden answered running up the hill towing Mystic behind him. He stopped and swooped Kat up in his arms and tossed her in air, catching her with two hands. "I believe I got you." He laughed and set her back on the ground.

Kat looked up and eyed Mystic suspiciously. "Who you, Cadn's?"

"I guess so," Mystic said with a laugh bending down to offer her hand to the little girl. "I'm Mystic. What's your name?"

"Kat." Her pudgy, dirt-caked hands reached for Mystic's hand for a moment then ran back toward her mom and dad.

"It's been a while since you've been able to do that." Nathanael observed, nodding in Caden's direction.

"Yep. Each day is better than the day before." He strode forward and grasped his legion commander's hand. He leaned over and kissed Alaia on the cheek, giving her a quick hug. "You keeping the big man in line?"

Alaia looked up at her husband and down at her diminutive size. "Yeah, right. You're looking good, compared to the last time I saw you."

"Geez, I was almost dead, the last time you saw me. I'll take that as a compliment anyway. Alaia, I would like you to meet the light of my life, Mystic. Mystic this is Alaia, the wife of Nathanael North, my legion commander."

The women nodded to each other. Mystic wiped her hand on her jeans, then extended her hand in greeting.

Alaia smiled knowingly, glanced at Kat, and shook the hand offered.

Mystic turned and offered her hand to Nat.

He smiled and graciously clasped her hand.

Caden glanced behind his legion commander. "Where's the rest of your band of merry men?"

Nat frowned, his eyes sparked. "I imagine Killian and Sean are making good use of a couple of the loungers in front of your trailer."

"Figures."

"We should probably join them."

"If you insist." He shoved a hand in his pocket.

Their little group walked up the path to the trailer, with Kat in the lead. Killian and Sean made no move to get up as they entered the campsite.

Caden turned to Mystic. "Any chance you could scare up some refreshments for our guests? I'll be in to help in a minute."

Alaia waived her hand at Mystic and smiled. "You want some real help?"

"Sure. Come on in." Mystic opened the trailer door and motioned Alaia inside.

"Nathanael, please put Kat in the playpen and watch her. You know she is a little escape artist," Alaia said over her shoulder as she entered the trailer.

Mystic paused for a moment standing in the doorway watching Nat.

"You bet." Nathanael swept his daughter off her wobbly little feet, kissed her on the nose, and plopped her in the enclosure with a large down-filled comforter.

Chapter Seven
Girl Talk and Warrior Angels

Once inside the trailer, Mystic sank to the couch and leaned back gingerly. She was exhausted, her backside hurt, and she was dizzy. The weather was so beautiful they had hiked twice as far as the day before. Caden had insisted that she rest before they started back, but that didn't help now. He'd seemed so preoccupied on the way back after learning Nat had arrived.

Alaia frowned. "Are you all right?" She leaned down on her knees in front of Mystic.

"I will be in a minute. I guess I pushed it a little too far today. But it was so beautiful."

"What do you mean? Pushed what too far?"

Caden yanked open the door and bounded inside. "I figured you'd be exhausted. How's the back?"

"It burns and aches pretty bad."

"Take your shirt off, I'll get some lotion and painkillers. You rest for a while, and you'll be right as rain. I'll get refreshments for the guys."

Mystic leaned forward and removed her shirt wrapping it around her front in case one of the guys came in without warning.

Alaia walked to the side to look at Mystic's back and sucked in her breath with a slight squeak. A look of horror crossed her features. "What in God's green earth happened to you?"

All the blood rushed to Mystic's face. "It's a long story." She sighed as the blood drained away and sweat beaded on her forehead.

Caden returned with a glass of water, a couple of pills and bottle of lotion. He handed her the water and medication then gently applied the lotion to her back. "Give it all about fifteen minutes to work, and you'll feel much better." He washed his hands and started getting glasses down from the cupboard, then whirled around to get sandwich fixings and crashed into Alaia. "Sorry."

Alaia glanced from Caden to Mystic. "So, who's going to tell me what on earth happened to you?"

Caden stared from Alaia to her and back again. "It's her story to tell. I'm sure she'll fill you in as soon as she is feeling better."

"Give me the short version," Alaia demanded hands fisted on her hips.

He raised his hands over his head in a gesture of surrender an eyebrow raised. "Hey, hey, hey, I'm not Nat. Ordering me around won't get what you want. Though I've heard you're a force to be reckoned with." He looked over at Mystic. "It's still her tale to tell." He turned back to the counter and got lunchmeat out of the fridge, grabbed mayo and spicy mustard, then began building sandwiches. He jerked his chin toward the fridge again. "Iced tea and beer is in there."

Her strength began to return, slowly. She smiled at him then nodded giving him permission to tell part of her tale.

While he got a plate out for the sandwiches, Alaia gathered cans of iced tea and a couple cold beers.

"Short version, one of her own people, a suitor she refused, almost killed her. Then he sent two hired guns to finish the job or find her body, I'm not sure which. I rescued her. Taking care of that situation is my next order of business as soon as I get your husband off my back."

"And does Nathanael know about this?" She waved her hand toward Mystic.

"Sort of, I was going to fill him in today, but I haven't had a chance, yet. He's offered divine intervention if I need it. Suppose that's why he's still hanging around here."

"Anything I can do to help, just let me know. I'll cold cock the bastard, if I get a chance," she said vehemently, hands fisted on her hips, her cheeks flushed in anger.

His eyebrows winged up. He smirked. "Thanks for the offer. We'll keep that in mind." He took the plate of sandwiches outside, and Alaia followed with the drinks.

Returning to the trailer, Alaia set about fixing sandwiches for them. "Your man didn't like no for an answer."

"Ethan didn't, but he never was my man. I really don't feel like talking about that right now." She snatched the sandwich from Alaia and took a bite, then sighed. "What I'd kinda like to know about is Caden and how all this works."

"I'll start off by saying, whatever spell you put on him, it's sure changed him. He was always the renegade of the renegade warriors. The guy I saw today…well… I wouldn't believe it, if I hadn't seen it with my own eyes." Alaia took a bite of her sandwich and chewed thoughtfully.

"I guess that's a good thing?" she said, picking up a glass of lemonade watching the condensation drip down the side of the glass. She took a sip and closed her eyes, the cool tart liquid tasted wonderful. She wiped the bottom of the glass on a napkin and sat the glass on a coaster.

"Sure is. Do you know the difference between the regular angels, I call them the white, fluffy, goody-two-shoes angels, Nat hates my reference, and the warrior angels?" Taking another bit of sandwich, Alaia reached for her glass of lemonade.

"No. I thought an angel was an angel."

Alaia sputtered, choked on the bite of sandwich she was chewing on, and nearly knocked over her drink. She grabbed her glass, took a gulp of lemonade, swallowed, then threw her head back and laughed until tears rolled down her cheeks. "Oh, no."

"Are you going to tell me the difference? Or just roll on the floor laughing?" She grinned, feeling better.

Alaia fanned herself with her hand and wiped the tears from her eyes. "Okay, okay. A white angel is just what you would expect of an angel. They help people in need, and other divine duties as called upon to perform. The warrior angels are beings who are good souls but extenuating circumstances made them unable to fit that mold. Most were soldiers, warriors, or misfits with a good heart and soul in their human life. Warrior angels are the renegade angels up above. They take on the dark demons or dark ones that rise from the bowels of Hell, or are caught in between, and leave death and destruction in their wake. Mortals have no idea such creatures walk among them or even exist. That's the way the big guy likes it." Alaia took another bite of her sandwich.

"I'd be dead without Caden's intervention," she said taking the last bite of her sandwich washing it down with a gulp of her drink. "He rescued me from certain death, took me back to his home, cared for me when I wasn't able." A shy smile crossed her lips. "He fixed delicious oatmeal when I regained consciousness."

Alaia's eyes sparkled with mischief. "And I'll bet he wasn't happy when that situation presented itself. Usually, warriors don't interact well with others. Although, there are exceptions to the rule, but Caden was never one of them. Warriors are considered outcasts by the white angels, but let one of those dark demons break through the perimeter and listen to the white one's squeal." Alaia snickered. "And believe it or not there are two categories of demons, the good or acceptable demons, and evil or dark demons. I personally know a few acceptable demons that share the earth with us. They are territory overlords that help control the dark demons and other paranormal creatures. You do know they exist? Right?"

Her eyes rounded, she chewed on her bottom lip and tried to neutralize her expression. "I always suspected such beings existed…" She paused and stared intently at Alaia.

"What…do I have food on my face or in my teeth?" Alaia snatched a napkin and dabbed at her mouth.

She snickered and shook her head. *This woman is so easy to talk to. It couldn't hurt to tell her the truth.* "I'm a shape-shifter."

Alaia's eyes widened, and the breath whooshed out

of her. "I knew it." She slapped her hand down on the table. "Native American, aren't you?" Without giving her a chance to respond, Alaia continued. "Your bronze skin and miles of black hair gave it away. No wonder Caden took such a shine to you. His father was Lakota/Sioux, I think. His mother was Irish. That's where he got those beautiful green eyes, and with his father's sculptured high cheek bones, it really makes him unique. Don't you think?"

"Yes, I find him quite…hmmm…attractive." Heat rose in her cheeks. She took another sip of her lemonade, swirling the remaining liquid in her glass.

"I bet you do. Caden's a bit taller and brawnier than Nat, and never lets him forget it. But he doesn't step over the line of disrespectful…too often." Alaia chuckled brushing the crumbs from the table. "Over the years, he learned how far he can push Nat without repercussions. When Nat was appointed Legion Commander, there was quite a test of wills and egos, but they worked it out."

"How long have they known each other?"

Alaia pursed her lips. "Hmmm…at least a couple hundred years."

"Good lord, how old is Caden?"

"Oh, I guess he didn't tell you that part. Maybe I better let him explain."

"Oh, no you don't. Spill it. The question of age didn't exactly come up between us. He said something about a hundred years without…well never mind…but I thought he was kidding. He looks to be about what thirty-five or so?"

"You might want to add about a century to that, give or take, but don't tell him I told you. Angels don't age. They remain the same physically as the day they became an angel. He died in one of the bloodiest battles in Sioux history, for what he considered a righteous cause. So Nat told me. Thusly, he became a warrior angel. We don't talk about Nat's business much. She waved her hand dismissively. "Back to the subject at hand. You are right in a way, he will not age."

"Whoa…wait He was at—what battle?"

"I've told you too much already." Alaia glanced at the door. "Need to get back to topic's I know about.

"If things work out between Caden and me, how does that work? I get old and wrinkled. He stays young and handsome? I die, and he lives on?"

"Another subject I'm not at liberty to discuss. Things are handled differently depending on the situation." Alaia paused for a beat, tilted her head, a puzzled expression crossed her face. "But isn't your life span different because you are a shapeshifter?"

"That I'm not at liberty to discuss." She smirked.

"Touché. Feel like joining the guys? If we leave them alone too long, they'll get into trouble. Believe me."

"Yeah, I'm feeling better. How well do you know the guys in Nathanael's legion?"

"Not well. I stay out of angel business. This is the first time I've been included, and I've mucked it up already." With a nervous giggle, Alaia spread her arms wide, let them fall into her lap.

"Was it tough for you and Nathanael when you first got together? I don't mean to pry, but I am a little worried about the forbidden rule." Getting to her feet, she walked to the cupboard and took out a package of chocolate striped cookies she'd seen earlier. "Want one?" She waved the package in front of Alaia on her way back to the couch.

"Of course." Alaia reached out, took a cookie from the package. Nibbled at the edge of the treat. "We are the reason that rule was enacted. The tribunal doesn't like warriors to have priorities above their job. Nathanael spends a third of his time up there and the rest down here with Kat and me unless he's called into battle. Although now days, the battles seem to be down here as much as up there."

"Down here, how is that possible?" She eased onto the couch, took a cookie, broke it in half and popped one-half in her mouth.

"You'd be surprised at the positions other worldly creature hold in our world. Some use their abilities illegally to manipulate mortals to do their bidding. If they refuse, there is trouble, and that's when the warriors and overlords step in. Enough said. I probably said too much already—again. You'll learn." Alaia put the last bite of cookie in her mouth, got up, and opened the door to the trailer.

"Hold on a moment, I need to put the"—she got to her feet and lowered her voice—"cookies back. Not enough for everyone."

****

"Well, well, well, they are going to grace us with their presence," Nat said as he greeted his wife with a kiss on the cheek.

Alaia glanced at Kat curled up in the play yard with her blanket, pieces of her sandwich squished between her fingers, a piece stuck in her hair.

Mystic giggled at the sight. "Want me to get a wash cloth?"

"No, we'll wait until she wakes up." Alaia turned her attention to Nat. "Glad to see you fed our daughter." Alaia pointed to the sleeping Kat.

"Unfortunately, Kat wore some of it, but she drank all of her juice from her sippy cup." Nat smiled.

Caden sprang up from his seat and reached for Mystic, putting a gentle arm around her waist. "Have a seat." He motioned to the lounge. "I'll get another chair." He walked a couple of feet over to the trailer and dragged out more chairs from the storage compartment under the trailer.

Nat and Alaia exchanged glances. "What happened to Caden? The rough spoken, self-centered, shattered warrior is missing," Alaia whispered.

"You guys know I can hear you." He grinned.

"Each time I've checked on him, I've seen changes, but this is the most drastic transformation yet," Nat said.

She smiled and nodded. "She's good for him." She breathed into Nat's ear. "Do you know what happened to her?"

He nodded and put his finger to his lips talking in her mind. *Caden filled us in, I'll tell you later.*

Caden carried over another chair and sat down. He narrowed his eyes at the couple. *It's rude to talk behind other's backs. Especially when one can hear you.*

As the words wafted through Nathanael's mind, he glared in his direction. *Listening to other's thoughts borders on insubordination in the ranks.* Nat shot him a scathing glance then stood and addressed everyone. "Now that we are all here, I want to discuss a few things."

He jumped to his feet also. "Shouldn't this be

between you and me?" His glance cut to Killian and Sean.

"No. They're aware of the situation and the decision."

"What decision?" Caden snapped.

"If you'd sit down and quit interrupting, I'll tell you," Nathanael said. "Keep your voice down or you'll wake Kat, then she's your responsibility to entertain."

He paced around behind his chair resting one hand on the back of it, the other on Mystic's. She reached behind her, put a hand over his, and waited for Nathanael to speak.

Used to his attitude, Nathanael waited for him to calm down then continued. "At your request, I addressed the council with the current situation you've created. I explained what happened, your only choice of intervention and the results. Needless to say, they were not happy and immediately determined that you violated the mortal relationship rule."

"Gee, now there's a shock," he said rocking back on his heels and murmured, "Meddling assholes."

Nat narrowed his eyes. "Before they passed judgment, I made them aware of the decisions you've made. The fact you were outside their jurisdiction and intended to remain so. There was a lot of disagreement and discussions, but eventually they decided to set aside a ruling until the situation with Mystic is concluded. Your relationship is not approved, but they didn't forbid it…yet. Again, this is uncharted territory for all of us."

He moved over to stand behind Mystic, his hands resting on her shoulders. He bent down, kissed the side of her neck, and whispered, "I told you it would be okay."

"Okay my foot. We're still in limbo." Mystic huffed, then put her hand to her mouth, glancing at Kat who shifted in her play yard.

Nat cleared his throat and continued. "As for Mystic's life remaining in danger and you still healing, the tribunal decided that it would be in everyone's best interest to assign a task force to assist in your pursuit of justice. Short of illegal activities or bringing attention to ourselves, of course."

"We've been assigned bodyguards?" Caden asked incredulously.

"Yes, until further notice, Killian, Sean and I are assigned to guard and assist you and Mystic in any way necessary."

"And what do they want in return?" Raising an eyebrow, he crossed his arms over his chest. "I'm not putting myself under their jurisdiction ever again."

"I believe someone reminded them of the centuries of dedicated service you gave them, even to your detriment. There is nothing required in return," Nat said. "While on the surface it appears this was a domestic situation, with power play overtones. The council agreed the threat of evil undercurrents not yet discovered might be on the horizon. Being caught unprepared was not an option."

He walked around his chair and sat silently for several minutes as he looked in the faces of everyone there. Finally, he took Mystic's hand in both of his holding it tight.

Without so much as cracking a smile Nat said, "This is one for the record books. I believe Caden Silverwind is speechless."

Killian grinned. "And it couldn't happen to a more deserving warrior."

Nat flashed a smile and continued. "I have rented a small lodge a few miles down the road. We'll be moving the rest of our belongings in later this evening or tomorrow morning."

"Mine and Kat's too?" Alaia wanted to know. "What a grand adventure."

The toddler rolled over and stretched rubbing her eyes.

"Yes. There is room for Caden and Mystic also, if the situation becomes too dangerous for them to be on their own."

"I am not…" Caden began.

"We are not trying to force you out of your home, only letting you know an alternative is available if necessary."

"Gotcha." He relaxed in his chair glancing at the woodpile. "Care to join Mystic and me around the campfire this evening? Tomorrow will be soon enough to get you moved and plan vengeance on the bastards that nearly killed her."

Alaia laughed. "There's the Caden I know."

Kat got to her hands and knees, stuck her butt up in the air then raised herself up, balanced on her feet, and shoved her arms in the air.

Alaia got up and reached in the play pen and picked up her daughter. Kat reached her hand out toward Nat. "Daddy."

"Daddy's busy," Alaia cooed.

Killian, Sean, and Nat helped him gather additional firewood. Soon blue and orange flames shot several feet high from the large fire pit.

Alaia handed Kat to Nat and followed Mystic into the trailer. Mystic brought a bag of marshmallows and Alaia came out with chocolate bars, graham crackers and bowl of warm water with a wash cloth.

He triumphantly held up six skewers and handed them out.

Nat held Kat out toward Alaia to wash up the toddler. "Not sure why we are bothering, she's soon be wearing marshmallow and chocolate."

After wiping Kat's hands and combing the bread out of her hair Alaia said, "At least she started out clean. I can't imagine that sandwiches and s'mores mix well." She grinned at the little girl and kissed her on the cheek. "Such a daddy's girl."

For the rest of the evening the guys told tales of the battles they'd fought and their heroic conquests.

The women roasted marshmallows and made s'mores, passing them out to everyone. Kat took her treat apart, picked at the marshmallow with her chubby little fingers until strings of marshmallow clung between her fingers like spider webs. Then she shoved the melty chocolate into her mouth and crumbled part of the graham cracker in her sticky fist.

Laughing, Alaia pointed to Nat. "Looks like you're wearing part of Kat's s'more too." She got up, grabbed up the wash cloth, rinsed it out in the bowl, and washed Kat's hands and face. After drying the child's hands with a paper towel, Alaia handed the toddler a small square of graham cracker. "See if you can eat that like a big girl."

Kat took the cracker, turned it over in her hand and nibbled on the corner, giving Alaia a wide smile.

Alaia returned to her seat, laid a hand on Mystic's

arm, and leaned over to whisper, "Don't believe all these testosterone induced tales."

"I don't. Males are males whether they're mortal, shapeshifter, or angel." She winked at Alaia, snickered, and looked affectionately over at Caden.

It was well after midnight when the fire died down. Nat, a sleeping child in his arms, suggested they head toward the lodge. He and Mystic folded up the chairs and put them away.

Nat settled Kat in her child seat, Alaia slid in beside her. The others piled into the SUV and started down the gravel road. Suddenly, gravel spewed everywhere as the vehicle came to a screeching halt. Red taillights gave way to bright white back up lights in the dark night, and the vehicle returned. Nat stepped out. "Caden, do you want one of the guys to stand guard tonight?"

"Why? We haven't had any problems here. Go on back to the lodge and get some rest."

Nat sighed heavily, glanced back at the SUV then over to Mystic.

"Whatever you want to say to me, you can say in front of her." Caden stood arms crossed over his chest leaning against the trailer. "Since it can't be warrior business. I'm not a warrior anymore."

"You are going to perform like one in the coming days. Believe me." Nat leaned one hand on the trailer.

"What do you mean?"

"The FBI is involved in Mystic's disappearance now. Apparently, there is another casino worker, a shift manager, who came up missing a week or two before Mystic. Foul play is suspected in the shift manager's disappearance. Of course, we know Mystic isn't missing. But once the FBI learns of the situation…" Nat shrugged. "He'll be a person of interest."

"Holy shit. That Ethan is a piece of work."

Mystic stiffly ambled into the trailer. At the top of the stairs she turned. "Good night gentlemen. I hope you'll excuse me, but I've had way too much fun for one night." She closed the door, and he watched the lights in the bedroom come on.

"Well I guess I'm sleeping on the couch tonight."

Nat raised an eyebrow, glanced to the window and back to him. "You're sleeping with her? I didn't know the relationship had—"

He interrupted. "No, we've not slept together in the sense that you mean. Not that I haven't given it considerable thought. I lay naked with her when I healed her, the best I could the day I found her. Otherwise, one of us sleeps on the couch in the living area, the other in the bedroom. As if it's any of your business."

"You healed her? Your healing abilities are intact?"

"Well, not completely, her injuries were too severe, but well enough to save her life. She's had to heal the rest on her own." He rolled his shoulders. *I need to get some flight time.*

"That's more than we hoped for when you were injured." Nat narrowed his eyes. "What other talents have returned?"

"Most of them. Wings are weak, so long flight is still difficult, but coming along. I haven't had a chance to practice daily like I did before she arrived. Now that everything is out in the open, I'll be able to continue my routine. I haven't tried shifting yet, but the feelings are there."

Nat nodded. "And we know your telepathic abilities are intact. I think all this can wait until morning. The FBI being involved will change my strategies. Knowing Ethan may have killed before makes a lot of difference in what we are dealing with."

He shifted from one foot to the other, tilted his head toward Nat. "How so? Mystic thought it was Ethan's anger and lack of control when he shifted to his wolf form that caused his actions. But if he's killed before…" Caden stiffened, his eyebrows drew together.

"We have no proof that he's killed before, just a missing employee and the FBI investigation." Nat shifted his stance, glanced over to Alaia in the SUV, and back to Caden.

"What's the FBI got on him? I imagine employees quit all the time." He waved his hand in a gesture of dismissal.

"Don't know, you'll need find out. Is Mystic able to participate in the investigation?"

He chuckled. "Just try to stop her. She is the most determined individual, I've ever met."

"You two should make a great pair, if you don't kill each other first." Nat grinned.

"You know everyone said the same thing about you and Alaia."

"Yes, but she is mortal. I have the upper hand most of the time. Mystic is a shapeshifter, and I'm willing to bet she has other magical abilities. She comes from a long line of powerful people. She'll keep you on your toes, or flat on your back." Nat laughed.

"I wouldn't say that first part too loud." He nodded toward the open window in the SUV where Alaia's smiling face peered out the window.

"Nat either get in the car or join us later at the lodge. Kat needs to go to bed. Now." Alaia insisted. The sounds of a whiny child floated in the night air.

"Be right there," Nat called to Alaia. "We'll see you tomorrow, probably be afternoon, since we need to get more of our stuff and get settled."

"Need any help? Mystic and I can meet you at the lodge about midmorning."

"Let's give that a try. See ya then." Nat strode quickly to the SUV and climbed in.

Alaia waved out the window, then leaned back inside as the dark tinted window went up.

****

Caden watched the vehicle's red tail lights bounce down the dusty gravel road. He leaned against the trailer considering the strange turn his life had taken during a few short days. In all his nearly two hundred years of existence, 'ready to settle down' was never in his vocabulary. Now he couldn't imagine one day without Mystic by his side.

He heaved a sigh of relief, trudged up the steps and tugged open the door. Glad the tribunal wasn't going to fight him. One problem solved, now on to the immediate matter at hand of how to keep Mystic alive. Not about to admit it, he was glad that Killian, Nat, and Sean would have his back as he tried to figure out what was going on and how to handle it.

Inside, he closed the door softly. Slow rhythmic breathing from the bedroom, told him Mystic was asleep. Silently he ascended the steps and eased himself onto the foot of the bed. Watching her sleep was somehow soothing. He kicked his sneakers off and lay across the end of the bed. *Just for a minute.*

When he opened his eyes again, warm sunlight streamed across his face. Mystic was lying on her side watching him with warm chocolate brown eyes, from under her long, thick, black eye lashes.

She smiled. "There's plenty of room for us both in your king-sized bed."

"I know I just don't want to rush you." He groaned as he stretched his arms above his head, arched his back, and rolled his shoulders side to side to ease the crick in his neck and back. He stifled a yawn with the back of his hand. "I offered our services to help Nat, Alaia, and the guys get settled in the lodge this afternoon. You up for it?"

She shrugged her right shoulder. "Sure, don't know how much help I can be. Each day is better, but my back is still a little stiff. I need to start stretching it out several times a day. My stamina seems to be lacking, too."

"I think we have waited as long as we dare. Are you ready to go after Ethan?"

"Oh, yeah. That weasel won't know what hit him."

"How do you feel about teleporting?"

"I've never done it. I'm not sure that's one of my talents, though in ancient times shapeshifters were said to have that ability among others."

"Really, how do you find out?"

"Find someone from the tribe who has that ability, and ask them to teach me."

"Not necessary. I can teach you."

"Can you now?" She sat up, scooched down the bed reaching around his waist and tugged him up beside her. "Now that's giving my back a good stretch." She put her hands on her lower back, leaned back and side to side grimacing. "I think the scabs are pulling the skin tight more than the muscles."

"Possible. What were you trying to do?" he said with feigned innocence. In the blink of an eye, his body was under the comforter next to hers. He gently slipped his arm around her bare waist pulling her to him, breathing a kiss just below her ear while trailing his lips farther down her body. "You know at this rate we'll be late to the lodge. How am I ever going to teach you to teleport?"

"How did you do that?"

"It's what you wanted, right?"

"Maybe…but…" When he brought his mouth up to hers, all attempts at conversation ceased as her body curved into him.

Chapter Eight
Things are not Always What They Appear—Get Used to It

Forty minutes later they stood outside the trailer hand in hand. "Hold tight onto me," Caden said. "Don't let go under any circumstances. I'll do the rest—this time. When we port individually, you'll visualize a reference point where we are going and lock onto it in the end location. Then close your eyes and see yourself in that place. With a little practice, you'll have it in no time."

"Now, hold tight, this will only take a minute." He held tight to her arms that were wrapped around him.

The sounds of twittering birds, scent of clean mountain air infused with the aroma of pine trees changed around him in the blink of an eye. Suddenly, melodic bells, excited voices, and the odor of stale air wafted around as they materialized in the casino hallway. He recognized they were standing beside the alcove a few yards from Ethan's office, exactly where he'd envisioned.

"Whoa, what a ride," Mystic whispered.

After making sure they weren't seen, he checked the power light on the surveillance camera. It was off. Killian had been successful in disabling the cameras as they'd discussed prior to teleporting. The team approach seemed to be working.

Mystic studied him for a moment then surveyed her surroundings. "Looks like Ethan made upgrades since I was here over a year or so ago. He's repainted in cream and added blue and gold carpeting. Looks nice."

Caden took Mystic's arm and tugged her down the hallway. "Come on, Ethan's office is just around the corner. We need to get in and out without being seen by anyone except Ethan." They paused at the door and listened to make sure Ethan was alone, then Caden knocked.

"It's open." Ethan growled.

Caden gave Mystic's arm a squeeze. "Remember, don't step any farther away from me than an arm's length. I'll fade into the background. Ethan won't be able to pick me out, but if he lunges for you, I'll grab you, and we're out of there. Got it."

"I got it." Mystic's voice had a slight tremor to it as she leaned against him.

He frowned. "You sure you're up to this?"

"Of course." She straightened her shoulders, turned the door handle, and walked through the door. "Hello Ethan," she said in a firm voice as she stepped farther into the office.

All the color drained out of his tanned face as he looked up. "Mystic. I thought…"

"Well—you thought wrong. You've got twenty-four hours to tender your resignation, or I'll have your ass hauled to jail and press charges for attempted murder. I may anyway."

Ethan swallowed hard, his eyes darting behind her. "Are you here alone?"

"No."

Ethan surveyed the room as he stood up from his

chair and moved from behind the desk. "Who came with you?" He edged closer to her.

"People you don't want to mess with. Now get back behind your desk and sit down." Mystic stood her ground but moved her back closer to Caden, shifting her weight a bit.

Ethan kept advancing toward her. "Mystic you shouldn't have come back," he growled.

"Don't say I didn't warn you." With a swift movement, she jumped up kicked out with a front kick and planted it just under Ethan's chin. His head jerked up as he stumbled back and flipped over the desk, crashing into the wall. With a groan, he slid down the wall.

Caden stepped out of the shadows, lifted his hand toward Ethan pinning him to the floor where he landed, on the off chance he was still able to get up.

"Remember twenty-four hours. I'll be watching." Mystic gripped Caden's arm and he teleported them back to the lodge.

Mystic fell into his's arms. "How'd I do?"

"Scared the shit out of him. That's how you did. He'll be moving a bit slow for a few days and out for your blood after that." Proudly, he hugged her tight and kissed her. "Now we wait."

"For what? Him to resign?"

"No, it won't be that easy. He'll call his people and tell them you're alive, probably put a professional hit out on you. Then he'll call the FBI, tell them you threatened him. If he doesn't check the surveillance footage first."

"If he checks it first?"

"Most people would think they're losing it and

won't say a thing to anyone. But Ethan's a loose cannon and desperate, he may press harder for his hired hit men to find you. He may also…well, let's wait and see. We need to disappear for a while and let the others handle things."

"I'm not running away."

"No, but you are leaving. We need to find out what is really going on here. Killian and Sean planted bugs in a few strategic places in the casino. Hopefully, they'll remain undetected long enough for us to find out what we need to know. Until then you'll remain missing."

"You're not going to tell me what to do." Mystic whirled around her hands fisted on her hips. "No man has ever controlled me and no one, not even a fallen warrior angel, ever will," she said emphasizing each word as she stalked out the door slamming it behind her.

****

He remained inside the lodge, shoved his hands in his pockets. "Women."

Nat blew out a breath. "That's one feisty female, and you broke the first rule of relationships." He shook his head and started to walk out the room.

"What you need to do, is…" Alaia said.

Nat interrupted. "Is come into the kitchen and see what there is to fix your very hungry husband." Arm firmly around her shoulder, he tried to guide her into the kitchen.

She whirled around in place. "What the hell are you doing? Trying to manage me? You know better than that Nathanael North." She grabbed his hand and flung it off her shoulder, her eyes narrowed.

Hand on the door knob, Caden paused to watch the

fireworks.

"Settle down, love. Caden and Mystic will figure it out on their own, if their relationship is going to work. I promised we'd not interfere. That includes you."

"I made no such promise. Caden's never been in a real relationship, he's going to muck it all up."

"Neither had I until you came along. One-night stands, sure. But…" He never saw it coming.

Fist balled, Alaia buried it in his stomach. "You've still got a lot to learn too." She stomped off in the direction of the front door. "Fix your own damn dinner!"

He slipped out the door several seconds before Alaia yanked open the door and stomped outside, down the steps and across the yard. He slunk around the corner glad to be out of her sight and possible wrath.

He skirted the outside of the lodge and returned via the back door into the kitchen. Slumped forward, Nathanael took a step backward, trying to catch his breath as the front door slammed. Nat straightened and leaned his hand on the kitchen counter to take in a full breath as he came in.

"This is all your fault," Nat said shoving past him as he hustled through the kitchen, into the living area and out the front door after his wife.

Killian and Sean stood at the end of the living room near the stone fireplace, watching the activities and grinned at each other.

"That's why it's forbidden to fraternize with mortal women," Killian said nodding his head, shifting his glance toward him.

"Sure, but females of any species can be difficult, however, the pleasure of their company is well worth the pain in my opinion." Sean rubbed his hand together in front of the roaring fire.

"You're entitled to your own stupid opinion." Killian grimaced.

They suddenly stopped their bantering to listen. Voices rose from the deck just outside the front door as a long, wail came from upstairs.

"Uh oh, Kat's awake. I don't know about you, but I'm going upstairs to my room, out of the line of fire." Killian hit the stairs at a run taking them two at a time.

"Right behind you. Bro."

Alaia rushed in the door and up the stairs.

Having had enough, he slipped out the back door, shrugged out of his green and black checked flannel shirt, tied it around his waist, and released his wings in the crisp night air. The breeze ruffled his feathers, and it felt good. He exercised them back and forth a couple of times then with powerful sweeps, he soared far above the treetops. Pleased at the strength and surprised at the lack of pain, he hovered for a moment, lowered his flight trajectory, and went to look for Mystic.

About a mile away from the lodge, he sensed her presence but failed to see her. Hovering over the area, he dropped lower to get a better look. That's when he saw a large, magnificent black wolf sitting alone atop a jagged rock ledge. The silver moonlight shimmered on her coat, casting shadows that disguised and blended her outline with the surroundings.

Unsure of how to proceed, he landed silently approximately a hundred yards away from her and down wind. *Now what? Don't tell her what to do and apologize. Yeah that should be a good course of action.* His expertise in this area was sorely lacking. He didn't want to fight with her anymore, but saying he was sorry, rankled too. For God sakes, he gave a sideways glance to the heavens. *I'm only trying to keep her alive. What thanks do I get?* His temper spiked. C*alm down. This kind of thinking is only going to make matters worse.*

Within ten feet of the wolf, he stepped on a branch, it snapped. The wolf turned her head, hackles raised, her haunting yellow eyes staring at him.

"Mystic, you are absolutely beautiful. I wasn't ordering you around, only meant to convey what we need to do to keep you safe." He took a couple more steps toward her. *I can't bear to lose you.*

The wolf's ears plastered to her head, upper lip curled in a silent snarl exposing her large canines as she watched him step carefully out of the shadows. Her yellow eyes registered surprise as they swept over his large dark wings, the marble gray feathers at the edge ruffling in the breeze.

"May I sit down?" he asked, sidling closer to her.

The wolf bowed her head for a moment as if granting permission then watched intently as he dropped to his knees, withdrew his wings, and sat cross-legged a few feet in front her.

"I'm used to giving commands and having them obeyed. Making decisions for others that are executed without question." He shoved his fingers through his already tousled hair. "Recently, I've been on my own, avoiding contact with others by choice. You come waltzing into my life changing everything. I'm still trying to get my footing. If I step on your toes, give me the benefit of the doubt, till I get it worked out."

The wolf's intense gaze softened, and she nodded

her massive head.

"I'll do the same for you. I know you are used to calling the shots and taking care of yourself. But right now, your life is at risk from your own people, you gotta let me take the lead here," he said, his voice rising in frustration.

The lines of the wolf blurred and shimmered, legs and arms lengthened, long flowing black hair blew in the breeze as Mystic returned to human form. He helped her into his shirt which hung midway to her thighs.

He watched in awe of the transformation. She had no trouble blending from wolf to human. It was a thing of beauty. "I know we'll have disagreements, we are two dominant beings, but I think it'll keep things interesting as our relationship grows." Not exactly what he wanted to say but couldn't bring himself to say the words he felt, not yet.

"I understand where you're coming from, but you can't simply order me around. Talk to me, tell me what is happening. What you have planned. I'm scared. I've never put my life in someone else's hands. It's not easy for me."

"I get that. Let's head back to the trailer. I caused enough trouble at the lodge. The morning will be soon enough to deal with the fallout." He took her hand carefully and picked their way off the ledge and on to the path leading back to the trailer.

Mystic tilted her head raising knitted brows. "What did you do?"

"I'm really not sure. Alaia started to give me advice, I think. Then Nat whisked her into the kitchen. The next thing I know they are yelling, and Alaia punches him in the stomach, then stomps out the front door into the yard. When I went around the lodge and came in through the kitchen, Nat was hunched over with his hand on the counter top trying to catch his breath. He stared daggers at me, claims it's all my fault, and sprints after Alaia. When I heard their voices on the front porch, Killian and Sean beat feet upstairs. Kat woke up from her nap, I guess, and started to cry. Alaia ran in the front door and upstairs. I skipped out the back door to exercise my wings."

"Oh, Caden, I didn't mean to cause all this. Are Alaia and Nat all right? It wasn't a big fight?"

"Hell, if I know. I left. You weren't the cause. I guess it was me. We'll find out tomorrow. They've weathered a lot worse, believe me, so don't worry." A lone light flickered against the moon lit shadows as the trailer came into view. He sprinted up the trailer stairs, opened the door.

Chapter Nine
She's in Trouble but Rescue is Risky. Will there be Another Body on Sacred Land?

Plopping on the couch, Mystic reached for her backpack and yanked out her cell phone. "I really need to check on Chinoah. I have a really bad feeling. Ethan knows she's the only person I'd trust if I was in hiding. He'll go after her now that he knows I'm alive. We've been friends all our lives. I'll never forgive myself if something happens to her."

Caden ran his fingers through his hair leaving furrows in it. "That's exactly why you can't contact her. He may use her as a trap."

"I can't let anything happen to her. Do you want another body on your hands?"

"You're positive there is no chance she would cooperate with him."

"Absolutely. I'd bet my life on it."

"That's exactly what you're doing." He frowned but said nothing else.

She pushed the power button on her phone, holding her breath hoping that it still worked. As the white apple with the bite out appeared on the screen, she sighed with relief. The icon disappeared, and a battery symbol appeared with a red line. She dumped the contents of her backpack on the floor, stirring through the items until she found the power cord. "Thank God," she whispered.

He took the phone charger and plugged it into a power outlet. "Shouldn't take long and you can at least check your messages." His mouth formed a thin line, and his forehead creased. "If something's wrong, we'll work it out together. You can't... I mean it would be better if you tell me, then we decide from there. Okay?"

She smiled, he was trying. "Agreed." She paced across the floor then checked the phone again. The main screen was up. She had fifty new voice messages and twenty text messages. The text screen popped up with 611 on it. She went pale and checked the rest of the texts. All 611 and all sent this afternoon.

"What is it?" Caden put his hand on her shoulder as he squinted at the screen.

"That's a code Chinoah and I used as children. It means she's in big trouble." She turned her worried eyes to Caden. "We have to find her. He may have killed her by now."

"Not if she doesn't know where you are. She is still leverage for him against you as long as she's alive. I'll contact Nat."

****

Holding her phone to her chest, she followed him into the bedroom. He slid open a closet door and reached far back in the wardrobe, his fingers rested on his celestial diamond sword and platinum spelled daggers. Grabbing the chest harness, he slipped his arms through and sheathed the daggers. Then he slung the leather scabbard over his back slipping the magical sword inside.

Never in his wildest dreams did he expect to wear his weapons again. In fact, he'd almost given them to

Killian, who refused, saying a warrior, even a retired warrior never parts with his weapons. Idly, he wondered if Killian had foreseen this situation. He'd heard rumors that Killian had inherited the second sight of his Scottish mother, which he retained through the angel transition. Killian never confirmed or denied such talent.

He sent a distraught message into Nat's mind. *Nat, I'm sorry to bother you, but we have an emergency, Mystic and I will be right over.*

No. Absolutely not. Nat shot back so strong, it reverberated in his mind.

He shook his head to stop the words. *It can't be helped, I'm really sorry, but this could mean some one's life or death.*

Yours. You have no idea how sorry, until I get my hands on you.

We're down stairs, I disabled the alarm on my way in.

"Shit." Nat hissed between his teeth. "Caden and Mystic are downstairs. There's some kind of emergency."

"What's wrong?"

"Hell, if I'd know." Nat growled. "He's going to pay for this. Don't forget where we left off, I'll be right back."

He grimaced at interrupting his boss, but it couldn't be helped. A door banged, and he looked up to see Nat exit the bedroom.

"I'm coming too." Alaia rushed out the door behind Nat, hopping on one foot as she pulled on fuzzy slippers. "Should I wake the guys?"

"No, let me find out what this is all about, first."

Nat took the stairs two and three at a time landing on the floor at the bottom of the stairs with a thud. He looked from an ashen faced Mystic to a flushed Caden standing near the stairway. "What's going on?"

Mystic held out her phone and pushed play. A shaken female voice said, "Myst what's going on? Ethan called, said you were missing. Wanted to know if I'd heard from you. He said you might be dead. I hate that guy; can't believe a word he says. He creeps me out. Call me."

She pushed play again. "Myst, I'm worried, call me."

She pushed the play button again. "Myst he keeps calling, claims I'm hiding something from him. I'm leaving the house, so he can't find me. Don't come around here. Call me."

She pushed play one final time, as tears glistened in her eyes. "Myst, I'm really scared he tracked me down at work. Co-workers are keeping him busy while I leave the back way. I made it to my car, and I'm pulling out of the parking lot. Call..." A woman's terrible scream resonated through the phone then silence.

"The voice mails were all from the days leading up to yesterday. Yesterday, I received twenty texts with the code 611, that is the code Chinoah and I used as children reserved for when we were in the most terrible trouble we could imagine and required adult intervention. Those texts originated after we returned from the River Winds."

"We believe that Ethan has Chinoah. Obviously, he is using her to try to lure Mystic to him. Any info from the bugs planted at the casino?"

"Nope, quiet as a church mouse. Ethan left his office and the casino via the back way shortly after you two left. I don't think he's returned," Killian said, entering the room with Sean on his heels. "What's going on?"

Caden filled Killian and Sean in as Nat and Alaia listened to the last voice message again.

Killian walked to the window watching outside for several minutes. "You know, I don't think Ethan has her. Oh yeah, he probably gave the order, but the feds are watching him, and he knows it. Nope, someone else has your friend."

Known for his battle strategies, Killian was the very best at figuring out what move the demons would make next and countering it successfully. Familiar with how Killian's mind worked, he knew by the look on his face the warrior had formulated a plan.

"Killian, out with it."

"First of all, it would depend on who has her, local thugs or professionals. If professionals have her, they already ascertained she doesn't know anything. She's dead." His voice was void of all emotion. "But I don't think that's the case. I think this is the work of locals. Where would locals take an individual that the Fed's couldn't follow without permission? Which would allow more time for interrogation?"

Mystic jumped up from her seat. "The FBI doesn't have broad jurisdiction over Indian tribal members inside the boundaries of an Indian reservation in the United States. Tribal land is considered sovereign land, owned and governed by the tribes and Tribal Police. They have total jurisdiction regarding their members. If tribal members are involved, they'd take her to the sacred lands on the Rez. Let's go." She grabbed her backpack and coat then headed for the door.

Caden caught her by the elbow. "Not yet."

"Exactly. Do you have a map of the Rez?" Killian asked.

"Yes, but it's on my phone."

"Send it to my e-mail address." Nat handed her a card. "I can download and print it upstairs."

"Wow, computer savvy angels," Mystic said in amazement.

"That's warrior angels, and we fight evil with everything at our disposal. I'm good, but Caden is better. Didn't you notice his media center on his desk in the living area of his trailer?"

Mystic shook her head slowly then snapped her fingers. "The midnight blue computer sitting on the desk? How long is this going to take?"

"Long enough for us to get it right the first time." Killian grumbled glaring at her. "As soon as Nat has the map printed out, I need you to point out the area where they may have taken her, including all access roads leading there. We'll need a quiet secluded area we can teleport to without being seen, as close as possible to the sacred land."

"I can do that." She leaned against Caden as he wrapped his arms around her.

Nathanael came flying down the stairs holding a large sheet of paper and handed it to Killian. "I printed it out on eleven by seventeen paper hoping it would be easier to read. It's still pretty small."

Mystic leaned over. "I can show you the roads surrounding the sacred land on that printout. She circled a smaller section on the paper. Nat can enlarge the suspected area, then I can find you a place to materialize unnoticed that won't desecrate the sacred lands." Mystic took out a magnifying glass, bent over the original map.

"Hey, we're angels, we tread lightly on sacred lands," Killian stated indignantly.

"But you are not Native American nor do you understand their beliefs. More specifically my people's spiritual beliefs and traditions."

"And your people are?" Killian asked.

"The Northern Arapahoe, we share the Wind River Rez with the Eastern Shoshone tribe, which by the way encompasses over two million acres."

He shrugged. "We have you, the daughter of a shaman to advise us."

"True. Now here are the roads leading into the area." She circled a large expanse on the map and handed it back to Nat. "Can you enlarge this area I have circled and print it?"

"Sure. Be right back."

When he returned, they spent an hour bending over the maps, heads together. A few heated discussions erupted but finally a search area was determined and a safe place for them to materialize was located. Mystic stuffed her phone into her backpack, slung it on her back, and stared at him.

He shook his head vehemently. "You're not going." He closed his eyes and clenched his jaw. "I mean, we can discuss this, but I think you'll agree by taking you we're providing him with exactly what he's after."

A corner of Mystic's mouth turned up in an almost

smile. "I want to help."

Nat shifted his gaze to Caden with a look that silenced him. "We understand that, but the warriors standing before you are the elite of the elite. Let us do our job. You can care for Chinoah when we bring her back. Now we're wasting valuable time. Suit up warriors."

She let her backpack slide to the floor. "How will I know you have arrived safely in the designated area?"

"Because we've been doing this for hundreds of years," Nat said.

Alaia reached out putting an arm around Mystic's shoulder. "It'll be all right." Alaia nodded to the group, and they disappeared.

Chapter Ten
Don't Tread on Sacred Ground

The group materialized in a thick group of trees. Standing still, they listened to the usual nocturnal sounds to make sure nothing was alerted to their arrival.

Nathanael spread the map out on the ground matching the sound of rustling leaves. He pointed out areas on the map to each warrior. After ensuring that nothing was in the way of direct mind to mind communication, they split up Sean was the first to detect human voices. He put a hand out to stop Caden's forward movement.

They crouched down in the brush, while he scanned the area for movement. A few minutes later a group of teenagers stumbled by unaware of their presence. Sean alerted the others to the unwelcome visitors. A shot rang out, followed by a man with a gun chasing the teenagers.

"What the hell are you doing here?" A thin man, of average height caught the slowest teenager by the back of his shirt and swung him around. The kid fell to the ground. "Answer me."

"Nothing man. We was drinkin with the spirits. Heard screamin. Figured the spirits were pissed, so we split." The boy stood listing to one side, then grabbed hold of the man and threw up on his shirt. "Sorry, man, I think I drank too much." He did a face plant directly into the dirt.

The man kicked him in the side. "Get the hell out of here before the spirits end your miserable life."

The kid pushed up, doubled over, half crawling, in an attempt to get away. There was no sign of his friends. The warriors remained motionless as another man approached. This one stocky with short cropped hair.

"What's going on? I heard a shot. What's that all over your shirt?" The stocky man wrinkled his nose and shoved the other man away. "You smell awful."

"It's exactly what it looks and smells like, smart ass." He pulled his shirt off over his head and wadded it up. "A group of drunk teenagers out taunting the spirits. I didn't see any reason to kill 'em. They ain't going to remember anything anyway. Been enough blood spilled tryin to cover the boss' ass."

"They see anything?"

"Naw, they might have heard her scream, but thought it was angry spirits. Bet they don't come back here again." He snorted.

"Idiot. What if they tell someone? We'll have the Tribal Police out here nosing around. Find them and eliminate them. Remember the boss man said no witnesses."

"They're only kids and so drunk they can't even walk."

"Do it. No witnesses. And don't throw your shirt on the ground."

The stocky man strode away, while the other one headed in the direction of the kids.

He connected with Nat, reporting what they'd seen and heard. *Anyone else see or hear anything?*

123

Yeah, she is definitely here and still alive. Close ranks slowly toward the center of the sacred ground until we can pin point her location. Nat replied in kind.

What about disturbing the sacred grounds? he countered.

"We'll ask forgiveness or pay the consequences tomorrow. I don't think the spirits want her killed on their grounds.

True.

The abductors seemed to disappear into the mist. There wasn't another sighting or sound for the next hour.

Let's rendezvous back at the starting point, we're missing something. I can feel her but it's like she's part of the ground.

Once they all returned to their point of arrival, Nat nodded to him. "Go back to Mystic. Ask her if there are any underground tunnels or if we need a blessing to start digging. I don't want to disturb the resting place of their ancestors, but we're not leaving here without Chinoah."

"Got it."

He materialized in the living area of the lodge. Mystic rushed to him. "Where's Chinoah? You didn't find her?"

"We know the area she'd being held but can't get a fix on her. It's like she is part of the ground, if that makes any sense."

She nodded, took a deep breath, and let it out slowly.

He relayed the legion commander's request, while holding her tight against him. The steady beat of her heart in time with his, settled him.

"I don't know of any, but then I didn't learn all I could have. Unfortunately, when I returned, my father was sick, and I focused on the healing arts, not in learning the secrets of the land. I do remember my father always reminding others to be respectful to the ghosts of the innocent killed in an 1864 massacre. Could be dealing with…"

He raised an eyebrow. "Really?"

Mystic lifted her right shoulder and moved to the computer, pulled up a search screen, typed in spirit legends and scrolled through the listings. "Nothing specific." She sighed. "I could contact a member of the tribal council."

"Not an option right now," he said shaking his head.

"I'll do what I can to appease the spirits from what I remember and hope they understand," she said chewing on her bottom lip. "Also realize there could be evil spirits in that area that are disguising the area from you."

Of the opinion that the problem was man made, he left armed with more maps of the area. He materialized in the trees and handed the maps to Nat, bringing him up-to-date with Mystic's efforts and thoughts. He also admitted he'd felt the evil, but still wasn't sure if it was real or imagined.

"Go with your gut. I'd trust your instincts, damaged or not, more than any other warrior out here."

A woman's blood curdling scream split the air, just as the warriors divided up preparing to close the circle of their search.

Hone in on that Caden, what are we dealing with? Nat's words wafted through his mind.

There are evil spirits protecting the area where she's being held. We must see through them to reach her and hope Mystic has worked the magic to allow it.

He felt a guiding hand pulling him toward an area away from where they were currently searching. He motioned Killian to follow. Self-doubt and darkness started closing in. He thought about Mystic, her steady heartbeat, and fought his way through the darkness, just as he heard voices. Killian nodded, and they closed in, alerting the others. The voices were coming from an anomaly in the rock wall straight ahead.

The warriors crowded around the area, he pushed, and his hand went through what appeared to be a solid rock wall. He slipped the rest of his body through, followed by Killian. The other side proved to be the entrance to an underground cave lit with wall torches.

The area opened to a large cavern, a fire burned in the center. Chained to a wall was a young woman. He recognized Chinoah from the pictures on Mystic's phone. Her clothes torn, her face bloody, her arms and legs bruised and burned. She was alive, but barely. Killian and Sean hugged the rock wall, fading into the shadows as they moved closer and closer to the open area. He and Nat faded into their surroundings and moved in from the opposite side.

He counted five men, no, three men and two demons disguised as mortals. *This is why we had so much trouble finding Chinoah, they were masking detection from the mortals.* The demons stood as the first line of defense, two men were huddled around a large fire, and the third stood next to Chinoah, leering at her.

He cut his gaze to the others. A slight nod from

each of them told him they were aware of the demons. Protocol required that they take out the demons first, sparing the mortals, if possible, for their own kind to deal with, and leave no evidence of battle. At the edge of the cavern, they stopped. Nat gave the signal to split up, then motioned he and Sean would take out the two demons closest to them. He and Killian should handle the mortals. With one jerk of his chin Nat and Sean disappeared.

First evidence anything was amiss was a severed demon head flying across the room, body slumped on the floor. The remaining demonic partner backed into the shadows and donned battle gear. He drew his sword and came out slashing. Sean materialized and attempted to knock the sword from the demon's hand. The creature ducked and came up under Sean, slicing his arm open as he tried to maneuver away.

A bright red stain quickly soaked the lower portion of Sean's shirt. "Shit, that was a brand-new shirt. You're going to pay for that you piece of crap."

"The demon's next blow deflected off Sean's armor. Sean brought his sword under the demon's, and with a swift upward motion the sword went flying. The demon fell forward, before he regained his balance Sean thrust his sword through the demon's lower torso jerking upward, splitting him from groin to throat. He withdrew his sword, and the demon hit the floor with a thud bursting into flames.

From opposite sides, he and Killian rushed the two mortals who had drawn their guns. The thin man squeezed off a round. He sidestepped it, bent down, and swept the mortal's feet out from underneath him. The man scrambled up, wildly firing again, this time barely grazing his shoulder. He jumped straight up pulling his knees to his chest then twisted, shot his left leg out in a sidekick connecting with the man's solar plexus, sending him flying across the room. The man's body smashed against the rock wall, skull hitting the wall with a sickening crack, blood splattered behind his head, trickling down the wall as he slid to the floor.

He leaned over checking for vitals. "Out of commission for the duration, but not dead."

He turned, throwing his dagger across the room, skewering a man's arm as he ran at Chinoah with a knife. Killian grabbed the man by the throat slamming him against a rock slab.

"Same here," Killian said as he let go of mortal's throat, reaching for the man's leg flipping him off the slab. The man landed face down on the floor spread eagle. Killian stepped over him and turned toward the sound of footsteps. The third man ran for the entrance, his right arm dangling uselessly at his side. Nat within close proximity, reached for his dagger.

"I got this commander." Killian stepped in the man's path. The thug pulled his gun and fired. Killian jumped sideways knocking the gun out of his opponent's hand, caught the weapon mid-air, and slammed him in the head with it, then shoved him to the floor.

"Killian, cut down Chinoah and get her back to Mystic. Use your healing power on her," Nat shouted. "Caden, Sean, and I will clean up. Killian drew his diamond sword from its leather pouch. It shimmered in the firelight as it sliced through the chains like a hot knife through butter. Chinoah fell into his arms, and he disappeared with her.

Nat checked their injuries and found that they were minor and would heal by tomorrow morning, without a scar. "All right guys, get the blood off the walls, this demon ash swept up, and let's get out of here."

"What the hell do you think the demons were cozied up with mortals for? Why were they involved at all? Kidnapping Mystic's friend to what end? What was or is in it for them? There's more to this than meets the eye." With a wave of his hand, the ash formed a pile, then disappeared.

"Unless, Ethan is mixed up in more than Tribal business," Nat suggested. "What is worth the Demon Overlord's wrath, should he find out? And he will. I'll see to it."

"Yeah, where there's a few demon's, you can bet there are more involved. I still don't see what could possibly be motivating them. The casino business? Not their style."

Forty-five minutes later, they materialized at the lodge where Mystic was waiting. "Chinoah was beat up but will survive. I cleaned her wounds and dressed her in one of my soft cotton gowns, before Killian carried her upstairs." She shook her head.

"Is he still up there with her?"

"Yes. He curled up next to her and wrapped her in his wings. A golden glow surrounded them. That's when I left." She sighed, padded toward him, and caressed him on the shoulder. "Is that how you healed me?"

"Yes. I was—" He leaned into her touch, then hesitated at the sounds of approaching footsteps.

Alaia rushed in with a large first aid kit and set it on the table. "How about you two?" She eyed him and

Sean. "Let's take a look at your injuries."

Nat watched his wife fuss over Sean's injury. Mystic cleaned and bandaged his without a word.

"Good work, tonight men." Nat eased onto the couch.

"Yeah, right, wounded by a mortal." He snorted shaking his head slowly.

"Grazed by a wild bullet shot by a crazed mortal. No time to figure out the trajectory, avoid it, and not kill the mortal. Your restraint is to be applauded. That sidekick could have sent him clean through the rock, if you hadn't held back your power. Nice job, considering you've been out of commission for a while. Reactions were great," Nat said wincing. "Too bad your warrior days are over."

"Thanks. Not an excuse, but I'm still not one hundred percent. I'm exhausted. After a little skirmish like that, I shouldn't even be winded." He chose to ignore his commander's last comment.

"That's the way it is when you get old," Sean said grinning.

"I'll show you old." He bounded out of his chair only to career into Mystic's arms, as she jumped between the two men.

"Don't use up all your energy on him. You might want to use it for something else later tonight," she said, breathing a kiss at the hollow of his neck.

Nat chuckled. "She's got your number, Caden."

"You could be right." He shot Mystic a seductive smile as he donned his weaponry. "We're going back to the trailer, so you can finish what we so rudely interrupted."

Alaia blushed as Nat reached for her hand tugging

her toward the stairs. "How does he always know?" she whispered.

He winked then swept Mystic up in his arms and disappeared.

****

Caden opened the trailer door to soft lights and strains of classical music. Stepping inside he lowered Mystic to her feet. She blinked in surprise. "Did you set this up before we left, or has someone been here? She sidled closer to him.

"I set it up. It's what I used to do before heading into battle. It helped me cope. I knew tonight would end in a fight. It was nothing like I was used to, but bad enough. It's like being on an adrenaline high and then when it ebbs away you've nothing left, muscles ache, any injuries sustained drain you. Many a time I woke several hours or even days later on the floor where I stumbled in." He stretched his arm behind him, slid the leather scabbard off, pulled the 9mm out of his boot and returned the weapons to the closet.

"That's not going to happen on my watch. Get in the shower, I'll fix you bowl of soup." First, she took off the blood-soaked bandage and examined the cut closer. "Just a nick, it's already healing. She tossed the bandage in the garbage and watched him undress. "Are you all right?" she asked as he stepped into the shower.

"Never better. I'm in my warm, comfortable home, with a beautiful woman, fixing me something hot, and she is going to lay with me, while I sleep. What more could I want?" Flashing a devastating smile, he turned on the water, stepped into the shower, and leaned against the shower wall. *She was safe, but for how long?*

"Hey, I didn't agree to sleep with you," she whispered back to him.

"I heard that." He cracked the shower door open. "Have no fear fair maiden, you are in no danger from me. I'm too tired even to contemplate what you are suggesting. Now…tomorrow morning may be a different story, we'll see." He left the door ajar letting the hot water cascade down his tired, aching body. His mouth watered when he heard her rip open a package of crackers, and the pot of soup bubble. She poured the soup into a bowl, sat it on a tray beside the crackers, then carried it into the bedroom, the silverware clinked against the bowl as she set it on the nightstand. Quiet footsteps came closer to the bathroom door.

His body flexed as he turned, soapy water ran in rivulets down his back. Through the rising steam, he saw her and raised a brow. "Like what you see?" He pushed the door to the shower farther open. "Care to join me?"

"I do like what I see, but I'll pass on the invitation for now. Can I get a rain check?"

"You bet."

"Come eat your soup while it's hot, then you can get some sleep."

The shower door snapped shut. He walked naked and dripping into the bedroom, leaned over her, and shook his wet hair all over her. She squealed shoving him backward. He caught her arm pulling her to him then winced when she landed against his sore shoulder.

"See that's what you get." She giggled wiggling under his arm to make her escape.

"I guess." His tired eyes met hers as his nostrils flared. "The soup smells delicious. Thank you." He eased down on the bed, brought the bowl to his lips, and drained it before she could hand him a spoon. "By the way, thanks for not fussing over me in front of the guys. It's embarrassing."

By the time, his head hit the pillow, he was out.

Chapter Eleven
Be Careful What You Wish For

Mystic cleaned up the dishes, showered, slipped one of his worn t-shirts over her body and crawled under the covers next to him, the only place she felt safe.

When her eyes blinked open the next morning, he was leaning on his elbow watching her.

"Like what you see?" She grinned sleepily at him, tugging at the t-shirt that wound up above her breasts while she slept.

"Oh, yes." He leaned over to her and kissed her. "The game you are playing is a dangerous. One of these days, I'll not be able to control myself."

Her lips formed a saucy smile. "I'll take my chances. Right now, next to you is the only place I feel safe. What happens next?"

The corners of his mouth curved up in a mischievous grin. "In this bed or outside of it?" A strand of raven hair fell across her face. He brushed it aside, his fingers lingering on her cheek as his thumb caressed her jaw line.

Leaning into his warm hand, she kissed his palm lightly, cupping her hand under his.

A frustrated groan escaped from his lips. "I want you so bad, I can taste it, but not until you are ready." He threw off the comforter, stood, and yanked on a pair of well-worn jeans. We'll talk about this over breakfast."

Surprised at his sudden business-like attitude, she stood and pulled on her maroon jogging suit. "Can someone go to my apartment and get some of my clothes?"

"Yeah, we'll port over there this morning. Let me see if I can get backup." The words no sooner out of his mouth and Sean materialized.

"Boss says, I'm to check out her apartment before you two port in." Killian made air quotes. "And no more shenanigans. Clear your actions through Nat. Demonic involvement has changed the rules. Now, give me a couple of minutes." Sean disappeared.

"Whoa. What was that all about?" Mystic stared at the spot where the other angel had been.

"Nat's pulling rank. Can't say as I blame him."

"Oookaaay." She glanced around the room then continued. "What happened to the guys who were holding Chinoah?"

Two of them were demons and three were mortals. That's why we had so much trouble finding them. The demons were masking their hiding place. We dispensed with the demons first and neutralized the mortals, leaving them tied up just inside perimeter of the sacred grounds. I called the Tribal Police and suggested they check the area. Told them about the drunk teenagers we saw last night then hung up before the call could be traced."

"Demons? On sacred lands." Her brow wrinkled as she chewed on her lip. *What the hell was Ethan into? I don't think this is just about me.*

"Yep. They were weak and actually under the

sacred lands. But, I'm sure retribution will be coming when word gets around."

"What kind or retribution?"

"Depends on why they were cooperating with the mortals and what consortium they belong to. Whatever the reason, it spells trouble. You're right, I don't think this is only about your slap to Ethan's male ego or losing control while shifting. Demons wouldn't throw their lot in with mortals over something like that. It has to be a big payoff to them."

"What…what do you mean?"

"I agree with you."

"You know what I mean. You can read my mind?" She stood her hand fisted on her hips, waiting for an answer.

"That's the hazards of running with a fallen warrior angel." He gave her a lopsided grin.

"Great. Read this."

"Don't believe I want to."

Sean reappeared. "All clear, for the moment. Let's get in and out. I'll play lookout."

Caden motioned to her. "Come here so we can port to your apartment and get back. Nat's waiting for us to join him at the lodge to discuss our next move." He held his arms out, she grudgingly allowed him to wrap his strong arms around her. "When we get there, don't say a word. Grab your stuff. We'll need to get out of there quickly in case Ethan or whoever is calling the shots is watching or having the place watched."

A few seconds later they materialized in her apartment. *Whoa that was a rush.* It was just like she left it. Dragging her bag on wheels out from under the bed, she hurriedly stuffed underwear, jeans, shirts and shoes, shampoo, lotion, toothbrush and toothpaste in it. She grabbed a garment bag from the closet, shoved some nicer clothes inside, and tossed it to Caden, giving him a thumb up sign. A key scrapped in the lock as the doorknob turned. Caden handed her the bag, grabbed the suitcase, and gripped her hand tightly as they disappeared.

"Whew that was close," she breathed once they were back in the trailer.

"Didn't see anyone from my vantage point," Sean said. "But I stepped inside as we all prepared to port. I'll see you at the lodge." With a whisper of air, Sean was gone.

"Who has a key to your apartment?"

"I've never given anyone a key. Except the landlord has one."

"I'd sure like to know who was coming in your apartment and why. We need to beat feet to the lodge. If we leave now, we can walk there. That'll burn off some of that excess adrenaline caused by our little adventure. I can hear your heart thundering from over here, your face is flushed and you're shaking."

"Let me splash water on my face, change into my jeans, a sweater and a pair comfy shoes." She swung the suitcase onto the bed and flipped it open.

"Make it quick or we won't have time to walk the distance. Nat is not a patient man."

****

He ambled outside and stretched his wings. The cool breeze wafting under the feathers in the warm sun felt good. Exercising his wings back and forth, he noticed the marble gray tips now extended up a third of the wing. *The charcoal black damage wasn't permanent. They feel almost strong enough to carry Mystic and me. She'd enjoy a moonlight flight tonight.*

In what seemed like only a few minutes, Mystic bounded out the door and down the stairs. "I'm ready."

It was only a few miles to the lodge, so they jogged up the path. By the time he knocked on the door, Mystic was breathing hard, but he sensed her jittery feeling was gone. She blew out a breath collapsing on the love seat in front of the fireplace, pulling him down beside her.

"Good afternoon," Nathanael called from upstairs. Kat came tearing down the stairs in front of him. "Whoa." He snagged her around the waist just as she stumbled and pitched forward. "One stair at a time, honey or you're really going to get hurt. Alaia, would you put up the baby gates at the top and bottom of the stairs."

"Not a good idea, she climbs right over them. Too much of her father in her." Came the answer from one of the rooms at the top of the stairs.

Nat smiled indulgently at the little girl dangling under his arm. He put her on the floor, and she ran for her rocking horse in the corner, climbed on, and began rocking furiously. "Wish I had that kind of energy."

"Where's Chinoah?" Mystic asked wringing her hands.

"They're not up yet. I imagine it was a rough night, with the fight and the drain of healing on his body." Nat nodded toward the den. We can review last night and kick around some ideas while we wait for him. Mystic, you're free to join us."

Alaia stood in the doorway wanting to hear what her husband had to say, but also keeping an eye on Kat.

"According to what I've heard, Mystic had a point this morning. It can't be just about her rejecting him or losing control while shifting. If Demons are involved, we know from experience, it's something more, much more." Nat rounded the desk and motioned for the others to sit.

Everyone's attention shifted to Mystic as they nodded in agreement and settled into their seats.

"Ethan must have cut some kind of deal with them. Now, his actions have jeopardized the deal. And you— my dear—are a liability," Nat said.

"Exactly," a soft voice said from across the room. Chinoah stood in the doorway next to Alaia supported by Killian. She was dwarfed by the larger warrior angel.

Mystic rushed in and hugged her. "I am so sorry this happened to you. It's all my fault."

"No, it's not. From what I overheard, they left you for dead. When your body couldn't be found they snatched me. Something changed."

"Yeah, Ethan found out Mystic was alive. We wanted to force his hand. But didn't realize he is mixed up in something much bigger than we thought. You got caught in the middle." He said disgustedly shoving up from his chair.

"What can you tell us?" Nat asked.

"Not much except, even Ethan was shocked at his actions when he attacked Mystic. He's an experienced shapeshifter, control is second nature to him. I don't think it was entirely that you spurred his advances, but rather whatever changes you requested in the way the casino operation. Requiring him to answer to the tribal council is the real problem." Chinoah closed her eyes and leaned on Killian.

"I think she's had enough for now," Killian said.

"No, just let me sit down for a bit. I'll be all right."

Killian swept Chinoah off her feet, carrying her to the couch. Mystic sat next to her, while Killian perched on the arm next to Chinoah protectively.

"Two guys, could have been demons, kept muttering to each other something about the consortium not liking the attention that Ethan was getting over Mystic going missing. They said the operation would be delayed due to the Feds snooping around. That's why Ethan was so intent upon finding you once he knew you were alive, but he couldn't prove it. Did you do something to the surveillance videos?"

He grinned. "Something like that."

For the first time, Chinoah looked around suspiciously. "Just who are you people?" She turned to Mystic. "And how are you mixed up with them?"

Mystic smiled. "It's a long story, but the short version is that Caden saved my life when Ethan left me for dead. It's been a long road back but I get stronger every day. Don't worry, you can trust these people."

Chinoah looked unconvinced as she narrowed her eyes examining each person critically, except Killian.

He moved to Mystic's side, putting his arm around her. "We're an elite security task force. A division of special forces, operating under a top-secret clearance. I was on extended leave when I found Mystic laying on the path. She almost bled out."

"Chinoah, have I ever lied to you?" Mystic asked.

"Noooo," Chinoah said, a slight hesitation in her voice.

"Then have a little faith. When this is all over, I'll

explain everything. Believe me these people are the good guys."

Nathanael interrupted. "I understand your concern, but right now our mission is to figure out what's going on, and how to keep Mystic safe until we do. That's our number one priority. If you can help in any way, it would be to everyone's benefit for you to do so."

Chinoah closed her eyes and sighed. "I've told you all I can remember. I'm really tired. If I think of anything else, I'll let you know. Can I go home?"

"'Fraid not, you're not safe at home any longer. You'll remain under our protection until its safe and our mission is complete," Nat said.

Chinoah opened her eyes and glared at Nat.

"It's not so bad." Mystic reassured her friend. "Surrounded by a group of good looking, guys here to protect you. This is what most woman's dreams are made of." She giggled, gently elbowing her in the ribs. "Enjoy it."

"For the time being, we'll prepare the spare room upstairs across from Killian for you, that way if you need anything, he'll be close. He's assigned to you for the next few days."

Chinoah cocked her head questioningly but said nothing.

"I've scheduled a meeting for this afternoon at the Colorado field office of the FBI with an acquaintance of mine." He paused for a moment, rubbed at the back of his neck. "I've worked with him previously. The field agents that visited Ethan earlier are out of that office. Caden and Mystic, I want you to join me," Nat said.

"But they're still treating me like a missing person.

They didn't believe Ethan when he told them he'd seen me."

"Well, then they'll know the truth after today. It won't make any difference now that Ethan is convinced that you're alive. The dem—individuals he's tangled up with are going to be searching for you too. That's one of the reasons I decided to go to the FBI, rather than the local Tribal Police."

"That and the fact you don't have any contacts in the Tribal Police. But I do," Mystic said.

"Don't be so sure where I have contacts." Nat glared at her then chuckled. "Lawyers, they are all the same, think they know everything. Believe me, it's best to let me handle this situation. I have a few hun…ah, years' experience on you."

He raised his eyebrows and rolled his eyes but remained silent.

"Are you sure pursuing a relationship with a lawyer is wise, Caden? You'll never win an argument. I know how you hate being wrong."

"I'm up to the task." He smiled thinking back to the boundaries they'd set the night she ran off and shifted. "She'll be an asset to our organization. Don't you think?"

"That remains to be seen. Things are changing. More activity here than we thought possible few months ago. Thanks in part to you."

"Hey, I didn't cause the problem," he said defensively. "The de…difficult ones, seem to be diversifying." *Keeping Chinoah in the dark about the existence of demons and the like is going to be a problem.*

Nat narrowed his eyes at his use of nonverbal

communication. "It would seem so. True, you didn't cause it. You just brought it to the attention of others."

It was his turn to glare at the commander.

Abruptly changing the topic, Nat said, "I think Alaia has prepared a feast for lunch, with the help of Kat of course. Let's enjoy." Nat motioned everyone toward the kitchen.

Upon hearing her name Kat ran into the room. Nat swept her up into his arms.

"If you'll excuse me, I think I'll just go lay down," Chinoah said her voice quivering.

"I'll get her settled in her room then bring up food for her before she goes to sleep." Killian looked at Chinoah, his eyes softening. "You must eat to gain strength."

He and Mystic took their plates out on the porch for a little privacy.

"Keeping things from your friend is going to be a problem."

"I noticed, but I don't see why we don't tell her. She's trustworthy."

"But there is no reason she needs to know. She's not involved with any of us. It was her connection to you that caused this."

"That's involvement. I'm…involved with…"

"Me. Why is that so hard to admit that you could be in a relationship? I know you care a great deal for me. I feel the same about you. I won't use the word love because it makes you crazy. But beware we are heading there, and there is nothing you can do to stop it," he said smugly.

Choosing to ignore his last comment, she changed the subject. "Chinoah has great talents that would be

Tena Stetler

useful. She's a shapeshifter too, has an accounting degree, and works for a public relations firm. Did you see the way Killian is looking at her? And she at him."

Caden snorted. "Killian is just doing his job. She's his responsibility until Nat says otherwise. Killian takes his responsibilities very seriously. Besides, I've known him for centuries, he's a confirmed bachelor."

"So were you, for centuries, and now look. You're lecturing me about relationship matters. Believe me, I know that look. The Tribunal is about to have another relationship problem."

"Care to wager on it?"

"What you gamble too? No saintly characteristics at all?"

"None. I told you I was a fallen warrior angel. I only wager when it's a sure thing I'll win."

"You're on. What are we wagering?"

"I'll do anything you want, within reason. If you win. If I win…we spend the night together not sleeping."

"What, oh. I'm not worried, this is in the bag." She smirked and kissed him lightly on the lips.

He pulled her into him, pressed her lips to his, caressing her mouth more than kissing it. She responded by running the soft tip of her tongue across his bottom lip, while her body curved into his.

He felt Nat approaching, and he pulled away slowly. "We'll just wait and see."

He looked up to see Nat striding purposely toward them and released Mystic. "Later. It appears duty calls."

"Promises, promises." She giggled.

"We have a choice. We can either take a four-hour

road trip to Denver or port to a familiar place just outside Denver, rent a car and drive to our destination. Either way, for appearances, we'll probably have to spend the night in a hotel. Pack a change of clothes, people."

"Let's port to a familiar place and rent a car. Four hours driving seems such a waste of time," he stated.

"I agree," Mystic chimed in.

"Done. We leave from here in an hour. Oh, Mystic, is there anything you'd like to see the FBI get their hands on?"

"Yes. All the financial records of the River Winds Casino, dating back to when Ethan took over as manager. He was visibly upset but restrained himself in front of the Tribal Council, when I asked that the tribal council have access to the records and approve any of Ethan's expenditures over ten thousand dollars. That wasn't an unusual request for a casino manager to be accountable to the Council."

"I'll see what I can do."

"Also, we should talk about Chinoah. Her accounting degree and background could be invaluable in this situation. Not to mention her gift for public relations."

Nat gave him an "I told you so" look. "I'll give it some thought."

Mystic shrugged her shoulders. "That's all I ask." She shot him a warning look.

"We better get back to the trailer and pack." With that, Caden reached around Mystic's waist.

"Alaia."

"I heard, and I've got you all packed. You should listen to Mystic about Chinoah, though."

"Not you too. I said I'd consider it, and I will."
"Okay, okay, don't get testy."
He grinned, pulled Mystic close, and disappeared.

Chapter Twelve
Angels, Demons, Shapeshifters and FBI, Oh My…

Mystic and Caden were waiting for Nat on the porch. Nat told him where they were going. He took Mystic's hand, and they all materialized in an isolated area a block from a rental car location.

"The girls and Kat going to be okay while we're gone?" Mystic narrowed her eyes at Nat.

Nat met her gaze and gave her a reassuring smile. "I'm sure they'll be fine. If anything unexpected happens, Sean and Killian have orders to port everyone to our hotel suite."

"How do we know the demons don't know where we're staying?"

"We don't. That's one reason I want to talk to the FBI, find out their thoughts on the situation."

"Why would they talk to us?" he asked. "What do they know about demons?"

"Nothing. I have friends in high places. Besides, they want to find out what we know as well. Coordination of information and resources will be useful to all of us."

"How much of what happened to Mystic are we going to tell them? Are they aware we aren't mortals? Mystic is a shifter?"

"No, I've told my contact nothing. I think he suspects I'm different from our previous dealings, but he doesn't ask, and I don't offer."

"We find out what he knows and offer part of what we know?"

"Exactly."

"Won't they be irritated that you didn't tell them that Mystic is alive and well?"

"Oh probably, but my stand is her safety first. After all, I will bring her in."

Nat pulled open the glass doors to the Aspen Car Rental, stepped inside and up to the counter, filled out the paperwork for a large SUV, and took the keys. He and Mystic waited outside in the warm sunshine.

Nat returned to the door and pushed it open a crack. "Caden, I need you to come and sign as a driver on the rental. I'm not as familiar with this area as you are." He knew it had been many years since Nat drove a vehicle. Porting was more convenient.

Mystic opened the door to the black SUV and slid into the soft leather seats.

He sniffed. The vehicle still had a new car smell and had every accessory known to man. When he turned the key, the dash lit up like the cockpit of a fighter jet.

"We'll check into the Brown Palace Hotel on 17th Street and stow our luggage. Then I'll call Chad at the FBI and let him know our ETA," Nat said.

"What are we going to divulge?"

"As little as possible. Mystic watch me for cues and don't volunteer anything! If I tell you not to answer, don't. Tell them you turned down his proposal, he lost his temper, and a physical fight ensued. You'd never seen such behavior from him and it scared you."

"Got it."

"Caden you found her, had medical training out of country, and nursed her back to health. By the time she could get around, you both thought it better to lay low until you could figure out what happened. Because Mystic told you his behavior was frightening and not at all like him."

"Okay."

He pulled up to the Field Office and parked. Two men in black suits and ties were waiting just inside the office door.

Nat climbed out of the SUV and started toward the building at a quick pace, they followed right behind. "I think we're ready, let's go in." Nat yanked the glass door open.

Once inside, Nat led the way with he and Mystic slightly behind.

Nat was stopped by the black suits.

"We're here to see Agent Chad Zarkou. He's expecting us."

"Your names and IDs please."

"Nathanael, Caden, and Mystic. And your name?" He handed over their IDs.

"Agent Jacks." He took their IDs, glanced at them, his eyebrows shot up, then his face went blank again, and he handed them back. "Let me clear security, and I'll take you back." He picked up the phone, said a few words, and disconnected. "Follow me."

The heavy metal door in the waiting area buzzed and they walked through. Agent Jacks led them through a narrow hallway with polished tile floors and light tan walls. He opened a door with no window and motioned them to three chairs. "Agent Zarkou, this is Caden Silverwind, Nathanael North, and Mystic Rayne.

Zarkou stood behind the desk and extended his hand. He shook hands with Caden and Nathanael, when he took Mystic's hand he looked her over and glanced down at a file lying open on his desk. Her picture, in full ceremonial dress, was stapled to the left side of the file.

He tapped his finger on the picture. "Ms. Rayne. Our missing person is found alive and well."

"It would seem, at least the alive part. The well is yet to be determined, but I am definitely much better than the condition Mr. Nix left me in." Mystic smiled sardonically and sat in the middle chair, he and Nat took the chairs on each side of her.

The agent narrowed his eyes. "Mr. North, just how long have you been aware we were looking for Ms. Rayne?"

In a calm voice, Nat replied, "I called you the night I learned that one of my men had found her on the trail. I guess it was a few days after he found her. Mr. Silverwind was on leave in a remote area of the Rocky Mountains. Due to her condition, he couldn't leave her to make contact."

"He didn't have a cell phone?"

"Yes, he did, but coverage is spotty at best in the area he was camping. He had to walk a mile or so up a steep embankment to get service."

"We'll come back to that." Zarkou eased down in the chair and turned his attention to Mystic.

"Ms. Rayne, Mr. Nix is responsible for your disappearance?"

"Yes, sir."

"What happened?" He picked up a pen and jotted down a couple of notes on a page in the file, then tapped the pen on the page.

"Several members of the tribe decided to enjoy a weekend at my father's land in Colorado. Ethan planned a celebration. I wasn't aware what we were celebrating, but a getaway sounded good."

"Ethan was your friend?"

"We grew up together."

"And the others that came with you?"

"Ethan's friends."

"Didn't you think that strange, one women and several men?"

"No, I'm a lawyer under contract to the Bureau of Indian Affairs, assigned to The Wind River Reservation. One of the tribes on that shared reservation is mine. Besides, Ethan is always surrounded by outcasts... I'm sorry acquaintances. There was nothing unusual."

"What happened next?" He took a yellow lined tablet out of his desk drawer and laid it on top the open file, made more notes on the pad.

"It's all still kinda blurry. Ethan asked me to marry him. I declined." Mystic shifted in her chair. "He got angry and attacked me. The rest I don't remember."

"You were romantically involved with Mr. Nix?"

"We dated a few times, but when he started to want more from the relationship, I told him I wasn't ready for a serious relationship."

He tapped the pen on the pad and gave her a hard look. "How did he take it?"

Mystic shrugged one shoulder. "He seemed okay with it at the time. My father died shortly thereafter. Ethan was a good friend during that time until I told him I was taking my father's place on the tribal council.

Afterward he became distant. But he got over it, or so I thought."

"Why didn't anyone come to your aid?"

"I don't know. Because they were his friends? And to be fair, they had been drinking most of the day. Ethan had quite a few himself."

"And you?"

"I don't drink."

"Not even a glass of wine?" A note of disbelief sounded in his voice, his eyes narrowed again.

"On very rare occasions, but this was not one of those."

"Really?"

"Really!" Her cheeks flushed. The vein at her temple throbbed in time to her rapid heartbeat, a sure sign her temper was rising.

He braced his hands on the chair arms and directed his voice quietly into her mind. *Calm down, he's only doing his job. If he gets out of line, I'll step in. Relax, you've nothing to hide.*

Still unaccustomed to the silent form of communication, her eyes widened. She cut her gaze first to Nat then to him, took a deep breath, and let it out slowly. "Could I have a drink of water, please?"

"Oh, sure." Agent Zarkou dropped the pen on the pad, got to his feet, then appeared to change his mind, and pushed the intercom button. "Could we have some bottles of cold water in here?" He dropped back into his seat and turned his attention back to them. "How about we wrap this up in about half an hour and get some dinner? I should have all I need by then." He paused and gave Nat a hard stare. "Or all you're going to tell me."

"We're more than happy to cooperate, but remember Mystic is the victim here. She voluntarily came out of hiding to assist with the investigation." Nat glanced from him to Mystic.

"Understood. Have you contacted your employer, Ms. Rayne?"

"No. I should probably check in tomorrow morning."

"Didn't you think they'd be worried about your absence at work? You know the Bureau was the one who reported you missing."

"No, I didn't. I'm gone from the office weeks at a time, when assigned to the Wind River Agency and help where needed. Who told them I was missing?"

"Their agency got the same anonymous call we received. Since they couldn't reach you and no one had seen you since you left with Mr. Nix, we were called in."

"You have no idea who made those calls?" she asked.

"No, not yet. It was a male caller both times. We're still working on that."

He felt Agent Zarkou turn his attention to him. "Did you take her to the hospital when you found her?"

"No, sir. It was a long way. I wasn't sure she would survive such a trip. She was in bad shape, lost a lot of blood."

"Are you a doctor?"

"No. I have traditional medical training and experience in the healing ways of my people."

"Your people?"

"Yes, the Sioux/Lakota."

"Did you take any pictures of her injuries?"

"No. Didn't have a camera."

"How are we supposed to prosecute or even investigate this crime? I have an anonymous phone call telling us about a murder committed by Ethan Nix. We go to the supposed crime scene, no body but a lot of blood over the area. Looks like someone tried to destroy the evidence. If we tested the DNA evidence we collected, would it match yours?"

"Probably. At least some of it."

Agent Zarkou's eyebrows shot up. "Some of it?"

"I wasn't the only one there and certainly didn't just stand there and let Ethan beat on me."

Nat interrupted, "No one is asking you to prosecute this crime. Ms. Rayne came forward at your request, after I contacted you."

"True. But as with cases you're involved in, this case has exploded from a simple missing person, now found, to desecration of sacred lands, and kidnapping. We can't find the person kidnapped but have three badly beaten men that admit to the kidnapping. The men claim that two of their companions were killed and turned to ash."

Zarkou shoved up from his chair, hands in the air. He let them fall to his side. "Then we have a missing employee from the River Winds Casino. Reports of three teenagers who swear they saw ghosts that night. Nix reported an attack in his casino office. When the Tribal Police check the surveillance tape, there is no one on it but him flying across the desk and sliding down the wall to the floor. What the hell am I supposed to do with a case like this? And why do I always get the cases involving you assigned to me? Huh?"

"The Tribal Police may be better equipped to

handle this," Nat suggested, tenting his fingers in front of him.

"Oh, no. Not going to let the locals take the lead on this. We'll have men turning into wolves, medicine men banishing evil spirits, and who knows what else."

Caden and Mystic exchanged glances and looked at Nat.

"I don't believe we said anything about shapeshifters. Do you have a problem with Native American beliefs or customs?" Nat's eyebrows drew together in concern.

Zarkou picked the file up and shook it a Nat. "No, not as long as the file doesn't land on my desk. How am I supposed to explain all this to my superiors?" He rubbed his temples and looked across his desk at the three individuals staring at him. "I'm sorry if I've insulted either of your beliefs and traditions. I should've declined the case, taken a leave of absence, and left town when I discovered Nathanael North was involved." He dropped the case file on the desk with a loud pop and shook his head.

He observed Nat's demeanor and smirked. *Yep, angel influence required here.*

"I believe you've been working too hard. Let's call it a night and get that dinner you were talking about." He hid his smile as Nat stared into Agent Zarkou's eyes and used just a little angel persuasion to calm him down. "One thing you might be interested in is the financial records of the River Winds Casino. It might help explain Nix's actions."

"I'll see about that tomorrow. I believe the Tribal Police were going to do exactly that. What kind of food are you hungry for?"

"A nice thick T-bone, baked potato loaded with butter and sour cream, maybe chives and bacon bits for starters," Mystic suggested. He and Nat nodded in agreement.

"I'll drive, you navigate Agent Zarkou." He took the keys out of his pocket and tossed them in the air, swung his hand behind his back and caught them, ignoring the disgruntled look he received from Agent Zarkou.

"Are the three of you headed back tonight, or will you be around tomorrow morning?" Zarkou wanted to know.

"We're staying the night. Plan to get an early start in the morning, unless you need something else, or Mystic's employer wants to see her after she talks to them tomorrow."

"Check with me before you leave."

"Sure thing," Nat agreed.

He held the front passenger door for Mystic, then walked to the driver's side. Nat and the agent slid into the back seat.

"You familiar with Denver at all?"

"Sort of, been a while," he admitted.

"Take the first left and head for 19th Street. The Chophouse has great steak and sea food. I think you'll like it."

He slid the SUV into traffic and followed the agent's directions.

As promised the food was fantastic, atmosphere charming, and the conversation light. The return trip was uneventful.

"Dinner was delicious, thanks." Nat shook hands with Chad Zarkou and then the agent exited the car.

"Talk to you tomorrow." Zarkou closed the door and walked to his car in the lot.

Within minutes, they pulled into the hotel's parking lot and got out of the vehicle.

"This is absolutely beautiful," Mystic said walking into the sweeping atrium lobby. "I always wondered what it would be like to stay here. It has a grand history. Several presidents have stayed here. In fact, did you know President Eisenhower actually was practicing his golf swing in his room and dented the fireplace mantle in the presidential suite?"

"Glad you approve. You'll get your chance to see if that's true. I booked the Eisenhower Suite for the night and tomorrow night should we need it. There are only two separate bedrooms, so Caden you'll be sleeping on the couch. Though I understand it's quite luxurious." Nat chuckled under his breath as they made their way to the assigned room.

He and Mystic exchanged glances as Nat opened the door to the suite.

"Not a problem. A presidential suite with all amenities and great morning sun, that I can handle. I'm dead on my feet, so if you two don't mind heading off to your rooms, I'd appreciate quiet on the couch."

"Me too." Nat pulled his cell phone out of his pocket, touched the #1 on speed dial, put the phone to his ear, and picked up his luggage. "We're back at the hotel. The meeting with Agent Zarkou is finished for now, and I'm headed off to bed. Got someone to watch Kat?" He paused and listened. "Good see you soon. You know how I hate to sleep alone." Nat closed the bedroom door behind him, and the lock clicked.

****

Caden tossed his overnight bag on the couch. Mystic grabbed her overnight bag and padded across the dark rose carpeting toward her bedroom, opened the door, and sucked in a breath. In the middle of the room was a tall four-poster, dark cherry wood bed, with a rose loveseat at the foot of the bed. Two chairs sat next to the three huge windows. Maroon and white designed wallpaper reminiscent of the 1950s adorned the walls. The king size bedspread matched the wallpaper. "Caden, you have got to see this."

He groaned as he got up off the sofa, pajama bottoms tossed over his shoulder. "What now?"

He joined her at the bedroom door, and his eyes grew round. "Wow, nice."

She flung her arms around his neck. "Isn't it elegant? Kinda makes you feel like you stepped back in time." She caressed the length of his back and instinctively arched her body toward his.

"Is this an invitation? If it is, I accept." His hands gently explored the soft lines of her back, her waist and hips pressing her closer. He closed the door with a bare foot. His lips pressed against hers, then gently covered her mouth, moving his mouth over hers devouring its softness.

She quivered at the sweet tenderness of his kiss, surprised at her own eager response to the touch of his lips. She'd survived the day dreaming about being alone with him. She hated to admit it, but he centered her and she loved him for it.

You're thinking too much.

She gave herself up to the kiss, lingering, savoring every moment.

Caden raised his mouth from hers and gazed into

her eyes. "You do realize that once I take you to bed, feeling the way I do, you will be mine forever, as I will be yours. Are you ready to make that commitment?"

"Mmmm…what…what commitment?" she murmured, brushing her lips, still warm and moist from the kiss, down his neck to the pulsing hollow at the base of his throat and breathed a kiss there.

"That's what I thought. You can't keep ignoring what is right in front of your face. I won't let you. My self-restraint is dangerously close to breaking. With that in mind, I'm going to take a shower and go to bed. I suggest you do the same." He took her hand turning it palm up and pressed a kiss there before sauntering to the bath off her bedroom.

She stood there for a moment savoring his scent and feel against her skin. He was the one, and she knew it with every fiber of her being. Her father told her that once it was right, there was no turning back.

The running water stopped, and Caden emerged from the bathroom, dressed in black silk pajama bottoms. He closed the door to the adjoining living room and crawled into the right side of her bed.

"Hey, aren't you supposed to be sleeping out there?" She pointed toward the door to the living area.

"Nope, I accepted your invitation. There were no conditions to the acceptance, so you sleep on your side and I'll sleep on mine. The bed is plenty big enough for both of us." He rolled over, his back to her, and closed his eyes.

"What will Nat think? He assigned us sleeping areas."

"Nat isn't my boss anymore. Besides, he knows we sleep together. He was just giving us the option of having our relationship out in the open, which I'm all for. Besides, at this moment, I don't think he cares what we do. He's snuggled in with his woman. Good night."

"But…" Mystic stood there not quite sure whether she wanted to crawl into bed and snuggle against him or punch him. She marched into the bathroom, flipped on the shower, and let the warm water ease the tensions of the day away, except for the one sleeping in her bed. That one she would deal with, after this was all over. Warm and relaxed, she slid into bed next to him.

He rolled over and banded an arm around her, burying his face in her long hair.

Chapter Thirteen
An Unexpected Night at the Theatre

The bright sun streamed through the windows and Mystic's phone chirped on the nightstand. "Rayne here."

"Well it's about time you answer this phone. Don't you check your messages?"

"Usually, sir. There's been some extenuating circumstances."

"I understand. I want you in the office within the hour to explain those extenuating circumstances. I want to know when one of my agents is hurt or missing."

"FBI contact you?"

"Yes."

"I'll be there, but it might be a bit longer than an hour. I'm dependent on someone else for transportation. I'm in Denver, as you know."

"Understood."

She crept out of bed, grabbed her overnight bag, and locked herself in the bathroom. Standing in front of the mirror, she took stock of what she saw. Dark circles under her tired brown eyes, prominent cheekbones due to weight loss, and mouth set in a determined thin line. The deep purple bruises on her face were fading to a sickly yellow and green. *I look like hell. I can't go into work looking like this. The boss will relieve me of duty on appearance alone.*

She dumped the contents of her bag on the bathroom counter. No mascara, no foundation, no concealer, or eyeliner, and no hair gel. She needed to visit a store with a decent makeup selection and fast.

A long-sleeved turtleneck sweater or blouse would cover the healing bruises and bite marks on her neck and arms.

Stepping into the shower, she scrubbed, shampooed, and conditioned. After turning the water off, she wrapped a towel around herself and padded out of the bathroom. "Caden."

"Finally awake sleeping beauty?"

"I am anything but beautiful. My boss called and wants to see me ASAP. I can't go in looking like this, and I left all the makeup we bought at the trailer." As she talked, she towel dried her long, thick hair. Peeking out from under the towel, she saw him trying to conceal a grin. "It's not funny."

"Honey, you look so much better than when I found you, but I understand. What can I do?"

"I need to get some makeup to cover up this." She pointed to her cheek and chin where the bruising was yellow and green.

"While you get dressed, I'll ask the concierge where the closest department store is that sells quality cosmetics. How long before you need to make an appearance at your job?"

"He gave me an hour, but I told him it would be a little longer."

He opened the bedroom door into the main living area and nearly ran into Nat. "Mystic and I need to run a few errands. Is it all right if I take the SUV? She also has to meet with her boss, Raymond Gray-Eagle shortly. Wanna come along?"

"Sure, give me five minutes to get ready? Maybe we can stop somewhere along the way to grab a bite to eat?" Nat asked hopefully.

"Maybe... Afterward. We're kinda short on time right now." He picked up the hotel phone and asked directions to the nearest department store that would fit her needs. "All set. Mystic you ready?"

"Almost." She came out the bedroom door, dressed in a light beige blouse with copper roses and dark brown slacks with beige heels. The sunlight played off strands of her rich raven hair giving it a polished gleam.

"You look great." He stepped to her and nuzzled her neck. "You smell wonderful too. The department store is only ten minutes away."

"Thanks for doing that for me. I appreciate it."

Twenty minutes later, she had the cosmetics she needed and applied them in the bathroom at the department store. She gave her reflection one more glance, satisfied that she had done all she could to cover the injuries and it looked pretty good.

Caden drove slowly down East Colfax until she pointed out the building that housed the Bureau of Indian Affairs.

"You can just drop me off. I'll call when I'm done," she said confidently.

He turned the SUV into the parking lot and shut off the engine. "You're not going in there alone."

"I have to."

"No, you don't," Nat said his voice stern, eyes dark. "After Mr. Gray-Eagle hears what happened to you, he'll understand your need for security."

"I'm not sure how much I'll tell him."

"It would be best for everyone concerned to tell him everything. Agent Zarkou has probably already done most of it for you."

She frowned and nodded her head in agreement. "You're probably right, but I'm still going in alone."

"No, you're not, end of discussion." Caden emphasized each word in a calm but firm voice. "I won't go into the room, if it has only one door, but I will be outside listening to every word. Keep in mind, you don't have any recollection of the condition in which I found you and the evidence at the scene. Nor what I saw when I returned to your father's land."

She opened her car door and stepped onto the parking lot. "Follow if you must, but don't embarrass me, or you'll regret it." Her dark eyes flashed in warning.

"We're your security guards, and as such will remain professional at all times," Nat assured her.

"We? No, no, no. Caden can come, but you— " she pointed at Nat, "wait in the SUV."

"That won't be possible. I need some clarifications from Mr. Gray-Eagle as to whose jurisdiction this falls under. Whether we need to coordinate with the BIA or the Tribal Police in Wyoming, or both." Nat crossed his arms across his chest.

"I can tell you this investigation belongs to the Tribal Police first, the BIA second, and the FBI third, unless someone overrides the locals, and that would be a really stupid idea. Since no one will trust the outsiders, cooperation will be nonexistent."

Caden looked thoughtful. "What are you going to suggest?"

"I remain on this case and coordinate the

investigation of the agencies involved. The people at the Wind River Agency and the Rez trust me. They'll talk to me. If there is anything to find out, I'm their best bet."

"Sounds like a plan. Now if you can get your boss to agree."

She pulled open the building's glass door and walked confidently inside. Caden and Nat just a few paces behind her. Mary and Martha were waiting for her.

"What on earth happened to you? Why didn't you call for help? The FBI said you just vanished for several days, then walked right into their offices." Mary frowned.

"The FBI, namely Agent Chad Zarkou, should mind his own affairs. Thanks for your concern, but I'm fine. Where's Mr. Gray-Eagle?"

"Waiting in his office for you and he is not happy. Didn't like finding out about his agent from the FBI," Mary said shaking her head.

"Understandable."

"You sure you're all right? You look tired, and you've lost so much weight," Martha said.

"Trust me, I'm fine. See you in a few."

Martha leaned closer and whispered, "Who are the two handsome men with you?"

"Security." She smiled to the women and strode toward Gray-Eagle's office. The last thing she needed was to be the topic of office gossip. That's one of the reasons she took the position of liaison and advisor. Very little contact with others in the office. She'd always been a loner.

The women talked quietly behind their hands, as

she and her security disappeared down the hall.

When she reached her boss's door, it opened.

"Ms. Rayne, how nice of you to grace us with your presence."

"Sorry, about the way you learned of my situation. Unfortunately, it was out of my control. My safety depended upon no one knowing I was alive."

His eyebrows shot up and motioned her into the office. Caden and Nat remained inconspicuously on either side of the door, arms crossed across their muscular chests, their stance wide and relaxed as she disappeared into the office.

"Have a seat." Raymond Gray-Eagle motioned to the chairs on the other side of his desk.

She told Raymond everything from Ethan's attack, to his sending thugs to find her body, the FBI's investigation, and her suspicions. She left out the possibility they were dealing with a consortium of demons and the implications of that situation.

"Well, Ms. Rayne, apparently you are lucky to be alive. While it is against my better judgment to allow you to take lead on this case, you make a great argument for continuing in your present capacity. Temporarily we'll leave things as they are, with the stipulation that you have security with you at all times and that you check in twice a week. Understood?"

"Yes sir. I am sorry for any trouble or inconvenience I have caused."

"Inconvenience. You would've died on my watch, if it hadn't been for Mr. Silverwind. He glanced at the door. "I am grateful for his help." Gray-Eagle stood indicating the meeting was over.

She got to her feet and followed him to the door.

After opening the door, he turned to Caden and Nat, his hand extended. "Good job." He shook their hands. "I imagine we'll meet again soon."

Nat's cell phone rang, and he looked at the ID. "I've got to take this call. It was a pleasure to meet you. I look forward to seeing you again." He hurried up the hall and out the door with phone to his ear.

When she and Caden exited the building, Nat was leaning against the SUV, still talking on the phone. A few fluffy white clouds floated across the blue sky, and the sun was warm on her face. "Let's take a short walk and let Nat finish his conversation. We should be safe outside the office. Right?"

Caden nodded. "I don't see the cream-colored sedan that tailed us yesterday when we left the FBI's office. I had Killian run the plate. He confirmed the vehicle belonged to the FBI's Denver Field Office, specifically assigned Agent Zarkou."

"We're being followed?"

"It would appear so."

"Where are they today, then?"

Caden raised his shoulders in a noncommittal shrug. "No idea. Got wind we were onto to them and backed off?"

They returned to the truck as Nat concluded his phone call and slammed his fist onto the hood of the SUV.

"Anything wrong boss?" Caden asked nonchalantly as he opened her door.

"No," Nat said curtly.

"Okay, but keep in mind this is a rental and any damage you do will be paid for when we turn it in."

With piercing hazel eyes, Nat returned Caden's

gaze. "I said nothing was wrong."

"And you lied. You always were a rotten liar," Caden said cheerfully.

Nat narrowed his eyes and stiffened. "The Demon Territory Overlord has requested a meeting. He's flying in this evening. I told him where we were staying, and he'll call from the lobby when he arrives."

"Why?"

"Hell if I know. All he told Killian was the situation required a face to face meeting."

"That can't be good. The last time we encountered him, or rather his enforcer, was at the Overlord's wedding. Right?"

Nat nodded. "And when Tristian saved your life in the Scottish Highlands. Years ago, we had some problems with a rogue demon/vampire group. He sent someone to take care of it, and we never heard another word," he said as an explanation to her.

"Well, I guess we'll find out." Caden shrugged again.

"In our dealings setting up the joint task force, his reputation is one of fairness, but he believes in swift justice for individuals stepping outside the Demon Rules of Conduct."

"The demons have rules of conduct?" She scrunched up her face.

"I guess it's really the otherworldly creatures that are held to a code set forth by a council made up of witches, demons, vampires, and shapeshifters. More recently, we've combined forces to stay on top of the situation, since we're on earth as much as up above these days."

"Do we need to check in with Zarkou? He's

dropped the tail." Caden stared at Nat. "Guess we won't be going back home tonight."

"Probably not. Depending on how long the meeting is with Bruce." Nat reached into his pocket, pulled out his cell phone, and tapped the screen, holding the phone out, it rang once. "Chad—Nathanael North here, you're on speaker phone. Any news on the request for financial records?"

"Yeah, should have them tomorrow. They've been made available to the Tribal Police in Riverton."

"I think we may bring in an accounting expert to take a look. Any problem with that?"

"Nope. But they're at your expense. We can have our expert available, if you'd like."

Nat was silent a couple of beats, as if considering the offer.

"Nathanael, you still there?"

"Yes. We appreciate the offer and will wait to hear from you tomorrow morning." Nat disconnected the call.

When they arrived back at the hotel, Nat walked through the atrium lobby to the front desk.

"We're staying in the Eisenhower Suite and will need a small meeting room with a Wi-Fi connection for late this evening." Nathanael leaned on the counter watching the hotel clerk type something into the computer.

"Yes, sir. I'll have someone contact you with the arrangements within the next thirty minutes. Will that be all right?"

"Thanks. That will be fine. I'll be in our suite."

No sooner had Caden slid the key card in the door and turned the handle, the room phone rang. Nat crossed the room and pushed the intercom button. "Hello."

A pleasant woman's voice greeted him. "We have the Aspen conference room reserved, water and refreshments will be provided."

"Thanks, that'll work." Nat disconnected the call and sat down on the couch.

Caden took a bottle of water out of the little fridge, took a swig, picked up the remote, and settled into an overstuffed chair. He flipped through the channels as she went into the bathroom to freshen her makeup, leaving the door open.

At nine p.m., the hotel phone rang.

Nat reached over and picked up the receiver. "Hello." He paused.

"Good evening, Bruce. Mind if I put you on speaker phone so Caden and Mystic can hear the conversation?" He pressed the conference button.

"Not at all. I'll be ready to meet as soon as my wife and I get settled in our suite. Tristian, my expert on renegade demons will be joining us if that's all right."

"That's fine. I've arranged for a meeting room on the first floor. It's called the Aspen Room."

"Wonderful. See you in about thirty minutes."

****

Caden, Mystic, and Nat sat at the long table in the conference room, when two tall, extremely, muscular men strode in. Nat and Caden stood. The tallest of the two had thick chestnut brown hair streaked with blonde that flowed over his collar. He smiled and reached for Caden's outstretched hand and then Nat's.

"Nice to see you again. You know my colleague, Tristian Shandie, the expert I mentioned earlier."

Tristian's chiseled features and no-nonsense demeanor set her nerves on edge as she sat quietly listening to the conversation. *I should be able to sense their magic signatures. But there's no trace of magic surrounding them.*

Tristian nodded, as he shook hands with Nat and Caden. His piercing gray-blue eyes swept the room then turned to acknowledge her.

Caden made the introductions. "The beautiful lady sitting at the table is Mystic Rayne."

Bruce's eyes glittered in appreciation. "Nice to meet you Ms. Rayne. Shall we get started?"

Bruce and Tristian took seats across the table from her and Caden.

Nat eased into his chair at the head of the table and began. "As one of my security officers told you, we encountered a pair of demons working with three mortals. They kidnapped and tortured Mystic's friend to lure Mystic to them. The demons masked their magic signature and location, which was in a tunnel under sacred ground. We found the site only because of Mystic's talent to overpower the demons masking abilities. The woman they kidnapped overheard bits of conversation between the two regarding some type of consortium of demons and that their plans would be delayed."

She saw Bruce and Tristan exchange glances. "That is extremely disturbing on a number of levels. The first and foremost being able to use their abilities on or under sacred ground. Someone had to give them permission to be there."

Tristian's rough voice interjected. "We have intel that rebel demon factions are operating in central

Wyoming. I was en route here to verify the info and neutralize the perpetrators, when Bruce called with a slight change of plans. Yours."

"I'm afraid the demons are acting together with a shapeshifter, Ethan Nix. How or why and to what benefit we don't know. We've launched an investigation, but without telling other agencies involved exactly what they're dealing with. As I'm sure you're aware, mortals would rather not know the things of their nightmares walk the streets daily." Nat rubbed the back of his neck and rolled his shoulders.

"Bet the demons were surprised to come up against warrior angels in Wyoming." Bruce's lips twitched. "As you know, mortals are to remain oblivious to magic and creatures who wield it."

"Probably, but it took our security team by surprise too. The demons were no match, but they got a couple of licks in."

"How did your shapeshifter, Mystic, become involved?" Bruce wanted to know.

She pursed her lips, narrowing her eyes. "I'm no one's shapeshifter." She shifted her gaze from Bruce to Tristian. When neither of them spoke, only nodded, she laid out the whole situation for them.

"During the fight, just you and Ethan shifted?" Tristian asked, his sharp gaze doing nothing to ease her misgivings.

"Yes, or at least I think so. I shifted for my own protection. Ethan attacked me while he was in the process of shifting and continued after his transformation was complete. I can't honestly say if anyone else shifted or was capable of shifting. Not all Ethan's friends are shifters. Why?"

"Just trying to figure out if the demons were involved at that point, or whether it was later after Ethan was unable to find your body or proof that you were still alive."

"The others were tribal members, so the demons weren't involved that night."

Tristian nodded, his lips set in a thin line, eyes scanning the room again.

"He wasn't only angry at my refusal, but because of my stance with the Tribal Council. I'd suggested earlier in the week that any expenditures over ten thousand dollars be discussed and approved by the council. That's not uncommon in casino management and wasn't meant as a reflection on Ethan's ability or trustworthiness. Just a way of protecting everyone's interests." She paused for a beat. "Though in retrospect, I don't think he can be trusted."

Bruce listened intently rubbing his hand over his chin. "As I am sure Nat and Caden have told you, demons don't just arbitrarily decide to assist another being. There must be something big in it for them. Figure out what that is and you'll have your motive for Ethan's behavior, at least part of it."

She blew out a breath. "We've tried." *If I sit here one more minute, I'm going to explode.* "Excuse me." She stood and paced around the perimeter of the conference room. The others stood as she left the table, then returned to their seats and resumed the discussion.

Bruce watched her for a moment then said in a low voice, "Wolf shifters don't handle being confined in a room for long. I'll make this as brief as possible. Am I to understand that before the attack on Ms. Rayne, another casino employee came up missing?"

"Just call me Mystic. And don't talk about me as if I'm not here," she called from across the room.

"My apologies, Mystic. I just meant, I understand and shall be brief. My wife is not a shifter, but a witch and absolutely hates to be confined to a room."

She returned to the table. "Your wife is a witch? And you are a demon?"

He gave her an appraising glance. "That's correct."

She eyed Tristian thoughtfully and took a chance. "He's a warlock too. Correct?" She cocked her head and examined Tristian more closely. *Still no trace of magic.*

"Now that we've all been identified, can we get back to the matter at hand?" Tristian snapped impatiently."

Bruce shot Tristian a steely, warning glance.

"Sorry," Tristian mumbled.

"That's okay, I was out of line." She couldn't keep the smirk from her lips. "Surprised that demons and witches associate so closely."

"You know my position, and as such I employ all different kinds of people, if you will, for security services as well, as at my Salon in DC. The Wycked Hair caters to even a wider variety of…people. Mortals make up a large percentage of the salon's patrons, without ever being aware of the paranormals that frequent or work at the salon."

"I understand. I'll take my foot out of my mouth and listen." She grinned as she felt her cheeks burn.

Caden coughed into his hand to hide a smile.

"Though you're taking all this in stride, I would wager that you had no idea that other paranormals existed, before tonight," Bruce said with a chuckle.

"You'd be surprised." She returned to her seat. "To answer your question, the FBI is investigating the disappearance of Toby Star. He worked for the casino for over ten years, an exemplary employee and simply failed to show up for work one day. No one has heard from him since. The Tribal Police think foul play is involved."

"I would agree with that assessment, especially when we know demons are involved." Bruce poured a glass of water and took a drink. "Educated guess, Mr. Star discovered something that got him killed."

Tristian leaned back in his chair, his arms folded over his chest and nodded slightly. "The Tribal Police aren't aware of the demon element?"

"No," Caden said grimacing. "I believe we are the only ones that have had any encounters with them."

"That you know of," Tristian said.

"What Tristian means is that the demons could have infiltrated the casino as workers, even security, which would allow them unrestricted access to all areas of River Winds. They could also be vendors, suppliers, or even customers. Demons can be shapeshifters of sorts, making it hard to pick them out if they're able to mask their magic signature," Bruce explained.

"Sounds like the place for us to start is the casino. Are any of you familiar with the lay out?" Tristian studied each person, finally his gaze landed on her.

"I am—but it's still risky for me to be there," Mystic said chewing on her bottom lip.

"Are you able to transfer your knowledge to Caden or Nat?" Tristian asked.

"I can help her with that," Caden volunteered. "I can walk the casino with you if that's what you have in mind."

"Possibly," Tristian said slowly as he appeared to work out a plan in his head. "I need to fine tune a couple of ideas. I'll get back to you. Telepathy a talent among you?"

Caden smiled. "Yes. Mystic is realizing her talent, but Nat and I are old hands at it."

"Good." Tristian rubbed his hands together.

"I think that we have all the information needed at the moment. We'll be in touch," Bruce said as he and Tristian stood to leave.

"Wait a minute. We didn't discuss the financial records that the Tribal Police will turn over to the FBI. We're going to review the records tomorrow morning with their expert and see if anything looks fishy. Is that something that would be of use to you?" Caden asked.

Bruce glanced at Tristian, who shook his head. "Not at this time, unless it gives us a reason the demons have hooked up with Ethan. We would like to be kept in the loop if you find anything suspicious."

"Will do. Is this your first time in Denver?" she asked.

"Yes," Bruce said, and Tristian nodded.

"Are you here for a couple of days, or are you leaving tomorrow?"

Bruce looked at her with a mixture of surprise and interest. "My wife and I were going to check out the city tomorrow then leave the next day or so. Tristian is leaving tomorrow morning. Why?"

Where are you going with this? Caden asked silently.

Don't worry. I want to get a feel for these people and thought we could invite them to a performance tomorrow night at the Denver Center for the Performing Arts.

Caden nodded.

"*The Phantom of the Opera* is playing in the Buell Theatre at the Denver Center for the Performing Arts. Granted it's not Broadway, but it's only a few blocks from here," she said.

Bruce rubbed his chin and smiled. "I'll check with Angie and get back to you tonight. I think she might enjoy it. Either way, thanks for the invitation, it was very kind of you," Bruce said looking genuinely pleased. He leaned over to her and whispered, "I've had centuries of experience at masking my magic signature and even the most experienced can't detect it unless it's to my benefit. Don't worry about your abilities." Smiling, he winked at her and turned his attention back to Nathanael.

Her eyes flew open, but she maintained her composure and said nothing.

The parties shook hands and left the conference room.

"What the hell are you doing?" Was the first thing out of Nat's mouth, once the door to their suite was closed and locked. "We are scheduled to leave tomorrow."

"Like I told Caden, I need to get a feel for these people. Will they just come in and try to run the show? Which as the FBI has learned doesn't work in our culture. Or will they let us take the lead and cooperate?"

"I can tell you one thing, if the demons are out of line and are involved in the casino worker's death, Tristian will take immediate action against the demons responsible. He may be Bruce's demon expert, but also his enforcer, and a damn good one," Nat said with a touch of admiration in his voice.

"Enforcer?" she asked.

"Assassin," Caden said bluntly. "I recognized him the minute he walked in. We met in a skirmish in the highlands a while back. We were acting as joint security at his sister's wedding."

"What? He kills people without provocation?" she said stunned.

"No, he hunts down and kills demons that have stepped outside their moral code. It's also my understanding that his expertise is not limited to demons gone wrong but other paranormal creatures as well."

"Welcome to the dark side, Mystic," Nat said grimly, frowning at Caden. "But Tristian's not out in the field as much as he was. Let's his teams do most the hands-on work now. Though I suspect he still calls the shots."

"Well, this situation gets darker and darker by the day," she mused.

Nat shrugged. "You might as well know what's really out there."

The hotel phone rang. Caden picked up the receiver, hit the intercom button. "Hello."

"Caden. It's Bruce. Angie and I would love to accept your invitation for tomorrow night. Tristian as we said will be gone. Angie wants to know if it's black tie or more casual attire."

"Attire is out of my league. Let me let you talk to Mystic." Caden nodded to her.

"Suit and tie for the guys, nice dresses or pant suits

for the ladies is the safe attire. You will see everything in between too."

"Thank you. What time is the show?"

"I'll check into that and get back to you. Maybe dinner before, depending on how long we are at the FBI in the morning." She disconnected the call and looked to Nat.

"You can get tickets to the show tomorrow evening."

Nathanael snorted. "Now you ask, but yes, I should be able to make that happen. I assume you will call Alaia and explain my delay."

"Nope. I figured that if you could port her here to share your bed at night. You can port her here to join us for dinner and the show." Her lips twitched in an attempt to keep the smirk at bay.

Nat's eyes narrowed and he stared hard at her.

"That look won't work on me either. I'm not under your control." She flounced toward her bedroom pausing in the doorway.

"Caden, control your woman," Nat demanded.

Caden stared incredulously at Nat then burst out laughing. "I'll get right on that." He crossed the room to where she stood. Still laughing, he looked back at Nat his eyes dancing with amusement then started toward the bedroom.

Nat took his cell phone out of his pocket and tapped the speed dial for Alaia. "Change of plans, we'll be here at least one more night. Can you get someone to watch Kat tomorrow evening? We are going to dinner if time allows, then attending a performance of *Phantom of the Opera*, with Caden, Mystic, and a couple business associates."

Chapter Fourteen
Security Detail in Need of Assistance

The sun was barely peeking over the mountains when Nat, Caden, and Mystic arrived at the FBI's office. Agent Zarkou, unlocked the main door allowing them inside, then locked the door, and escorted the trio into his office.

"Mr. Tayor is our resident expert on financial records. He's reviewed the records received and finds nothing out of the ordinary."

"May we take a look?" Mystic asked.

"Sure, just wanted to advise you of his findings."

A laptop was set up on a table with three chairs surrounding it. Chad inserted a USB drive into the computer and waited for the spreadsheets to come up. "Here you go, have at it." He returned to his desk and began filling out paperwork.

She stared at page after page of the records. Then she stopped, paged backward, wrote down an account number, fast forwarded, and wrote another number on the legal pad provided. "I think something weird is going on with the account numbers the money for the educational fund is being transferred to."

"What do you mean?" Caden asked, leaning closer to the computer screen.

"Well, last time I knew, the transfers were made twice a month. These transfers are every week. Two of the transfers are the same amount, which is unusual, since a percentage of the profit is how the amount is calculated. The reoccurring transfer of the same amount is going to a different account than the others. Why would there be two different accounts for the same fund?" She shook her head. "It doesn't make sense, and they are at different banks."

"Maybe they opened a new account for some reason. You know like spread the wealth or better interest rate," Caden suggested.

"Another council member would have had to sign along with Ethan. I don't remember that being addressed recently, but it could have happened before I joined the council." She took her phone out of her backpack. "I need to make some calls before I jump to any conclusions. It could be all above board."

"Since when do you look before you leap?" Caden winked at her as the corners of his mouth curved into a wide smile.

Mystic shot him an irritated glance and sauntered out of the room to conduct her conversation in private.

When she returned, fear and anger knotted inside her roiling belly. "My hunch was right." Her voice void of emotion.

"What's wrong?" Caden asked hurrying to her side. "Who did you call?"

"Archer Clearwater. He's acting head of the tribal council. There is only one account for the education fund. He was pretty sure bimonthly transfers were made as usual. Arch is going to check on it and get back to me." She paced across the floor.

"Where are the other two transfers going?"

She paused and locked eyes with him then shifted

her gaze to Chad Zarkou. "Certainly not where they should be. Archer didn't know about any other account. He didn't sign for another account at a new bank. Again, he is checking with the other council members to see if any of them knew about any addition accounts."

"I can subpoena records on the questionable accounts based on what you learned," Chad offered.

"No. That would put Ethan on notice that we discovered the unauthorized transfers. I'd rather investigate myself and then confront him. We need the element of surprise on our side."

"Right now, you can bet he's sitting on pins and needles, hoping that we miss the additional account and just note the educational fund, as the FBI's expert did," Caden said. "Myst, you're not going to the new bank alone, nor are you going to be the one to confront him."

"Who else would have that kind of knowledge to be able to back him into a corner?" she challenged.

"Mr. Clearwater," Nat said.

"I have an idea," Chad Zarkou said drumming his fingers on the desk. "How about we contact the bank and freeze the account so withdrawals are not allowed, but transfers and deposits are?"

"If Ethan tries to make a withdrawal, he'll know the jig is up at that point," Mystic said. "Not a good idea. He'll go underground with the help of whoever he's mixed up with."

"I'd need approval for any other plan. I'll contact my superior and see what options we have available. Be right back." Agent Zarkou strode out of the room.

"We may have to compromise with the FBI," Caden suggested.

"No, I want to see what Arch finds out first." Making sure the agent was out of ear shot, she looked pleadingly at Caden. "Can we port to National Wyoming Bank in Riverton and meet Arch? I'd like to look at the transaction register. See if the money sits there or is transferred somewhere else. Since the account appears to have been opened under the Tribe's corporation, Arch has the paperwork to allow him access to the account records."

"Sure. But we can't be seen upon arrival," Caden cautioned.

She jumped when her phone chirped. She tapped on the screen to see who was calling. "Arch, what did you find out?" she asked walking from the room, pulling Caden with her.

"That other account is unknown to anyone on the council," Arch answered in a bewildered voice.

"Arch, would you meet us at that bank in a few minutes?"

"Sure. I'm outside Bank of the West right now. How are you going to get here, you're still in Denver, right? And who is us?"

"Is there any one with you, or around you?"

"No, it's pretty quiet right now."

"As my father used to say. It's on a need to know basis and right now you don't need to know." She handed the phone to Caden. He got a fix on the location, and they disappeared out of the deserted hallway, leaving Nat to deal with Agent Zarkou.

"Some things defy explanation," she whispered as she laid a hand on Arch's shoulder.

"Holy shit. Where did you come from?" He grabbed at his chest as he leaned against the bank building gasping for air. "You nearly gave me a heart attack?"

"Sorry, but you know as well as anyone there are forces in the world that are difficult to explain." She smiled using her preternatural abilities to access his condition.

Arch left his hand on his chest as his breathing slowed and waited for his heart rate to return to normal. "I've known you since before you could walk. I'll help you no questions asked, but after this is all over, whatever this is, I will expect a full explanation." He shifted his gaze to Caden. "I assume this young man is one of the forces you refer to?"

"Oh, Arch, you're one of the wisest men I know." She flung her arms around him and kissed him on the cheek.

"Let's go in. I assume time is of the essence, or you wouldn't take such a risk." He glanced up and down the still empty sidewalk.

Caden opened the door, and they strode into the bank. Arch asked to speak to the manger and showed his credentials.

After reviewing Arch's paperwork, the bank manager nodded. "All your documents are in order, but I still need to call Mr. Nix for authorization. He left strict instructions that no one was to have access to these records without his express written consent."

Archer's eyes went wide and said, "He did…"

She laid her hand on Arch's arm, barely shaking her head. Caden used a bit of angel influence to convince the manager to give them immediate access to the transaction records, without contacting Ethan.

She looked over at Caden and whispered, "Using

this much magic must extract a heavy toll."

"Not when it's used for the good of mankind. Personal and selfish purposes are another story, I'll explain later. Now can we get on with it before my suggestion wears off?" he whispered in return.

In a quiet voice, Arch said, "We need to change Ethan's instructions before we leave here today."

They followed the bank manager to a small glass office off the lobby and sat down at a computer terminal to review the records.

She drew in her breath sharply as she looked at the balance. "Wow," she said quietly releasing her breath. She looked from Arch to Caden, who were both slack jawed.

At first, the money accumulated in periodic transfers of $9999.00 or $8999.00 to an out of state bank for credit to an account owned by BGE. Even more surprising were the additional transfers in from BGE in the same amounts, only to be withdrawn a week later.

"Looks like money laundering is going on here," Archer said flatly.

"Yes, but more is going out than coming in," Caden observed. "And the amounts are sporadic as are the transfers. Can we download this information without compromising the case against Nix?"

"No, we can't download the info. The bank has to voluntarily transfer the records to the Tribal Police, at the request of a council member." She glanced at Archer. "You got this. You're a council member, and acting Council Chief."

"You bet I can," Archer said.

"And we need to do it before my influence wears

off," Caden said fidgeting, then moving toward the door.

They strolled back to the manager's desk. Archer made the request, signed the necessary documents, paused, and requested the deletion of Ethan's instructions, then watched the manager complete the transactions.

"Will there be anything else, Mr. Clearwater?"

"Nope, you've been very helpful. Thank you."

Once outside the bank, Caden caught her hand and squeezed. The words *So far so good,* slid into her mind in Caden's deep smooth voice.

Archer's eyebrows rose as he looked from her to Caden. "Is there something you want to tell me, Ms. Rayne?"

"No, not right now, but later." She raised up on her tiptoes and kissed him on the cheek.

"Your father would be proud. Let me know if you need anything else. I suppose this whole thing is to be kept just between us."

"For now. Everyone will know soon enough."

"Ethan has gotten his hand caught in the money jar?" Archer raised an eyebrow and pressed his lips into a thin line.

"It would appear so. Thanks for your help."

"No problem." He turned around and strolled down the sidewalk in the opposite direction, without looking back.

She and Caden materialized in a deserted alcove of the FBI.

Caden pushed Agent Zarkou's office door open for her and followed her inside. Three pairs of eyes watched them cross the carpet and take their seats in front of the computer.

"That's all Patti. Thanks," Agent Zarkou said. A woman in her mid-forties, dark brown hair chopped short in business attire exited the room carrying several file folders.

"My assistant," Zarkou said by way of explanation.

"You might want to contact the Tribal Police and request the records they just received electronically on the additional education fund account at Bank of the West," Mystic suggested.

Agent Zarkou heaved a heavy sigh. "Do I want to know how this information was obtained?"

"No."

"Please tell me it's not illegal." Agent Zarkou cut his gaze to Nathanael North.

She smiled and patted Zarkou on the shoulder. "No, the case will not be compromised. But please don't move on it until you hear from one of us."

"I can only give you thirty-six hours. Then I'll have to answer to my superiors."

"Understood." She picked up her backpack and joined Caden and Nathanael as they walked toward the office door. "Thanks for everything. We'll be in touch soon."

Agent Zarkou walked them to the outer door. The group stepped out into the warm sunshine, turned right, and started toward the parking lot. Pop. The car windshield in front of them exploded. Pop. Pop. A couple bullets bounced off the glass door to the FBI building and bounced across the sidewalk in front of Caden. Another whizzed past her ear as Caden grabbed her waist and pulled her to the ground. Nathanael hit the ground and rolled in time to see security swarm out of all the building's exits like angry bees.

"Get us out of here," she screamed.

Can't port, too much security and security cameras. Caden's words flowed through her mind.

Security officers yanked them to their feet and hustled them back into the building. Agent Zarkou shoved open the door quickly pulling them inside.

"What the hell?" Zarkou looked accusingly at Nat.

"Don't know. Didn't see any one. Apparently, someone knew we were here. Got a leak in your office?"

"No. Got one in your ranks?"

"No. For reasons I can't divulge, that isn't possible, under any circumstances."

"Really?" Agent Zarkou asked incredulously.

"Really," Nat said.

"What about the men you met with last night at the hotel?"

"They're my experts I am working with from another angle of this case and are above reproach." Nathanael's back stiffened, and his eye twitched.

"We ran their faces through our computer and came up empty. They don't exist," Zarkou shot back.

"Then your database is out-of-date or just plain defective. One of them is a prominent business man in DC."

"And the other?"

"His head of security."

"And their names?"

"That you'll need to discover on your own. I've fed you enough information, especially if you have a leak."

Two security guards walked past Zarkou and gave the all clear sign.

"Did you find anyone?" Zarkou asked.

"Not yet, but we got the license number of the car they fled in. Wyoming plates. It won't be long."

Nathanael frowned. "Now, if we could get an armed escort to our vehicle, we'll be on our way."

"Still staying in the B…" Zarko hesitated a moment. "Uh…location you were previously?"

"Yes. If you need us, you have my cell number."

After a thorough search of their SUV turned up nothing, as did a scan for incendiary devices, four armed security guards escorted she, Nat, and Caden to their vehicle.

"Nat, are you leaving your cell phone on? We can be tracked that way." Caden pulled into traffic, then looked in the rearview mirror. "We got company. Want me to shake 'em?"

"No, the FBI knows where we're going and staying. No advantage at this time," Nat said. "Phone's off. I'll check it periodically from a remote location."

"Unless we lose them, park the SUV in the parking lot at the Denver Center for the Performing Arts and port back to the room. That way this evening, we all can port to the SUV, eat dinner in the area, see the performance, and drive back to the hotel. It'll keep them scrambling to find us. The dark tint to the SUV's windows will cover our arrivals and departures," Caden suggested.

"Actually, I think we may want to cancel tonight," Nat said.

"Why? We're sitting ducks in the hotel, if there is a leak. With my plan, they won't be able to track us as quickly," Caden insisted.

"Let's give Bruce and his wife the choice. We'll

fill them in, and they can decide. Bruce knows the score only too well." Nat shifted in his seat to glance at the vehicle following them.

"Good point. If worse comes to worse, all attending tonight, apart from Alaia, are capable of magic, we'll escape that way." Caden smiled. The hotel phone rang as she entered the suite, followed by Caden and Nat.

Caden picked up the receiver and pushed speaker. "Hello."

Agent Zarkou here. "The cell number we have is turned off because it goes directly to voice mail."

"Yeah, better to use this phone. Don't want to be tracked."

Zarkou huffed into the phone. "Great." He paused for a couple beats. "Wanted to let you know we've captured the men that shot at you this afternoon. Ballistics on the guns found in the car confirms the weapons are the ones used. Appears they're just a couple of guns for hire, working alone. Haven't been able to connect the men to anyone involved in the case yet. Still working on it. But they aren't talking."

"Thanks. We appreciate the update."

"No problem, thought you'd sleep easier tonight, with the information. Are you leaving tomorrow morning?"

"Not sure. We'll be in touch." Caden disconnected the call and blew out a breath. "Sounds like they were cheap hired guns."

"Yeah, but we still need to be on our guard and inform Bruce." Nathanael crossed the room to look out the window.

She and Caden nodded in agreement.

Nathanael pulled his cell phone out of his pocket and called Bruce. He filled him in on the morning's events. "How about we meet in our suite in about an hour? That will give us plenty of time for dinner and to get to the theatre early."

Nat ended the call, then let everyone know Bruce concurred with their assessment of the situation. Nat touched the phone's screen again. "You ready, Alaia?"

Nate smiled wide and ended the call. With a wave, he sauntered into his room, closing the door.

****

A soft knock sounded on the suite's door. Caden checked the peep hole, then opened the door to a petite woman with hair like spun gold cascading down her back standing in front of Bruce.

"Hi, I'm Angelique, Bruce's wife." She smiled up at him with sparkling violet eyes full of mischief.

He moved aside to allow Bruce and Angelique to enter.

"This is nice and decorated much brighter than the Roosevelt Suite. That's where we're staying," Angie said.

Bruce stood behind Angie and motioned to him. "Angie, this is Caden. He is one of the business associates that brought us here and graciously invited us to join them at the theatre."

"Pleasure to meet you, Caden Silverwind, is it?" Angelique extended her hand.

Caden shook Angelique's hand and gathered Mystic to him with the other. "This is Mystic Rayne. Nathanael and Alaia North are in the adjoining room getting ready. They should only be a minute. May I get you something to drink?" He released Mystic and reached for one of the six crystal wine glasses arranged around the bottle of Pinot Noir 2003.

"Yes, red wine would be nice," Angelique said eyeing the bottle, then looking up at Bruce. "Same for you?"

He nodded and flashed a brilliant smile at her.

Angelique grinned as she surveyed Mystic. "That is a beautiful name. Native American family name?"

"Yes, it is," Mystic said.

"Thanks for inviting us. *Phantom* it's one of our favorites," Angie said her voice warm and friendly. "It's not often we get to enjoy an evening with couples that we have things in common with, if you know what I mean. Bruce is always busy with work and well, his work doesn't mix well with socializing."

"I totally understand," Mystic said warming to Angelique. "We are so glad you decided to join us."

"That we are." Nat's rich voice sounded from across the room as he and Alaia crossed the living area to meet their guests. "I'm Nathanael North, and this is my wife, Alaia." He reached for the two wine glasses sitting on the bar and handed one to Alaia.

Caden raised his wine glass. "To a relaxing and enjoyable evening."

"Yes," everyone answered in unison. The crystal sang as they all touched the rims of their glasses and then took a sip.

"Delicious, one of my favorites," Bruce declared as his nostrils flared taking in the scent of the Pinot Noir.

"Glad you approve," he said.

Arriving at the theatre early, Nathanael handed the tickets to the attendant.

"This way, sir," she said and led them down the

main aisle to the middle of the front row. "Here we are, enjoy the show."

Angie's eyes widened. "Wow, nice seats, how'd you do that on such short notice?"

Nathanael snorted. "Really?"

He snickered. "Call it divine intervention."

Angie's eyes darted from him to Nathanial and finally locked on Bruce.

Bruce's lips twitched and curved at the corners. He leaned over and whispered, "They're angels, remember?"

"You were serious about that?" She sucked in a breath, glanced toward him, and Nathanael gave a slight nod. Her cheeks flushed as she realized the others were aware of her conversation.

"What kind of angel attends the theatre with a 9mm tucked in his waist band and a dagger strapped at his ankle?" Angie asked keeping her voice low.

He chuckled. "A warrior angel, with security issues," he whispered back.

The couples took their seats, taking in the full orchestra in the pit just below them and stage in front of them.

"Would you look at this?" he whispered to Mystic with a hint of a smile. "I could reach out and touch the conductor's head." He stretched his arm down in front of him and started to lean toward the pit. He glanced over Mystic and met Bruce's amused look.

"Don't you dare," she tersely whispered back, yanking on the back of his shirt.

"Is that a challenge?" he asked his lips curling up into a full smile.

She narrowed her eyes and pursed her lips.

"Caden," she warned.

"Only kidding." He relented and relaxed against the back of the seat.

Bruce studied the stage as the curtains opened and the lights dimmed. He leaned back in his chair and caught Caden's eye. "Bet that chandelier will pass right over our heads on that line." He pointed above their heads.

"Possibly," he agreed as the actors took the stage.

Mystic sent them both a scathing look. Both he and Bruce shrugged their shoulders and turned their attention to the stage.

During the intermission, he and Mystic excused themselves for a few private minutes.

"Are you feeling more comfortable with Bruce on our security team?" Caden asked. "We really have no other choice."

"Why? You kicked ass the other night on the Rez."

"And how would you know? You were safely ensconced at the lodge," Caden taunted.

"Chinoah told me what happened." She absently curled a strand of hair around her finger.

"But she was so out of it she didn't see the demons explode and their ashes float to the cavern floor. She still doesn't know the battle was between demons and angels with a few dangerous humans thrown in." He narrowed his eyes and looked sternly at Mystic. "Unless you shared information you shouldn't have."

"Of course I didn't. I keep my word," she said, her voice rising above the crowd noise.

"Keep your voice down. You're attracting attention." He laid his hand on her lower back and pulled her toward him. "We can have this discussion later. Right now, Nat and I need to know if you are comfortable with our alliance with Bruce and his people. Or if you want to go it on our own."

"Since it appears that demons may be entrenched in the situation with Ethan, I have to be okay with it."

"You really do. When we get to Wyoming, we'll be working closely with Tristian. If you can't trust him, this won't work. Otherwise, Bruce will give the order for Tristian and his team to hunt out and neutralize the demons that are out of control."

"But then we will never find out exactly what Ethan is up to or get the money back he's misappropriated." Chewing on her bottom lip, she paused. "We can terminate him and then try to follow the money trail to recoup what he appears to have taken. Then hope there are no repercussions from whatever he is mixed up in."

"Exactly my point."

"Ookkay," Mystic said drawing out the word. "What difference does it make whether the warrior angels take them on, or demons like Bruce and his entourage take them out?"

"Bruce is the Territory Overlord and has the authority to enforce the rules laid down for the paranormal creatures to peaceful cohabitate with the mortals. He earned the respect of the demons, vampires, and witches who want to exist amicably with the humans. For those who don't, justice is swift and deadly."

Mystic's eyes widened, her lips formed an O. "I'm glad he's on our side."

"He has the support of the others to do exactly what it takes to maintain the necessary balance and has the individuals and tools to do so. Leaving no trace of their activities."

"I'm okay with Bruce, and I really like Angie. Tristian makes me uncomfortable, he exudes danger and violence."

"That's exactly why he's so good. The only other option is to take this situation on ourselves and hope we're dealing with more humans than paranormals. We were just lucky that night on the Rez. We had the element of surprise on our side, and that gave us an edge. Now they know and will be prepared next time. I doubt Nat wants to engage the entire legion in the situation."

Mystic winced and blew out a sigh. "Of course, you're right."

"How 'bout this? If you have questions about Tristian, why not be up front about it with Bruce and ask him. Worst thing that can happen is he'll tell you it's none of your business and he'd be right." He glanced around as the lights dimmed off and on indicating the production was about to resume.

"Great plan. Make me the fool."

"Hear me out. The best thing that could come of it is that he'll understand your difficulties with Tristian and answer your questions."

"I guess."

"Bruce requested this meeting to warn us and volunteer his expertise rather than just coming in here, neutralizing the offenders and leaving without a trace. Which is business as usual for Tristian and his teams. Nat agreed to the meeting and for Bruce's expertise, not to question his methods," he said as the lights in the theatre lobby dimmed. "It's time to return to our seats.

Think about what I've said." He brushed a strand of her silky black hair from her face and kissed her. "It will all work out. Trust me."

He returned to his seat. Mystic stopped a couple of seats away to talk to Angie. Bruce reached across the empty seat and tapped Caden on the shoulder. Bruce jerked his chin upward and eyed the chandelier, which earlier in the production swung across the stage, above the audience, a few feet above their heads. Now it waited held high behind them. He smiled and nodded. Mystic slipped into her seat just as the lights went down.

Mist floated across the stage, and flames sparked from the burning opera house set as the story came to its climatic end. The chandelier careened back toward the stage as he and Bruce started to raise their arms. Angie and Mystic shrieked each grabbing a raised arm as the chandelier passed just inches as planned above their fingertips. The men leaned back in their chairs and roared with laughter, the sound covered by the chandelier's scripted crash to the stage in the final minutes of the production.

As they left the theatre, Mystic was still glaring at him, even as she suggested stopping somewhere for a drink and a snack.

"Good idea," he said. "Let's go back to our suite. I've several more bottles of vintage wine, and we could order room service for late night snacks."

Bruce looked at Angie who nodded. "Sounds like a great idea. Will we need to port from the SUV back to the hotel?" Bruce asked.

"No. We'll just drive back to the hotel. This afternoon we needed a subterfuge so we parked the

SUV in the DCPA's parking lot and ported to the hotel. Thank you for going along with the plan for arrival this evening."

"Not a problem. It was fun," Angie said.

Back at the hotel, the men excused themselves to talk business for a few minutes.

****

Mystic stayed with Angie, while Alaia called in the room service order.

"Is something bothering you?" Angie asked. "Other than the behavior of our dates."

"I can't believe they actually did that, and we fell for it."

Angie stifled a small giggle. "Bruce used to cut up like that once in a while when we were dating and alone. With recent resurgence of frequent illegal demon activity, he hasn't behaved like that in a long time. It felt good to see him enjoy himself. Sorry he put Caden up to it."

"Believe me, Caden didn't need any encouragement. He probably needed a little light-hearted fun too. It's been quite a day."

"So I've heard. I understand you were in a shootout this afternoon. That would have scared the shit out of me."

"Yeah, this has not been one of my best weeks."

"I've had those kinds of weeks. Like when I had to tell my brother, who is an enforcer by profession, that I intended to marry a demon and his boss. He hit the roof. There was quite a fight between Bruce and Tristian." Angie blew out a breath. "It took a while, but eventually, it all worked out."

Her eyes flew open, and she sucked in a breath.

"Tristian, the warlock that was here with Bruce, is your brother?"

"Yeah. I had no idea Tristian worked for Bruce when I first met him at The Wycked Hair Salon. That's a story for another time." Angie waved her hand in a dismissive gesture.

"Bet that was interesting."

Angie laughed. "It was, to say the least. Anyway, Bruce thought you might have trouble accepting Tristian."

"Good guess. Tristian's aura is a bit domineering."

"He does lack in certain social skills, but he's a good guy with a hard job. Since he moved into management and married Hannah, she's softened his rough edges. You should have seen him before." Angie rolled her eyes and shook her head. "No, on second thought, you shouldn't have seen him before."

She cocked her head and looked quizzically at Angie.

"Oh, don't misunderstand. Tristian is a wonderful brother and did his best to raise me after our parents died. He was a little…no…a lot overprotective." Angie giggled. "The things he's done…well…again a story for another time."

Caden strode into the room and flipped the crystal wine glasses up in the air catching each one by its stem, then motioned to several different bottles of wine. "Pick your poison. Alaia said food should be here any minute."

Caden winked at her and began pouring the wine.

Bruce walked over to where Angie was sitting and stood behind her. He laid his large hands gently on her petite shoulders, leaned down, nuzzled her neck, and brushed his lips lightly over her cheek. She crooked her arm around his neck affectionately and whispered something in his ear. He smiled and gave a slight nod.

Straightening up, Bruce took two glasses from Caden filled with rich amber liquid. He handed one to Angie, the other he waved under his nose and sniffed lightly. "Splendid floral bouquet," Bruce murmured then he closed his eyes and took a sip. Under a raised brow his eye sparkled. "Domaine Ramonet Montrachet Grand Cru, Cote de Beaune?"

Caden nodded.

"I've been trying to locate a bottle of this wine. Expensive and elusive."

"We have our sources." Caden grinned.

Bruce nodded. "We'll talk later." He took another sip and set the glass on a nearby table. The crystal facets shimmered through the amber liquid in the fire light. When he turned his attention to her, Caden watched Bruce intently. "As you know Tristian took off this morning for Wyoming. I've left a message for him to call, so I can bring him up to speed on the shooting this morning. Cell coverage in Wyoming is a challenge." Bruce grimaced.

"What will he be doing in Wyoming?" she asked.

"Checking up on the demon population in Riverton. He wanted to wait until you arrived in Wyoming to visit River Winds Casino. Unless you object, he would like to accompany you to the casino. If he goes alone, he would be an outsider and at a disadvantage, as you pointed out last evening. But with Tristian things always change."

She hesitated for a moment. "I don't know…"

"Is there something about Tristian that bothers

you?" Bruce asked his eyebrows scrunched together.

"I don't know him well enough to trust him to have my back, after all that has happened." Her cheeks heated. "I'm sorry. I know you are here to help, but…"

"Tristian can be intimidating at times and his rough mannerism puts people off, but he's working on it. It's also why he's so good at his job. There is none better. I trust him with my life and to make the right decisions for his teams in the field. He also takes my place when I'm unavailable. He has quite a varied skill set."

"But he's a paid assassin." *There, I finally said it, what bothers me about Tristian.*

"He is also my body guard, the enforcer of the rules that keep everyone safe, a most trusted friend and the hardest of all, my brother-in-law. That gave me more than a few lost nights of sleep." The corners of Bruce's mouth twitched then curved into an almost smile.

"Yeah. Angie told me." She cut her gaze to Angie then back to Bruce. "Said you two had one hell of a fight."

"Yes, Tristian and I both sustained serious injuries that put us out of commission for a couple of weeks. The use of deadly magic and defending magic also drained us as well. But eventually we worked it out. Still, I would rather have him protecting my back than anyone else."

Her eyes grew round, and she blew out a breath. "After all that, you still trust him with your life? Even when he tried to take yours at one time?"

"Yes."

"You've made me feel a lot better about Tristian. Still wary of him, but I think I can work with him. I'd still like Caden at my side."

"Of course, I assumed as much." Bruce turned to Nat and Alaia. "Will you be accompanying them to Wyoming?

"No, I think we'll stay at the lodge near Aspen, in case we need to call for reinforcements. Alaia isn't usually involved in my business. We have a young daughter that keeps her busy."

"I understand."

"Will you be assisting Tristian?"

"Not right now. He has his own team. Angie and I need to return to DC and handle some other pressing matters. But we will be available to either Caden or Mystic, if they need us."

"Thanks," she said, her voice quiet, looking first to Bruce and then to Angie.

"Tristian and I will be in constant communication once he obtains a smart phone and establishes cell service that works in Wyoming." Bruce rolled his eyes. "You'd think Wyoming was in a different country or dimension at least. Not an eight-hour drive or few minutes should we decided to port." He shook his head in amazement.

Chapter Fifteen
A Quick Detour, a Proposal and All Hell Breaks Loose

Up before dawn, he knew the eight-hour drive to Riverton would do little to calm Mystic's nerves. While driving, Caden quietly considered all the angles in the upcoming confrontation and ways to protect her from herself as well as others.

They checked into the Riverton Cozy Inn and unpacked their bags, showered, and sat down to relax while waiting for Tristian's phone call. It wasn't long before Mystic restlessly paced the room, took the remote from him, flipped through the channels, then flopped on the bed.

She planned to wait for the moon to rise and then shift into wolf form to snoop around the Rez before contacting Tristian and heading to the casino. Something wasn't right, she felt it in her gut since before Ethan asked her to accompany him to Colorado. *And look how that turned out.*

"Mystic, let's take a walk," Caden suggested after inadvertently intercepting her thoughts.

"Yes, but I'm not sure it's safe. What if our arrival was detected and reported? There could be a hired assassin waiting to take me out. I want my life back or at least some part of it. I'm tired of hiding, tired of being afraid, tired of being shot at, and most of all tired of not having control over my own life."

"Not where I'm going to take you. Close your eyes." He wrapped his hands around her waist and teleported them out of the room. The sound of waves lapping against the shore and the scream of a bald eagle warning others away from his territory replaced the drone of the television.

"Where are we?" she asked without opening her eyes.

"On the secluded north shore of Leigh Lake. You can open your eyes now," he whispered, his hand caressing slowly up and down her spine as he held her tightly against his body.

She opened her eyes slowly and sucked in a breath. "Oh, wow, it's beautiful. We'll be safe here for a while? Where exactly are we?" Her body melted against his, and she tucked her head under his chin. The fresh scent of Lodge Pole Pine and Blue Spruce wafted on the breeze.

"What does it matter?" He laughed. "We're inside Teton National Park, southeast of Mount Moran. Paintbrush and Leigh Canyons end here. Thought we'd explore for a while then follow the hiking trail back to String Lake, it's about a mile or so then find a quiet place and relax. It was apparent the hotel room wasn't having that effect on you."

Mystic giggled and stretched her arms out wide while still leaning into him. "You got that right. Do we have to go back?"

"Not if you don't want to." He paused for a beat. "But I imagine Tristian will notify everyone that we are missing and launch an all-out search for us shortly after dark if we don't return. I didn't tell anyone we were leaving. And I don't want to deal with Tristian if he's pissed."

"Me either, but such irresponsible behavior. I love it." She sighed and turned around in his arms, her back to his warm chest, her hips curved into his as they watched the swooping and diving eagles in search of their dinner.

"I brought you here so we could share what should be a spectacular sunset this evening. Then I want you to consider agreeing to be my mate or wife whatever you want to call it. I'm falling in love with you and want to spend the rest of my life with you. When you're ready."

She hesitated for a moment then sighed. "After this is all over, ask me again." She stood on tiptoe, leaned her head back, and brushed her lips against his, running her tongue along his bottom lip.

He turned her to face him, and his mouth covered hers hungrily. The kiss sent new spirals of lust and desire through him. She returned his kiss with reckless abandon as if she didn't care that she was confusing the hell out of him. Talk about mixed messages.

Hand in hand, they started up the trail to Paintbrush Canyon at a brisk run. Suddenly she withdrew her hand, stripped where she stood, her body shimmered around the edges and blurred, fluidly changing from woman to a majestic black wolf. Increasing her speed, she thundered down the path, four paws flying and disappeared around a bend in the path. His wings unfurled and he followed, watching her every move.

She slowed and came to a stop at the edge of a clearing where she smoothly transitioned into her human form. Feet in a wide stance, she bent at the waist stretching her long legs and slender arms from side to side, hand touching the opposite foot as the other reached to the sky then alternating. She straightened and put her hands at the small of her back stretching backward slightly.

Feel better? He touched her mind. She twisted looking skyward.

He touched down a few feet from her, wings swaying in the breeze as he strolled toward her. "Your wolf is absolutely breathtaking, as you are right now. He bent and brushed his lips across her neck, working his way to her warm moist lips where he lingered, listening to their synchronized heartbeats, holding her snug against him. "I brought your clothes, but you don't have to put them on, if you don't want to."

"Thanks." She reached for the items, just as he yanked them out of her reach. Frowning, she bounced on the balls of her feet and grabbed the clothes, narrowing her eyes as she glared at him.

"Just having a little fun." He shrugged.

"It's fun, if we're both naked," she retorted. "Not when you try to get the upper hand."

As the sun disappeared behind the mountains in a fiery glow of red, orange, and yellow, he slid one arm around her shoulders and the other under her knees, and then lifted her into his arms while he unfurled his wings. Lifting slowly at first, hovering just a few feet off the ground, his wings beat harder and stronger to lift them above the treetops, and then out across the sparkling lake.

Mystic sucked in a breath. "What if someone sees us?"

"They won't," he assured her.

"Your wings, they're stronger. Healed? And such

beautiful gray marble feathers mixed with charcoal, so unique. Just like you." She laid her head on his chest. Attuned to her feelings as she enjoyed being in his arms, he projected protection from all that could harm her, at least for a little while. *This is just what I needed.*

Glad I could oblige. His words floated through her mind a satisfied smile curving the corners of his lips.

Time suspended, they floated on the evening breeze. As the moon rose, slivers of silver shimmered across the rippling waves of the lake's surface.

"Jellybean, it's time to return to the Riverton. I'm sure Tristian is trying to get in touch with us," he said.

"What's with the Jellybean?"

With a mischievous tone to his voice, he said, "Because on the outside you're all hard and smooth, but on the inside, you're soft and tasty. Not to mention the array of color displayed on your skin when I first saw you." His lips twitched as the smile twisted into a wicked grin. He leaned far left as her hand glanced off his shoulder He grabbed her wrist and they disappeared.

One minute the cool breeze caught her hair, sending strands across his face and the wolf song echoed through the canyons. The next, a television droned on, lemon-scented furniture polish wafted in the air mingled with an unfamiliar male scent. Mystic's eyes flew wide open as he shielded her from Tristian who stood in the middle of the room, fisted hands on his hips, his mouth drawn into a tight thin line, eyes blazing with anger, mingled with a hint of concern.

"Where the fuck have you two been? I tried calling two hours ago, no answer. I came over here knocked, no answer. Entered your room, all your stuff was neatly arranged, but no sign of you." He flexed his hands and paced the room like a caged animal.

"Mystic needed a break from it all, before diving head long into whatever is awaiting her…us."

"Haven't you heard of leaving a message? If you two were under my command, you'd be—gone."

Caden set Mystic on her feet, immediately regretting releasing her.

Hands fisted at her hips, she stared defiantly at Tristian. "We're not under your command. Nor will we ever be trained, unfeeling, cold-hearted, professional assassins." It was immediately apparent on her face, she regretted her words and the bitterness of their delivery.

"The past weeks have taken a toll on all of us," Caden said hoping to smooth over the hateful words Mystic spewed.

Tristian's gray-blue eyes flashed with anger and concern then returned to cold and calculating. "No, I don't believe that either of you will, but without us cold-hearted killers, there might be a lot less damaged warrior angels and shapeshifter's in denial. Shall we address you playing lawyer of the downtrodden rather than facing your own destiny." He paused for a couple beats. "I thought not." Turning on his heel, his black duster billowing out behind him, he strode out the door, shutting it quietly behind him.

"Well, that went well," Caden quipped as he reached for his cell phone feeling Mystic's glare bore into his back. He touched the #1 and immediately connected to Nathanael.

"Where the hell have you been? Do you have any idea how close to calling in reinforcements I was, not to mention Tristian and Bruce?"

"Nat, you know me better than that," Caden

answered. "I felt you touch my mind an hour or so ago. We've already encountered Tristian."

"I knew your mind wasn't in battle mode, as it would have been if something bad had happened. But that didn't tell me where you were or if you were in some drug induced state meant to deceive me."

"I'm sorry. I've been out of the security loop too long. It didn't even occur to me until we were gone to leave a message. It won't happen again."

"Make damn sure it doesn't. Tristian threatened to handle things on his own. I believe Bruce advised against it, at this time."

"Yeah, Tristian gave us a briefing. Then he and Mystic had words."

"Oh, I bet they did." Nat tried to keep the smile out of his voice, but Caden wasn't fooled.

His lips twitched, but he returned his attention to the matter at hand. "Tristian and Mystic are an explosive combination. I've had my hands full keeping the peace on a good day, let alone after one like today. We'll give Tristian space and time to cool his jets. Tomorrow will be soon enough to start poking around."

"Sounds like a good plan. You and Mystic get a good night's sleep and don't let her shift and explore on her own. That would just add more fuel to the fire."

"I'll see to it." He turned to her. "Myst, for tonight, do me and yourself a favor and get a good night's sleep. Tomorrow night you can shift and sniff around, tonight would just anger Tristian. Okay?"

"How does everyone know my business?" Mystic asked.

"Because you were broadcasting so loudly when we first arrived. You've toned it down so our little adventure must have been worth it."

"You have no idea." She yawned wide as she lay across the bed then scooted next to Caden burying her face in his shoulder. She sighed softly.

****

Before dawn, a loud knock on the door awakened them.

"Tristian?" Caden called out sleepily.

"Are you expecting someone else?" His voice boomed in the quiet predawn morning.

"No. I'll be right there." He rolled out of bed, yanked on his jeans, and flipped the light switch on his way across the floor. He looked through the peephole to verify Tristian and opened the door.

Mystic grabbed the clothes laid out last night and ran into the bathroom, leaving the door open a crack.

Tristian strode in. "Well at least you had the common sense to make sure it was me before you opened the door."

"Tristian, if we're going to work together, you're going to need to tone it down. I'm used to taking commands, but Mystic isn't. It doesn't do any good to antagonize her. You don't like working with us. I got that. But you have your orders."

Tristian stood silent for a few moments, then grunted. "I guess I deserved that. Working with you two is not the problem. Your blatant disregard for safety is."

"Understood. I've already told my legion commander it won't happen again and give you the same assurances. Fair enough?"

"Yep." Tristian gave him a quick overview of his plan. "Think we can all adhere to the arrangements? A couple of my people will be stationed outside the casino."

Caden raised an eyebrow in question.

"I assure you they will blend in. We've run this type of operation many times before," Tristian said.

Dressed in the copper slacks that fit like a glove, black and copper striped cream sweater, Mystic stepped out of the bathroom a half hour later. Her long straight shiny black hair cascaded down her back and over her shoulders. He let out a low whistle. "Wow, you look great."

"Yeah." Tristian let his glaze slide slowly from her head to her feet and then blew out a breath. "Nice. You'll turn heads today. Bet your ex will wish he behaved better." After a short pause he said, "In more ways than one when I'm finished with him."

"You're not going to do anything today, are you? We're just going to walk through the River Winds, so you can get the lay of the land. I'll talk with a few employees while you check for demonic activities inside. If we draw Ethan's attention, he'll make an appearance. It will be easier to deal with him in front of a crowd of people." Mystic brushed her hair away from her face, tucking it behind her ear.

"That's the plan. Since I won't be recognized, I'll walk in just ahead of you and wander around. If the casino employs demons or other worldly creatures, we need to be prepared. Two of my men will be stationed outside the doors. I won't be too far from you at any one time. Caden will walk in with you. Ethan won't want another confrontation with witnesses."

"I'll just carry on pleasant conversation with the employees as I walk through," Mystic said.

"Yes, as the newest tribal council member. Ask questions about working conditions, employee relations, co-workers' attitudes anything you think might help. If anyone gets antsy, back off, could be a demon. Can you feel their magic signature?" Tristian wanted to know.

"I have the ability. I don't think I ever met one, except Bruce."

"Yeah and he masks his magic signature well. You will soon. Caden, you do, right?"

"More experience with them than I'd like to remember. I'll stay close to Mystic. We can use telepathic communication to avoid being over heard."

"Good. Let's move out." Tristian swung the door open then stopped. "Mystic, I want you in sight at all times. That may present a problem if you need to use the ladies' room. If that happens, you and Caden should leave the casino, or Caden will accompany you into the room."

"That's ridiculous. I will be all right for a couple of minutes. He can stand outside."

"No. In sight at all times. No exceptions. What if we encounter a female demon? She can lay in wait for you in any restroom you choose. Only takes a couple seconds for her to disable you and port you elsewhere."

"I didn't realize they had those kinds of powers," Mystic said.

"And a lot more. There are some very powerful demons. Unfortunately, it appears a group of them have joined forces here." He scrubbed his hand over his chin. "I haven't seen anything yet that would attract such a gathering."

"I can blend into the surroundings and not be seen

in the ladies' room, if it's necessary," Caden offered.

"Great. Can't even go to the ladies' room by myself." Mystic huffed.

"We'll arrange to have lunch away from the casino and stop back by the hotel. I'll take my car. It's less conspicuous than that huge SUV you're driving."

They walked out into the unlit parking lot. Parked several rows over from the SUV was a dark blue metallic low-slung sports car.

"Less conspicuous. Are you insane? This is Wyoming. If it's not a pickup truck or SUV it sticks out like a sore thumb." Mystic jerked her chin in the direction of the only sports car in the parking lot. "Not to mention that car is over one hundred grand. Ever seen the movie about stealing cars in sixty seconds? Speaking of gone, I thought this parking lot was lit."

"It was. Until I arrived—will be again after we leave. And yes, I've seen the movie, but the car is not going anywhere," Tristian said with confidence. "Besides I want Ethan to think I'm a big spender."

"No, Ethan will be suspicious of you. Why would a person that could afford a one hundred thirty-thousand-dollar vehicle, stop in Riverton, Wyoming, at a little tribal owned casino?"

"Because Native Americans are my cause. If he checks my background, he will discover I am involved in several Native American non-profits."

"Pretty smart. I underestimated you," Mystic said a slight smile turning up the corners of her mouth. "What if there is surveillance in this parking lot, or someone recognizes you? Your cover is blown."

"Duh. I've done my homework. No working camera's. If there were, I'd have disabled them. Also,

I'm able to change my appearance at will. I've spent most of my life outwitting the criminal mind. Believe it or not, I'm not just Bruce's assassin. I've climbed… Never mind. If Ethan is bilking the educational fund here, he may consider me another possible patsy." Tristian swaggered toward the sports car.

"That way you can find out where the funds are going, and maybe what they are being used for. Nice," Mystic said, climbing into the passenger side of the SUV.

Caden closed the door and walked around to the driver's side, still admiring Tristian's ride. "Is that really your car?" The orange glow over the horizon bounced off the vehicle.

"Yep, one of the perks of the job. When I bust a demon whether is it necessary to neutralize him or send him down under, and I don't mean to Australia, all his belongings are forfeited to me. Except if rehabilitation is an option, then his assets are held until he completed the rehabilitation requirements."

"Impressive." He climbed into the SUV.

Tristian ambled to his vehicle, opened the car door, and slid in. He turned the key, and the motor purred with raw power. The vehicle pulled out of the lot and turned down the highway toward River Winds Casino.

Chapter Sixteen
The River Winds Casino Operations are in Question and Someone Doesn't Like It

Caden gave him a few minutes head start and then followed. "Don't want to let them know he's with us, at least initially. We'll hope no interested parties saw him come to our room or watched our parking lot conversation."

"He's pretty thorough, doubt he would have shown up at our door if there were any questionable people around. Just in case, we can take an alternative route to the casino. Turn here."

They parked in the opposite end of the casino's lot away from Tristian's car. He opened Mystic's door and wrapped an arm around her shoulders. "This time we'll give the impression we are a couple. Okay with you?"

"Sure. Aren't we?"

"Yep, as far as I am concerned. You haven't told me your position." He grinned down at her.

"I will when the time is right," Mystic said, smiling up at him, with a mischievous glint in her eyes.

"I'll hold you to that. Ready?" He pulled open the casino door and watched her sashay through it. He blew out a breath and followed her inside.

She walked up to the cashier's cage. "Good morning, I'm Mystic Rayne, tribal council member. Looks like you get to play with money all day. My dream job."

"My name is Rusti, and it's not a fun job at all. Very stressful. Either you're counting out the winner's money and management is watching me like a hawk, or displeased at the amount won. I'm always glad for the winners. Then you have people that have no business gambling their money away. I feel sorry for them when they get advances hoping to break even." She shook her head.

"I understand. What could we do to make the job easier, less stressful?"

"It would be nice if the new floor manager, Sage, would do the winner's payout confirmation. She's happy to help."

"I see. Thanks for your frankness. We're considering making a few changes and appreciate your input."

Rusti's forehead creased with worry. "What kind of changes?"

"Oh, don't worry, it's not with the employees, just procedural changes to make things run smoother. That's why your input is so important. You work here, we don't."

Rusti smiled, and the crease between her eyes smoothed out. "Oh, happy to help. Will you be talking to others?"

"Yes, as many as I have time for today. Thanks again for taking time to talk with me." Mystic walked away from the cage and started across the main floor.

A statuesque woman with long thick black hair and strands of gray peppered through it stood rooted to the floor staring at Mystic like she'd seen a ghost. The color drained out of the woman's face, and she wobbled a bit on her feet.

"It's Flora Rose, isn't it? Are you okay?" Mystic laid a hand on the older woman's shoulder to steady her.

The woman's hand flew to her heart. She blinked and heaved a long sigh. "Thank God," she murmured reaching for Mystic's hand. Then in a quiet voice meant only for Mystic to hear, she said, "They said you went missing after your trip with Mr. Nix, and you were probably dead."

"As you can see, I'm very much alive. Now who put those silly ideas in your head and scared you half to death?"

"Joey and Colt, you know they went to Colorado with you but didn't remember much about it when they came back. Guess they drank too much. Then several of the workers around here kept repeating rumors they heard, I guess. The other two guys never did come back. I don't remember their names right now." Flora clasped her shaking hands together. "I need to sit down. I don't feel so good."

Caden put a hand under Flora's elbow. Flora jumped and tried to brush his hand away.

"It's all right Flora. This is Caden my friend."

Flora's eyes widened. "I thought you and Mr. Nix…"

"No," Mystic said more sharply than she intended. "Mr. Nix and I were never more than acquaintances. We grew up together. That's all."

Caden led Flora across the floor to a chair.

"Mark another one up to the rumor mill. They had you engaged to Mr. Nix." Flora leaned her hand on the desk and sat down. "I thought you were too sensible a young woman to fall for him." Flora leaned over and whispered into Mystic's ear. "That man's not right. Hangs with a bad crowd and shuns his own kind. You know what I mean?"

"You mean they don't have the gene?" Mystic smiled. Flora was one of the older generation that felt the shapeshifter gene made them different.

He had a glass of water and some crackers brought over. "Take a sip and eat a few crackers, you'll feel better."

"No. They're not," she dropped her voice to a whisper. "Shifters. They're not human either. Bad feeling when they're around. Not right." Flora took the glass from him and drank half of it, then munched a couple of crackers. "I better get back to work. Mr. Nix will have a fit if he sees me sitting. He has cameras all over River Winds. Not just for watching the gamblers either. He'll dock my pay and might even fire me. I need this job." She got unsteadily to her feet and stood for a moment. He slid his hand under her elbow again. "I'm okay." She took a couple of steady steps, looked back, and smiled then hurried off.

"That was an interesting conversation. Do you know her well?"

"Not really, she belongs to my tribe. Her husband liked the drink too well and died from it. Her two sons followed in his footsteps. She's all alone now."

"Hard life, and now she's worried for her job." He shook his head.

"We might want to meet up with her away from work and see exactly what she meant by not human."

"You know what she meant, but I'd like to clarify if these people are working at the casino, or she's seen him outside of work with them," he said.

They talked with a few more employees that would talk to them and got basically the same story. Ethan Nix was a difficult boss. He kept the employee's in line by threatening their jobs.

As he and Mystic rounded a corner, Ethan came hurrying from the other direction. He lunged at Mystic, and Caden stepped in front of her.

"I don't think you want to do that," he said, putting his hands out in front to keep Ethan at arm's length.

"What, I was just going to hug her. Glad to see that she is all right," Ethan said.

"No thanks to you," Mystic said viciously staring at Ethan. "To what do I owe the pleasure of your visit?" Ethan asked.

"As you know, I'm the newest member of the Tribal Council. They've appointed me their liaison to the River Winds Casino."

"Who gave you that authority?" Ethan hissed.

"Archer Clearwater. You know—he's the acting Council Chief," Mystic said smugly.

"Get out of my casino," Ethan said pointing to the door.

Mystic raised an index finger and wagged it in front of him. "I might point out this is not your casino. It belongs to the Northern Arapahoe Tribe. There'll be two more liaisons appointed and eventually a gaming commission. They'll oversee the safe, lawful, and honest operation of the tribe's gaming operations and activities on the reservation."

"Oh, you think—so do you?" He raised his arms out from his sides and turned in a semi-circle. "Look around. I've built a successful business."

"For the tribe."

"I've kept it looking good and welcoming. Employee morale is good."

"You're also under investigation by the Tribal Police and the FBI. Then there's the matter of the missing floor manager."

"Employees quit. I don't have time to chase each one down and find out why."

"Then there have been other discrepancies reported."

Ethan's eyebrow winged up. "Lies. Plain and simple."

Mystic ignored his outburst and continued. "The three liaisons will also revise and review the rules, and procedures to govern, facilitate, and protect the gaming assets of the tribe, and environment. We'll share the authority to disseminate and enforce technical standards and rules of each game of chance operated by the tribe. Mr. Nix, you're on your way out."

"I'm not the only one." Ethan shoved him and grabbed Mystic's shoulder. "I'd hate to make a scene and call security to have you removed."

He took hold of Mystic, pushed her behind him, and jerked his chin toward the door.

Ethan glanced around. Everyone was staring at them as Ethan straightened his suit jacket.

"I think you have already done enough. We're leaving, but your troubles have just begun," Mystic said. "Oh, by the way, effective immediately, you'll not hire or fire anyone without the council's approval. Clear?"

"Of course." Ethan tugged at his tie as his face reddened.

He banded an arm around her waist and led her to the door. "You've pushed him hard enough."

"Need him riled up enough to cause problems with whoever is calling the shots. I don't think it's him. He's scared. I can feel it."

"Agreed. Still, I don't like you putting yourself in harm's way. You just upped the bounty on your head."

"But I have two wonderful protectors." She smiled and looked up at him from under her long thick black eyelashes.

"That you do, if you'd just listen to them. Now let's get the hell out of here before Ethan's reinforcements arrive."

He caught Tristian's gaze, jerked his chin toward the door, then whisked Mystic out the door and across the parking lot. He pushed the remote and opened the passenger door for her, hauled her into the seat, and shut the door. Mystic pushed the driver side door open. Bounding over the hood of the SUV, he slid into the leather driver's seat, turned the key in the ignition, and drove out of the parking lot, careful not to draw unwanted attention. As he turned the corner back on to Highway 789, four high-end pickup trucks pulled into the River Winds parking lot.

"Predictable." He snorted. "When we get back to the hotel, we'll check and see if the bugs are still working that we planted last time we were in Mr. Nix's office." Caden chuckled.

"Aren't the receivers back at the lodge?" Mystic asked looking over her shoulder.

"Nope, took 'em with me. Figured they might come in handy. Tristian and Bruce agreed."

"River Winds has camera's outside in the parking

lot. It won't take long to get a plate number and trace the SUV back to you."

"Not if Tristian was successful in disabling the surveillance system while we were in there. It should be back on line now."

"Oh, so you are still messing with Ethan's head too." She grinned.

"Yep, I'm sure he knows we are messing with the surveillance system, by the way it stops when we arrive and starts after we leave. It will be impossible for him to figure out. It's not humanly possible."

"I've been meaning to ask you about your talents and use of magic. My grandfather told me that use of magic was a very powerful and dangerous thing. That its use always exacted a price from the wielder, regardless of the reason."

"That's true."

"From where I stand, it appears that you, Nat, Killian, and Sean use it constantly. Well almost. Teleporting at will and taking others with you, telepathic communication you use between yourselves and others, not to mention things I haven't seen."

"That's because as warrior angels, we've paid the price to wield magic a thousand times over during our battles with the dark ones to protect mankind. As far as creatures like you, Tristian, Bruce, and the demons we'll face, the use of magic will exact a price. I'm sure Bruce, Tristian and probably Angelique weigh the benefits against the costs before they use their magic. The dark ones never do, and we use that to our advantage in a fight."

"But you aren't a warrior angel anymore. How does that work?"

"No, I'm not, but believe me, I've more than paid the price for several lifetimes of magic."

When he drove into the parking lot at the motel, he noticed that Tristian's sports car was back. He circled the parking lot and parked in the corner closest to the room.

Tristian sat in a chair, his feet propped on the bed. He'd set up the receivers and was listening to the conversations taking place in Ethan's office. Then he switched back and forth to other conversations elsewhere in the casino. The computer and flat screen monitor were up and running on the small desk.

"Just make yourself at home," Caden said sarcastically.

"Thanks. I just figured you might need a little help this evening, if they figure out you're here," Tristian said polishing the blade of his ivory handled dagger with a motel hand towel. He sheathed it in a harness strapped to his ankle. "You might want to cloak your vehicle for the night."

"I can make it blend into the asphalt and hope no one runs into it by accident. It's parked in a corner, so it should be fine."

"We should sleep in shifts. I'll take the first one," Tristian volunteered. You and your woman might want to get some shut eye."

He cut his gaze to the one king size bed in the bedroom and back to Tristian. "Am I to understand we're all expected to share the bed?"

"Nope. I took the liberty of switching rooms with you and moved your stuff to the adjoining room next door when I set up the receiver in here. Figured you'd want your intimate moments in private and all."

"We don't have int…" Mystic said taking a defensive stance.

He cut her off by pulling her to him and brushing his lips across hers lightly. "We appreciate that, but there are no adjoining rooms in the motel."

Mystic narrowed her eyes at him and tried to pull away but said nothing. He held her tight with little effort.

"There is now. Tristian reached sideways and stuck his arm right through the wall and pulled it back, grinning.

He released Mystic and stared at the wall. "Wow, that's a cool trick. Is the whole wall that way?" he asked as he stood and poked his hands through various places in the same wall.

"Yeah, comes in handy," Tristian said absently. The loud bang of a door slamming yanked his attention to the receiver tuned into Ethan's office.

"The woman is still alive. What does she remember?"

"Everything," Ethan answered.

"Why haven't the police paid you a visit?"

"How the hell should I know?"

"Let me handle it and get out of my office," Ethan said deadly calm.

"Sorry. You had your chance. Now, we'll take care of her and her companion, just like we did your nosy floor manager. Our association with you is becoming less and less profitable. We're tired of cleaning up your messes."

"But Black Gold Enterprise can't operate without association with the casino. Thereby tribal permission to conduct business on reservation land," Ethan shot back. "And I'm the key to that association."

A loud thud sounded and then a crash sounding like something hit the wall and then quiet.

"We'll just see about that." The menacing voice echoed in the room then snickered. A door opened and closed then nothing but silence again.

Tristian rubbed his hand across his jaw. "Gee that didn't sound good." He tapped the keys on the computer keyboard, and the monitor came to life with a view through the front entrance and into River Winds parking lot. Tristian watched attentively until a man of average height, dressed in a dark suit, his light brown hair pulled back in a ponytail and dark sunglasses appeared. He walked out of the River Winds door and got into the shiny black pickup with temporary tags parked in the lot and roared out onto the street.

He pointed to the screen. "I recognize that truck. It was one of four that entered the parking lot after we left. They were sitting at the corner waiting to turn. Hey, did you tap into the casino's surveillance system?"

"Not exactly, I didn't have enough time to tap in and cover my tracks, so it wouldn't be found. But I was able to add an additional remote feed that should take them a while to find."

"Nice."

"I don't want to sound macho, or like I don't want your help, but I'd really like you two to port back to Colorado just for tonight. Then I'll bring in my team. Caden, I understand you have battled demons for centuries, but you're still not one-hundred percent. My team is, and I would rather know you are protecting Mystic far away from here. My team and I can neutralize what comes here tonight. The big boss won't come. He'll send his minions first. When they don't return..." Tristian raised his hands in a dismissive gesture.

Caden shoved his hands in his pockets and paced the floor.

"No way are we leaving you here to battle heaven knows what," Mystic protested.

He heaved a heavy sigh, his eyes fixed on Mystic. "Tristian's right. The last thing the demons expect is to run up against a team of demon slayers. Besides, with us gone, the demons' attention will be split, looking for us and battling Tristian and his team. That will give him a huge advantage."

"Exactly," Tristian said. "You know your battle strategy. No wonder you've been a force to be reckoned with for centuries."

A sad smiled crossed his lips. "Those days are gone, for now." He paused. "Maybe forever."

"That's not what I heard," Tristian said fiddling with his dagger again.

"Then you heard wrong," Caden said fiercely. "Mystic grab what you need for tonight. We better leave now, so our magic signature can't be followed. It'll give Tristian a chance to get his team in place."

Mystic opened her mouth to protest.

"Don't argue. This is my area of expertise," Caden said.

She disappeared through the wall and returned with her backpack. "Ready. Good luck, Tristian."

As he wrapped his arms around Mystic's waist, he glanced back at Tristian. "We'll be back in the morning unless we hear otherwise.

Tristian nodded in agreement. "I'll be in touch."

He cut his gaze to the main room's entrance just a second before there was a loud knock on the door. Mystic and Caden disappeared from the room.

Chapter Seventeen
Surprise, We're Back!

Mystic and Caden materialized on the front porch of the lodge. Caden turned the handle on the door and poked his head in. Killian and Chinoah where sitting on the couch in front of the crackling fire. Killian's arm lay across the back of the couch.

"Mind if we join you?" Caden said, holding the door open for Mystic.

"Wh…what?" Chinoah jumped off the couch, mug in hand, nearly spilling her coffee and turned around prepared to sprint upstairs.

"Caden. What are you two doing back?" Killian asked in a slow easy drawl, his eyes locked on Chinoah and then shifted to Caden and Mystic. I thought you were gone for the duration. I know it can't be over already."

"No, it's just beginning. Mystic talked with some of the casino's employees, one was under the impression she was dead. She had a confrontation with Ethan, and we left immediately afterward." He looked over at her and shook his head. "Antagonized the bastard, is what she did."

"I didn't. I told him like it was," she protested.

He rolled his eyes and blew out a breath. "Okay. Did Nat fill you in on the particulars of what happened while we were gone?"

"Yeah. Sounds like we've a mess on our hands, with not enough intel."

"Tristian acts as the enforcer for Bruce, the expert in these things. We met with them both and agreed to work together."

"Bruce is an unknown to us. How can we trust him?"

"He's trustworthy. We have it on good authority. Anyway, while we were gathering information in the casino, Tristian was tapping into their surveillance system. Then he verified that the bugs planted during an earlier trip worked. By the time we returned to the room, Tristian had the receiver working and the remote to their surveillance system connected to his computer system. The man knows his stuff."

"I told you," Nat said coming down the stairs. "Back so soon?"

"Long story short, Tristian wanted to move his team in and wait to see who showed up to neutralize Mystic and me. He wanted us out of his way."

Nat's eyes narrowed. "And you agreed?"

"Yeah. He listed numerous valid points." Caden filled Nat in on what happened since he left Wyoming and the conversation overheard in Ethan's office.

"Wise move. Will you be returning tomorrow?" The legion commander motioned Caden into the den.

"As far as I know, that's the plan," he said, following Nat into the den.

He lowered his voice while glancing meaningfully in Chinoah's direction in the other room. "No chance they'll follow your magic signature here?"

"Nope, we left in plenty of time and masked the signature as an extra precaution. We won't know for sure until we hear from Tristian," he said over his shoulder leaving the den, and heading to the kitchen. "Got any coffee around here?"

Mystic followed him into the kitchen and grabbed a couple of mugs. He reached for the coffee pot, but it was empty.

She stretched over to take the glass pot from him. "I'll make the coffee and bring you a cup when it's done."

"No reason for you to make it. I'm quite capable." He held on tight to the pot, raised it out of her reach.

"No argument there. I just figured you'd want to talk with Nat. I'd rather have hot chocolate than coffee, so while I wait for the coffee, I'll make my hot chocolate and join you shortly." She gave a slight nod toward Chinoah who had padded into the kitchen behind Mystic.

"Oh, got ya." Caden kissed her on the cheek, handed the pot over, and exited the kitchen.

****

She turned to Chinoah. "How are you feeling? You look much better," she said her eyes taking in the flush of color on Chinoah's cheeks and her relaxed stance.

"I am feeling much better. Killian won't let me out of his sight, except to sleep. Even then, I think he checks in on me during the night. The man is a puzzle."

"How so?" she asked pouring a packet of hot chocolate into one of the mugs Caden set on the counter.

"One minute he is warm and friendly, the next he's chilly and distant. When he holds me…" Chinoah let out a sigh. "It's like heaven."

Oh, boy, you have no idea how close to the truth

that is. She pursed her lips and braced her hands on the counter for a beat. "Is there a problem? He just wants to make sure you're okay. Probably doesn't want to get mixed up in that Florence Nightingale Effect."

"I understand what you mean, but it's not like that. I'm attracted to the man, not the caregiver." Chinoah shot back. "I do know the difference."

"How do you know for sure?" She poured the last of the steaming hot water over the hot chocolate mixture. After getting a spoon out of the drawer, she stirred the mixture until it was smooth and creamy. Then she added a dollop of whip cream and breathed the chocolaty concoction in. "Mmmm." She discretely watched Chinoah's reaction. "You barely know Killian." She winked at her. "He is a very handsome man. I can see why you're physically attracted to him."

"It's more than that, and I know he feels the same way. But for some reason he's hiding it and pushing me away." Chinoah eyed the mug of hot chocolate.

"Have you talked to him about it?" she asked, holding her mug in two hands and blowing on the hot chocolate then taking a careful sip. "Want something to drink?"

"No. Thought I'd talk to you first. There is something different about the people here. You seem to take it all in stride."

"You want to know what I think? I think you're tired, recovering from a terrible ordeal, and not up to dealing with all the stress." She took a couple more sips, set the cup on the counter, and put her arm around Chinoah's shoulders. "Tomorrow things will look better and the day after even better."

"You're not telling me something. I have always

been able to tell when you're not being completely truthful, even when we were little kids." Chinoah snorted. "You're no better at it now than you were then."

"You need to talk with Killian. That's all I can tell you." She wished she could tell Chinoah the truth, but knowing this was Killian's battle…and Chinoah's.

Caden swaggered into the kitchen. "What's taking so long? I need coffee, my caffeine fix."

"Oh, you'll live, probably be up all night because of it." She poured him a mug of coffee and handed it to him. "Can we go home when you finish your coffee?"

"You bet. Give me a couple more minutes to wrap up some loose ends with Nat and we'll be off. Okay?" He took the cup and returned to the den.

"Sure." She looked over at Chinoah, reaching up in the cupboard for another mug, grabbing two. "You want coffee or hot chocolate?"

"Hot chocolate, please," Chinoah said, her lower lip fixed in a pout.

This time Mystic poured milk in the mugs, adding Dutch chocolate and sugar, then stirred the mixture. She put the cups in the microwave and turned to her friend. "I like this version, richer with milk, rather than the packaged hot chocolate. But the packages work in a pinch when you have hot water." She shook the can of whipped cream. "Empty. Huh?" She took the bag of mini marshmallows out of the cupboard and cut the corner open. The microwave dinged. She took the mugs out, gave each a stir then sprinkled the marshmallows in the mugs, and handed one to Chinoah. Mystic sipped from the new mug, closing her eyes. "Perfect." She glanced up at hearing footsteps.

"Have you seen Chinoah?" Killian pushed through the kitchen door. "Oh, there you are. It's late, and you need your sleep to fully recover." He smiled down at her. "What's with the pouty look?"

"Nothing." Chinoah turned on her heel taking her mug with her as she strode out of the room.

"What's going on?" Killian wanted to know. He leaned against the counter, crossed his arms, brown eyes switching from the kitchen door to Mystic.

Her hands fisted on hips, she stared at him. "You know what's going on. Don't play with Chinoah, or you will live to regret it. I promise you," she threatened pushing past Killian, one of his eyebrows raised in question.

"Ready?" she asked as she grabbed Caden by the waist when he sauntered into the living area.

"Yeah."

"Caden, could I have a minute of your time?" Killian asked as he stuck his head out of the kitchen door.

"Sure." Caden pried her fingers loose. "One more minute." Holding up one finger, he paused for a beat, then walked into the kitchen.

Nat watched Chinoah hurry up the stairs then turned his attention to Mystic. "Something wrong?"

"Now there's a question. Think over the last forty-eight hours, and I bet you'll have your answer," she said, sarcasm dripping off each word.

"I meant other than the obvious. Mystic there is no need for attitude," Nat said.

"I know, sorry. I'm tired."

"Understandable." Nat raised his voice and said, "Caden, get out here and take Mystic to the trailer, or I

233

will." Nat smiled mischievously. "That'll get his attention."

"No, you won't, I'll be right there," Caden called from the kitchen.

Nathanael winked at Mystic. "We warriors are very protective of our mates."

"But I'm not..." she protested.

Nat put his finger over Mystic's lip and shook his head. He dropped his hand quickly as the kitchen door swung open.

Caden and Killian strode through the kitchen door. Caden turned and clapped his hand on Killian's shoulder. "I understand exactly." Caden looked meaningfully at Nat then cut his gaze toward Killian.

Nat made a quiet sound of acknowledgement. "Stop by here in the morning before you return to Riverton. Call if anything develops tonight."

"Will do." Caden took hold of her hand, and they disappeared.

****

They materialized in the warm golden glow of firelight from the gas fireplace in Caden's fifth wheel. Two crystal glasses with deep burgundy liquid sat on the table in front of the couch, a bottle of wine between them.

In the kitchen, the oven door stood slightly open, a pan of steaming macaroni and cheese topped with toasted breadcrumbs and bacon bits barely visible. Two plates, appropriate silver wear and napkins sat on the kitchen table, in the middle a large serving spoon rested on a ceramic trivet. Two white candles in crystal candleholders were on either side of the trivet with matches.

"Alaia has been busy since we arrived at the lodge, with Nat's help," he said. "I'll have to thank her."

Mystic stood, hand still held tightly in Caden's, looking around. "She is amazing. How'd they do it?"

"I suspect that Nat ported Alaia here—" he picked up a stuffed bear off the floor "—and Kat—with all the fixings and then ported them back when Alaia was done."

"Oh, Kat is not going to be happy." She paused taking the bear from him. "But they didn't even know we were coming back tonight?"

"No, but we spent quite a bit of time at the lodge this evening before coming here."

"Alaia was at the lodge. Wasn't she?"

"Well, apparently she was here early enough to turn the heat up and get it toasty in here. Then return with food and wine." Mystic laid the bear on the counter closest to the door.

"How'd she know we'd come back here and not stay at the lodge?"

"Because that is exactly what they'd do, to get some alone time." Caden grinned picking up the glass, swirling the liquid as his nostrils flared. "Ah violets, rose petals, spices, raspberries and cherries, must be 2002 Bourchard Pere et Fils La Romanee, excellent choice," he murmured reaching down and picking up the other glass, the crystal facets winking in the firelight, and handed it to her.

"I can go close the oven door and keep dinner warm while we enjoy our wine, or I can bring the food in here, eat and then enjoy our wine. What is your pleasure, my lil' wolf?"

She returned her glass to the table. "I'm starved.

Let's light the candles and enjoy our meal in the kitchen then relax with our wine in front of the fireplace."

"Your wish is my command." He placed his wine glass on the coffee table and followed her to the kitchen. Striking the match, he touched the flame to each candle then dimmed the lights. His fingers sifted through her long hair and tucked it behind her ear as he bent to kiss her affectionately on the lips.

After dinner, they cleaned the dishes and relaxed in front of the welcoming fire, the horrific day forgotten, if only temporarily.

She cuddled into Caden, her arm loosely around his waist and tilted her head up until her gaze, met his sparkling green eyes. "I could live in this moment forever." She sighed.

"Me too." He nuzzled his face in her hair, breathing deeply. "I love your rose and lavender scent tonight. But I promise there will be years of moments like this ahead of us," he whispered.

"I'm going to hold you to that promise," she murmured.

Taking her face in his hands, he softly kissed her eyes, nose, and cheeks, finally taking her mouth with his. He slid his arm under her knees, wrapped the other around her shoulders, and stood.

Her cheek rested against his warm muscular chest, while she raised her arms to encircle his neck. Her heart thundered in her chest as she realized how badly she wanted to be his.

Making his way up the steps to the bedroom, he shouldered the curtain aside and eased her onto the king-sized bed. His lips recaptured hers, more demanding this time as his mouth covered hers hungrily. He nipped at her bottom lip, soothed it with his tongue and slid it between her parted lips.

The touch of his lips on hers sent a shock wave crashing through her body. She returned his kiss eagerly, the tip of her tongue exploring his as they entwined

Raising his mouth from hers, he gazed into her eyes. His fingers brushed over her jawbone then lightly down her neck until he reached the buttons on her sweater.

She didn't protest as his fingers unbuttoned the first one.

Keeping his eyes on hers, he continued to release a few more. He slid his hand inside her sweater and cupped her firm breast through the shimmering soft fabric of her lilac bra. Indecision had allowed him access to her body. Now her body had a mind of its own and reveled in his arousing touch. She stroked the strong tendons in the back of his neck with her fingers then caressed the powerful muscles down his back.

His head bent, he trailed his lips to the swell of her breast. Nudging the bra aside, his tongue caressed her sensitive swollen nipple, caught it between his teeth then covered her breast with his warm, wet mouth sucking softly. Instinctively her breasts arched up against him, encouraging his lips intimate exploration. A quiet whimper escaped her as his mouth kissed its way to the other breast.

Her fingers reached for the top button on his jeans, popped it open, and slid the zipper down as her hand lingered over the thick hard ridge straining for release. She tugged the denim over his hips and peeled them off his powerful thighs.

When his hands slowly moved downward skimming either side of her body, one hand slid over her taut stomach to the swell of her hips. He reached for the button on her jeans. His smoldering gaze flicked to her face, wanton lust shot through her at his touch.

Magically the zipper slipped down, he eased the material over her hips in a matter of seconds. His tongue made a path down her ribs to her stomach licking in soft arousing swirls sliding farther down with each passing moment. His hands caressed the inside of her thighs and spread her wide.

"You are absolutely beautiful," he breathed against her skin.

Her hands explored his muscular backside as he moved over her and slipped between her legs.

Heat rippled under her skin as she recognized the flush of feral sexual desire. The wolf prowled inside the confines of her body urging her on as her legs spread wider allowing Caden access to where she was already hot and already wet.

Breathlessly Mystic murmured, "Caden, do you have condoms?"

Caden cut his gaze to her, the corners of his mouth turned up and grunted. "No worries. I can control my seed, so don't worry about getting pregnant." At her amazed look, he paused, shot her a cheeky grin. It's an angel thing. Nor do I contract or pass on STDs."

"Good to know." Mystic gasped as Caden's fingers intimately expertly explored, teased. She moaned and arched against his hand. *No one has ever made me feel this way.*

Oh, lil' wolf, I'm just getting started. Don't hold your wolf back you're in for the ride of your life.

Her pleasure burned so intense she failed to notice her fangs were unsheathed and her claws poked through her fingertips. She tried to will them back as the first wave of ecstasy crashed through her. "Oh—my God—Caden." She raised her head and let loose a possessive howl as her wolf took over. Wanting what she had so long withheld from the wolf, now it would have everything.

She grabbed hold of Caden's waist with claws extended, rolled him onto his back and straddled him. Mystic lowered herself down slowly enjoying the full feeling of him.

Moaning, he grabbed her hips and thrust into her. "You feel so good." He seized her shoulders and flipped her over onto back and pumped into her until she howled again. This time she took him with her riding the crest of pleasure until they were both wet from sweat and exhausted. They lay entwined together sleepily satisfied, drifting into a deep sleep.

Chapter Eighteen
The Calm before the Storm

The rain pinged on the roof as Caden awoke. Out the windows, he saw black storm clouds gathered on the horizon, promising one hell of a thunderstorm.

He sighed and looked down at the beautiful woman in his bed. Her long black hair fanned out over her pillow and across his shoulder where her cheek rested, her body curled into his curves. Mystic fit him perfectly. Wow what a ride she'd given him last night.

She blinked and smiled sleepily up at him. "You're damn good."

"Nice to know." He leaned over and kissed her deeply. "As much as I'd like to continue where we left off last night, we'd better get up and call Tristian then head over to the lodge before Nat is on our doorstep."

"The ramifications of last night, don't we need to talk about them?"

"Talk is over rated. Your actions into the wee hours of the morning spoke volumes."

"That's what I'm afraid of. I think we need to sort…"

He interrupted. "Sorting it out can wait. Join me in the shower?" He didn't want her to analyze or rationalize last night. She was his now, like it or not. And he liked it a lot. The consequences of bedding a warrior angel were quite clear. Yet, he knew the wolf took over and how that affected the whole consensual act, he had no flaming idea.

"It's a little small for both of us," she said rolling over and sitting up.

"No, it's not. I'll show you." He grinned, got to his feet, and padded toward the shower.

His back turned to her, she sucked in a sharp breath, appalled she asked, "Did I do that?" She pointed to the red marks and scratches around his waist and down the length of his back.

"Yep," he said. "I've never had such mind blowing, raw sex in all my years. Of course, you're the first shapeshifter I've taken to my bed."

"And the last," she said possessively, following him into the shower.

"As you wish." He held the shower door open for her.

She slid her arms around his neck and gasped, her bare breasts crushed against his hard chest. She pressed her open lips to his taunting him wordlessly. *You can't give me too much trouble in here after last night.*

He cupped his hands under her fine ass and lifted her up. *Wanna bet?* He leaned back against the shower wall fitting his groin to her crotch as she wrapped her legs around him.

Twenty minutes later, he stepped out of the shower followed by Mystic. He pulled on jeans and a sweater. Locating his cell phone, he checked for messages watching her wriggle into her red bikini panties with a rhinestone heart on the front and fastened the matching red lace bra. Legs spread slightly apart, she bent over searching for her jeans.

"If you don't stop teasing me, we are going to be

really late," Caden said reaching over snapping the elastic band on her panties.

"Sorry, I thought I'd left my jeans on the floor, but I must have hung them up. She brushed past him deliberately rubbing against him on the way to the closet. He felt her wolf prowl under her skin, a sensation like nothing he'd ever experienced. *A real turn on.* She'd let the wolf out last night, but it was apparent she was having trouble keeping it contained this morning.

He reached for her and pulled her to him, rubbing his hand intimately over her body. "Tonight." Then he released her.

Too aroused to remain close to her, he walked out of the trailer to cool off and dialed Tristian's phone number. It rang several times then went to voice mail. He tapped disconnect, tried again with the same results, his brows drew together. Something was wrong; he could feel the darkness. The trailer door stood open, he sprinted up the stairs, into the bedroom and jerked the panel open to his secret weapon stash.

He pulled the leather scabbard over his royal blue sweater and sheathed his sword and daggers. Picked up the subcompact 9mm he slid it into the harness inside his boot and tucked the .357 in the back waistband of his black jeans. "Come on Mystic, we gotta go."

She quickly appeared in the living area, dressed in black jeans, a black and white stretchy V-neck sweater and running shoes. "What's wrong?" Her eyes swept over the arsenal tucked across his body.

"Nothing. I need to talk with Nat."

"You're lying to me."

He blew out a breath. "Tristian isn't answering his

cell phone and no messages from him this morning."

"Maybe he slept in?" Mystic said hopefully, rushing to gather her things. A quick smile crossed her lips as she picked up Kat's bear. "I know a little girl who'll be glad to get this back."

"I imagine she will. But it's doubtful that Tristian slept in." He waited for her exit, locked the trailer door, and set the alarm system. His arms encircled her waist. Suddenly, several voices replaced the quiet of the trailer. The scent of coffee wafted through the air.

"Well, it's about time," Sean greeted the pair. "Late night or early morning?" He raised a brow questioningly and grinned. "Oh, Kat will be so glad you found her bear. We looked all over the house for it last night."

"None of your business. Where's Nathanael?"

"Uh oh, testy this morning. The little woman giving you grief already?" Sean teased and then saw the serious look on Caden's face. "They took Kat outside to burn off excess energy. She's bouncing off the walls and driving everyone nuts." Sean grimaced and rolled his eyes. "What's up?"

"Not sure. Probably nothing." Caden rolled his shoulders and stretched his arms above his head, wondering if his warriors sixth sense still overacted to stimulus. "Anyone heard from Tristian?"

Sean picked up a mug and took a swig. "Not that I know of, but Nat could have talked to him and not said anything." He wrinkled his nose and looked in his mug. "Things sure cool off fast here."

"That's what microwaves are for. It takes longer to cook food up here, and it cools off a lot faster than if you're at sea level." Mystic smirked.

Killian strolled into the room with Chinoah tucked protectively under his arm. "They should be back any time. Do you want to go look for them?"

"No, I'll just wait." He shoved his hand in his pockets and stared at the floor. *I've got to keep a grip on myself, cool head and calm nerves, just like before I flamed out.* He blew out a breath slowly and listened for Mystic's heartbeat. The woman centered him. However, the feeling of foreboding remained. He paced then paused in front of the window.

"There's fresh coffee in the kitchen," Chinoah offered, looking at Mystic and then cutting her gaze to the kitchen door. "Alaia made a huge batch of cinnamon apple oatmeal this morning and insisted that we leave some for you two."

Mystic walked up behind him, put her arms around his waist, and leaned her chin on his shoulder. "Want some breakfast?"

"Not really…okay…gotta eat. Thanks." He turned his head and brushed his lips over hers.

Mystic patted him on the shoulder and scooted into the kitchen behind Chinoah, careful to prop the door open. Bowls, mugs, and spoons clanged together as Mystic took them out of the cabinets. Chinoah removed the ceramic bowl of oatmeal from the oven, the door closed with a whoosh, then she sat the bowl on the table.

"Well, how'd it go with Killian?" Mystic asked scooping oatmeal into two bowls and inhaling deeply. "That smells wonderful," she said putting the bowls on a tray.

"Not bad. After a long talk with Nathanael, he seemed more settled. He wants me in his life but says it's complicated right now and asked me to be patient." Chinoah poured steaming coffee into mugs and set them on another tray.

"That's a good start. The way he looks at you, it's obvious he cares a great deal for you." Mystic warmed milk in her mug and stirred in the hot cocoa packet.

"Mystic, you know what's going on around here. Why can't you tell me?"

In the other room, Caden held his breath listening to the conversation after Mystic left the room.

"It's not my tale to tell. Killian will confide in you when the time is right. The wait will be worth it, I promise." Mystic picked up the tray of food and made her way through the doorway, followed by Chinoah with the tray of drinks.

They set the food and drinks down on the coffee table in front of the fireplace. He and Mystic ate hungrily while the others enjoyed their hot drinks.

Kat burst through the front door. Her slicker's hood pushed back and hair soaked, carrying a basket full of pinecones. "Looky what I found," she said proudly. Promptly dropping the basket, she squealed and rushed to Mystic. "You found bear." She snatched the stuffed animal and hugged it tight against her, then raised it up for her mom and dad to see. "Bear," she announced, smiling.

"I see." Alaia said, as she and Nate followed in their daughter's wake.

"Good morning." Nat removed his raincoat and handed it to Alaia.

"Thanks for all you did last night." Mystic hugged Alaia. "I don't know how you do it."

"I trust you had a good night?" Nat ran his fingers

through his wet hair.

"Yes, we did. Have you heard from Tristian?"

"No, but I didn't expect to," Nat said easily, then noticed Caden's worried expression. "Is there a problem?"

"Not sure. I haven't heard from him either. When we left, he said he'd be in touch, I assumed that meant this morning."

"The plan was for you and Mystic to return to Riverton this morning, right?"

He nodded, taking a gulp of his coffee.

"Then maybe he's waiting for you to return, to discuss further developments." Nat accepted a mug of steaming coffee from Alaia and took a sip. "Perfect." He smiled at his wife.

He pushed his half-eaten bowl of oatmeal aside. "He was expecting trouble last night. I'm concerned about walking into the unknown with Mystic."

"Do you want one of us go with you and Mystic stay here?"

"Oh, no. I'm not staying here," Mystic interrupted defiantly. "I'm armed, know how to defend myself, and won't be blindsided again."

Nat raised an eyebrow and looked at Caden. "I believe you have your answer. We'll remain ready, should you need assistance. Report to me the minute you materialize at the motel and keep communication open."

"What if it's a trap, and I don't have time to respond?"

"Do you feel a trap or darkness? You've got to trust your instincts."

"I don't feel a trap, but I can't shake the feeling

that something is wrong."

"Then find out what it is and report back."

"Okay." He glared toward Mystic. Stepped behind her and unzipped her backpack. He dropped three speed loaders for her .357 in the pack. Patting her waist, he felt her holstered gun, then extended his hand. The fact that she'd put the gun on, ratcheted up his anxiety. *Did she feel it too?* "Ready?" He grasped her hand, and they disappeared.

Chapter Nineteen
A Less than Welcoming Arrival

Dark clouds swirled overhead, as Caden peered out from behind the fencing that surrounded the dumpster. "Tristian's car isn't in the parking lot," he whispered to Mystic crouched behind him.

She crept to his side and looked out across the parking lot. "Does that mean that Tristian took it? I don't see the SUV either. But, I don't see anything out of the ordinary. Should we check our room?"

"Possibly, but why didn't he call us? Our vehicle is still blended. If you look real hard over in the corner you can see a kind of an outline near the pavement. Yeah, let's check out the room."

As they approached the room, he looked down at the floor in front of the door. Piled neatly against the door were clean towels and bedding. He glanced over at Mystic, who shrugged and then put his palm against the door. "Something has happened here, but no one is inside now. We're going to rely on mortal means and minimum magic. Ready?"

She nodded touching her holstered weapon.

Key card in hand, he inserted it in in the slot next to the door handle, heard the click and a green light flashed. He motioned Mystic to get behind him and pulled the gun from his waistband. His other hand on the door, he turned the handle and pushed the door open. The stench of burned flesh assaulted his senses. In the darkened room, he crept silently checking around corners, behind doors and the bathroom. His eyes went wide as he flipped on the light and involuntarily sucked in a breath.

Mystic, gun in hand aimed to the side, peered over his shoulder and stifled a scream.

In slow motion, he took in the scene before him, committing everything to memory. There was no one here, yet he kept his gun drawn. Large amounts of demon ash covered the carpet and darkened the unmade bed linens. Blood splatters dotted and streaked three walls. The chair in the corner reduced to splinters and one of the curtains drawn across the windows shredded.

Mystic edged into the room behind him and closed the door.

His eyes shifted to the corner where Tristian set up the command center. The computer, flat screen monitor, receivers, and other electronic equipment were the only items untouched. A soft blue light glowed on the computer console indicating the power was on, but the equipment was in sleep mode. The receivers appeared to be off. A low humming vibrated as he moved closer to the equipment. He tapped the keyboard, and the monitor blinked on requesting a password as the computer came to life.

Mystic walked to the wall that had adjoined the two rooms together and gingerly touched it in several places. Solid. She swung her backpack to her knee and plucked out the key card to the room.

He cut his gaze to her and jerked his head toward the door. She followed him outside and down the hall to the other room.

"What the hell happened in there?" she whispered.

"I don't know, but it didn't happen long ago."

A do not disturb sign hung on the handle. He followed the same procedures as before as they entered the room. It was exactly as they'd left it. Nothing out of place, not even foot prints in the newly vacuumed carpet. Fresh linens hung in the bathroom, there were no wrinkles on the neatly made bed and curtains were open.

He and Mystic returned to the other room. He yanked the phone out of his pocket along with a business card. The screen lit up on his phone as he entered the number and touched the green call icon. "Bruce, it's Caden. We've got a problem." He described the situation to Bruce in detail. "There is no sign of Tristian. Have you heard from him?"

"No, but from what you described, I wouldn't expect to hear from him. Tristian has gone undercover and taken his team with him," Bruce said.

"How can you be so calm, after what I've just told you?" he asked incredulously.

"Tristian is a professional, and he's extremely good at his job. If something happened to him, the computer system and all the surveillance equipment would be destroyed or missing. This is his way of letting us know, he and his team are all right."

"A similar thought actually crossed my mind when I discovered the equipment undamaged, in the middle of all the chaos. It's something I would expect one of my men to do. But I don't know Tristian well enough to make such an assumption."

"I'll get a cleanup crew out there right away. Until then, stay clear of the room and make sure no one enters."

"We can do that. Meanwhile, thought we'd talk with the desk clerk and manager to see what they know. Afterward, we are going to find somewhere else to stay and set up the equipment."

"Good plan. Just to be on the safe side, I'll touch base with Tristian's wife and see if she's talked to him."

"Tristian is married?" He couldn't keep the surprise out of his voice.

"Yes," Bruce said impatiently.

"Wow." He shook his head. "I know it's none of my business, but does she know what line of work he's in?"

"Of course," he said his voice flat. "Keep me in the loop as you investigate further. I'll do the same. Caden, don't hesitate to call me if something seems amiss." Bruce severed the connection.

"Hmmm," he said after a long silence. "Bruce and Tristian aren't so different from Nat and I."

Puzzled, she pursed her lips while tilting her head to one side. "Why do you say that?"

"Battle strategy is the same. Kinda. And so are the expectations."

"Hadn't you better call Nat and fill him in before he shows up here and reams your ass for failing to contact him when you arrived?"

"Oh, lil' wolf, but I did. Telepathically. But you're right, an update is in order." He smiled over at her and touched the speed dial to Nat. Nat answered on the first ring, and he quickly filled him in on the latest developments and disconnected the call.

Mystic blew out a breath and returned his smile.

"What are we going to do about that room? We can't leave it like that. All the ash, Caden, it's a nonsmoking room. Not to mention the blood and the stench."

He chuckled. "I'm glad you can see the humor in this situation. Bruce is sending a cleanup crew. We need to stick around until they arrive and make sure no one enters the room."

"Well, if I don't laugh, I might cry, and that wouldn't do much for my tough woman image." She grinned at him, then tapped her finger to her lips. "Why do you suppose no one has entered that room? Yet it's quite apparent someone has cleaned the other room?"

"Not sure. I think we better load the equipment in the SUV and go talk to the desk clerk." He turned off the surge protector power strip and begun unplugging the equipment.

"Is that the last of it?" he asked as Mystic put the monitor into the back of the SUV.

"Yep." She closed the rear door and leaned against it. "Now what?"

"You all right to go talk to the desk clerk and manager or do you want to stay here?" Caden asked, scrunching up his forehead in concern.

"I'm fine. I'll go see what I can find out." Mystic slung her backpack over her shoulder and started toward the office.

"I'll join you as soon as the cleanup crew gets here," Caden called after her.

****

Mystic yanked open the glass door and strode across the lobby. A man smiled at her from behind the front desk as she approached.

She returned his friendly smile. "Hi. I'm Mystic

Rayne. My partner, Caden Silverwind, and I rented a room yesterday. An associate of ours rented the room next to ours. I want to take care of the bill now since we'll be leaving before dawn in the morning."

The young man tapped a few keys on the computer keyboard and frowned. "It appears Mr. Shandie, paid for both your rooms through next week. He also left strict instructions that motel personal were not to enter either room, even to clean them. Fresh towels and linens were to be left outside the door."

"Oh. Tristian wasn't here when we arrived, so plans must have changed."

The clerk shifted from one foot to the other nervously. "It appears that we cleaned the other room before Mr. Shandie's message was relayed to the housekeeping staff. I hope that didn't create a problem. Let me get the manager."

"No worries. Make sure it doesn't happen again," she said in her most reassuring voice.

A woman dressed in a navy pinstriped pantsuit, in her mid-thirties, with short black hair joined the desk clerk. "I'm Abby Rich, the day manager. Ms. Rayne, we can talk in my office? Please follow me."

"Okay," Mystic said hesitantly, looking around to see if Caden had arrived yet. She touched the small of her back to make sure the weapon was still in place.

Ms. Rich led her to a room just to the right of the front desk and motioned her to one of two beige chairs positioned in front of a modern cherry wood desk. The office was small with light beige walls, wallpapered in light blue with a dark blue diamond design on the upper half of the walls.

Ms. Rich sat on the edge of a beige leather chair

behind the desk. "Mr. Shandie briefed us early this morning on the very basics of your security assignment for Homeland Security. He wasn't pleased that the room was cleaned but said nothing was compromised. Has something changed? I gave Mr. Shandie my personal guarantee no one else would enter the room."

Mystic put her backpack on the floor in front of her, settled into the chair and relaxed. "No, not at all. As I was telling your clerk, we returned this morning after Tristian left, so we haven't had a chance to talk with him. Apparently, things changed while we were gone, and we will be here longer than originally thought. That's all."

"I am relieved. Wouldn't want to be the cause of a security breach. The industry Mr. Shandie is investigating is one of the main employers around here. Especially the newest one just outside the Rez, it's supposed to be a secret, but you already know that. Tristian, uh, I mean Mr. Shandie indicated it's part of your investigation." Ms. Rich slid back in the seat and leaned against the back of the chair.

"Industry?" Mystic raised one eyebrow. *Could she mean the River Winds? It's not a secret. Unless Ethan is involved in opening another casino off Rez?* "If it's a secret, you really shouldn't be discussing it with anyone. What if your office was bugged?"

"Oh, dear, I hadn't thought of that." She jerked upright, her spine rigid and shoulders straight, as her eyes darted around the office from item to item, lingering on the telephone.

"Tristian's very thorough, so he wouldn't have discussed anything with you unless he'd swept this office first." She let her eyes slowly scan the room as if checking it.

"Well, uh, he didn't really say anything about the new site. I guessed that was what he was here for since it's so close to federal land and the Rez. He was relieved that I was aware and that no explanation was necessary."

"I bet he was." She considered asking Abby for the location of the site they were talking about but decided against it. If Tristian led Ms. Rich to believe he already knew about it, she didn't want to compromise whatever Tristian had discovered.

There was a soft knock on the door, and Caden stuck his head in. "Oh, there you are. The reservation specialist said he thought you were still in here with the manager."

"Caden, this is Ms. Abby Rich. She was very helpful to Tristian before we returned this morning. I think everything's under control for now, until we talk with Tristian."

Caden stepped inside the room far enough to shake hands with Ms. Rich. "Nice to meet you." Then he returned to the door and looked over at Mystic. "We need to be on our way. The other shift of agents just arrived."

She picked up her backpack and slung it over her shoulder as she stood and shook hands with Abby. "It was nice to meet you. We'll just check in periodically and let you know when we will be vacating the rooms."

They walked out, and Caden closed the door behind them. "What was that all about?"

As they walked toward the rooms, she filled him in on her conversation with Ms. Rich. "I still don't see where the industry comes in to play here. Apparently,

Tristian did or let her think he did. Could Ethan be planning to open a competing casino outside the Rez. Would the River Winds Casino be considered one of the main employers or industries around here?"

"Interesting. Maybe you should show me around the Rez. If we find a new construction site just outside the Rez border, it would require further investigation and maybe a hint to why Tristian disappeared," Caden said rubbing his chin, the corners of his mouth turned up slightly.

"Caden, you saw the map of the Rez. It's huge, that could take days," she said hands on hips, stopping a couple doors down from their rooms to turn and look at him. "I don't think we have days."

"Okay, we ask around a bit first and see if someone will volunteer any information we could use."

Mystic snorted. "Not likely with you around. The people on the Rez, well, don't like outsiders."

"Not if that outsider is your fiancé." Caden's eyes sparkled with mischief. He caught her hand and pulled her against him, planting a warm, wet kiss on her mouth with a little tongue.

"What are you doing? People will talk," Mystic said against his inviting lips as she tried to wriggle out of his tight hold. Her heart not in the struggle, she melted against him.

He pulled back just enough to whisper against her ear. "Exactly. That's what we want them to do. A conversation starter for you, leading to any information you can glean from your friends and acquaintances."

Chapter Twenty
Where do We Go From Here?

A tall slender man with thick black hair that almost covered his sharp pointed ears, with a full beard and elongated fingers, cleared his throat stepping out of the shadows as he slid his hands in his pockets. "Excuse me. I'm looking for Caden Silverwind."

"You found him. Are you all done with the rooms?" Caden asked releasing his hold on Mystic but keeping her hand clasped tightly in his.

"Yes. You can move back in now. There are no traces that anything unusual happened in the one room, and the other was already clean."

"Thanks, we'll lock up and look for other accommodations. Mystic is a little uncomfortable staying after what she saw. You checked for electronic bugs?"

He nodded. "Understandable. I don't mean to interfere, but you might want to talk with Tristian or Bruce before making that decision." The man lowered his voice. "Someone put a very strong protection spell on both rooms as recently as this morning. Probably the safest place you can stay given the situation."

"And just what is the situation?"

The man glanced up and down the sidewalk as well as scanning the parking lot. Keeping his voice low, he said, "Rogue demons, witches, and a few vampires have infiltrated businesses in this area. Their discovery and subsequent neutralization of some of their numbers has led to dangerous circumstances."

"This from the cleaning crew? Who are you?" Caden demanded.

"Dameon Parks. I work for Bruce and Tristian as director of the sanitation crews. I usually don't work a scene, but Bruce insisted I oversee this cleanup personally."

Caden detected the magic when they'd first arrived but thought it was left over from whatever happened. "How would you know what form the magic was meant to take?"

"Detecting and destroying magic without a trace is my business," Dameon said, trying to keep the irritation out of his voice. "Now if you'll check the rooms, I'll be on my way."

"Sure." He tugged Mystic behind him and opened the door to the first room. His nostrils flared as they stepped inside, and the mild aroma of citrus drifted through the air. The room was immaculate, furniture all in one piece and back where it belonged. A crystal vase with fresh flowers sat on the desk. Mystic leaned her hand against the wall, it was solid. They checked the other room, and the wall was the same.

"You did a great job." Caden extended his hand in a friendly gesture.

Dameon grasped it and smiled. "Thanks, we take pride in our work. Now I need you to put your index finger on my screen in the highlighted box." He held out an electronic tablet toward him. "Bruce will know the job is done."

Caden's phone vibrated in his pocket for the third

time since they left Ms. Rich's office. This time he pulled it out of his pocket and checked the screen. "I need to take this. Excuse me." He walked out into the parking lot, touched the phone's screen, and put it to his ear, all the while keeping his eyes on Mystic. "Caden."

The conversation was short. He returned to the doorway, pressed his finger in the highlighted area. Dameon and his crew disappeared behind the fenced off area around the dumpster.

Mystic glanced at him, one brow arched in question.

"It was Bruce. He confirmed what Dameon said. Bruce also thought I would be hesitant to sign off on the work order as requested without corroboration from him." He ran his fingers though his hair and rubbed the back of his neck, rolling his shoulders.

"Are we staying here?"

"Looks like. You okay with that?"

"I guess. The evil aura I felt when we arrived is gone. Still I'd rather stay in the other suite."

"Good enough." He put his hand at the small of her back, guided her into the room, and shut the door, sliding the lock into place. With a satisfied nod, he sat down in the chair beside the desk and kicked off his boots, stretching his long legs, rotating his ankles, wiggling his toes. They were tired of boots. He pinched the bridge of his nose with thumb and forefinger, his forehead creased in concentration. Upper most in his mind was formulating a plan going forward. *The locals won't talk to Mystic when I'm around, and I can't let her out of my sight.*

As if reading his mind, Mystic put her backpack on the bed and walked around behind him to lay her soft warm hands at his neck, her thumbs moved in a circular motion at the base of his neck.

"Ahhh—that feels good." He leaned his head to one side and then the other allowing Mystic's magic fingers to smooth out his knotted muscles.

"I have an idea. Hear me out before you veto it. Okay?" She worked out a final knot at the base of his neck and patted his shoulder.

"Sure." He craned his neck to see her face.

"How about we ask Killian and Chinoah to join us? Chinoah and I can question the locals while you and Killian can drive the Rez during the day. Have Killian bring the maps Nat and I created. We can divide the area into search sectors. Some we can all do together at night, Chinoah and I can shift, you and Killian, can shift into, you know, into angel mode. We'll cover more ground that way and still stay safely in range of each other."

"You're assuming Killian has confided in Chinoah. If not, your nocturnal plan is not feasible."

"Under cover of darkness, lots of things are possible," Mystic said smiling secretively.

"We can't join forces and keep secrets. It's too dangerous."

"It's up to Killian to step up and explain everything to Chinoah, as you did to me."

"It's not that easy, and you know it. There's the tribunal and laws to consider. Killian is still an active warrior on special assignment."

"And Chinoah is deeply involved in this situation whether you like it or not."

"Not up to me to like it or not." He shrugged his shoulders and reached for his boots. "Nat calls the shots as the tribunal instructs him."

"He doesn't have any input?" She took a step back, crossed her arms and stared incredulously at him.

He shrugged again. "Not sure how much influence he has with the tribunal. We'll run your idea by him and see what he says." He pulled on his boots and stood. "We need to get all the surveillance equipment out of the SUV and set it up in this room. See what info we can get that way."

"Chinoah and Killian?" Mystic asked as she opened the door and stepped outside.

"I'll contact Nathanael in the morning and set up a meeting unless we hear from Tristian sooner."

Surveying the parking lot and surrounding area, Caden deemed it safe and uncloaked the SUV. He didn't want it to look like they were pulling equipment out of nowhere and opened the back door. Computer under one arm and the flat screen under the other, he waited for Mystic to get the remaining equipment and close the door.

"Do you know how to set all this up like Tristian had it?" Mystic asked setting the box of cables, connectors, and the receiver equipment on the desk.

"Yeah, I think so." He hooked up the screen, computer, and printer. Then dropped the cords behind the desk, crawled under the desk and plugged in the power strip making sure the switch was off. "Hand me the cables."

"Caden, you are laying right where I need to stand," Mystic complained.

"Then step over me, I need to be right here to get everything hooked up," he said.

For a minute, she just stood there. Then sidled next

to him, put one hand on the desk for support, and stepped over him straddling his prone body as she bent over to feed the cables behind the desk.

"Thanks, got it. Now connect the black USB cord to the printer and drop it down here."

She plugged the small square with on flat side into the printer then slid the cord with the USB end down the wall into his hand and he connected it to the computer. Putting her hand at the small of her back, she straightened up.

He shoved out from underneath the desk between her long, shapely legs and grabbed her ankles, holding her in place. "Nice view." He grinned up at her.

"Caden, let me go." She squealed.

"No way." He chuckled playfully.

Eyes narrowed and glinting with malice, she said, "You had this planned all along."

"And I love when a plan comes together." A wide grin spread over his face. Leaning up on his elbows, he kept one hand on her ankle and let the other slide up to caress the inside of her thigh and farther up until his fingers brushed the crotch of her jeans.

He sensed the desired effect when her pulse suddenly leapt and her heart thumped erratically. She wanted him. Leaning into his touch, she let a soft moan escape her lips.

In a flash of movement, he sat up and hooked his fingers inside the waistband of her jeans. His hands slid toward the front and unfastened the top button on her jeans as his breath warmed the area between her thighs.

"Caden, I don't think…"

"Good, don't think, just feel," he said peeling her jeans down her slender legs.

Chapter Twenty-One
Seeing is Believing, it's the Easiest Way

Caden's phone chirped on the nightstand drawing him slowly from a deep slumber. Thick gray clouds hid the sun and encased the suite in darkness with only a thin line of filtered light spilling through the crack between the insulated curtains.

He stared at the phone uncomprehendingly for several seconds, then realization hit and he grabbed it. Trying not to disturb Mystic, her warm naked body still snuggled against him, long legs intertwined with his, he touched the screen. "Caden," he whispered into the phone.

"Didn't wake you, did I?" Nat said, the smile in his voice coming though the phone.

"What do you think?" He growled as Mystic looked at him sleepily from under her long raven lashes.

"Any sign of Tristian?"

"No."

"Any movement in the investigation?"

"Nat, I'm not even coherent. Let me call you back in a couple of minutes so I can get my thoughts together."

"Could have reported in last night," Nat replied.

"I was busy. It was a very stressful day," Caden snapped, drawing Mystic closer.

"I bet you were. Remember we're here at your request," Nat chided.

"Sorry. Didn't mean to sound ungrateful. I appreciate your assistance. Give me a couple of minutes, and I'll call you back." He rubbed the back of his hand over his eyes, his brain clearing from sleep. "Better yet, I was going to call you this morning to set up a meeting. Killian and Chinoah need to be available also."

"I'm about to go into a meeting with the tribunal. I should be able meet with you shortly after noon. Will that work?"

"Is there trouble?" Caden asked, fully awake now.

"Nothing I can't handle. Meet you at the lodge or should we come there?"

"The lodge."

"See you this afternoon." Nat disconnected the call.

Mystic nibbled at the pulsing hollow at his neck then followed the jugular to just behind his ear. "Do we have to get up?"

"I'm afraid so." He wrapped both arms around her possessively and kissed the top of her head. "My lil' wolf." He sighed.

"What do you mean, your lil' wolf? I don't belong to anyone." She wriggled out of his hold.

He leaned up on one elbow, his eyes meeting hers. "Guess you've forgotten our conversation that day on the trail. By Angel Tribunal Law, you're my mate." The words were no sooner out of his mouth and the flash of fire in her eyes confirmed trouble.

"I'm what?" The words flew out of her mouth then the light dawned, he saw it in her eyes. "Mate?" she asked.

"Actions speak louder than words and your actions spoke volumes." He smiled uncertainly in a struggle to salvage their morning. "Both times."

Flustered, she couldn't voice what she was feeling. "Yes, but the words, I need the words, so I know it's not just lust or oh, I don't know what." Her eyes glistened with unshed tears. "What about my beliefs, a ceremonial wedding, and engagement ring, you didn't even propose."

"Myst, honey, I never would have made love to you without being head over heels in love with you. I've been a warrior so long, perhaps I've forgotten the emotional needs of the body and soul. We'll arrange a tribal ceremonial wedding that will honor our commitment to each other and our people when it's safe. As far as a proposal…" He wrapped his arms around her again and tried to avert the emotional storm rising in her.

She pushed him away, crawled out of bed, and rushed into the bathroom. The door slammed and the lock clicked.

He swore as he slid out of bed and pulled on black jeans, a deep burgundy and white cable knit sweater, black socks and stepped into black sneakers. He closed his eyes tight and let out a heavy sigh as he ran his fingers through his hair. *I don't have time for this. Someone is trying to kill her and all she can think about is...* He stopped short considering the conversation they'd had high on the cliff after she returned to human form. W*hat is important to her? I can't believe I did it again.*

Waiting until she turned the shower off, he knocked softly on the bathroom door. "Mystic, I'm sorry, I didn't consider your feelings. I got caught up in the moment, but that's no excuse. I love you and know you feel the same about me. That's what is most important."

She made a noncommittal noise from behind the closed door.

"We'll arrange a beautiful Arapahoe/Sioux wedding ceremony, and my proposal to you will be worth waiting for. Unfortunately, right now we're dealing with life and death issues that can't wait. We have a meeting with Nathanael in a couple hours. If you want Killian and Chinoah to help us, we need to have a darn good plan to present to Nat. He's the one that will take the heat for Chinoah's enlightenment." *If he hasn't already.*

****

The door to the bathroom creaked open. Mystic stood wrapped in a white towel, water droplets rolling down her cheeks and neck from the strands of her wet hair, damping the edge of her towel. *When he's right, he's right. I still don't like it.* She told herself, knowing she would cave the minute he put those big warm hands on her. *No one has ever made me feel like he does.*

He cupped her face in his hands wiping the droplets from her cheeks with his thumbs. "You are absolutely beautiful, and I want to spend eternity with you by my side."

"I'll be there." *Geesh, why can't I just say I love you.* She stood on tippy toes and brushed her lips over his affectionately. "Now let's get to work on that plan."

He looked her up and down then tugged at the towel. "Not my first choice for strategic planning attire, but I like it."

She put her hand over his holding the now damp towel in place. "I bet you do, but we'll get a lot more done, if you let me get dressed."

"Depends on what our focus is," he said in a suggestive tone and waggled his eyebrows.

"Mumm, getting Killian and Chinoah's assistance."

"Oh, yeah." He argued but caved. "You're right, but my plans would be a lot more fun."

"We'll get to that later." She crossed the room and snatched her clothes off the chair and shimmied into her underwear, jeans, and sweater.

"I'll hold you to it."

Caden shoved a gun in his waistband and snugged one in his boot. Then he slung the harness that held his sword and daggers over his shoulder. "Make sure you grab your backpack. Don't want to leave our weapons unsecured."

She reached for her backpack, slid her arms through the straps, and grasped his hand. The foreboding gray atmosphere of Wyoming gave way to slivers of sunshine dancing on the floor and walls of the lodge.

"Well, well look who's decided to grace us with their presence." Killian drawled, his Scottish brogue deliberately exaggerated.

"Is Nat back yet?" Caden asked impatiently.

"Not yet," Sean answered sauntering down the stairs. "You know, I'm not sure you and Killian are worth the trouble." He shrugged one shoulder. "But apparently Nat does."

"What trouble?"

"Female trouble. You two keep Nat busy running interference between you with the tribunal." Sean skipped the last three stairs and landed with a thud at the base of the stairs, hand on the newel post.

Alaia came up behind Sean and swiped at him. "Sean, I don't believe what Nathanael does is any of your business." She crossed to where she and Caden stood, giving them each a hug, and then turned back to Sean. "At least we don't have to worry about you, no woman will have you."

Caden let out a bark of laughter. "Good one, Alaia." He returned her hug and asked, "Now what has Killian done to cause Nat to be summoned?"

"I'll let him explain. Little ears you know." Alaia jerked her chin toward the kitchen as Kat raced through the doorway. Alaia grabbed her shoulder as she passed by slowing her progress. "Nat should be back any minute now."

Kat still ran head long into Caden's legs as he bent down to catch her and toss her into the air. "I missed you too," he said smiling into her beaming little face smeared with peanut butter. Kat leaned over to hug Mystic, almost knocking Caden off balance in the process. He swung her down to the floor.

Before the girl could take off again, Alaia firmly grasped her by the shoulders and smiled down at the squirming child. Alaia leaned down and whispered something in Kat's ear.

Kat quit squirming immediately and looked around cautiously. "Daddy?"

"You will soon." The words barely left Alaia's lips, and Nat materialized in the room beside the fireplace.

Kat wriggled out of Alaia's hold and propelled herself at Nathanael. He caught her in the air, whirled her around and kissed her on the cheek before shifting her to his hip, holding her tight as he stroked her curly blond hair. Alaia reached up and wrapped her arms around them both. Giving him a lingering kiss, she ran her fingers up his neck into his course blond hair.

"How'd it go?" she asked taking a defiant Kat out of Nat's arms and setting her feet first on the floor. "Daddy has business to attend to, after that he'll come with us for a walk down the path and you can show him what you found."

"Okay. Work not too long?" Kat inquired, scrunching up her face.

"Not long." Nathanael grinned and ruffled his daughter's hair before she ran for the rocking horse in the corner of the room. He turned his attention to his wife. "About as I expected, they did give him some leeway. At the end of this assignment, he'll have a tough decision to make, unless they take my recommendation." Nathanael's eyes were dark, and his lips pulled tight as he observed each person in the room.

"You presented it to the tribunal? Were they receptive?" Alaia asked.

"Maybe. It seems the extent of this situation has given them reason for concern."

"What recommendation are we talking about?" Caden asked.

"One that doesn't include you at the moment. Hard as that is to believe. Now what's on your mind?" Nat took the steaming mug offered by Alaia. The aroma of the freshly brewed coffee wafted through the room.

"Mystic and I have come up with a plan that will hopefully uncover what is going on at the Rez and the

River Winds Casino. But we need the help of Chinoah and Killian, possibly Sean, if Tristian doesn't show himself soon."

"Still not heard from Tristian. Huh?"

"No, but when I talked with Bruce, he wasn't concerned. Thought Tristian was probably in the wind and wouldn't surface until he found what he's looking for. Have you heard from Bruce recently?"

Nat shook his head. "But I've been kinda busy with things here. I'll give him a call now that we have a secure phone line in place. Bruce doesn't like to discuss sensitive topics on an unsecured line."

"Understandable. It might be a good idea to fill him in on our plans and see if he has any suggestions."

"Mystic, would you see if you can roundup Chinoah and Killian, then the three of you join Caden and me in the office. I think we'll make a conference call to Bruce once we've discussed your plan." Nat led the way to the office as she bounded up the stairs following the sounds of Killian's deep voice.

She padded up to a closed door and raised her hand to knock.

Killian's voice boomed from inside room with a note of frustration. "It's not that I don't have feelings for you, because I do. But I am a warrior first, and that is where my allegiance should be. Nat has gone to the tribunal over our relationship, such as it is. I can't ask him to continue and jeopardize his position or mine."

"But Caden and Mystic are working things out. Why can't we do the same?" Chinoah pleaded. "You said your allegiance should be with the legion as a warrior, does that mean it's not?"

"Caden and Mystic are in a different situation.

Caden is no longer a warrior and isn't under the tribunal's jurisdiction. I am, and our relationship is forbidden. End of story."

"How can the tribunal expect you to live without love? According to what I heard, that's what happened to Caden. The darkness of battle tried to take over his being. If he'd had someone…"

"Chinoah, don't go there. We all learned a valuable lesson at Caden's expense. He may never be the same or fit for battle. And that's a damn shame. He was one of the best."

"You can't do this."

"I can and I am." Killian yanked the door open and barreled headlong into her, knocking her across the hallway. His quick reflexes caught her as she rebounded off the wall. "What the hell are you doing skulking out here?"

"Ah, what language from ah, around a lady." She tried a small smile to defuse the situation.

Killian narrowed his eyes and glared at her. "Is there something I can do for you?" He growled.

"Yeah, I was sent up here to find you two. Nat and Caden want to see both of you." She cut her gaze to Chinoah, who was sitting on the bed, arms crossed over her chest, eyes flashing in anger. Yet her lower lip trembled as the muscle at her temple pulsed. "Caught you at a bad time? I can tell Nat and Caden you'll be along in a minute."

"We're through talking." Killian took the stairs two at a time and strode across the floor to the office.

"You all right?" she asked one eyebrow arched.

"Yeah. How much did you hear?" Chinoah asked narrowing her eyes at Mystic.

"I didn't mean to eavesdrop. I just didn't want to knock and interrupt. I was leaving when Killian opened the door."

"And?"

"I heard enough to know there's trouble between you two. And unfortunately, we're about to make matters worse."

"I don't' see how."

"Come downstairs, and you'll find out. I'm not sure what Caden and Nat have decided. But I believe that you and Killian are going to Wyoming with Caden and me." Mystic ambled toward the stairway.

"Oh, that's just great. Killian will refuse the assignment, if I'm involved." She got up from the bed, shoulders slumped, and followed Mystic downstairs. "Why do I get the distinct impression something more is going on here than meets the eye?"

Choosing to ignore her last question, she replied, "I don't think he has a choice. Caden needs someone to watch his back while he scouts the perimeter of the Rez. At the same time, I need someone who the locals trust, to help me poke around and find out what's going on."

Chinoah put her hand on her shoulder and turned her around. "Going on where? This is bigger than just Ethan's attack on you, isn't it? The perimeter of the Rez is huge, it could take weeks, if not months."

"Not if, well, I'll let Caden fill you in on the rest."

When she and Chinoah walked through the doorway into the office, Killian stood just inside the room, his face flushed, hands fisted at his sides, and eyes staring down at the floor. He didn't look up as the women entered the room.

She exchanged looks with Caden, and he shook his head sliding a glance toward Chinoah.

"Come in and have a seat." Nathanael motioned to empty chairs in front of his desk. "We have a lot to discuss, but first Killian has something to say."

All eyes turned toward Killian. She and Caden settled back in their chairs as Chinoah sat on the edge of hers. Alaia came to stand in the doorway wiping her hands on a dishtowel.

"Chinoah, the elite security force that we belong too, is very unusual in its structure and personnel." Killian unbuttoned his shirt and slipped it off baring his muscular chest, wide shoulders and washboard abs accentuating his narrow hips still covered in tight jeans.

Mystic leaned over and whispered in Caden's ear. "Killian's going to shock Chinoah, like you did me. Are you sure that's a good idea?"

Caden turned his head slightly, eyes shifting from Killian to Chinoah while he answered in her mind. *It appears you survived the shock fine. It's the only way to make it quick and avoid the disbelief scenario trying to explain it to her.*

Her eyes went wide for a moment, still not used to the causal use of telepathy then nodded. *He's almost as well built and good looking as you are.* A smile played at the corner of her lips.

Caden covered his mouth quickly and coughed to keep from laughing. *In his dreams.*

Killian rolled his shoulders forward and unfurled his wings from his back. They were frosty gray, the black tips brushed the floor while the top of the wings were several inches above his head. He stretched them out for a total wing span of over nine feet.

Chinoah gasped, her hand flew to her mouth but not before she blurted out, "Holy shit." She closed her eyes for a couple of seconds as her face reddened all the way to the tips of her ears and down to the base of her neck. Opening her eyes, she stared openly at Killian for several seconds and then glanced at Nat, Caden, Alaia, and finally Mystic. "You knew," Chinoah accused once she found her voice, pointing a finger at Mystic.

"Of course I knew. But I'm sworn to secrecy as you will be too." She stifled a giggle. "It's not every day you fall in love with an angel. How's it feel?"

"Not very damn good, since he doesn't return the feelings." Chinoah crossed her arms across her chest refusing to meet Killian's gaze.

He rolled his eyes and blew out a heavy sigh. "Not true. Could you guys leave us alone for a few minutes?"

Nat looked at his watch and shifted his gaze to Caden for confirmation then said, "You've got five minutes Killian, ten tops."

They stepped outside the door and closed it behind them. Nat's shoulders shook has he laughed silently and shook his head. "Killian's in for a rough ride with that one," Nat said to no one in particular then collapsed in the nearest chair.

****

Another one bites the dust. Sean's disgusted voice seared through Nathanael's mind, echoing in Caden's. *How long can you use the tribunal's guilt over Caden to sway them to your wishes?*

Until the laws the tribunal make and enforce reflect the blood, sweat, psyche, and even tears of the warriors. They are not unfeeling or programmable machines, nor are the warriors expendable. Nat fired back silently, his face darkened with determination.

Relief was written all over Nat's face after the bitter confrontation with the tribunal. "I secured Killian's right to a relationship with Chinoah, for the time being. After this assignment Killian will have a rough decision to make." Nat let out a heavy sigh, his exhaustion was evident to all and the day was far from over. "If I'd known this legion commander position would eventually entail responsibility for my warriors' emotional and psychological wellbeing as well as their ability to fight, I would have reconsidered my decision. Touchy feely is not my forte."

"But you're good at it, and I'm proud of you," Alaia whispered in his ear as she wrapped her arms around his neck and laid her cheek on his broad shoulders. "I'll see if we can work out a reward later tonight." She snuggled a kiss at his neck and winked as she pulled away.

"Listening in again?" He grumbled at her as the corners of his mouth turned up and he reached up gently running his fingers through her hair.

"Always. It's the only way I find out anything. Heaven knows you certainly won't tell me."

After his outburst, Sean, the newest member of Nathanael North's command stood shifting his gaze from the legion commander to Caden.

"A little overwhelming huh?" he said slapping Sean on the back.

"No kidding. It's a little disconcerting to see everyone outside the warrior realm away from the battle scene. Seeing Commander North, my demanding, rough, battle tough commander as a gentle loving husband and father is a little unsettling. Let alone the complications you and Killian have caused." He shook his head. "If you won't need me for a while, I'm going for a walk," Sean announced and started for the door.

Nathanael grasped Sean's shoulder as he walked by. "Everyone needs to know what is going on, so I'd like you to stay. Caden and Mystic have a plan that requires the assistance of Killian and Chinoah. We'll review this plan with Bruce, who already has a team on the ground, for his input, then put the final plan in action. If further assistance is needed, you'll be the next to go and need to hit the ground running."

Sean nodded.

Nat knocked on the den door then opened it. Killian and Chinoah broke apart though Killian kept his arm around her waist. Nat smiled at them and walked to the desk. He punched in the code on the phone to secure the line then tapped in Bruce's cell number.

Chapter Twenty-Two
Nothing is as it Appears, or is It?

Caden, Mystic, Killian, and Chinoah materialized behind the privacy fence that hid the dumpster from view at the Cozy Inn.

"We'll walk in from here," Caden said surveying the half-empty parking lot and his SUV parked in the corner. He tossed the key card to Killian. "This is your suite. We're right next door. Get yourselves settled then come on over. The surveillance system Tristian set up is in our suite. I want to familiarize you with the system so we can take shifts monitoring it when necessary."

"You got it. See you in a few." Killian took Chinoah by the hand and sauntered toward the adjunct room.

Once inside their room, he tapped the keyboard and the monitor blinked on. Several windows opened and spread across the screen, he sifted through all the camera views and angles Tristian had been able to tap into, nothing unusual going on. He flipped the power switch on the receiver, silence. Ethan wasn't in his office or on any of the surveillance cameras. He made a mental note to check out which cameras Tristian had been unable to tap into, next time he was in the casino.

Mystic wrapped herself around him and began unbuttoning his shirt as her hands caressed the muscles that flexed across his chest each time he moved.

"Mystic, I don't think you want to start something we can't finish." He snaked his hand around her and feathered his fingers across her breast. His lips brushed hers as he said, "Killian and Chinoah will be here soon."

Standing on tiptoe she touched her lips lightly to his. "I don't think so. They have a lot to talk about, and Killian is dead on his feet. Chinoah isn't far behind. We'll talk with them in the morning." She finished unbuttoning his shirt and started with the top button on his jeans.

He swept her off her feet and tossed her on the bed. She giggled and caught his arm pulling him down beside her. "Don't try to escape, you're good and caught."

"Wouldn't dream of it, but just remember we have an early day and a busy day tomorrow. A good night's sleep wouldn't be a bad idea."

****

Mystic awoke with Caden's arm slung over her chest his fingers lightly curled around her. She studied his face, long, thick dark lashes fringed his closed eyes, chiseled square jaw and chin with a slight cleft, and flawless bronze skin stretched over high cheekbones gave him a ruggedly handsome look. A slight smile curved his full sensual lips as if he was enjoying his dreams and the tension lines gone from around his eyes and corners of his mouth. This was the most relaxed she'd seen him, well, since they'd met. She laid there watching him sleep, soaking in the calm and quiet, considering the day that lay before them.

Not wanting to disturb him, she inched out of bed before the first golden rays of sun crept over the horizon. Glad she'd had the foresight to bring two business suits with her. She padded into the bathroom and closed the door quietly. The garment bag hung on the back of the door where she'd left it last night. She surveyed the suits, pleased that they were unwrinkled and ready to wear. When she bent over turning the shower on full, an arm snaked around her waist. She squealed.

"Sneaking out on me?" Caden chided playfully, kissing the back of her neck.

She blew out a breath. "You scared me." Slapping at him, she grinned. "Not at all, trying to let you get some much needed sleep."

"I sleep much better with you beside me. I don't like waking up to a cold, empty bed." His deep rich voice sent shivers up her spine. "What do you have planned today?"

"After we shower." She pulled him into the shower with her and closed the glass door. "I thought we'd check the assessor's offices and building departments in Riverton and Landers."

"Looking for?" he asked as he slid his soapy hands over the curves of her body.

"Building permits, land use permits, any records pertaining to new construction outside the boundaries of the Rez. Don't think I don't know what you're doing." She moved directly under the shower spray and watched the streams of soapy water swirl down the drain.

"Hey, I wasn't finished," Caden protested.

"You are now. Hand me the shampoo and turn your attention to washing your own body."

"I thought I'd let you do that." He grinned

lathering the shampoo into the long black hair piled on top her head. "Your curves are much more interesting that mine."

"I'll take a rain check. We need to get moving, if you're going with me today." She rinsed her hair and stepped out of the shower, wrapped a towel around her hair and used another to dry off. "Did you bring any casual business attire with you? Slacks, button down shirt, shoes other than boots or sneakers?"

"Of course." He stepped out of the shower and into the bedroom, standing in front of the closet.

"Good, let's hope Chinoah and Killian did too."

She used a blow dryer first and then a roller brush to style her hair. She clipped her waist length hair at the nap of her neck with a turquoise and pearl encrusted hair clasp. Next, she pulled on cream-colored pants and slipped into a turquoise blouse with tiny pink rosebuds embroidered on it. She put on cream, peep-toe heels, draped the matching suit jacket over her arm then surveyed the results in the mirror. Professional, exactly the look she was after when representing the Bureau of Indian Affairs. Pausing for a moment, she sighed. *I don't miss those days.*

For good measure, she applied a minimum amount of eye shadow, liner, a bit of blush to accentuate her cheekbones, and smoothed a lightly tinted pink lip-gloss on her lips. She didn't care for lipstick.

Caden let out a low whistle when she stepped into the living area. "Nice. Very professional looking. Lawyer like. And sexy as hell, the suit fits your curves like a glove."

"Thanks. I'm glad you like it." She took in his attractive male physique, dressed in light brown linen trousers, a maroon and brown striped shirt left open at the neck, brown dress shoes and light brown sport jacket. "You look quite handsome. I've never seen you in anything but jeans and a t-shirt or sweater. I like what I see."

With a bark of laughter, Caden said, "Now that the mutual admiration society has convened, let's get some breakfast and get on the road."

"I'll walk over and see if Killian and Chinoah are ready," she offered. She opened the door to Killian standing with his hand poised to knock.

Killian looked Mystic up and down and grinned. "You look great. Sorry we didn't make it back over here last night. We were both beat and fell asleep."

She stepped aside and opened the door wide. "Figured. Come on in. We're about to go find some breakfast. Care to join us?"

Killian stopped just inside the door. "Sure." He glanced at her and Caden. "I think, I'm underdressed. Thought we were going over the surveillance system." His gaze shifted to the corner of the room where the electronic equipment sat.

"Nope, you missed it. We're going to check for building permits, land sales, etc. in Riverton and Landers today," Caden said.

"Give me a couple of minutes. I'll get changed. Let Chinoah know and we'll be right back."

"Take your time. We'll stop at the front desk and see who has the best breakfast in town."

Caden turned the SUV onto N. Federal Blvd. and drove slowly. "Keep your eyes open for a full parking lot and a restaurant named Trailhead. The desk clerk said they have the biggest and best cinnamon rolls in the state. I need to appease my sweet tooth, and that sounds like the way to do it."

"What about the rest of the food?" Killian wanted to know. "I'm starved."

"The clerk assured me the rest of the menu is good," Caden said.

"There it is. Turn right here," she said, pointing to the right side. "The parking lot is full and running over. There's going to be a wait."

"Hopefully not too long," Killian grumbled.

Friendly chatter greeted them as they entered the establishment. A western theme predominated throughout the restaurant. Seating was a mixture of well-worn, dark, wooden tables, and chairs, comfortable, brown leather, upholstered booths and brown, leather stools at the counter. The commercial grade tile of blues, greens, and creams set in a repeating pattern covered the floor. A huge matching brown mat lay in front of the door to help keep mud from tracking inside.

Caden gave the hostess his name and took the menu to look over while they waited. After about ten minutes, the waitress led them to a booth beside the front window. "Ready to order?"

"Yep," Caden said as the others in the group nodded.

In short order, Julie, their server brought piping-hot heaping plates of eggs, bacon, sausage, hash browns, biscuits, and gravy to the table. She placed glasses of orange juice in front of her and Chinoah. Caden and Killian had ordered steaming cups of coffee and an extra pot was left in the middle of the table.

"Smells wonderful. Thank you," Caden said as the

others nodded in agreement.

"If you need anything else, just holler. I'll be back to check on you later." She smiled and winked at Caden while giving Killian a long appreciative look.

She put her hand on Caden's arm possessively. "Do mortal women always act like that around you?"

"Well, I know of one that gives me nothing but a hard time. But then again, she's only part mortal," he said with a mischievous grin. "But for the most part they do, that is one of the reasons for the tribunal's law."

"It's a boost to your self-esteem after dealing with shapeshifters," Killian said, his lips twitching as he dodged a blow from Chinoah.

They finished breakfast and ordered four cinnamon rolls to go with frosting on the side. Caden left a generous tip, and they were on their way.

First stop was Riverton's Community Development Department. She asked to see a recent list of commercial building permits and any land use change requests. The list was short with nothing of interest on it. She thanked the clerk and joined Caden in the hallway. "Any rumors among the employees you talked with?"

"Not a thing. This is a little town and news travels fast, but no one seems to know of any new commercial building projects fitting our description. That includes any new businesses moving into town."

Killian and Chinoah reported the same from the business people they'd talk to on Main Street. Everyone returned to the SUV. Caden eased the vehicle into traffic toward State Highway 789 and Landers. It was farther from the Rez but was the Fremont County seat.

After pouring over the records and talking with the clerk in Landers' building department, they returned to the SUV, climbed in, and headed to Riverton.

Once inside the hotel, Mystic plopped down on the chair and kicked her shoes off. "The day was a total bust. I get the feeling we're asking the wrong questions."

"Or maybe we're asking the wrong people," Chinoah suggested.

"There's something here, in Riverton. I can feel it. I just can't find the right route. Know what I mean?" She leaned back in the chair.

"We can take a road trip to Cheyenne, check the state records required for building permits or land use. You still thinking Ethan is siphoning off money from the River Winds to get seed money for one off the Rez?" Chinoah asked watching Caden demonstrate the basics of the surveillance system to Killian.

"Makes sense in some ways but not in others." She pulled her phone out of her backpack and tapped in Archer Clearwater's cell number.

"Mystic, to what do I owe the pleasure? More sleuthing?"

"Yeah, kinda, but I keep coming up empty. Any leads on what BGE does?"

"No. It's not registered in the State of Wyoming. I've not had a chance to do an in-depth national or international search. Been pretty busy at the trucking company. I can see if someone else has time to run the search."

"Glad to hear business is good. I'd rather keep this situation between us for now, until we're sure who else is involved. Assuming BGE is a corporation licensed outside Wyoming, they'd still be required to register their corporation as a foreign entity with the Wyoming Secretary of State," she said more to herself than to Archer.

"You'd know more about that than me. Seems the FBI should have run a search after their review of the financials? You told them the Tribal Council didn't know or authorize anything to do with BGE. Right?"

"I did. Good question though. I'll check back with the FBI and see what they turned up."

Archer was quiet for a couple of beats then said uneasily, "Mystic, we need to bring the unauthorized transfers before the council soon. I don't like keeping them in the dark."

"I know. Right now, the less people who know something is wrong the better. Telling the council won't get the money back. Finding out who is behind this might."

"Okay. You be at the council meeting next month. We need to tell them then unless you have more proof of wrongdoing by one of the council or someone close to the council members."

"Fair enough. I'll be in touch. And thanks!"

"Any time."

She touched the end call icon and looked in Caden's direction. He was still engrossed in watching the surveillance footage with Killian. "Can I call Nathanael?"

"Sure. Why?" Caden answered absently.

"Has he contacted you with any information regarding the FBI's investigation into the financial records for River Winds?"

Caden looked up from the computer screen. "No,

he hasn't."

"Could you give me his number? I'd like an update."

Caden gave one more sideways glance at the computer screen as he reached into his pocket for his phone. "Holy shit!" He slammed his hand on the keyboard. "Mystic come look at this." He tapped the keys to rewind the footage then checked the date stamp.

She leaned over his shoulder. "Look at what?"

"Right here the man walking in the casino doors flanked by two men. Isn't that Tristian?"

"What? Let me see." Mystic pushed Caden aside to get a better look at the screen. "Yes, I believe it is, but there's something different about him, darker hair? Who is that with him? Part of his team? He looks at ease, strong confident strides, and relaxed expression on his face. I'd say he's in command of the other two men, wouldn't you?"

"I don't know him well enough to tell. He probably wouldn't show any emotion if he was about to be filleted and fed to the wolves. We need Bruce to see this footage."

"But we can't send it to him over a non-secure line. Do you think Tristian set this system up with a scrambler?"

"No way to know for sure." Caden pulled a USB flash drive out of his pocket, inserted in into the computer, and copied the file. He tapped his phone against his jaw for a beat, then touched #1 on speed dial. "Nat, just checking in."

"Since when do…good day?"

"Interesting day."

"I think it's about time you get caught up with your

reports."

"Yep. I'm on it." Caden ended the call. He tossed the flash drive in the air then pocketed it. He looked over at Mystic. "Put some shoes on, the lodge is calling. Killian, mind checking the rest of the footage? I'll call you."

She looked down at her sore aching feet. "Do I have too?"

"Unless you want to walk barefooted over rough terrain."

"I've done it before," she replied saucily. Slipping on her sneakers, she grasped Caden's hand.

"We'll be back shortly." And they were gone.

****

Mystic and Caden materialized in the office of the lodge where Nat was waiting for them.

"Pretty cryptic conversation." Nat leaned back in his chair and looked over his coffee mug at them.

"You seemed to catch on. Didn't want to say anything without a secure line. Have you heard from the FBI regarding the unauthorized transfers and the initials BGE?"

"As a matter of fact, I haven't. Let me see, I believe I have Chad Zarko's cell phone number." Nat pulled out a business card from his wallet and punched in a number. No one answered, so Nat left a message to call him, leaving no other details.

"What else is on your mind?" Nat wanted to know.

"While watching the River Winds surveillance feed that Tristian tapped into, we believe we saw him enter the casino early this evening. He didn't look the same as the last time we saw him, his hair was black, and he was accompanied by two other men."

Nat's eyebrows drew together as he looked from Mystic to Caden. "Was he being escorted by these men or was he in charge of the situation?"

Caden pulled the thumb drive out of his pocket and tossed it to Nat. "I don't know for sure. Seemed pretty at ease on the video, but it's hard to tell. See for yourself."

Nathanael caught the flash drive and inserted it into the computer. Caden leaned over and punched a couple of keys on the keyboard, the footage blinked onto the screen. He fast forwarded it to a few minutes before Tristian's entrance.

Nat stared at the screen, his forehead creased in concentration. "You could be right, it looks like him, his hair is dark. It doesn't seem the man is in any distress, but I can't say for sure it's Tristian," he said, rewinding the footage and watching it again in slow motion. "Have you seen the two guys accompanying him anywhere else in your travels?"

"No, but we haven't canvassed Riverton yet, just the building department, the assessor's office, and a few businesses on Main Street. We haven't spent a lot of time in the casino either. Thought we should verify if it's Tristian or not before proceeding. Don't want to screw up Tristian's gig. We should send the footage to Bruce over your secure line. Maybe he knows the two men and can positively identify Tristian."

"Good call." Nat picked up his phone, scrolling through the contacts. "What were you looking for in Riverton? Got a theory?"

"Maybe, but nothing concrete. Can't get any of the puzzle pieces to fit."

"Care to share?"

"One thought is that Ethan is siphoning off money to invest into building another casino or business outside the boundaries of the Rez. As Bruce pointed out, whatever he is involved in must be lucrative or the demons and other worldly creatures wouldn't be involved."

"Gambling isn't legal except on the Wind River Reservation," Nat pointed out.

"But what if part of it was on Indian land, the other part on private land?"

Nat rubbed his chin. "I don't think that could be done, legally. The gaming commission rules are strict."

"Ethan has never played by the rules. He isn't about to start now," Mystic chimed in. "There is something bad going on here, and my gut tells me it's in or near Riverton."

"Did you turn up anything at the building department or assessor's office?"

"No, hit dead ends both places. According to the business owners we talked to, there haven't been any new businesses interested in setting up shop either."

"Then maybe you're looking down the wrong rabbit hole."

"Yeah, our next step is to investigate what industries feed Riverton's local economy."

"That's easy," Mystic said, giving her forehead a slap. "I don't know why I didn't think of it before. Oil."

The room was quiet. All eyes were on Mystic.

Caden was the first to speak. "That is a very lucrative industry. One that would spark a demon's interest in power, money, and influence."

The oil industry and its riches could finance any endeavor the demons wanted worldwide. If they'd aligned themselves with those wielding power and influence within that industry there would be no limit to what could be accomplished.

Now he knew where to look. It had never been only about Mystic and Ethan. It was about what Mystic represented, the power she'd hold. If she wasn't aligned with Ethan, she would be a major problem. *How could I've have been so blind?*

"Nat, can I use your computer?" he asked.

"Sure." Nat got out of the chair as he searched the contacts in his cell phone. "I'll call Bruce, bring him up to speed, and see how he wants us to proceed." Nat reached for the phone on the desk, punched in Bruce's number, hit speaker, and pocketed the cell phone.

The phone rang only once, and Bruce answered. "How are you Nathanael?"

"You're on speaker. I'm doing well. Thanks. Yourself?"

"Up to my neck in demon spawn. To what do I owe this honor, business or pleasure?"

"Have you heard?" He started then paused for a moment. "Business before pleasure unfortunately."

"I understand. Let me call you right back." Bruce disconnected the call.

Five minutes later, Nathanael reached for the phone on his desk before the first ring ended. "Hello."

"Is it all right if I put you back on speaker phone? Only Caden, Mystic, and Alaia are in the room with me."

"Not a problem, as long as the room and phone line are secure."

Nat touched a button, and Bruce's smooth deep voice sounded over the speaker.

"What can I do for you?" Bruce asked.

"Has Tristian checked in with you?"

"No. I told Caden, he would be the first to know, if I had contact with Tristian," Bruce said.

"Don't mean to interfere in your business. Earlier this evening, Caden checked the surveillance system that's tapped into the casino in real time. He was surprised to see a man that looked like Tristian walk into the River Winds Casino accompanied by two other men."

"And."

Caden moved closer to the speaker. "I'd like you to look at the footage and see if you can verify that person is Tristian. He's changed his appearance. I'd like to upload the video to you over the secure network we have here."

"Okay, make sure it is encrypted before you e-mail it to me."

Caden plugged in the flash drive and converted the video into an attachment. "It's on the way."

A few clicks of Bruce's keyboard were audible. "Got it. Give me a second to take a look." After a couple of minutes, Bruce's voice came back on the line. "Yes, that's definitely Tristian."

"Do you recognize the two men with him?"

"Nooo… I don't believe so, but I don't know all of Tristian's team members. Normally, I give him an assignment, and he executes it, filing a report with me within forty-eight hours of its completion. This operation is different because of your group's involvement."

"Sir, I don't want to compromise Tristian's operation. However, I'd also like to know if the two men with him are friend or foe?"

"It's not sir, it's Bruce. I can tell you by Tristian's body language he is in charge of the situation. Therefore, it's safe to assume they're part of his team or working with him. They are not his captors, if that is what you're asking."

"Would it be safe to resume our investigations?" Mystic asked while he continued his search on the computer.

"Yes, if you run across Tristian, act like you don't know him. I can assure you that's exactly what he'll do unless it's to his benefit to act differently. Then you can play it by ear."

"We can do that."

"What progress have you made?" Bruce wanted to know.

Mystic filled him in with their progress so far. Nat informed him that they were waiting for a call from the FBI as to the outcome of their search for the entity that was receiving the unauthorized money transfers.

"I got it," he yelped, pumping his fist in the air. "Black Gold Environmental, BGE, filed a foreign corporation request with the Wyoming Secretary of State last month, stating their business as oil exploration. The company rented an office in Riverton, and Ethan Nix is listed on their board of directors." He whirled around in the desk chair, barely missing Mystic when she came over to look at the computer screen. He printed out all the information on the corporation.

"Nice job, Caden, could you send me a copy of what you've found?" Bruce asked. "Will you need someone that won't be recognized to infiltrate their office?"

Caden looked around, neither he nor Mystic could do it because Ethan would recognize them. Chinoah, was out for the same reason, that left Killian, who could be associated with Chinoah since they canvased the businesses in Riverton together.

"We could probably use someone like that. Are you offering?"

Bruce snorted. "Not exactly. I was thinking of Angie. She could apply for a job in the company's front office. If you'd like our help, we could take the company jet and be in Riverton in a couple of days."

"Not a bad plan." He looked to the others for approval and got nods from all of them. "How about we coordinate plans when you arrive? We could pick you up at the airport."

"I don't think we should be seen together in public. Angie and I will find a house to rent tonight. Come to think of it, you might want to do the same when you return to Wyoming. The motel could become a liability. Too many people around there are aware of your routine."

"When we returned, that was a consideration. The room was trashed, and Tristian was missing. But the head of your cleaning crew, suggested it was the safest place, since Tristian apparently cast a protection spell before leaving."

"Yes, that was then. Now, Angie can cast the same spell when she arrives. We'll be in contact with Nat. He can give us your new address, then relay ours to you. Communications should be only through Nat, don't you agree? That way there is no connection between us."

"Agreed," he said.

"Talk to you later. Good night, Bruce," Nat said.

"Good night and good luck. We'll be in touch." With that, the connection was broken, and silence fell over the room.

Nat handed him a piece of paper. "I took the liberty of finding a house when the motel room was trashed. Didn't like where things were headed."

He glanced at the paper. "Tomorrow will be soon enough to move. Mystic and I are going to spend the night in our trailer. We're in need of a good night's sleep. In the morning, we'll port back to the motel and move our stuff into the rental." He waved the piece of paper and stuffed it into his pocket. "Thanks."

Nat nodded. "You might want to have Killian keep a low profile, since he's the only one that Ethan doesn't know. If Black Gold has a field operation, Killian may be useful in that capacity," Nat suggested before they left.

Mystic stifled a yawned and nodded her head. He gave the two thumbs up sign. "Anything else before we leave?" He gathered up the research paperwork on Black Gold Environmental and handed it to Mystic. She stuffed it in her backpack. He bookmarked the sites and stood returning control of the computer to Nat.

"Nope, looks like you two could use some shut eye. Talk to you tomorrow," Nat said.

He wrapped his arm around Mystic's waist. The hardwood floor creaked under their footsteps as they crossed to the door. He opened it, and they stepped out on to the porch. Turning, they said their goodbyes and disappeared into the trees alongside the road. Mystic slipped out of her clothes. In one great leap, she blurred into her wolf form landing silently on the damp forest floor on all fours.

Powerful, yet graceful and so beautiful, he sighed, watching her bound through the trees, silver light from the full moon shimmered across her sleek black coat. He leaned over and picked up her clothes. Tugging his own shirt over his head, he unfurled his wings and lifted effortlessly off the ground, his now silver wings tipped in a frosty gray stroked the air with ease. The breeze was crisp but refreshing as he soared above tracking her the few miles to their trailer.

"Feel better?" he asked unlocking the door and pulling it open. She swept past him deliberately rubbing her naked human form against him.

She nodded and murmured, "The full moon always makes me restless."

His wing tips brushed the stairs as he slipped in behind her, grabbing her wrist and pulling her to him, his mouth hot and hungry over hers. The touch of her warm tongue against his sent shivers of desire careening through him. She quivered against him.

"Cold?" He stared down at her, reluctantly releasing her.

"Not really," she said still plastered against him.

"You're trembling," he said a twinge of concern in his voice.

"I assure you, it's not because I'm cold."

He took the quilt off the couch and draped it around her shoulders.

It was chilly in the trailer. He had turned the heat down the last time they left. Reaching above her to the control panel, he turned the heat up, flipped the water heater on, and smiled when he checked the propane levels. Someone had filled both cylinders in their absence. The fresh water tank was full, and the black tank read empty. "Nice."

"Nice what?" Mystic slowly climbed the stairs to the bedroom, the quilt still wrapped around her.

"Someone cleaned and filled the water tanks while we were gone."

"Probably Sean, he said he'd keep an eye on the trailer when we left last time. Remember?"

"Yeah, but I didn't figure he'd do all that. I'll thank him tomorrow before we leave."

"Good idea. Now, I could use some of your heat up here in the bedroom until the trailer warms up." She grinned seductively as she sat on the bed, the quilt falling open in the front.

He grabbed the bottle of wine he'd swiped from the lodge, two crystal glasses, kicked off his shoes, and shimmied out of his jeans, bounding up the steps.

The lights dimmed. He handed her the glasses and poured wine, carefully setting the bottle on the nightstand. A soft melodic sound rang out as they touched rims and took a small sip, not taking their eyes off each other. It felt good to leave the recent week's stress behind and just enjoy being with each other.

He took her glass and set it next to his then gently began a series of slow smoldering kisses down her neck and across her breastbone, reveling in the wonderful scent and taste of her. His tongue teased her nipple until it was taut, the tip of his tongue caressed her belly button and slid lower, while his hands stroked her lower abdomen and massaged her inner thighs, fingers exploring her tenderly. He loved to kiss and when he made love, his lips lingered over every inch of her, until it seemed steam rose from their bodies. He kept her balanced on that precarious edge until the swell of passion took them both crashing over into a mind-blowing orgasm. He rolled to his side and cradled her body against his.

"Comfortable?"

"Mmmmm. Never better," she murmured half asleep.

Their bodies intertwined in a tangle of damp sheets, he smiled, relaxed, and drifted off to sleep. Only a couple of hours later he awoke with a start, the flaming building still scorched in his brain. *A dream.* He ran his fingers through his hair and glanced around. In the darkness, nothing seemed amiss. He eased out of bed, the blue light on the security system blinked indicating no breach. Peeking out the window all seemed quiet. *What the hell?* Taking a deep breath, he settled on the couch, pulled out his phone, punched in a number.

After several rings, a sleepy voice answered. "This better be good."

"Gather up the computers, our stuff, and get out of there. Got a bad feeling."

Chapter Twenty-Three
In Riverton Things Go Boom!

Two days later, Caden stood out of sight at the Riverton Regional Airport as the sleek, gleaming white jet streaked across the bright blue sky strewn with wispy clouds. Sunlight glistened off the silver and navy stripes along the lower side of the aircraft as it dropped the landing gear on its final approach to the airport.

The plane, emblazoned with Wycked in red and silver across its tailfin, touched down lightly on the runway, turned on the taxiway, and came to a stop beside a black SUV with dark tinted windows. A driver got out and stood impassively beside the open rear passenger door.

Pushing his new cowboy hat back to get a better look at the driver, he memorized the man's features.

The door to the aircraft slowly opened as the steps unfolded. Two large men dressed in dark suits with white silk shirts open at the neck and dark sunglasses emerged from the plane. They looked in all directions before one descended the steps. Half-way down, he turned and gave a small nod, and his partner started after him. A tall muscular man with shoulder length chestnut hair streaked with blond followed the two men. The tall one had a petite woman on his arm, her waist length straight blonde hair blowing gently in the warm breeze.

I'm aware you're here. Bruce's deep, smooth voice whispered through Caden's mind. *Don't obey orders, huh?*

A small smile curved his lips. *Didn't know they were orders. Seemed more like a request. Sorry if I misunderstood. Glad you arrived safely.*

As long as you're here, I'll allow communication, for now. Any problems?

None so far. He leaned his back against the corner of the building watching as Angie paused after exiting the plane.

Her bright violet eyes swept the early morning landscape as her mouth curved into a bright smile. "Bruce, isn't this spectacular? Not one high-rise in sight, and you can see for miles." She took in a deep breath and blew it out. "Smells a lot different than DC too." She turned to glance at her husband. "Bruce, are you paying attention?"

"I am. It's a lot quieter here also." He scanned the plains surrounding the airport while he offered his hand to Angie as an assist into the SUV. Before he joined her inside, he gave a slight nod to the driver. "Galen, nice to see you again. You've been well?"

Galen nodded as Bruce ducked into the vehicle and closed the door behind him. The driver walked to the driver's side, opened the door and, slid behind the wheel.

Bruce leaned forward and said, "Pinnacle Drive, please."

After watching and listening to the interaction, he pulled his cowboy hat low over his face and walked to the truck he'd rented this morning. Turning his attention to his own situation, he decided one vehicle between him, Killian, and the women wasn't enough. He climbed into the truck, started the engine, turned left onto Airport Road, then left onto Main Street. He slowed and turned right onto South 2nd Street, made another right onto West Monroe. He turned the corner onto Spire Drive and slowed. Halfway down the block, Killian stood at the rear of their SUV, back door open, boxes and computer gear stacked on the ground. Mystic watched from the middle of the front yard.

She turned and shaded her eyes as he pulled up in front. Fisting her hands on her hips, she asked, "Where have you been? You call Killian in the wee hours of the morning. We port to the motel. Move everything out. Say you'll be right back and disappear, then reappear in a new truck? What's going on?"

Killian picked up a box and carried it into the house.

"Needed more vehicles. A truck in this town blends in better. Especially if Killian has to do some undercover work." He picked up a computer and monitor. Mystic picked up the box of cords and started toward the house. She paused, glancing up the street at the two figures walking toward them. A smile spread across her face as recognition dawned. "Caden, we have company."

He whirled around box in hand to follow Mystic's gaze. Pleased but perplexed at the sight of Bruce and Angie. *Hadn't Bruce just called me out for being at the airport?*

Sure did. Bruce's voice boomed in Caden's head.

Yet, here you are walking right toward us. What gives? Want to be ignored? He looked back at Mystic, too late, she was already waving in acknowledgment.

As she brushed by him, he grasped hold of her arm. "Remember what Nat said. No contact."

Bruce's low chuckle wafted through his mind. *Angie will use a disguising spell. Makes it easier to work together. She'll also be adding a protection spell to the houses.*

Caden nodded in understanding and felt the connection snap shut.

Mystic glared at him for a moment, jerking her arm free. "Nat's not here, and they're obviously coming to visit. Plans must have changed—again. Where'd they rent a house?"

"I'm not sure, but since it looks like they're out for a stroll, must be around here." He shifted the box from his hip and set it down on top the others.

"Hey, what's taking you two so long? I have all Chinoah's and my stuff inside and put away. Want me to start the barbeque? We're starved." Killian paused in the front doorway of the house and turned to see what caught the other couple's attention.

"Good afternoon, Caden." Bruce extended his hand and then nodded toward Mystic. "Mystic, good to see you again." His voice friendly and calm, no hint of the authoritarian tone used during previous conversations. The corners of his lips curved in a lazy smile, tilting his head slightly to the left, brow raised in question. "Surprised?" he asked with a slight chuckle as he caught his wife around the waist and pulled her to him.

"Yes," he said truthfully. "Didn't expect to see you so soon. Welcome." Caden shook Bruce's hand and did the same to Angie. "Nice to see you too."

Mystic rushed over and gave Angie a quick hug, then tugged her out of Bruce's grasp and toward the house.

"Things change. Apparently, we have the same taste in housing. Need some help getting your stuff inside?" Bruce did a quick visual check of the surroundings and jerked his chin toward the house. Returning his gaze possessively back to Angie as she made her way to the house.

"Sure." He stacked Mystic's bag on top of the box he'd put down earlier and picked it back up, resting it against his hip. Leaning over, he easily hoisted up the computer CPU tucking it under his other arm. "If you'd grab the computer peripherals, Killian can get what is left."

Killian strode from the door to Caden's side.

He cut his gaze to Killian and nodded. *Relax Killian; they're friends.* "I'll make the introductions once we're inside."

"It figures, you'd wait for someone to come along to help move your things," Killian said in mock disgust, handing the printer and cords to Bruce while scooping up the last box containing the rest of the surveillance equipment.

Once inside, introductions where made. Caden and Bruce set up the surveillance equipment while Killian tended to the grilling duties. Angie and Chinoah unpacked the dishes they'd purchased earlier in the morning and washed them. Mystic cut and sliced veggies for a green salad then spread a red-checked, vinyl cloth over the picnic table on the back deck.

Killian hollered through the back door. "How does everyone want their Porterhouse steaks?"

"Rare," Bruce said, licking his lips.

"Rare for mine too," Mystic added.

"Medium rare," Angie sang out.

"Medium," he added. "And don't overcook it. There is a difference between medium and well done."

"Got it. Someone want to come get the baked potatoes. I think they're done." Killian used the tongs to move the potatoes from the grill onto a platter.

Once the food was spread out on the table, everyone grabbed a cold drink out of the cooler and sat down to enjoy the meal.

****

After dinner, Bruce pushed back from the table stretching his long sinewy arms over his head and leaning his chair back on two legs. "Thanks for a wonderful dinner and interesting conversation. Now, I'd like to discuss what you've learned about Black Gold Environment and how we can assist with the investigation."

Caden retrieved the research folder and spread the documents out on the table. They reviewed the corporation information and the staff at the storefront location. He set out where the suspected field operation was located and how many otherworldly creatures appeared to be employed.

"We hoped that Angie could infiltrate the office and were considering sending Killian into the field. What do you think?"

"What are you hoping to find?" Bruce shifted his gaze from the paperwork to Killian. "This could get real messy, real fast allowing the mortals a glimpse into our world. Which I don't need to tell you is strictly forbidden. How does this fit in with Ethan's attack on Mystic? Not just personal anymore? Huh?"

His sharp amber eyes, tinged with orange, shifted

again staring directly into Mystic's. The strength and power he exuded was downright scary. Mystic shifted in her chair uncomfortably and looked away. She was already antsy again.

Even if he thinks he's the biggest, baddest demon on this planet, I'm not going let him intimidate me. She squared her shoulders and brought her gaze back to meet his. "Personal or not, we'll find a way to recover the tribal funds that Ethan siphoned off."

Jellybean, he is the biggest, baddest demon on earth and in heaven. I've seen him in action. Don't want to tangle with him. Caden's words floated through Mystic's mind.

Bruce's lips twitched with amusement as though he could hear their thoughts. "I meant no disrespect, Ms. Rayne. Only need to get my head around what triggered your involvement. There are other aspects at play here, and I don't want them to get out of hand. I'm sure you understand."

His tone seemed a bit condescending and Mystic countered. "No, I don't. Please elaborate for us mere mortals."

Eyes narrowed and his mouth set in a firm line, Bruce said dangerously calm, "First, you are not a mere mortal, but a talented shapeshifter aligned with one of the fiercest warriors I've ever had the pleasure to meet. Second, I'm merely warning you of the terrible dangers that could lie ahead if my intel is correct. I'm still waiting to hear from Tristian."

"Enlighten us," Mystic said shifting in place.

"Mystic, that's enough. Bruce is not the enemy. He and Angie volunteered to help us," Caden said aware of the signs Mystic's need to release her wolf again to disperse the excess adrenalin building up in her body.

Bruce smiled. "I understand. Perhaps this should wait until morning."

"No, the sooner we get a plan in place and know what we are dealing with, the better chance we have of success," she insisted.

"I couldn't agree more, but let's take a break." Bruce glanced at his wife as she fidgeted in her chair. "The long flight and unpacking in the confines of the house hasn't left much time to get the wiggles out, as she says." He grinned. "Seems you and Angie have a few things in common."

Mystic's glance shifted from Bruce to a smiling Angie, nodding in agreement.

The guys scraped and rinsed the dishes and handed them to Chinoah and Mystic to arrange in the dishwasher. Angie wiped down the counters and folded the tablecloth.

So, being seen together is not a problem? Caden asked.

Angie nodded. "Actually, with the disguising spell, what people see is nondescript couples walking down the street. Magical creatures won't be able to identify us either. I've added subterfuge by also masking our magic signatures. I've used the same trick to mask the protection spells on our homes.

Chinoah raised a brow in question. "So, our houses can't be seen?"

Laughing, Angie clarified. "The protection spell allows only the home's resident to use magic within a one-hundred-foot radius outside or inside the home. The magic signature used to maintain that spell is masked to other magic creatures as is the signature of those inside the home."

"Sounds complicated and draining on your magic abilities."

A smile curved Angie's lips. "Not really. It's being used for the good of all, not for my personal gain. Besides there is plenty of power to draw on in this group."

Caden opened the door, and the three couples took to the street for a brisk walk familiarizing themselves with their surroundings, allowing her and Angie to work off their excess energy.

As they turned the corner at the end of the block, a large explosion rocked the ground underfoot. A tall, black, billowing plume of smoke accompanied fifty-foot flames shooting into the night sky.

"What the hell was that?" Caden exclaimed.

Bruce stared off into the distance as a black plume of smoke rose in the distance. "I think the Cozy Inn you vacated just exploded."

"Convenient. I removed the protection spell, as we drove by on our way from the airport this morning. It would have been awkward to explain why an explosion of that magnitude left two middle suites standing unharmed," Angie said.

Bruce cursed under his breath, pulled his phone out of his pocket, and strode ahead of the group. Phone to his ear, he changed his mind and placed the phone back in his pocket returning to the group. "I think it might be best if we went back to the house. Caden, do you have secure telephone lines?"

"Nat had them installed this morning."

"Angie, did you cast the protection spell for Caden's home as well as our own?" Bruce asked.

Angie rolled her eyes. "Weren't you listening? Already in place." She smiled rubbing her nails against the front of her blouse.

She felt herself losing her battle to her wolf and her human form shimmered and blurred around the edges as she morphed into wolf form, leaving bits of clothing in her wake. Her speed was unbelievably fast as was her agility, and she left the others in the dust. They stared after her then Angie let out a low giggle and raced after her.

****

Caden shrugged nonchalantly. "The full moon makes her restless. Guess she needed to release the wolf before being confined in the house again."

Bruce's forehead creased in concern. "She shouldn't go running off. It puts her in danger alone in the dark. Not to mention my wife."

"Don't worry. If Mystic sensed danger she wouldn't have run off to the house. She has a good sixth sense about lurking danger."

"Yeah, that's why her boyfriend nearly killed her," Bruce growled.

"Ex-acquaintance," he corrected. "They were never romantically involved. Grew up together on the Rez."

Eyebrows quirked in question, Bruce considered him for a moment, then deliberately slowed his pace, letting Chinoah and Killian continue ahead. "Then why the crime of passion, nearly ending her life?"

He slowed to keep in step with Bruce. "If we knew the answer to that, we'd be a lot closer to solving the mysteries surrounding the illegal transfers and missing persons. My theory…it wasn't only that she refused his proposal but her support of the tribe's involvement in the management of the River Winds Casino that caused him to attack her. His smoke screen is he lost control of his wolf during the shift."

Bruce raised his eyebrows and nodded.

"Mystic says that's bullshit. Once you learn to control the transition, the ability never leaves you, even under extreme duress. It's second nature. Feel free to discuss the matter with her." Caden shrugged and scanned the area under the silvery light of the full moon for his wolf. When he finally located her outside the front door of their house, he relaxed. Angie stood beside her bent over at the waist, hands on hips, trying to catch her breath. He turned his attention back to Bruce.

"She seems a bit touchy to my questioning." Bruce frowned.

"It's the full moon, and she's not sleeping well. This whole mess is wearing on her. There is one other theory I've kicked around but never mentioned to anyone. What if the demons or other creatures mixed up with Ethan were close enough to influence his behavior when he transitioned? Perhaps directing his rage and bruised ego into attempted murder. Would he know the difference or he'd been played? Is that even possible?"

Bruce rubbed his chin thoughtfully. "Possible— maybe. If they were familiar with the process of shifting. You may be onto something, but still motive, makes it iffy. How would the demons benefit? Seems no one knew the council's plans at that time."

"I don't know. That's why I haven't voiced that particular scenario, except nothing else makes sense either. Maybe Angie can find the missing puzzle pieces once she is able to snoop around at BGE."

"I'd like Angie to be aware of this newest theory before she attempts to get hired on at BGE," Bruce said increasing his pace.

They caught up with Killian and Chinoah a block from the house. By the time they reached the house, Mystic had transitioned back to human form, dressed in jeans and a t-shirt. She and Angie were setting bowls of chips, dip, and nuts on the table. Six crystal wine glasses sat next to a bottle of Road Kill Red wine. Maps of Riverton, the Rez, and surrounding areas spread across the table.

He put his arm around Mystic's shoulders and pulled her against him, brushing his lips tenderly across her temple. "Guess the girls think it's time to get down to business."

They each pulled up a chair and listened as Mystic described the layout of the town and the pertinent areas of the Rez. She passed around maps of the cretaceous sandstone reservoirs, which produced significant quantities of oil and gas adjacent to Riverton's boundaries. She handed out sheets of research gathered on the corporations that owned and operated the drill rigs.

Then she shared the copies obtained from the bank of the unauthorized transfers. After everyone had a chance to peruse the documents, she passed around what little information Caden dug up on Black Gold Environmental.

Bruce leafed through the BGE documents, stopped and stared intently at one diagram and explanation of a drill rig attached to some kind of permit paperwork. It set out the benefits of horizontal /directional drilling and hydraulic fracturing in shale, like the black shale of the Phosphorus and Movry formations, a source of petroleum for most of the Wind River basin reservoirs.

"Find something?" he asked leaning over to exam more closely the documentation Bruce was holding.

Bruce handed the papers to him, and he felt his eyes widen as he followed Bruce's train of thought. "Angie, I think we found what you need to confirm once you get access to the BGE offices." He handed the documents to Mystic. "Could you make a couple of copies of these pages and give one set to Angie and the other to Killian?"

"Sure." Mystic took the papers and glanced at them as she walked to the copier. "What do you see?"

"Don't want to say yet, until I can confirm my speculation. But see here…" He pointed to the location of several drill rigs then drew his finger horizontally across the county line and into the federal land of the Wind River Reservation.

Understanding slid across Mystic's face. "That would explain a lot of things."

Chapter Twenty-Four
Love it When a Plan Comes Together

"Caden, don't you think we should check out what happened at the Cozy Inn." Mystic pursed her lips.

Chinoah grabbed her bag. "I'm coming too."

"Sure." Caden looked up from the computer and smiled. "Give me a couple of minutes to finish checking the casino surveillance video. I haven't seen any sign of Ethan or Tristian in several days. Maybe we should check there too. Depending on what we discover at the motel."

"Okay, but they could be using the back entrance and avoiding the surveillance cameras," she suggested, looking over his shoulder at the feed. "Don't think heading to the casino is a good idea without Tristian's knowledge or protection."

"True enough." He pushed back from the desk, stretched his long arms above his head, and stood. "Checking out the motel is risky enough." Wrapping his arm around her waist, he brushed his lips across the shell of her ear and whispered, "You look ravishing this morning."

She felt his warm breath against her neck and shivered. A ripple of excitement shot straight south. "Well, thanks. What do you want?" She giggled.

"Nothing, can't a man compliment his woman without an ulterior motive?" He gave her his best wide-

311

eyed innocent look.

"Maybe, but not you." She purred.

Slowly and seductively, his gaze slid downward. "You got me. I want to rip your clothes off and make wild passionate love to you."

"All right guys, get a room or let's get going." Chinoah tapped her foot impatiently.

"Got a room, gotta get her to it." He tugged playfully at her waist.

Heat crept up her neck and spread across her face. "Knock it off, Caden. There is a time and a place, and this isn't it."

He shrugged. A look of indignation crossed his features. "You started it. I was just going to finish…"

She jerked out of his grip, grabbed her sweater, and shot a disgusted look over her shoulder.

"She loves me." Caden chuckled. "Killian, what's on your agenda today?"

Dressed in work jeans, T-shirt, black steel-toed boots, dark sunglasses and an attitude to match, Killian, said, "I'm going to go to the BGE office and see about getting on their field crew. Thought someone should check on Angie, see if she is still there. Bruce won't be with her." Killian put a ball cap on his head and reached for the keys to the other rental car. "Okay if I use the truck? Don't want to just pop in when I'm not familiar with the layout."

"Good idea. We'll take the SUV for the same reason. Just FYI bro, Bruce and Angie communicate telepathically and long range. Any trouble, Bruce would be there in a flash, and it wouldn't be pretty. Regardless of the toll it took on him. Good luck getting on the crew. You up to the work of a roustabout or roughneck?"

"Sure am, piece of cake compared to our usual line of work." Killian grinned back at him. "This assignment is making me soft." He kissed Chinoah and hugged her to him. "See ya later, be careful."

Caden parked the SUV in front of Cozy Inn. "Not as bad as I thought it would be. Damage seems to be confined to the west end of the building and the adjacent land." Crime scene tape remained at that section of the site. The last law enforcement officer got in his car and drove off.

She nodded her head and climbed out of the vehicle with Chinoah right behind her. "We should split up. I'll find the manager on sight. Caden, how about you talk to the desk clerk and other employees still here? Chinoah, could you wander around and see what you can find out from the workers?"

She walked toward the lobby area, which was still intact and the doors were propped open. Caden hung back surveying the work area situation outside the lobby to keep an eye on both girls.

She paused before going inside and glanced at Caden. Chinoah checked her makeup in the side mirror, applied lip-gloss, and sashayed toward a couple of men cleaning up the burnt and water soaked debris. She saw her wrinkle her nose at the stench. It made her chuckle as she headed inside.

****

By evening, everyone was assembled at Caden and Mystic's place. Mystic prepared dinner of roast beef with mashed garlic potatoes, and Chinoah whipped up green beans and homemade rolls. Bruce and Angie brought wine. After the meal, they retired to the living room to compare notes on the day's activities.

Caden started. "It appears that the explosion at Cozy Inn was unrelated to our actions or investigations. Apparently, the explosion was caused by out of town drug dealers cooking meth in the last room, next to the propane tank. Something went wrong. A small explosion and fire in the room caused the large propane tank to explode. One of the dealers is hospitalized in critical condition. The other two, died in the explosion. It's a police matter."

"One less thing on our plate." Mystic grinned. "Continue."

"The damage to the motel was limited to the west end and the adjacent property. Burned a wide area of vacant land. Chinoah talked to a couple of workers who said the Tribal Police had been alerted, so maybe some connection there. I just learned that a Detective Micah Rayne is assigned to the case."

Chinoah sucked in air and cut her gaze to Mystic.

Caden surprised by the reaction, switched his gaze between the two women. "Do either of you girls know him?"

Mystic glared at Chinoah, narrowed her eyes at him, and in a dismissive tone said, "We can address this later. It has nothing to do with the case. And he'll be no help, trust me."

"Is he going to be a problem?"

"No. I don't want to discuss it anymore."

"Okay," he said baffled at Mystic's sudden hostility, then changed the subject. "Mystic, Chinoah, and I didn't get a chance to check out the River Winds today. That's on our agenda for tomorrow. Angie, how did you make out?"

Angie sat tucked under Bruce's arm on the couch. "Good. I start tomorrow. The man who hired me, Murad Siry is a demon. The two others in the office are vampire and some kind of hybrid, demon, and something else…witch maybe, or werewolf. I couldn't get a fix on him. Seems I'll be alone in the office a lot of the time, since even the suits spend quite a bit of time in the field. I should have plenty of opportunity to snoop around. There are rows of file cabinets and blueprints in the plan room which is in the back of the office. I'll start there. My gut says we're on the right track, but motive is still a mystery."

Bruce, you okay with this?" he asked.

"Yes, so far, but I reserve the right to pull Angie out if things get volatile. I won't put her at risk for any one."

"Understood. I think we're all on the same page as far as our…ah…the women are concerned." Caden glanced at Killian.

Killian nodded. "I stopped by the BGE office this afternoon. Ran into a brick wall at first. But after I let slip that I was considered one of the best at setup, teardown and moving of drilling rigs, I got Mr. Siry's attention. I completed an employment application and now am waiting on a call from him. Any background search he runs will be exactly as I presented. Now, all I have to do is figure out how those rigs go together."

Bruce jerked his head around and shot Killian a dark look. Before Bruce could get a word out of his mouth…

Killian grinned. "Got ya. Only kidding. I know enough to handle myself."

Caden shot Killian a withering glance. "Please

excuse Killian. He has issues."

"Not a problem. I understand such urges myself." Bruce grinned. "But don't have occasion often to act on them."

Angie looked from Bruce to Killian as her forehead creased in concern.

The corners of Bruce's mouth twitched in amusement as his gaze shifted from Angie to Killian.

Choosing to ignore whatever was transpiring between Angie and Bruce, he decided to wind up the business and move on to more wine and friendly conversation. "Then we're agreed to let things play out on the course we've set up."

Everyone nodded.

"Good, let's have some more of that exceptional wine Bruce and Angie so graciously provided." He stood, moved to the kitchen to get wine and clean glasses. Mystic followed, took the six glasses, and set them on a tray. Her cell phone rang. She yanked it out of her pocket and stared at the screen. Her gaze flicked to him, her brow furrowed, lips pressed close together for a second, then she blew out a breath. "Hello."

Chapter Twenty-Five
Infiltrating the Casino and Oil Field—a Slippery Slope

The next morning, Caden and Mystic stood in the kitchen preparing breakfast. Bacon sizzled in a cast iron skillet on the stove under Caden's watchful eye. Mystic opened the oven door and inhaled deeply as she removed the cinnamon rolls. A full pot of freshly brewed coffee sat on the warmer in the middle of the kitchen table surrounded by four mugs. She placed the pan of rolls on the table beside the bowl of frosting and took the pitcher of orange juice out of the refrigerator. Chinoah reached for the glasses and set them on the counter next to the orange juice.

"Where's Killian?" She wanted to know, setting out plates and silverware.

"He got a phone call just as I was leaving the bedroom to come in here. He should be in shortly," Chinoah said, pouring herself a steaming mug of coffee, adding a little cream and numerous spoons of sugar.

"Gee, like a little coffee with your sugar?" Caden grinned cutting his gaze from Chinoah toward the doorway at the sound of footsteps. "I'll go ahead and put on the eggs and pancakes. The bacon is done," he said as he slid several pieces of bacon onto a platter lined with paper towels, folding over another and pressing down against the strips.

317

Killian sauntered into the kitchen, grabbed a mug filling it with coffee, poured a little cream into it, and took a drink. "Mmmm, Mystic must have made the coffee. My spoon won't stand alone in it." He grinned toward Chinoah, who promptly swiped at him with her freshly painted lavender fingernails. Smoothly he caught her hand before it made contact and examined her hand. "Nice shade."

"Well, I'm in," Killian said. "Murad called this morning. Start work tomorrow on the graveyard shift. Supposed to meet some guy named Ryan a half hour before my shift. He'll show me around." Killian took another gulp of coffee and picked up a plate, helping himself to eggs, a couple pancakes, and two slices of bacon. "Syrup?" he asked, looking over the table as he buttered the pancakes.

"I'll get it," Chinoah said reaching into the refrigerator for the fresh maple syrup.

"Myst, Chinoah, and I are headed to the casino this morning. Want to tag along?" he asked, sitting down in front of the plate Mystic had heaped with eggs, bacon, and cinnamon rolls. "Hey, don't I get pancakes too? After all I made them."

"Too many carbs. You want to keep your studly angelic physique. Right?" Mystic chuckled.

"Give me those pancakes, woman, before I show you just how…"

Mystic moved the plate of pancakes out of his reach and giggled, handing the plate to Killian. "He needs the carbs. He'll be doing hard labor, unlike others seated at this table."

"Yeah." Killian snatched the plate smacking his lips.

"True enough," he agreed frowning at Killian. "Not much for you girls to do recently." He reached across the table and stuck his fork in a stack of two pancakes plopping them on his plate as he shifted his gaze to Mystic daring her to make a move.

"Such table manners." She clicked her tongue and sat down in front of her own plate of one egg, one slice of bacon, and a cinnamon roll.

"Sounds like fun, but being seen with you is now a no-go since I'll be working on the rig. Besides, I'm meeting Murad at the office to fill out a new hire packet and take a drug test." Killian forked another bite of egg into his mouth.

"The drug test is going to be a problem. No way to hide your DNA differences."

"Not a problem. Talked to Angie this morning, the lab that BGE uses has a mortal staff. Use a little persuasion on the tech, and they complete the form without the blood draw, at least it worked for her."

"She's a lot cuter that you are," he chided.

"Then we better hope I get a female tech. She won't be able to resist me," Killian shot back.

"The testosterone in this kitchen is reaching lethal levels." Mystic popped the last piece of cinnamon roll in her mouth and started clearing the table. "Chinoah and I are leaving as soon as the dishwasher is loaded, with or without you Caden. By the way you two need to rinse and stack your dishes in the dishwasher before I start it."

"Okay, okay." Caden sopped up the syrup from his plate with the last bite of pancake, slipping it into his mouth as he stood.

Killian made a face, picked up his plate, and

319

moved toward the sink.

"Good luck today," he said smiling as he followed the girls to the door.

Water splashed inside the dishwasher as Killian shrugged into his jacket, closed, and locked the door behind the others.

"Did you check the surveillance videos this morning?" Mystic asked.

"Yeah, still no sign of Ethan or Tristian." He opened the vehicle door for her. "Finally spoke to Tristian on the phone late last night. He called after you were asleep. He'll be ready for us today at River Winds."

"Good to know." Mystic pulled her cell phone out of her pocket and quietly said, "Archer." The phone dialed a number, and she put the phone to her ear as he started the SUV and turned onto the road.

"Arch, you busy?"

"Yeah, kinda. What's up?"

"If you can break free, would you meet us at the casino in a half hour or so?"

"Sure, I can do that. I won't be able to stay long. One of the drivers called in sick today, so I need to fill in."

"Okay, shouldn't take too long. Fill you in when you get there. Meet you at the cashier's cage in about half an hour." She disconnected the phone and without a word watched the businesses and homes pass by.

When Caden pulled into the casino parking lot, she pushed open the door and stepped out of the vehicle, crashing into his broad chest as he stepped in front of her.

He caught her by the shoulders, narrowed his eyes

as he looked down at her. "Just what are you up to?"

She stood on tiptoe and whispered a few words into his ear.

He blew out a breath as his expression turned grim and lips formed a thin line. He released her. "Risky. Especially if Ethan still has spies on the inside."

"I have to do something. We can't risk the tribe's money any longer."

"All right. But neither of you are leaving my sight." He put his arm around Mystic's waist. "Let's see what kind of trouble we can stir up." They strode across the parking lot and caught up with Chinoah just outside the casino door.

"Show time," Mystic murmured.

He yanked open the door, and they walked through into the River Winds slowly. Mystic waved at the hidden surveillance camera as they passed it in the lobby entrance. No reaction. The security guards remained at their stations. Rusti smiled and nodded in their direction.

Mystic walked over to where Rusti stood behind the cashier's cage. "Good morning. How's things?"

"Strange. Really strange," Rusti replied, glancing nervously around then lowered her voice to just above a whisper. "Haven't seen or heard from Ethan in several days. Sage said he was going out of town on business and left her in charge." Rusti shifted her gaze to the door as Tristian strode in flanked by two men. All dressed in black Armani suits, white striped silk shirts, and dark glasses.

She moved away from Mystic and started arranging chips. Without looking up Rusti said, "That's the new head of security. He's a mean one, so I've heard. Brought in his own security team. Gotta get back to work. Find Sage, she can fill you in. She's always here since Ethan left and looks ready to drop if you ask me."

Tristian flicked his dark glasses up and stared at Mystic. He jerked his head toward his and Chinoah's direction. The two men split up and walked toward them, while Tristian moved to Mystic's side. He placed his hand under her elbow. "A word, Ms. Rayne." He steered her toward the back of the casino while the other two men detained Caden and Chinoah.

"How do you know my name?" Mystic asked playing along while others could over hear.

"It's my business." Tristian pushed open the door that led down a hallway to the offices. Standing with his back to the security camera, his tall muscular form obscured her identity from the cameras. He reached for his keys and tapped a button on his key ring. "Shuts the security cameras off for a few minutes. Not much time, something is going down. I'm sure Rusti filled you in before I came in."

"She didn't know much, only that things were strange."

Tristian waited a couple of beats as if trying to decide just how much to confide. "Stay alert. The vendors unknowingly hire demons or vamps sent to intimidate or spy. Their credentials are a damn good forgery, and they rotate so they don't draw attention. A witch or two enjoyed Ethan's favors and are among the employees. Be careful. Sage can be trusted. Keep her in the loop." Tristian's face was unreadable as he studied her, then eased her hand through his bent arm and opened the door to the casino floor. "Sorry for the misunderstanding, Ms. Rayne, I didn't realize you represented the tribe. Will Mr. Clearwater be joining you soon?"

Stunned into silence for a beat, she wondered how Tristian knew about Archer. "Yes, as a matter of fact he will. Would you contact the department supervisors and have them meet Mr. Clearwater and my entourage in Ethan's office in twenty minutes?"

"Of course. Be aware. I have hired a member of your tribe as casino security. I've had dealings with him in the middle east. I think he will be a good asset to leave in place once this operation is completed." Tristian escorted her back to where Caden and Chinoah were waiting impatiently under the watchful eye of his men.

"I'd like you to join our little impromptu meeting. Things are about to change around here." She smiled sweetly at Tristian and then switched her gaze to his two men. "They can stand guard outside the office, but only you will be privy to the meeting. Make sure all the recording devices, audio and video are off, inside the office. Leave instructions we are not to be interrupted."

Tristian narrowed his eyes and nodded. "Understood." At some unseen command from Tristian, both men moved away from Caden and Chinoah, crossing the casino floor and disappearing between aisles of slot machines. Tristian looked to her once more, nodded then turned on his heel, strode across the floor, and through the door to the office hallway.

"Wow, what do you make of that?" Caden wanted to know.

She blew out a breath and leaned against the warm comfort of his broad chest for a beat. "I'm not sure, but

I think we should wait for Archer outside."

Chinoah had watched the events of the past twenty minutes in silence but now narrowed her eyes at Mystic. "Myst, why do I feel like I did when we were kids and you were about to spring one of your hair brained schemes?"

"Ever the clairvoyant. I hope you weren't planning on leaving the area any time soon." She looked at her childhood friend and flashed a tight-lipped smile.

"No, not really." Chinoah shrugged. "Wherever Killian is calling home is where I'll be. That's our pact. For the time being." She smiled twisting her favorite ring round and round her finger. A habit she'd had since childhood when nervous.

"Good. Relax. We've got this."

The group crossed to the front door just as Archer Clearwater came in. Caden jerked his head toward the parking lot, and Archer followed them outside.

He took in the group's somber looks and asked. "Who died?"

Mystic's lips twitched, and the creases in her forehead disappeared. "No one, I hope. Ethan appears to have taken an unannounced leave of absence without informing the council. Since you're acting head of the council, I want your blessing and backing for what I'm about to do," Mystic said.

Archer cocked his head and raised an eyebrow. "Is this something I'm going to regret? Or something we should bring before the council?"

"No, and eventually, when we're ready to make the changes permanent. Right now, the fewer who know about it the better. On the off chance we have a leak in the council."

"I've known everyone on the Council of Elders since you were in diapers. I would trust them with my life."

"Are you sure? It may come down to that, if you're wrong," she said gravely. "Convene a meeting for tonight, but today we're going forward with temporary arrangements in Ethan's absence. It's my understanding Sage is running on fumes."

"I heard the same thing from my wife this morning, just before your call. Apparently, she learned something while she was at the market yesterday."

She let out an exasperated sigh. "You could have told me."

"I figured that was why you called and wanted to meet," Archer said.

Quickly she laid out the changes she felt necessary and asked if anyone had suggestions or if they agreed. Caden and Archer nodded. Chinoah just stood there blinking. "Chinoah, you on board with this?" Mystic asked.

Slowly Chinoah nodded her head. "But I'm not so sure about Killian."

"He'll be fine with it. Tristian and Caden will be close, and it's only temporary. I've requested the supervisory staff meet us in Ethan's office." She looked at her watch, quickening her steps. "Now." She sucked in a deep breath, and Caden squeezed her shoulder encouragingly. *This is either the stupidest thing I've ever done or the smartest, wish I knew which for sure.*

Caden smiled, his comforting voice drifting through her mind. *We'll know soon.*

Gee, that's makes me feel a whole lot better. She shot him a chagrined look.

Have a little faith. You're on the right track. Caden patted her arm and opened the door to Ethan's office.

First glance at the people gathered gave her a plethora of info about each individual. Inside looking wary and uncomfortable stood Sage Runner, the floor manager, dark circles under her tired eyes. She was dead on her feet. Rusti Fox, the day pit supervisor, slouched next to her checking her cell phone.

Joey Moon, night pit supervisor, was perched on a bar stool impatiently tapping his foot against the rug, as if wanting to get this over with and get home. She couldn't blame him. Food service supervisor, Kindred Shaw, kept his eyes on her as she entered the room and Julian Hawk stood next to Tristian.

She recognized Julian as a member of her tribe. He recently returned from the Middle East where he served in black ops. Now he apparently acted as Tristian's second in command.

Tristian was the first to speak. "Ms. Rayne, I need to let you know up front that I'm leaving in a few minutes, prior commitment." He motioned to the tall, bronze skinned man with straight black hair standing next to him. "This is Julian. He takes care of things while I am out of the casino. He'll relay any information necessary to the security staff and make sure any directives are understood and implemented, immediately. I'll be in touch."

She nodded to Tristian, then directed her attention to the others, meeting the eyes of each employee. "Thanks for coming on such short notice. I know you have things to do, so I'll be brief. The tribal council has released Mr. Nix from his position as manager of the River Winds, effective immediately. That position will be temporarily filled by Sage, who you all know. Chinoah Grace…" Mystic motioned to where Chinoah was standing next to the wall, "…and myself. Sage will handle the day-to-day operations once she has a few well-deserved days off."

Sage's tired eyes flew open as her forehead creased and her shoulders stiffened.

She smiled understandingly at Sage. "Be aware that this decision has the blessing of the tribe's council and the acting Chief, Archer Clearwater." She shifted her gaze to Arch, he gave a small nod in agreement.

"Should Mr. Nix return to the casino, you're to report his appearance immediately to security. They will escort him from the premises. Otherwise, it will be business as usual. I want this information conveyed to the rest of the employees. My security consultant, Caden Silverwind in conjunction with Julian…"

She motioned to Caden who stood arms crossed over his chest leaning one shoulder against the doorframe. "…or myself will be sitting down with each of you to discuss any concerns in the next week or so. If something comes up that can't wait, don't hesitate to contact Sage, Ms. Grace, or me. You'll have our contact numbers before you leave this meeting."

She hesitated, her attention flicking to the closing door. She scanned the room and discovered Tristian was missing. She glanced at Caden who smiled at her inclining his head slightly. "That's all for now. You can head back to work or go home and get some rest." Her gaze swept over the employees, lingering a moment on Joey, and she nodded. "Thanks. I appreciate your time. Sage, if you have a minute or two, I'd like to talk with you."

"Sure, I guess," Sage said hesitantly as she crossed the room.

"Let's take a walk." She headed toward the door, grabbing Caden's hand as he opened the door for them. "Join us."

They walked down the hallway and out the back door to the benches lining the grassy courtyard area. Sage followed doggedly, shoulders slumped.

"It's my understanding you were the council's pick to eventually replace Ethan. Unfortunately, Ethan wasn't on board with the decision and undermined you at every turn." She shook her head. "Not a good working environment. I'm sorry about that. It's no wonder you're exhausted, overwhelmed, and ready to shit can it all. But if you'll hang in there a little longer, things are about to change."

"I guess I can do that." Sage nodded.

"I appreciate it." She eased down on one of the benches away from the building and motioned for Sage to sit beside her. Caden positioned himself directly behind their bench in a relaxed stance.

"Sage, can you fill us in on what's going on around here? If you feel more comfortable, I can have Archer join us."

"That won't be necessary," Sage said with a heavy sigh.

Chapter Twenty-Six
Infiltrating the Enemy's Camp can be Dangerous

Caden strolled through the front door of the house followed closely by Mystic and Chinoah, who closed the door behind her. Killian sprawled on the couch watching TV, looked up as they entered.

"Got your note this morning, so we split early. What's up?" he asked settling down on the loveseat next to where Mystic plopped down.

Killian stretched his arms above his head, swung his feet to the ground. He smiled at Chinoah as she slid in next to him. He curled his arm around her shoulder. "I've missed you. Working nights sucks." He nuzzled her neck kissing her lightly then whispered, "Later."

He cleared his throat loudly. "You wanted to talk?"

"Yeah." With difficulty, he tore his gaze from Chinoah. "I finally had some time to snoop around night before last. Got a good look at the field maps. Lucky for me the boss hates paperwork. After spending night after frigging night checking every inch of the drill rig, then cleaning and checking every one of the rig tools, making repairs where necessary, he finally decided to show me how to complete the nightly reports, and left me to it."

"Didn't you think it was a bit strange, he'd train a new employee on the paperwork?"

Killian shook his head. "Most of the guys don't

329

want anything to do with pushing paper or office work. The money is made working the rig. BGE's rigs are well outside federal boundaries, but they're drilling diagonally into black shales right under the Rez. I think that's why BGE, which by the way is a demon-controlled corporation, was interested in Ethan."

"As we surmised." He glanced at Mystic.

Killian continued, "Originally, BGE's board of directors thought Ethan held the power and authority of the tribal council, probably the purse strings to the casino, too. That's why he was listed as a board member. After the Mystic fiasco, they knew better, and Ethan was more of a liability than an asset."

"The demons have Ethan?" Mystic asked chewing on her bottom lip, molding herself against Caden.

"Not sure. There was a signed amendment to the corporate minutes on the fax machine when I went in the office to fill out my employment packet. The amendment removed Ethan but left the Northern Arapahoe Nation without a representative, I think. Murad came in and ripped the paper from the fax machine before I had a chance to get a really good look. I heard him coming and was busy working on my packet when he rushed in muttering something in an unfamiliar language. Then he turned, shrugged, sent me a tight-lipped smile, and said incompetence was all around him. But…that is just the tip of the iceberg."

"There's more?" Caden asked.

"Yeah. The BGE western regional corporate headquarters is here. They produce the permits and necessary paperwork locally. It's possible there's another national headquarters who oversee all the locations. There are permits and notices pending with the Oil & Gas Conservation Commission of the State of Colorado for Aurora and Colorado Springs where oil exploration is expanding. Several of the guys are hoping to transfer to Colorado if the tests pan out."

His brows knitted together as he tented his fingers in front of his chest. "Are the other locations operated by other worldly creatures too?"

"Don't know. That's a question for Angie. Hopefully, she's had time to check out the office. The plan room in the back has several four drawer locked file cabinets sitting side-by-side. My gut says BGE is involved in more than oil or using oil for a cover. Whatever it is, it's lucrative and spreading rapidly. It almost feels like they're gearing up for something big. Numerous demons, vamps, and a few witches pass through looking for Thamuz. Not sure who that is."

"That name sounds familiar." Caden stood up, he thought better on his feet, and paced back and forth across the room. Finally, unable to remember where he'd heard that name before, he decided to enlist the help of the resident demon overlord. "We need to invite Bruce and Angie over for a barbeque." He paused for a beat creasing his forehead, "Maybe tomorrow night, depending on their schedules. I'll give him a call."

"My thoughts exactly," Killian said nodding his head. "I stopped by the market on my way home and picked up steaks, potatoes, a bag o' salad, and devils food cupcakes." He snickered as the rest of the group groaned.

"Bad, bad, bad." He shook his head and grinned at Killian, thankful for his partner's ability for humor in this sobering discussion.

"I also bought a few six packs of beer, a bottle of

that red Burgundy you like. Since I noticed the supply Bruce and Angie brought over is dwindling—quickly."

"Good thinking."

"And that, ladies and gent, concludes my status update. Now, I need to attend to some long-neglected duties." Killian turned to Chinoah sending her a wicked grin as he got to his feet and swept her up in his arms.

Chinoah squealed and flung her arms around Killian's neck, snuggling into his chest.

Killian laid his cheek on the top of her head. "Good evening, Mystic, Caden, see you sometime tomorrow. FYI, after working nearly fifteen nights straight, I've four days off, so don't expect Chinoah at work."

"Hey, you big lug, she's a working girl again. People depend on her," Mystic informed him, shaking her index finger at him in mock irritation.

Killian snickered. "Not for the next four days." He turned on his heel, moving silently across the floor and down the stairs to the room he shared with Chinoah, closing the door quietly.

"You know what this means, don't you?"

Mystic huffed out a breath. "Yeah, I have to do Chinoah's job for the next four days."

"Nooo… I believe we're off for the next two. Isn't that what you told Sage when she came back to work, well rested and ready to take on the world?"

"Yes…but…"

"No buts. You've put in an amazing number of hours and deserve a warm bubble bath and after that an all-over body massage."

"You hired a masseuse?" she asked, batting her long lashes at him.

"Of sorts." He smiled seductively. "He's strong,

gentle, and desires only to pleasure you."

"Are you going to watch?" Mystic asked, covering her mouth to keep a giggle from escaping.

Unruffled, he countered, "Nope, I'm going to participate." He slid his hand under her bent knees and snaked his arm around her shoulders, folding her tight against his chest as he stood. He leaned in to nuzzle her neck, his warm breath teasing the pulsing hollow of her throat.

"You worked the same hours I did. Don't you deserve a bubble bath and massage too?" Mystic asked, her chocolate brown eyes dancing with mischief.

"Standing against the wall with my arms crossed looking formidable isn't what I'd call work. But if you decide to share your bubble bath and reciprocate on the massage… I wouldn't object," he whispered nibbling at the soft shell of her ear as he ambled toward the bedroom.

She unbuttoned his shirt and rubbed her cheek against his bare chest.

He carried her into the bedroom and gently settled her on the bed. Kneeling, he removed her shoes and socks. Massaging first one foot then the other in slow little circles with his thumbs, he caressed her slender ankles, then moved slowly to her smooth firm thighs. Brushing the side of her hips with his fingertips, he slid his hand into her waistband easing her pants down until they pooled at her feet.

He rose from his kneeling position, leaning into her, his lips brushed against hers as he spoke. "You wait right here while I prepare your bath. I'll call you when it's ready." His bare feet left imprints in the plush bedroom carpet, then softly slapped the cool light blue tile floor as he crossed into the bathroom. He flicked on the light and hit the dimmer.

She closed her eyes and leaned back on her elbows, a sigh escaped her lips.

Turning on the water, he watched it cascade into the large old-fashioned claw foot tub. He sprinkled lavender scented bath salts along with bubble bath into the steaming water. From under the sink cabinet, he retrieved the candles he'd left there early this morning while she was dressing.

He placed two on the countertop between the double sinks, and two on the ledge above the gleaming white tub. When he lit them, a hint of lavender mixed with vanilla wafted through the room as the candlelight danced over the walls. He dimmed the lights further.

Stepping to the doorway, in a husky voice he said, "Your bath awaits, my lady." Crossing the distance between them, he held out his hand.

Her fingertips brushed his palm as she reached for his support and stood, like a princess in a grown-up fairy tale. His lips skimmed the back of her hand lightly lingering to kiss each knuckle. He unfastened the buttons on her blouse and slid it from her shoulders, reached around and unfastened her bra, her soft mounds spilled into his waiting hands.

He steadied her as she perched on one foot and touched the toe of her other foot to the water. "Perfect," she murmured easing into the deliciously warm water until only her neck and head remained visible.

Positioning himself at the end of the tub, he skimmed his hands along the water and massaged her neck and shoulders. She moaned softly and relaxed against his fingers, then turned her face and brushed her lips against the wrist of his right hand. She looked up at him and said quietly, "Thanks for letting me handle the casino in my own way. I appreciate your strong silent support. I know it was hard."

He grinned. *You have no idea how hard I am.* He flicked his gaze downward then up to her and felt a slow burn as he leisurely took in every inch of her naked body.

She sat up, brought her cupped hand out of the water, bubbles streaming through her fingers and down her arm and threw the water covered in bubbles at him. "You know what I meant. I was being serious."

"So am I." His lips twitched. "But thank you. It's your show, but keep in mind if things head south, I won't hesitate to step in and protect what's mine." He eased her back down into the water, leaned over, and traced the soft fullness of her lips with his tongue. "Now, where was I?'

"You were about to disrobe and join me." She snatched the towel wrapped low around his hips and tossed it across the room.

"Thought, you'd never ask, my lady." He leaned his hands on each side of the tub and stepped in straddling her.

****

Mystic's tossing, turning, and fidgeting in her sleep awakened Caden just before dawn. He yawned and started to roll toward her as his cell phone rang on the nightstand. In an effort to silent the intrusion before it woke her, he grabbed for the phone, missed, and it tumbled to the floor.

Aren't you going to get that?" she asked in a sleepy voice.

Tena Stetler

The bath and intimate activities of the night before should have soothed the increased restlessness he'd observed in her over the last few days. She'd worked from dawn well into the night for the last couple of weeks at the River Winds then fell into a restless sleep only to repeat it day after day.

"Nope." He drew her closer against him, their legs entwined together. "If it's important, they'll leave a message or call back.

She gently nuzzled his neck and licked at the bite mark she'd inflicted last night at the height of their passion. "Do you mind?"

"Do I mind that you marked me as your mate? That you finally admitted you loved me enough to want to spend your life with me on your own terms? Hell no, I don't mind. I'll wear it proudly." He winced touching the wound. "You could have warned me."

"It would have hurt more." Mystic lifted one shoulder in a shrug. "Besides it was more instinct, than planning, the time felt right." She yawned wide and stretched her arms above her head and rolled over. Getting to her knees she leaned forward on her hands and stretched her back in an arch, getting the kinks out.

"Oh, don't tempt me. We'll never get out of bed." He placed his big warm hand on her bottom giving it a squeeze.

She pushed his hand aside, bounced up and stood, knees bent, legs wobbling on the bed for a moment straddling over him, then vaulted to the floor, and scurried toward the bathroom giggling. "Catch me if you can."

"Hey, you're not getting off that easy." He bolted after her, pinning her against the wall, his mouth

336

devouring hers, catching her squeal of delight as his naked body pressed tight against hers.

****

Caden pulled on his jeans, leaving the top button still undone, wiggling his eyebrows and thrusting his hips playfully at Mystic.

She laughed. "Caden Silverwind, you've had enough for one day."

"Oh, I beg to differ with you, I never get enough." He reached for her. She slapped his cell phone in his hand. He stared at it sadly for a beat and raised his eyes to her. "Can't keep up with me, huh?"

She rolled her eyes and sighed. "Whatever…" Wriggling into her jeans, she pulled a stretchy blue top with a deep V-neck over her head. "What time did you suggest they come over?"

"I like that top." He ran his fingers just inside the neckline and pulled the material toward him to look inside.

She backed away and caught his hand bringing it to her lips. "Later."

"I'll hold you to it." He grinned and tapped the screen to recall the message on his phone. "I told him around four. Thought that'd give us time to discuss things before dinner and wine." He put the phone to his ear and listened, then touched the screen and slid it back in his pocket. "They'll be here between four and four-thirty."

There was light rap on the door. "Caden, you decent?" Killian asked.

"Yeah, come on in."

Killian pushed the door open and stood in the doorway his silvery wings open, frosty gray tips brushing the floor. "I need some flight time. How about you?"

"Not a bad idea, but your timing sucks. Bruce and Angie will be here by four-thirty, and in case you haven't noticed, it's bright daylight outside. A couple of angels winging their way across Wyoming's bright blue sky might draw a bit of attention." Caden shifted his own shoulders. "It has been…way too long since I've had significant flight time. We'd have Nathanael on our backs for breaking the rules, then the whole domino effect coming down on us from on high. No thank you."

"But what if we ported to somewhere it's dark already, Australia, maybe Ireland," Mystic interjected.

He smiled shaking his head slightly. "Sounds good in theory, but to be comfortable, it should be somewhere either Killian or I are quite familiar with, know the current surroundings, the dangers and the safe havens, especially in the dark." He slid his hand in his pocket and pulled out his tube of lip balm, uncapped it thoughtfully, and smoothed it over his lips, trying to determine a place that would be safe. He looked to Killian whose forehead creased in concentration.

"Can't come up with a thing," Killian said. "Been too long since I've walked the earth in search of peace and quiet. I wouldn't feel confident in any places that come to mind."

"Teton National?" Mystic offered. "In the less populated areas and dense forest. You know, like the place you took me when we first arrived in Wyoming."

"What's this we? You got a mouse in your pocket?" He laughed.

Mystic grinned and reached into her pocket, pulling it inside out, shaking her head. She batted her long raven lashes and glanced out from under them at Caden, her brown eyes sparkling. "I could use a run au′ natural, if you know what I mean, I'm sure Chinoah could too."

"You got that right, girlfriend. The walls are closing in around me as we speak." Chinoah bounded up the stairs and stopped just outside the bedroom door. She rolled her shoulders and arched her back, supporting the small of her back with her hands, stretching her muscles.

He looked at his watch. "We could do that. Should take turns at look out, but it would still give us all some relief. Good call." He ran his hand through her hair affectionately, letting strands fall between his fingers.

They materialized at the edge of Leigh Lake, under the cover of pine trees and scrub oak. He turned and let the magic wash from the portal sweep over him, to make sure no one followed them. The warriors removed their shirts, unfurled their wings, and took to the sky, careful to blend into the surroundings and hovering low. After scouting the area around the lake for mortals and other creatures, they lightly touched the ground, their wings swaying back and forth in the light breeze.

"Not much of a work out, but better than nothing," Killian grumbled.

"You'll live. We'll make time for a more strenuous work out tonight," he said, watching both girls shimmer and the edges of their body's blur. "I never tire of Mystic's transformation. It's breathtaking."

Killian smirked. "I like Chinoah's return to human form. Her skin glistens after her run."

A laugh rumbled in his chest. "You just like to see her naked."

"Yeah, so what. You're no different."

He nodded, pushing off the ground lightly to hover just behind Mystic on the rocky path, masking his magic signature. Suddenly she skidded to a stop, ears flat to her head and nose in the air, nostrils flaring. Not more than fifty feet ahead of the girls, a muscular male, little over six-foot-tall, dark hair and black eyes, stepped out of the trees directly into their path. Instinct took over, Mystic veered to the left disappearing in the underbrush as Chinoah cut to the right behind the large pines. Without a sound, they circled around out of sight until they were behind the stranger.

He silently touched down, tucking his wings halfway behind his back, to have full use of his magic, if necessary. He remained slightly behind a tree trunk, hands on the daggers harnessed across his chest. Killian's wings vanished as he reached over his shoulder to unsheathe his celestial diamond sword and stepped into the path of the stranger.

The man stood arms loose at his side for a moment, then raised his hands, palms up in surrender. "That's a mean blade you wield. Expecting trouble on the trail, Killian?" The corner of the man's mouth twitched in a wry half smile, as his eyes remained fixed on sword.

Killian let his sword slid back into its leather sheath and stepped toward the man, hand extended. "Gabe, what are you doing here?"

Gabe clasped Killian's hand, relief reflected in his eyes. "Same as you, I think." He hesitated a beat, his eyebrow raised staring over Killian's shoulder. "A little R & R away from the rig. I didn't mean to startle you, didn't even see you. Was watching two massive wolves running up the path right in front of me. Did you see them?"

"Yeah, I saw you step directly in front of them. That was a stupid thing to do. Could've been lunch." Killian shifted his weight from the ball of his feet to his heels and leaned his head from side to side releasing the tension in his neck.

"Good point. I guess I wasn't thinking. Just doing a few trails and taking in the sights before heading back to Riverton. Best be on my way. Enjoy your time off." Gabe turned and strolled down the path.

Killian blew out a breath and stared at Caden. "Got a funny feeling 'bout that." He jerked his chin toward the path where Gabe had been.

Both men turned and stared down the path. Gabe was nowhere in sight.

Chapter Twenty-Seven
A Surprise Reunion and Explanation.

The lapping waves of the lake and fresh clean mountain air pungent with pine aroma faded to the whir of an air conditioner spreading lemon fresh fragrance throughout the house in Riverton. Caden flipped off the air and opened the front door to get a breeze flowing through the house when a business card fluttered to the ground. He stooped and picked up the card, a hand-written note on the back and the Tribal Police's insignia on the front.

He turned the card over and read the name. *Micah again. Need to get to the bottom of this.* "Hey, Mystic, do you know a Tribal Police Detective by the name of Micah Rayne? Any relation?"

Mystic hesitated, looking from his determined expression to the card and back again, then sighed. "Yeah, he's my twin brother."

He raised an eyebrow. "And…you never thought to mention him?"

"It's complicated."

He turned the card over and read the hand-written note. "He wants you to call him, ASAP. He wrote his cell phone number on the back, in addition to the numbers on the front of the card."

She took the card from him and stared at it. "Detective, huh," she said, a note of pride in her voice as she turned the card over.

"Killian, mind helping me with the barbeque?" He nudged Killian out the door in front of him.

"Since when do you need help starting the barbeque?" Killian grumbled snatching the bag of charcoal from under the shelf on the grill and pouring half the bag on the grate. A large puff of black charcoal dust rose in the air. "Shit. I left the cooler with the steaks in it inside."

"Since I imagine Mystic wants to return that phone call in private. Chinoah will get it." he shot back.

"But Chinoah…" He left the rest of the words unsaid, as Chinoah rounded the corner with a plate of steaks in a cooler and potatoes wrapped in foil balanced precariously on top along with a salt shaker and pepper grinder.

"What's the deal with Mystic and her brother?" Killian asked Chinoah, reaching out in time to catch the pepper grinder as it rolled off the top of the cooler.

"It's a long story, one that's hers to tell," Chinoah said sitting the cooler on the picnic table then waving her hand in a dismissive gesture. She picked up the salt shaker and the potatoes and placed them on the tray at the side of the barbeque.

****

Mystic watched her friends walk out to the porch, leaving the door open. She pulled out her phone and slowly tapped in the number on the front of the card. Quickly she touched the screen and disconnected the call just as it started to ring. She blew out a breath and paced across the room, her heart thundering in her chest.

The last time she'd talked with her brother was

when she returned after their father had fallen ill. They'd both said things they didn't mean, but the words still stung. *Oh, grow up, stick and stones and all that stuff.* She wiped her sweaty palms on her jeans and again called Micah's number, absently drawing her bottom lip though her front teeth, waiting for it to connect.

"Detective Rayne." A deep, confidant male voice boomed through the phone.

"Micah?" She worked hard to make sure her voice was nonchalant, business like.

"Mystic. Glad you called. Apparently, shortly after you left the casino today, Ethan returned. I don't know what you said to the staff, but security detained him while Rusti called us and demanded that we remove him immediately. I asked her on what grounds, she said because he was a rotten son of a bitch and an MF and well, I don't need to go on. You get the drift." He chuckled. "Anyway, she said you had taken over the management duties at the River Winds along with Sage and wanted him arrested if he returned. Sage met us inside the door and directed us to the security office where Ethan was being held."

"I didn't say I wanted him arrested. I said he wasn't to set foot inside the casino, and if he did to have security remove him. I don't think we have enough on him to hold him. Yet."

"Well, actually between your statement of the attack, Chinoah's abduction, and the FBI's seizure of the casino's books, we have strong probable cause to detain him on numerous state and federal charges. We'd about wrapped up the investigation when he appeared. Good timing on his part. I'm just sorry you didn't get to see the arrest."

"Well, I've seen enough of him to last a life time. What now?"

"We've turned the investigation results over to the D.A. The FBI is sending a man down with their investigation findings. We expect to file charges within the next day or two. Federal charges will trump the state, but until then, he'll cool his heals in our jail."

"Sounds good. Did you get in touch with Arch?" She picked at a piece of lint on her shirt.

"Yeah, he thanked me. Asked I contact you and gave me your address."

"That's how you found me?"

"Mystic, give me a little credit. I'm a cop. I knew where to find you."

"Did you know?" She paused for a long minute, shook her head. *Not going there.*

"Myst, you still there?"

"Still here." She paused again, hoping like hell that this was the right thing to do. "Micah, we're having a barbeque this evening. I'd like you to join us and fill me in on everything. Then I'd like you to meet someone. Can you be here around six?"

"Sure, I've the night off."

"And Micah, I'm really sorry the way we left things."

"Water under the bridge. I said some things I'm not proud of too, so let's just leave it at that and start over tonight. Dad was right in appointing you. I can't investigate crimes and protect the best interest of the tribe at the same time. Sooner or later there'd be a conflict."

"Dad was a wise man. Too bad it took me so long

to learn that," she said.

"He'd be proud of the way things have turned out." Micah paused for a beat. "For both of us."

"I think so. See you tonight. Oh, and you're free to bring a guest."

"Not this time, too many things to discuss, but another time, I promise."

"I'll hold you to it."

"I know, like Dad always said about you. Mind like an elephant in a steel trap. You never forget and never let it go."

"I'd almost forgotten that, wish you had. See ya."

"Nope, still need something to push your buttons. Bye for now."

She held the phone to her ear a minute longer until she was sure he'd disconnected. She tapped the screen to clear the call, held the phone to her chest, and sighed. He sounded so different from the last time they'd talked. She blew out a breath and started toward the open door. "Caden?" She listened for a moment and walked out the door. "Caden," she said louder as she came around the corner of the house.

"Out here," he called turning toward the sound of her voice, laying aside the wire brush he'd been scrapping the barbeque grate with.

"Ethan's been arrested. Apparently, he returned to the casino, and Rusti called the police. That's where Micah came in." She scooted up onto the top of the picnic table, her feet on the bench, arms braced behind her, and looked up at Caden.

"On what charges?" Caden asked.

"I'm not sure. But Micah said his and the FBI's investigations would lead to state and federal charges against him."

"Couldn't happen to a more deserving man," Caden said vehemently. "Care to shed a little light on those of us in the dark about Micah?"

"You'll get to meet him this evening. I've invited him to dinner, hope that was all right."

"Even more reason to fill us in. We don't want to embarrass you." He chuckled.

"You wouldn't."

"Well, depends."

She huffed out a breath and narrowed her eyes. "Okay. The last time I saw Micah was when our dad got sick. He'd made some decisions that weren't popular with Micah, involving me. I'm five minutes older than Micah." She rolled her eyes at the ridiculousness of it all, now. "Therefore, according to family tradition, I'm the oldest and expected to take over for my father as chief and shaman of our tribe. Well, I'm female."

"You know, I noticed that about you." The corners of his lips twitched in amusement.

"Do you want to know the story or not," she said haughtily crossing her arms over her chest.

"Yes, of course, sorry for the interruption," he said with a bark of laughter. "Sorry, you're just so cute."

"Geez. Anyway, Micah felt it should be him as the male heir. At the time, he was new on the force. Dad told him his job with the Tribal Police would be a conflict of interest with the duties of shaman and chief. Micah vehemently disagreed. Then he brought up the fact that I'd left the tribe and ran off to college swearing never to return. Which I don't remember saying, but it's possible. Dad tried to mediate the situation by bringing up that my job was looking out for the best interests of the tribe under any situation. Unfortunately, it had the opposite effect and enraged Micah worse."

"We all say things we regret. Especially, when we're young and don't consider the consequences of our actions," Caden said.

"True. The meeting went downhill from there. We both said terrible things to each other, and Micah stormed out. Eventually, he returned to make peace with our dad but never came around when I was there."

"Sounds like you both grew up and see things differently now," Killian said. As he opened the barbeque lid, smoke and heat bellowed out. He closed the lid with a quick flick of his wrist. "I think it's ready."

She waved the smoke away with her hand. "Yeah, Micah even said on the phone that Dad was right. There was no way he could protect the members of the tribe while investigating a crime that may involve them. I think given the situation, Arch has done a fine job leading the tribe and should continue to do so, until he is unable or unwilling. When that happens, Micah and I can see where we are in our own lives and decide the best course of action, together."

"Chief and Shaman aren't always the same person. Are they?" Caden asked.

"No, but it was with my great grandfather, grandfather, and my dad. He expected the same from me. But times change and the structure may need a little tweaking." She paused for a couple of beats. "I don't think as legal representative I would have a problem with either. I can remain as Shaman because my job will allow me to be based out of here if conditions warrant it. With BGE and the oil situation, there should be no problem convincing the Bureau of Indian Affairs that a representative needs to be present to sort it all out and stay on top of it. Whatever it is."

"Good point," Caden said. "I was thinking along the same lines, only as far as demon control and containment. It wouldn't hurt to have a contingent of warrior angels keeping an eye on things down here. It would be the answer to Killian's dilemma with leaving Chinoah for large chunks of time as he fulfilled his obligation to the legion. Not to mention ease the situation with Nat and his growing family." He rubbed his chin and paused. "Ah well, a topic for another time." He turned back to her as she focused her gaze more intently upon him.

"Really?" she asked her brow arched in question.

"Thinking out loud. Please continue." Caden grinned.

She held his gaze for a couple of beats. "I told Micah to be here about six. That way the discussion with Bruce and Angie should be over, and we can enjoy the rest of the evening."

"What discussions with Bruce and Angie are we talking about?" Bruce grinned as he came around the corner of the house with two bottles of wine under each arm. "We heard voices and thought we'd just join you out here."

"Glad you could make it." Caden clasped Bruce's hand and kissed Angie on the cheek as he took the plate of deviled eggs from her and set them next to her.

Killian took the wine from Bruce with a questioning look.

"These two should be chilled, and the other two are

best served room temperature," Bruce said.

"Gee, didn't know mind reading was one of your skills," Killian teased looking at the labels. "Nice."

"Oh, I have many skills, but reading the mind of friends isn't something I use. Your expression said it all." A laugh rumbled deep in Bruce's chest.

Angie arched her eyebrows and shot him a doubtful look. "Really?"

"Oh, now reading the minds of spouses is a whole different thing. That's always acceptable. Otherwise how would we stay out of trouble?" Bruce leaned back to avoid Angie's swing and caught her fist in his large hand pulling her to him. "You wouldn't have it any other way, and you know it." He leaned down and kissed her on the nose wrapping his arms around her, laying his cheek on the top of her head. "It's nice to kick back and be a couple enjoying a night out with friends. A luxury we rarely get. Though tonight, business discussions will come before dinner, wine, and pleasant conversation."

Angie wriggled away and glared at him. "Oh, I can keep you out if I want. It's easy to derail the male mind, demon or angel since it has only one track where the female is concerned." She chortled, her eyes darting from Mystic to Chinoah.

The women solemnly nodded in agreement, then collapsed into gales of laughter. "Right you are," Mystic said in between gulps of air, trying to catch her breath and control her laughter.

"I think we've been dissed," Killian said looking from Caden to Bruce.

"Yeah, but when they're right, they're right," Caden said with a smile and wink at Mystic.

Bruce let out a small sigh as his expression became unreadable. "On that note, shall we get back to the discussions being referred to as we barged in?"

"Sure, let's get the business out of the way, so we can enjoy the evening and the wine." Caden gave a longing glance toward the house where the expensive bottles of wine Bruce had so graciously provided resided. He reiterated the discussions they'd had yesterday morning with Killian filling in missed information. Mystic brought them up to speed with her brother's involvement, Ethan's arrest, and the FBI's investigation.

"I have some things to add," Angie said, after listening to everyone and discreetly weaving a privacy spell. "You were right, Killian. There was a change form executed and faxed to the secretary of state. A copy of that document and the fax confirmation happened to find its way into my bag. I also have documents I believe Ethan forged Archer Clearwater's signature on. When I compared Ethan's signature to the documents, that I considered forged, the letter formation was the same, but I'm not an expert. We probably need to turn over those documents to the FBI, once we've decided on a plan of action."

Mystic nodded. "We figured that Ethan represented himself as tribal agent. It all started to unravel after it became apparent he wasn't the legal delegate. After Ethan's botched attempt at my life, Archer was appointed temporary representative until things could be sorted out. He's pushing now for me to take my rightful place, but I think he's the right man for the job in the short term."

"BGE did apply for and was granted a permit for

horizontal drilling, with what appears to be the tribes' blessing, Ethan Nix being the tribes' legal representative, which we know is a lie. I captured those documents on my phone because recently there's been too much activity at the office to blatantly copy the pages. Using magic was out of the question since I've been able to keep my identity and status under wraps." Angie paused to glance at Killian.

"You're right. Most of upper management are demons with vampires providing security." She produced her phone and pulled up the copies of the documents. "I'll print these off and get them to you."

"Actually, our printer has the wireless ability to print documents from your phone over Wi-Fi. Do you have a print app?" Caden asked.

"Sure, give me the codes to your printer, I'll give it a try." Angie followed Caden into the house. "We'll be right back," she said over her shoulder.

A few minutes later, they returned with hard copies in hand. Angie passed the documents around the table.

"I see what you mean. It looks like Ethan forged them all. This is just what we need to confront the powers that be for BGE," Mystic said grinning.

She laid out the plan she had in mind. Caden added his thoughts as did Bruce and Killian. Angie indicated who usually was in the BGE office and what time they arrived. She also brought up that some big wig from the national office was supposed to be there this week.

"Big wig is supposed to review the filing for Wyoming and Colorado, check on staffing needs, and possible transfers."

The doorbell rang, and Mystic hurried off to greet Micah. Business concluded, Caden followed her into the house to retrieve the wine and glasses. She returned with Micah in tow as her friend announced that dinner would be on the picnic table. Chinoah gathered up the dishes, silverware, tablecloth, and kicked the door open. Killian held it for her taking the plates from her, setting them on the picnic table. Mystic exited the house with a bowl of salad. Caden carried a bottle of wine in one hand and three crystal wine glasses in the other. Micah held the remaining four wine glasses.

She made the introductions. Killian sat the plate of steaks in the center of the table, and everyone grabbed a napkin, plate, and silverware then sat down to eat.

After dinner, Caden brought out the lawn chairs. and she arranged them in a circle in the yard with small tables interspersed between them. He laid a bag of marshmallows, along with skewers, chocolate bars, and a box of graham crackers next to the barbeque. When he turned around to face the others, the corners of his mouth turned up in a wide grin. "Bruce what kind of dessert wine goes with s'mores?"

Bruce eyed him and chuckled. "Any kind you want. S'mores go well with everything." Bruce drew out a bottle of Chateau d'Yquem and sat it on the picnic table. "I think we'll save this for after s'mores."

Her eyes widened as she reached for the bottle. "I would say so. At three hundred seventy-five dollars a bottle, what are we celebrating?"

"Ah…life, great friends, and battles yet to be fought." Bruce paused for a moment. "And won. Tomorrow my friends may be a challenge." The corners of his mouth turned up in a slight smile while his eyes were dark amber and unreadable.

A dangerous combination, she thought, noticing

Angie's somber nod, but she said nothing.

Chapter Twenty-Eight
Oil Hits the Fan When Mystic Comes Calling

Caden and Mystic stepped into the offices of BGE. Angie sat in a black fabric high-back chair positioned behind a glass top work center. Computer monitor to her right, a headset lay next to a phone, and a stack of files neatly arranged to her left.

Angie looked up from a file she was reading and smiled courteously. "May I help you?"

"Yes, we're looking for Mr. Siry. We have an urgent matter to discuss with him."

Angie looked bored. "I'm sorry. Mr. Siry is not available. Can I schedule an appointment for you tomorrow?"

"No," Mystic said patiently. "We need to talk to him now."

"That isn't possible he's in conferences all day. I'd be happy to set an appointment for you tomorrow."

"Miss, my name is Mystic Rayne. I'm a consultant for the Bureau of Indian Affairs, and it has come to our attention BGE is operating on or more accurately under the Wind River Reservation." She pulled a file out of her bag. "We can discuss what is in this file before we go to the feds or after. Your choice."

Mr. Siry stepped out of his office and strode down the hallway, stopping slightly behind Angie's desk. "Is there a problem, Ms. Riley?"

"No, Mr. Siry, these people were just leaving." Angie beamed up at Murad Siry batting her long, mascara enhanced eyelashes, then turned, narrowing her eyes at her and Caden.

"Murad Siry? No, we're not just leaving," she said opening her file.

"Yes, I'm Murad Siry, but I've no time to meet with you today. Set an appointment with Ms. Riley for tomorrow." Mr. Siry crossed the floor to the door and held it open smiling.

She handed him a copy of the corporate change as she started through the door, then turned to face him. "And this is just the beginning. I've obtained questionable maps, possible forged signatures, and several more items I believe will be of interest to the Wyoming Oil and Gas Conservation Commission. In fact, it may even have consequences in your dealings with Oil & Gas Conservation Commission of the State of Colorado. Out of common courtesy, I wanted to see if there was a misunderstanding or miscommunication involved before I brought these reports to the attention of the commission, not to mention the local tribal leaders and the police."

Murad narrowed his eyes. "Follow me." Over his shoulder, he barked the instructions to Angie. "Hold all calls. I do not want to be disturbed." He led them down the hallway to the conference room at the back of the office and pulled out a chair for her, gesturing for Caden to sit beside her. Then he walked around to the other side of the table facing them, put both hands flat on the table, and leaned toward her. "Those are very serious accusations."

"I am aware of that, and that's why I'm here." She

took maps and signed documents out of her file and spread them out on the table. "If you can give me a reasonable explanation for the documentation or show me recent arrangements made with the tribe that can be verified, I'll make notes of our meeting in the file and be on my way."

Siry was silent for a beat, then sat down slowly reviewing the items spread across the table. "I think you know I can't provide such documentation on short notice. These things take time. I will contact Mr. Thamuz right away and see what we can do for you possibly tomorrow or at the latest a couple of days."

She smiled and shook her head. "Gee, I'm sorry. Tomorrow, I'll be in Denver with my report. I thank you for your time. I'll be in touch." She stood and pushed away from the table.

"What do you want?" Siry growled again leaning over the table toward Mystic.

"The truth."

"You know the truth."

"It appears that each oil exploration location has its own holding company under the BGE umbrella. In light of your deception and on behalf of the Northern Arapahoe Nation, I request the transfer of forty-nine percent of the stock for Wyoming Holdings Corporation to the tribe. In addition, the registered director representing the Northern Arapahoe Nation must be listed as Mystic Rayne." She pointed to the area left blank on the change form. "Archer Clearwater will sign the form in person, giving his approval as acting chief."

"You know I can't do that." He smiled menacingly his squinty eyes glowing red. "You don't know who you're dealing with."

Caden moved so he was slightly in front of her. "I believe that goes both ways."

Ignoring Caden, Siry continued, "Think you can just waltz in here, intimidate me with these documents." He swept his hand across the table and the paperwork fluttered to the floor. "Make your demands and BGE will just fall in line."

He laughed manically, pulled a gun from his waistband, and walked backward toward the conference room door keeping both she and Caden in his sight. He shoved the door with his foot and rather than closing, it bounced back. He turned and Micah was standing in the doorway, gun drawn.

****

Caden took the opportunity to push her out of the line of fire, leapt over the table, wings unfurling as he touched down lightly on the floor at an angle to Siry. He raised his arms in front of him palms out and sent a burst of energy that sent Siry flying across the room crashing into the file cabinets, finally crumpling in a heap on the floor.

He lowered his hands cautiously as Siry disappeared from the floor, only to reappear nose to nose with him, landing a blow to his jaw. Caden's head snapped back, and he stumbled a couple of steps backward. A ball of white-hot energy formed in Siry's hand as he prepared to lunge, hand held high. Crouching down to avoid Siry's lunge, he came up behind Siry, using his own momentum to shove him against the wall, the ball of energy flew out of Siry's hand exploding against the floor at the demon's feet.

Angie rushed to the door, arms extended, sparks

snapping at her finger tips. "Need help?"

"Nope, I got this. Thanks."

The explosion's concussion shook the walls of the room and debris fell from the ceiling covering the floor, furniture, and individuals with fine white dust.

Mystic emerged from behind a large file cabinet brushing the drywall powder from her face and hair. She sidled along the wall to where Angie stood bouncing a ball of energy from one hand to the other.

A smell of burnt flesh and hair permeated the room, as tendrils of smoke curled out of Siry's ears, floated above his head, and finally faded away toward the ceiling. In a whisper of movement, Caden pinned the demon against the wall, positioned his magic daggers at either side of Siry's neck, points penetrating the skin enough that a trickle of blood wound its way down his neck and pooled in the crevice formed by his collarbone. The daggers held Siry in place neutralizing his supernatural abilities.

After verifying Mystic was safe, he shot a quick sideways glance at Micah whose eyes were wide with disbelief, his gun still trained on the demon.

A sudden crack sounded as Bruce materialized in the center of the room. "Where's Thamuz?"

Frozen to the spot, Micah's jaw dropped, and his fingers tightened around his gun.

He glanced from Bruce to Micah and gave an almost unperceivable shake of his head. Turning his attention back to Siry, Caden said, "Sir, I believe the man asked you a question."

Siry's limp body stiffened. His hand fisted so tightly his knuckles turned white. Micah, pulling handcuffs out of his belt, moved toward him and Siry.

"Micah, don't bother, they won't hold him. Bruce, do you have a control collar on you?"

"Never travel without 'em." Bruce produced a crystal collar with a thin red vein running horizontally though the middle of it and tossed the collar toward Micah. "Now that's got teeth."

In an automatic reaction, Micah reached up and snagged the collar out of midair. He brought it down to eye level and examined it carefully.

"Nice catch. Pass your finger over the seam. It will slide open. Then push the collar against our friend's throat at the base of his neck."

He moved the daggers points up a couple of inches to make room for the collar. "Come on man. We don't have all day."

Micah did as instructed, and the collar slid around Siry's neck, glowed deep red, snapped shut, and locked. "Holy shit," Micah said, stepped back, and stared. "I gotta get me some of these."

Caden swung the daggers away, wiped the tips on the demon's shirt, and sheathed them across his chest in one smooth swift movement. With nowhere to go, Siry stood still, jaw clenched, eyes blazing angry red with flicks of orange. He shoved Siry into a chair. "Your eyes complement your collar nicely." He smirked.

"A demon with fashion sense. Who'd have guessed," Mystic quipped leaning over toward Angie.

The witch snickered and extinguished the ball of energy floating in her palm.

Bruce ambled over, brushing the dust off his suit, and roughly grabbed Siry's chin with his thumb and forefinger, tilting it upward so he was forced to look directly at Bruce. "I'm only going to ask you one more time."

Bruce ran a finger over the red vein in the collar. It pulsed through the crystal sending light shards through Siry's body. He screamed, writhing in pain. Bruce tapped the collar again, and the red vein returned to normal. Still holding Siry's chin, slowly with each word accentuated, Bruce repeated his question. "Where is Thamuz, and how is he armed?"

Murad Siry slumped back against the chair, head down, and mumbled something.

Another chunk of the ceiling fell to the floor with a thud. "I didn't hear you." Bruce drew his hand near the collar again.

Murad's red eyes flamed orange with hatred as he flinched. "He's at the rig."

"Weapons?"

Murad nodded. "Fully armed, I assume, he always is."

"Alone?" Bruce asked.

"Maybe." Siry snarled, shrugging his shoulders.

Bruce reached for the collar.

Eyes wide, Murad Siry jerked back. "I don't know. He doesn't come here often and rarely checks in with me. When he does, sometimes he brings his own security, and other times he uses the security officers here. Regardless, you're a dead man," Murad spat.

"Really. Huh?" Bruce rubbed his chin. "I don't have that scheduled today. Do you Caden?"

He thought for a moment and pulled out his phone and touched the screen, a calendar popped up. "Nope."

"Guess you're wrong." Bruce swiped the collar with a finger. Murad screeched and slumped unconscious in the chair.

Tena Stetler

"Angie." Bruce turned to check on her.

"Yes?" Angie entered the conference room, hands on hips, and clicked her tongue. "What a mess." She glanced at Mystic. "You okay?"

"I'm fine." Mystic brushed the remaining debris that fell from the ceiling during the fight off her clothes.

A slight breeze through the room was the only indication of movement as Cade appeared at Mystic's side. He took her face in his hands and searched her eyes with his. "You really all right?"

"Yes."

He held her close and kissed the top of her white dusted head.

She pushed against him so she could look into his face. "But you're going to explain this whole thing to my brother. Don't expect me to." She glanced at her brother whose deep bronze face was getting paler by the minute, his brown eyes still wide with shock.

"Wait until later. Gotta check on Killian at the rig. You coming Micah?" he asked as if nothing out of the ordinary had occurred.

"Yeah, um—" Micah scrubbed a hand over his face and his eyebrows squished together. "What the hell?" His eyes flicked to Mystic.

She shot him a wide grin meant to reassure. "Welcome to my world, bro."

Bruce raised a brow and looked from Angie to Mystic. "Mind keeping an eye on Siry for a bit?"

"Not a problem," Angie said without hesitation. "Let me get Mystic a cup of tea first. She looks like she could use it." She snapped her fingers, and two steaming cups appeared.

"Of course." Bruce's gaze swept over Mystic. He

362

grinned at his wife then turned his attention to the men. "Ready to roll?"

"Yeah," Caden said his lips drawn tight. "Micah, we may need law enforcement at the rig. You up to it?" He watched as Micah's stiff stance shifted to a more relaxed one, an aura of confidence returning.

"Depends on what you have planned," Micah said. "My authority extends only to the Rez and our people, maybe we should call in the feds."

"Trust me. The feds are the last thing we need right now. Let's hope your people are not involved. If we need your authority, we'll make sure your feet are firmly planted on the Rez." Bruce paused for a beat. "One way or the other, fair enough?"

Micah paused for a beat glancing around at the group. "I suppose."

Caden clapped his hand on Micah's shoulder, and all three disappeared from the room.

****

"Micah is never going to be the same after this." Mystic shook her head.

"None of us ever are, but it'll be fine. He's a cop. He's tough. I bet he's seen worse," Angie said patting her shoulder.

Her eyebrows shot up, and she stared at Angie.

"Okay, well, maybe not." Angie shrugged. "Depends on how Thamuz takes his demotion and deportation."

"Who's Thamuz?" Mystic leaned over and shook her head, brushing the remaining white dust from her hair.

Angie chewed on her lip as if debating how much to tell Mystic. "Ambassador of Hell, demon master of dark magic weaponry, and a long-time pain in Bruce's ass. I imagine this will be the final showdown. They'll unceremoniously hurl Thamuz back to the fire and brimstone permanently. Not to mention strip his title or possibly neutralize him as Tristian would put it."

"Kill him?"

"It's probable. Demons and other worldly creatures are allowed to live in the mortal world only if they follow the three main rules. Don't use mortals for monetary gain. Don't put innocent mortals in harm's way or worst yet cause their death, and finally, our existence must be kept secret from mortals. Thamuz has been treading on the cusp of these rules for years. Now, he's stepped over the line and flagrantly obliterated all the fundamental rules. It's lights out for him. Bruce will have no choice."

"Aren't you worried?"

"Oh, honey, Bruce was taking care of things like this hundreds of years before you and I were born. He'll be fine." Angie took in a breath and let it out.

"Liar," she said matter-of-factly. "You're as worried as I am, just more practiced at not showing it."

Angie shrugged again. "Comes with the territory."

She took out her phone. "I better check in with Chinoah. She's helping Sage at the River Winds. I'm sure she is wondering what's going on. Maybe she's got news from Killian."

"Not likely," Angie said under her breath. Checking to make sure Murad Siry was still out.

"I heard that." She pursed her lips and glanced at the door.

Chapter Twenty-Nine
Dark Forces are Gathering

Caden's mouth fell open in surprise as they materialized beside Bruce's leased SUV outside his rented tri-level home in Riverton. Tristian's sports car was in front of the SUV. Bruce frowned at Tristian's car for a moment then fobbed the doors open on the SUV.

"Appears the dark forces are gathering." Bruce jerked his chin toward the car. "Tristian's warning. He's gone ahead of us to the oil rig."

He tilted his head and raised an eyebrow at Bruce, but said nothing.

"I felt the dark currents strengthening in the portal causing an imbalance in the natural flow between dark and light. That's why I chose to continue on to the oil field by mortal means."

"The magic fault lines feel distorted to me. It started last night at least that was when I first noticed it," he said, his mouth set in a grim line. He felt the darkness seeping in and rage building to invade his psyche.

Bruce opened the door to the SUV. A gleam of silver sparkled in the sunlight. A set of car keys lay on the driver's seat, the sleek cat insignia imbedded in the leather tab attached to the key ring. He picked up the keys and fingered them for a beat, then tossed the SUV keys to Caden. "You and Micah go ahead. I'll follow in Tristian's car. Park behind the buildings away from the main site. We'll walk in from there."

"Don't want to let them know we're coming, huh?" Micah said finally acting a little less odd man out.

"Oh, I'm afraid it may be too late for that, but timing is everything." He turned toward Micah.

"Caden, are you able to project a mortal signature as subterfuge?" Bruce asked

"Yes, but not for long without being in angel form," he acknowledged.

"Do your best. It'll have to be enough," Bruce said. "The wings would definitely give the indication something was up." The corner of his mouth curved in an almost smile. "Let's get changed out of these dirty clothes and head out."

They parked and emerged from the back of the onsite buildings. Caden and Bruce dressed in jeans, denim shirts layered over worn T-shirts and work boots. Micah was in uniform, and Caden held a clipboard with the maps and paperwork previously shown to Murad Siry.

They stopped short of the work area, put on hard hats and ID badges that Angie had provided. He surveyed the location of the workers, possible weapons, and dangerous areas.

He nodded to the guard on duty, flashed his badge, and strode toward what appeared to be the main area. Only a couple of yards past the signs warning No Visitors Past This Point, a man with piercing dark eyes, stringy shoulder-length, brown hair pulled away from his face and tucked under a ball cap stepped directly into their path.

He extended his hand and said, "We're looking for Mr. Thamuz. It's our understanding he's visiting this BGE location today."

The man reached for a gun tucked in his waistband and glanced at Caden's hand then stared into his face. "What's your business? There are no visitors allowed in the area." The man took a menacing step toward him. "I don't recognize you, and I know everyone assigned here." Then he glanced at Micah. "You're out of your jurisdiction, Officer." He sneered, and his glance slid to Bruce, back to him, and a full-on stare back at Bruce.

He took a casual step toward the man drawing his attention. "I already told you our business. The girl at the office issued these badges and said to ask for Mr. Thamuz." He waved his clipboard. "I have important documents and maps for him." Using a bit of persuasion on the man, Caden tried again. "He won't like us being detained in this matter." The magic had no effect. *Demon, and he masks his signature well.* Caden glanced at Bruce who gave a slight nod in confirmation.

Killian sauntered by carrying his lunch cooler. "Is there a problem?"

"Naw. Just going to escort these trespassers off the site. Did you clock out?"

Killian narrowed his eyes and nodded. "Can I see you for a minute?" He cut his gaze away from the area.

The man frowned "Don't move." and stepped a few feet away from the group. Still keeping eye contact with them.

Killian leaned toward the man. "Tom, I don't want any trouble, but those men were in the office this morning talking with Mr. Siry. Their conversation became heated as I was leaving. Siry told Angie to issue temp badges, and Thamuz could handle the situation. Maybe you should check with someone before escorting them off." Killian shrugged and ambled away, pocketing Tom's communicator.

Tom moved his hand from his gun to his belt, then to the clip, there was no device. "Shit." He looked around. "You stay here." He glared at the three of them. "I'll be right back."

"Sure," Caden said.

Tom turned and strode toward the office. Bruce merely raised his hand. Tom slammed into the side of the building, face first. He slid to the ground, gurgling sounds coming from his throat. They stepped over the body, only Micah looked back at Tom.

"So much for the element of surprise," Bruce mused. The ground beneath their feet began to rumble. Steam curled and hissed from fissures that split the earth in widening crevasses. Searing heat spewed from the bowels of Hell, incinerating several of the men on the rigs. Others ran for cover or tried escape by out running or jumping clear of the widening ravines quickly forming a cavernous moat surrounding the platform.

"Well, he knows we're here," Bruce said reluctantly. "We'll wait until he comes to us."

A tall lanky form appeared a few feet from them, his sable hair curled at the neck of his black denim work shirt, strands fell across his leathery forehead almost covering one eye. He shook the hair out of his dark eyes as he looked from Caden to Micah, finally settling on Bruce.

Bowing his head slightly, his eyes shifted to the ground. "My lord," Thamuz murmured, his voice dripping with sarcasm. Suddenly, his head snapped up, and his eyes whirled to an unearthly yellow glowing brightly out of red-rimmed sockets. "I see you brought divine intervention. I'm honored that you consider it necessary, but it won't alter the outcome. You've had your chance at leadership and have failed. Fear and violence will always trump respect and fairness when it comes to ruling those with an evil nature. Your time is over, my lord." Thamuz sneered, glancing around at the horde of vampires, demons, and witches gathering menacingly around them.

Standing beside Bruce, he shifted, feet planted firmly in a wide stance, ready for a fight. He watched and listened as the events unfolded. Mortal workers emerged from behind the protective shields on the platform to fade into the shadows, while others drifted over to stand with Killian, watching in horror as the scene unfolded in front of Caden. Killian still in human form shifted from foot to foot and rolled his shoulders anxiously.

Bruce ran his large hand over the auburn stubble at his jaw. His skin took on a deep red-orange glow with scaly texture as ancient black runes moved under the skin of his arms, neck, and partially exposed brawny chest.

Blood dripped from his fingertips as sharp claws worked their way through the skin. Bruce's eyes were dark, the pupil dilated so only a sliver of the normal deep amber iris was visible and even that was rapidly changing to raging orange.

He'd never experienced this side of Bruce. No wonder the Overlord was feared.

The pulsing vein in Bruce's temple was the only

outward appearance of tension. A wave of dangerous calm washed over his face. The corners of Bruce's lips curled, baring his sharp pointed teeth in a vicious but knowing smile "More powerful creatures than you have tried and died a tortured death for their deeds."

Thamuz clicked his tongue, the corner of his mouth slightly upturned. "My lord, your demon is showing. Isn't that a violation of your own rules, allowing the humans to be aware of our presence?" Thamuz's gaze momentarily flicked to the mortals standing beside Killian.

Bruce raised his hands, palms out firing bolts of energy into Thamuz. The creature fell back, regaining his balance and screamed orders.

That was all he needed, taking a second to step forward, a small net of white hot energy forming between his outstretched hands. The net grew wider and crackled with power as he released it. Before the net could settle around Thamuz and the creatures closest in proximity to him, Thamuz disappeared.

A fiery rope and lasso blazed from Thamuz's hand as he reappeared a few yards between the trio and Killian's group. He flung the lasso toward Killian and the mortals standing with him. Killian threw up a shield, but he hesitated a split second too long, and three of the men ran blindly forward trying to escape, landing them in the path of the burning rope. It constricted around them as they screamed in terror, flames shot up ten feet high and died down leaving only ash where the men had stood. Killian cursed.

Thamuz cackled, waving his arms in the air like a mad man. "Evil triumphs over good every time in the real world," the demon screeched motioning for his vampire security force to advance on Bruce and the others. Fangs bared and bloody claws at their fingertips, the vampires moved swiftly and silently taking out anyone in their path.

He heard an audible crack, and the air shimmered while Angie materialized on the outer edge of the searing moat, a large black wolf at her side. Angie dropped the clothing she was carrying and swung her arms in a semi-circle silently chanting, several wooden stakes pierced the air flying directly toward the marauding vampires. Earth shattering shrieks rose from the vampires' throats as the stakes found their marks. The stench of burning flesh filled his nostril, and more ash whirled in the wind.

He threw his arms out, widening and reforming the net. This time Thamuz was caught inside, along with his underlings. Deep purple and black tendrils of energy raced through the woven white-hot strands of expanding energy drawing power and strength from the dark magic wielded from its prisoners they combined their powers attempting to escape. Thamuz bellowed in frustration striking out at those captured along with him.

Caden strengthened the white magic in the net destroying the purple and black tendrils of dark magic before they released its masters.

Thunder rumbled and Bruce reached his hands up, palms out, directing lightning bolts as they split the ominous black clouds gathering in the darkened sky above the oil rig. Each electrically charged bolt struck its intended victim, obliterating the creatures caught in the net one-by-one until only Thamuz and a couple of demons were left. Ash from the creatures remains swirled in the ferocious winds battering the combatants.

Wrinkling his nose as the stench of sulfur filled the air, he blew out a breath. The net wasn't going to hold much longer.

Thamuz brought his arms straight out to the side then slowly raised them above his head. Invisible forces from the inside pushed the dome net out of shape straining its ability to remain intact. Points of weakness sparked red then weakened allowing a hole to form at that juncture in the net.

He sent streams of energy to reinforce the vulnerable points, but it wasn't enough. There were too many failing points.

Thamuz kept pouring his life force into the power destroying the net. Finally, the net exploded sending Caden, Bruce, and Micah flying in opposite directions across the platform. Thamuz released conjured black crystal daggers sending them in all directions, but they quickly homed in on the overlord, angel, and officer.

Even in Thamuz's weakened condition, his concentration was deadly accurate. Caden and Bruce tried to dodge the daggers while shielding Micah, but a few of them found their intended targets. One lodged in Bruce's collarbone dangerously close to his jugular, and another sunk deep inside the tissue in his shoulder. He reached up in a futile endeavor to dislodge it. Sweat streamed down his face as tremors shot threw his arms and across his chest. He fell to one knee moaning in agony.

Searing pain screamed through Caden's muscles as another penetrated his outstretched wing at the juncture where it connected to his back. Micah swore vehemently as a dagger embedded itself inside his thigh tearing muscle and nerves. He crumpled to the ground.

The mortals at Killian's side ran for cover. Killian unfurled his wings, two powerful beats, and he was aloft looking down at the scene. His arms were outstretched in front of him. Streams of fire exploded from his fingertips as he breathed fire all around.

On the battlefield, he'd seen Killian's ability to control or breath fire only once, and Killian had requested he keep the ability to himself. After hundreds of years, Killian's talent was now out in the open.

At that same moment, Caden staggered to his feet, his blood-stained wing hung limp at his side. He stared in Thamuz's direction making direct eye contact. Thamuz's magic signature was weakening. His life force was unable to sustain both the dark magic mayhem and his body strength.

Caden, his strength spent, drew his 9mm from his ankle holster, unloaded the entire clip in Thamuz's upper torso, reloaded, took aim, and fired again. The demon howled as the bullets ripped through his upper torso sending large chunks of flesh and body pieces into the smoke laden air.

Killian incinerated the demon's body parts with a steady stream of fire from his fingertips without endangering others. Thamuz's reign of terror was at an end. Caden gave Killian double thumbs up as they both watched Thamuz's ashes be sucked into the molten moat as the ground shifted and the fissure closed leaving the scorched platform connected to the ground once more.

"That's one less thorn in my side," Bruce said wryly, the corners of his mouth curved in a weak smile as he slipped into unconsciousness.

Tena Stetler

He turned his attention to Angie and his black wolf who were sprinting across the smoldering ground. Angie tossed the clothes she'd been carrying into a small building still partially standing and motioned the black wolf inside. "I'll see what I can do for the men while you change." The large wolf lowered its head in agreement and loped into the building.

Angie rushed over to where Killian and a few men were standing around Bruce and Micah. Caden moved to keep an eye on the disappearing form of his wolf. Angie shoved her way through and assessed their injuries. "Stand back," she hollered at the small crowd, then glowered at Killian. "Killian, get these guys out of the way. I need room to work."

****

Against the one standing wall of the building, Mystic blurred around the edges of her wolf form, and her limbs lengthened. Returning to human form she slipped on the clothes Angie flung in the building. Then she hurried across the platform where Killian was trying to disperse the crowd. "How badly are they hurt?" she asked.

He shrugged. "Angie is working on them."

She jostled him aside. Her stomach lurched and did a sickly roll as she got her first good look at the injured men laying on the ground. "What do we need to do first, Angie?" she asked kneeling beside Caden. "Should I pull the blade out? Wound looks like it could be infected already."

Angie removed the nasty serrated blade from Bruce's shoulder, studied it. She winced and examined the tissue around the wound, prodding the skin with her fingers, thankful that Bruce was still unconscious. "It

374

looks like this dagger was conjured with a deadly poison on the blade." She pointed to the jagged edges of the wound now turning dark.

She glanced over to the area where Angie was pointing. Caden's injury looked identical.

"Yank the blade out quickly and push on the area try to get it to bleed freely, maybe keep the poison from traveling into his blood stream," Angie said.

She did as instructed and called Killian over to keep Caden's wound open. She moved over to Micah who was sprawled near Angie. Scraping her bottom lip through her front teeth, she knelt and examined Micah's injury. "Angie, I think that dagger may have penetrated Micah's femoral artery. If I pull it out, he may bleed out before I could get it stopped."

Angie glanced at Micah and back to Bruce. She removed the daggers and began a healing spell. Her hands held lightly over Bruce's wounds, the glow beneath her hand and over the wound was green with a rose edge. The rose glow intermingled with the green until most of the green disappeared.

Angie gave a little sigh and reached out her hand indicating she should move back to Caden. "Grab my hand then place yours over Caden's wound, but don't touch the skin. Hold it there until the glow is completely rose, no trace of the green."

"Killian, would you carefully move Micah over here so I can reach him." Angie swiveled her head around quickly in all directions. "Where the hell is my brother when I need him?" She gave another glance at Micah. Sweat was pouring off him, his upper body flushed as he began to shake uncontrollably. "Shit, he's going into shock." She shouted at the top of her lungs,

"Tristian."

Tristian materialized at her side. "What do you need, sis?"

"Finish healing Bruce. The blades of the daggers were poison. I've just about got it all, but the dagger in Micah's thigh may have cut the femoral artery. The poison will move directly into the blood stream once the blade is pulled, if it hasn't already," she said grimly, putting her hand to her head, wiping away the sweat.

"I think that's got it," she said to Angie. "There's no green, and the rose glow is quite dark on Caden's wound. It's already starting to heal." She glanced back to where Caden sat on the ground propped up on his elbows watching her and Angie work.

Caden switched his gaze back to Killian, a slight grimace on his face, forehead creased as Angie and Killian seemed to be conversing telepathically. Killian shook his head and glanced at Micah.

"Good, come over here and help me with Micah. I know you're twins. Do you share the same blood type?"

"Yes," she said, forehead creased with worry.

"Good." Leaving Bruce peacefully resting under Tristian's watchful eye, Angie placed her hand above Micah's wound and tried to extract the poison without removing the dagger. The wound glowed deep green with a slice of rose that faded in and out. "This isn't going to work," she murmured, as a wide swath of rose cut through the green dividing it and absorbing the green a little at a time.

She glanced at Angie as she wobbled, putting her hand to her head momentarily. "Angie, you can't continue this way. Keeping the magic strong is taking its toll. Is there a first aid station on this rig?"

"Yeah," a rough voice in the crowd shouted. "I'm a paramedic here. What do you need?"

"Transfusion supplies," Angie said.

Tristian stood and moved to his sister. "Bruce is fine. He'll be a little under the weather for a while, I suspect. Let me take over here," Tristian said, concern shown in his eyes as he slid his hand under hers, the wound glowing more rose than green, now with his added strength.

"We're going to need to set up a direct transfusion from Mystic to Micah, in case he starts to bleed out when you remove the knife." She looked up at Tristian, then shifted her gaze to Mystic. "You up for this?" Angie asked.

"Yes," she said in a determined voice.

The burly man with bright red hair, freckles, and straining biceps rushed back with a large metal box, a bag of sterile dressing, extra tubing, and clear surgical tape. He had blankets tucked under his arm. "This should do the job." He stared from Tristian to a chalk faced Angie. "Miss, I don't mean to be telling you what to do, but I think you need to sit down and let me take over." He reached for her arm and guided her to a scorched wooden box. "Take a load off. I've got it from here."

Angie nodded. "I'm grateful for the assist." Tristian and Killian nodded in agreement.

The man snapped on surgical gloves and turned to Mystic. "Name's Jessop McGerry," he said grinning. "Ain't never seen anything like this, but I guess people get uppity and need to be taken down a notch or two." He looked around and let out a low whistle. "Glad I'm moving on to Colorado, cleanup and recertification is going to a son-of-a..." He swallowed the rest of his words and turned his attention back to Micah. "Can't move this fellow, so we'll hook up the tubing right here." He quickly set up pumps, tubes, and suction, then hooked up the IV between her and Micah. "Now lie quietly, miss."

"You there." He pointed to Tristian. "On my count of three, pull the blade out with a smooth continual motion, don't jerk or stop unless I say so. Killian, monitor her vitals. You know how?"

Killian nodded.

"Okay, here we go." Jessop mopped his brow with a wad of sterile gaze as thunder rumbled and lightning streaked across the sky. "One, Two, Three."

She held her breath as they worked on her brother. Sirens wailed in the distance, red and blue strobes lit the night sky as emergency vehicles traveled rain slickened highways to the chaotic scene. Finally, she blew out a breath. The big burly man was between her and Micah obscuring her view. Did it slice the artery? She couldn't see, couldn't tell what was happening. She looked at Killian—his gaze was downcast.

Chapter Thirty

Life Goes on with Fewer Demons and a New Set
of Rules

Bruce and Caden leaned back in the recliners lining
Caden's living room. Micah sprawled out on the couch
beside his wife who held their three-month-old son.
Killian slouched against the door frame leading into the
kitchen where Chinoah, Mystic, and Angie were
preparing lunch. A loud knock on the door sounded.

"Killian, would you get that?" Mystic said, wiping
her wet hands on the dishtowel tucked in the waistband
of her jeans.

Sure," Killian said sauntering toward the front
door. He pulled the door open, and his eyes widened.
Nathanael and Sean stood in the doorway. "Boss, what
are you doing here?"

"Is that anyway to greet your legion commander?"
Nat said his lips set in a thin line.

"Uh. No sir, won't you come in?" Killian opened
the door wider shifting his gaze to Caden then to Bruce.
Sean jostled Killian deliberately as he followed Nat
inside.

"This is what happens, when I give you a little
leeway and let you out from underneath my
supervision." He threw his arms wide open.
"Explosions, mayhem, failing miserably at keeping our
existence a secret, allowing the devil's ambassador to

call up a fiery inferno, and joining forces with the Territory Demon Overlord of the Western Hemisphere. Need I list more?"

Killian stood opening and shutting his mouth not a word coming out.

Nat strode inside. "I can't think of one rule the Angel Tribunal set out that you left intact. Congratulations." He burst into a smile that sparkled in his blue eyes.

"Excuse me, sir?" he said.

"While we have a standing agreement to assist other factions, you and your group of renegades have demonstrated the need for an Angel Task Force on Earth. The elite groups will assist Lord Bruce and the other Overlords in the control of undesirable creatures. The Tribunal has authorized eight consortiums to be set up, two in each of the four hemispheres.

"I'll be responsible for the two set up in the Western region, the first consisting of Killian and Sean with you provided you agree, as advisor when necessary. The others will be assigned and report to me. There will also be legions above appointed as backup."

"Whew, I guess we turned the Tribunal on its ear," he said, the corners of his mouth twitching.

Nat glared at him. "May I continue?"

"Sure," he said unabashed.

"Thanks." Nat growled. "I've purchased the lodge we were renting near Aspen. Killian may stay there or remain here. Sean will remain at the lodge until he sees fit to make other arrangements. Caden, you are technically free from all tethers to the Tribunal but will still report to me on an advisory basis."

He nodded. "I'd like that. For the time being, I'll

be staying here in Riverton while Mystic's on assignment to straighten out the rights of her people and BGE."

Killian looked thoughtful then cut his gaze to Chinoah. "I'll be staying here with Chinoah. She is the new CFO for the River Winds and adviser to Mystic regarding the affairs of the tribes shares of BGE, in Wyoming."

A slow smile curved the legion commander's lips as his eyes danced. "I took the liberty of informing the Tribunal that was probably going to be the case."

"We'll be returning to DC as soon as Bruce is healed enough to travel," Angie said.

"I'm ready to travel," Bruce protested.

Angie shot him a warning glance.

"In a couple of days," Bruce said amicably.

"Our house is available next week, Killian." Angie grinned.

"Under the circumstances, I'll take you up on the offer. Fully furnished?" Killian said.

Angie smirked. "Cost you more, but we'll work something out."

Caden got up slowly from the recliner. "Mystic, a word." He grasped her by the elbow and led her out the back door, eased down on the bench to the picnic table. "I'd like that answer now."

"What answer?" Mystic turned to him a puzzled expression on her face.

"Will you spend eternity with me as my wife? You said to ask again when this was all over. I believe it's as over as it will ever be in our lives."

She smiled, wound her arms around his neck, and whispered against his ear, "Of course I'll be your wife."

"After you get things settled with the River Winds and the Council, could you take a couple weeks off?" he asked.

"What… There's so much to do here."

"And that will always be the case. Right now, we have a wedding to plan, sooner rather than later is my preference. Afterward, I want to take you away from all this for a couple weeks where we can concentrate on beginning our life together in peace and tranquility."

She raised a dark eyebrow. A hint of a smile curved her full lips. "Right."

"At least for a little while." He grinned enveloping her in a warm, loving, embrace. *Eternity would never be the same.*

**If you enjoyed
AN ANGELS UNINTENTIONAL
ENTANGLEMENT,
following is a preview of Tena Stetler's next
book.**

A Magic Redemption

by

Tena Stetler

Demon's Witch Series, Book 5

Chapter One
Freedom a Choice? A Responsibility? A Way of Life—She Didn't Know

Synn lounged in the front window seat of her cottage, one leg tucked under her, the other dangling, bouncing a stream of gold electrical current between her thumb and fingertips. *What am I doing here?*

The voices in her head had been silent since defecting to the side of the Demon Overlord of the Western Hemisphere. *It was the right thing to do.* Her reward for a job well done, "freedom with a few conditions" to quote the Overlord's words. *But am I really free?* She scrunched up her face, lips pursed.

A question she still didn't know what to do with. Impatiently, she pushed her long hair over her shoulders, tucking a few shorter wisps around her face, behind her ears. Tobi, a hairdresser at The Wycked Hair Salon had tamed her tresses before she'd accompanied Bruce and Angie to Ireland, giving her a short-layered look around her "pixie-like" face—Tobi's words not hers—and leaving the back long.

Tobi claimed it softened her sharp features and made her look cute. Back then she didn't want cute, she was a warrior, wounded but warrior still the same. Tobi insisted cute could give her the drop on an enemy. Now— she wasn't sure what she was and that was disconcerting.

Staring out the window, the mist thick as pea soup, she couldn't see the ocean, but the constant beat of waves crashing against the shore made her restless. She uncurled her leg and stood, padding over to the door and opening it. A cold wind made her eyes water and whipped her hair around her face in stinging tendrils.

The door slipped out of her hand and crashed against the wall with a bang. Sucking in a breath, she shrugged into her coat, pulled a red, yellow, and orange knitted hat over her unruly raven hair, tugged gloves out of her coat pockets, and slipped them on.

She shivered zipping her coat up, tucked her feet into warm boots Gavin had given her, all the while telling her the north wind off the coast could be bitter. *He was right— about a lot of things. Most of all that she needed her own space.* She wrestled the door closed behind her and locked it, pocketing the keys.

As she picked her way down the trail, the wind died down to a friendly breeze heavy with brine, except for an occasional brutal gust. Screaming sea birds swooped and dived into the white capped waves hunting for food. Wrapping her arms around her body more for a secure feeling than for warmth, she continued down the path to the ocean shoreline.

She breathed in the crisp air and skipped along the beach, skirting the incoming waves and chasing them out, her limp was barely noticeable. A calm replaced her restlessness. *Is this what it's like to be free? Make your own decisions, take action without permission? It's nice, but lonely in a way.*

Time seemed to go on forever as she slowed and walked backward for a while, her foot steps in the sand filling with water as she traveled along the shoreline, as if nature erased her intrusion. She turned around and continued her trek. Unaware of how long or how far she'd walked, the sudden outline of a figure, cloaked in the fog, jogging toward her caused panic to set in.

Her heart pounded rapidly in her chest, she swallowed hard, adrenalin pumping through her veins as flight or fight response kicked in. Digging her good foot into the sand she prepared to attempt a sprint...to where. *Where the hell am I?* A quick glance around, she spied a familiar building far off on the bluffs, as the figure burst from the fog. A tall, wide-shouldered male with long muscular legs. She froze.

Once lithe, strong and agile, her former life, and boss had taken a toll on her body. Now tired her gait was uneven and unsteady, even a slow sprint would likely end with her face planted in the sand.

"Synn, are you all right? You're a long way from the cottage." A male voice called to her.

A familiar male voice. She blew out a breath as her heartbeat slowed a bit. "Am I?"

"Aye, It's bitter out here. The pub's only over the ridge. Want to get something hot to eat and drink? With a gentle brush of his fingers over her cheeks, he said, "You're freezing." Gathering her into his arms, he held her tight for a moment, before loosening his hold. "Let's get you to Shaughnessy's where there's a roaring fire. You'll be warm in no time."

"I'm okay, just out for a walk. The walls were closing in." She stomped her feet, they were so cold there wasn't any feeling.

He narrowed his eyes. "How long you been out walking?"

"A while." She pushed his arms away and trudged

toward the lights in the pub.

He grabbed her by the shoulders and whirled her around to face him. "You promised to call me when things got too difficult."

She tried to shrug out of his hold, but his hands were so warm. "You also said I need to learn to stand on my own two feet. Discover who I really am in this new world I've been dropped in."

"Okay, I'll admit, those words were said in frustration."

"Anger." She shot back, giving him a defiant stare.

"Aye. You're right." He scooped her up and sprinted for the pub ignoring her objections and flailing limbs. "We can argue in the warm pub."

He was right—again. Relaxing against his muscular body sent spikes of desire through her. Feelings she had no business acting on. At least until she could hold her own without leaning on anyone for anything. She needed to earn his family's respect—*his* respect. The fact she was a demon with a terrible history that everyone was aware of was an obstacle she may never overcome. At least the townspeople were oblivious. That was a start.

The heavy wooden door to the pub groaned as he kicked it open. Warmth and laughter spilled out into the frosty night along with the mouthwatering aroma of Mulligan stew and yeasty scent of the pub. All the tables in the center of the floor were full as were most the booths along the wall.

"Put me down, don't embarrass me by carrying me into the bar like a mid-evil knight with his conquest."

"Where the hell did you come up with that?" His lips twitched as he set her on her feet and steadied her.

Grasping her gloved hand, he strode toward the two empty chairs at the bar and motioned for her to sit.

She straightened her shoulders and remained standing though she was starting to shiver.

"I'm going to go in the back and get a couple of extra chairs and put them by the fire." His da, Tim and ma, Mary, sidled over to where he stood. Mary touched her cheek. "She's chilled to the bone."

Gavin grabbed her around the waist and thrust her into the last chair at the end of the bar. "Be right back." He sent a significant glance to his Ma and Da. Mary nodded and bustled into the kitchen. Before he returned Mary emerged with a mug and teapot on a tray. She sat the tray down and shoved up the pass through at the opposite end of the bar.

Darlin' you look frozen," Mary murmured. "What were you doing out on an evening like this." She poured the steaming dark brew into the mug. "Cream or sugar?" Mary asked raising a brow."

"A little of both. I can do it myself." She picked up the spoon, added sugar and poured cream into the mug. "Thanks. I lost track of time. Sorry. Needed to get out of the cottage for a bit."

"Gavin saw you walking along the shore, after a while when you didn't turn back he got worried." Mary shook her head. "We were talking about..." Then she reached out and touched her hat. "Glad you like the hat I made. Looks great on you."

"I like it a lot. Makes me feel cheery when it's gloomy outside." She smiled. "Thank you."

"You're welcome." Mary smiled and returned to take orders at the bar. "Check on you later." She said over her shoulder.

Tim came up behind his wife with a bowl, spoon, and large piece of bread on a plate. "Thought you could use a bowl of stew and freshly baked soda bread." He set the bowl and plate on the bar in front of her.

Gavin swung out of the back room with two chairs and sat them in front of the fireplace, then arranged a small table in front. "Now Kevin, and Will, don't you think these are for you." He winked at two men ambling toward him. "My lass and me be occupying these for a bit of a while. Go on with you."

They gave a hearty laugh and returned to the bar with their half empty pints.

She scooped up a spoonful of stew, slipped it in her mouth, and swallowed. "Mmm, this is delicious. Thank you." She took a couple more spoonful's, and bit into the bread, chewing slowly.

He sauntered up behind her. "Want to move over to the fire?"

"Sure." By his smiling face, she could tell the argument was far from his mind and that was fine with her. She picked up the mug, it was deliciously warm and wrapped both hands around it. He carried the bowl and plate of bread to the little table, waited for her to take a seat, then eased down in the chair next to her.

Finishing the stew, she licked the spoon. "That was wonderful." She nibbled on the bread.

His face grew serious. "I have an idea. Hear me out before you answer. Okay?"

She hesitated for a moment, hoping he wasn't going to bring up…

"It's been a couple months since you moved into the cottage. I've given you space as we agreed. You're comfortable there?"

"Yes, it's quite cozy. I love the ocean so close. Somehow the crashing of the waves is comforting."

"Maybe it's time for you to move forward. By that I mean, think about getting a job, meeting people. Making this your home."

"Who's going to hire me? The skills I have are not what most people are looking for." She lowered her voice, "Demon warrior or assassin for hire."

"Well about that. Ma and Da want to hire a couple people during the upcoming tourist season."

"Stop right there." She held her hand out in front of her. "I'll not take any more charity from your Ma and Da."

"It's not charity. Bridget will be happy to train you. A dependable employee is what we need and think you would fit right in. April, May, and early June we'll be swamped, then again in October. Ma wants to help Brandy plan the wedding. Especially since Brandy and Stefan had to postpone the wedding for nearly a year due to Randy's fall."

Synn shook her head slowly, what an unfortunate turn of events. Brandy, Gavin's sister was engaged to Stefan, a vampire. They'd planned a big wedding in Ireland the first of this year, but the plans were derailed due to her boss's accident. Brandy worked as a park ranger in Glacier National Park. During an inspection trip, her boss Randy lost his footing on a steep trail, and tumbled down the side of a mountain. Due to complications, his injuries had taken longer to heal than anticipated, putting their plans on hold indefinitely.

"Yeah what a freak accident. Lucky he only sustained a few broken bones. Messed up Brandy's plans." She shrugged. "I could help. If Brandy would let me."

"I imagine Ma's going to need it." He paused a beat. "What Brandy doesn't know won't… Anyway—according to Ma, Brandy's leave has now been approved for mid to late December. It got pushed back again. Stefan's radio station is more flexible, he's free to leave anytime, but they want remotes once a week. That should be a bugger."

"A remote?"

"Yeah, he'll broadcast from here to his station at a certain time. Don't have any idea how he'll pull that off." He waved his hand dismissively. "Not my problem. The wedding is set for the end of December now. It's off-season, but prep in October or November is going to drive Ma nuts. Especially with Christmas festivities and the wedding celebration all taking place in the pub. Bridget will cover for Ma, but someone has to cover for Bridget." He stood, brushed the wrinkles out of his pants. "I'll be right back."

"Brandy won't be here until maybe December and the wedding is scheduled for the end of the month?" Her eyes widened. "That's not much time for final details."

"Nope. Possibly mid-December," he called over his shoulder. After making his way to the bar he said a couple of words to his da before his ma joined the conversation. Tim turned, drew a pint and handed it to his son.

When Gavin returned a smile brightened his face. "All we ask is that you think about the offer."

Staying cooped up in the cottage wasn't doing her any good. As a teen, she hadn't been idle after Baltizar murdered her family and forced her to do his bidding.

Growing up, her parents were proud of her many talents. If they'd kept that information to themselves, they might still be alive and her life oh so different. She sighed.

"Hey how about it?"

His voice brought her back to the present. The music, laughter, chatter, she could—would enjoy—but what if someone found out? "I don't know. I'm a stranger and a yank to boot." She unzipped her coat, tucked her hat and gloves in the pockets, glad she'd worn new black jeans and a turquoise sweater today.

He grinned. "Oh, you're more than a yank…That's why you're so damn attractive." He leaned over and kissed her on the cheek.

"I'm anything but." She put her hands to her cheeks as they warmed. "Don't do that in public."

Ignoring her comment, he continued. "So you say. Don't over think it. You're brilliant. You'll learn the duties in no time. Bridget isn't much older than you, might enjoy the company. Da, Ma, and I will always have your back. You'll be great."

With a mischievous twinkle in his eyes, he grinned wider. She should have anticipated what came next, that Irishman had an ornery streak a mile wide.

Quick as a wink he bent over and brushed his lips over hers murmuring, "Don't want any of these lad's trying to steal me girl."

Her lips parted to object, he covered her mouth with his and his tongue swept inside. Her traitorous body responded before she could think, arms wrapping around his neck, her lips responding to his kiss. Hell her body had a mind of its own. *He felt so good.* Desire spiraled through her body warming her lower regions as he eased away, stroking her lips with the tip of his tongue.

"Way to go laddie. Kiss her again," demanded the crowd through whistles and friendly shouts.

Her hands flew to her face and she rushed into the ladies' room. *How could I ever face anyone again, let alone work here?*

After a couple of minutes, Bridget bounced in face flushed and laughing. "Looks like you've taken the most eligible bachelor out of circulation." She patted her back. "Well done."

"What? I'm sure I don't know what you're talking about."

"Lass, I've never seen him kiss a woman like that in all my life. And I've known him since he was in nappies." She lowered her voice. "There was a time I yearned for him to kiss me like that." Bridget's expression went dreamy for a second, then she waved her hand dismissively. "Those times are long gone since I met me Quinn." Bridget fanned herself with a paper towel. "That man's got moves. Know what I mean?"

She had no idea how to react, she gave a quick nod, shoved her sweaty hands in her pockets and stood there.

Without missing a beat, Bridget said, "Mary tells me you might be helping out around here while she plans Brandy's wedding." She snickered. "Says she's gonna help her plan the wedding, but we all know the truth." Bridget cackled again grabbing her by the arm. "Come on let's get out of here. 'Tis early and Gavin has the night off, he'll be waiting on you." She waggled her eyebrows. "And Tim will take me to task for disappearing during my shift."

Stumbling as Bridget dragged her out of the ladies'

room, Synn regained her footing, but couldn't avoid bumping into Bridget when she stopped short. "See, what'd I tell you." Pointing to Gavin waiting outside the doorway, she gave her a little shove and winked at him. "Best keep track of your lass, boyo, less other lads get ideas."

Bridget sashayed through the crowd, batted a couple men's wandering hands away from her ass, stopped at the bar, picked up a tray of pints, and delivered them to a table in the center of the room. On her way back, she thrust a piece of paper in Synn's hand. "'Give me a call, we'll get together on my day off and have some fun."

When she unfolded the paper, Bridget's name and phone number were scribble inside.

"Well looks like you've met Bridget. Making friends already, are ya?" He glanced toward the fireplace. "We seemed to have lost our seats. How about a dance?"

She shook her head, even as he swung her into a jig, the band played a lively tune.

She tried to keep up, but her bum leg kept her off balance at times. No one seemed to notice. At the end of the dance, he put his hands around her waist, picked her up, whirled her around and kissed her again before setting her on her feet. Quick and flirty, not like the soul-searching kiss he'd planted on her earlier. Still he left her tingling to her toes. She smiled. *This was fun.*

He grabbed a couple of pints, handed one to her, and introduced her around the pub. It was well past midnight when he swung his arm around her shoulder and pulled her to him. "Ready to get out of here? You can talk with Ma tomorrow about a job."

"Back to my cottage?"

"Of course. Unless you want to come home with me?" He teased.

Eyes wide she stared at him too tired to come up with a witty answer.

"Only kidding." He paused his expression turned serious. "But one day I won't be." He helped her on with her coat and waited for her to put on her hat and gloves.

When they reached the car, he turned her to face him and pressed her against the passenger door with the length of his body, his mouth took hers with heated passion. She was shocked at her own eager response to his lips, her body melted into him. Through their winter attire, she could feel his heat.

With hesitation he lifted his mouth from hers, trailed kisses down her neck, his hand slid up her side, then he raised his head pursing his lips. "I think we better get you home, before I…"

The last thing she wanted to do was return to her empty cottage. But the alternative was even more scary—or was it?

A word about the author…

Tena Stetler is a best-selling author of paranormal romance. She has an over-active imagination, which led to writing her first vampire romance as a tween to the chagrin of her mother and delight of her friends. After many years a paralegal, then an IT Manager, she decided to live out her dream of pursuing a publishing career.

With the Rocky Mountains outside her window, she sits at her computer surrounded by a wide array of witches, shapeshifters, demons, faeries, and gryphons, with a Navy SEAL or two mixed in telling their tales. Her award winning books tell stories of magical kick-ass women and mystical alpha males that dare to love them. Well, okay there are a few companion animals to round out the tales.

Colorado is home; shared with her husband of many moons, a brilliant Chow Chow, a spoiled parrot, and a forty-five-year-old box turtle. When she's not writing, her time is spent kayaking, camping, hiking, biking, or just relaxing in the great Colorado outdoors. During the winter you can find her curled up in front of a crackling fire with a good book, a mug of hot chocolate, and a big bowl of popcorn.

http://www.tenastetler.com